Sam Llewellyn is himself a very keen and experienced sailor. He was born in the Isles of Scilly in 1948 and now lives with his wife and two sons in Herefordshire.

Great Circle

Sam Llewellyn

HEADLINE

ISBN 0 7472 3132 X

Printed and bound in Great Britain by
Collins, Glasgow

HEADLINE BOOK PUBLISHING PLC
Headline House
79 Great Titchfield Street
London W1P 7FN

To Karen, with love

PRINCIPAL CREW MEMBERS AND CAMPAIGNERS

CHINAMITE
Henry Harper, Captain
Ed Cole, Sailing Master
Nicholas Eason, journalist, spare radio operator
Horace Pembury, cook
Noddy Jones, winch grinder
Slicer Bailey, winch grinder
Bones Ede, ship's doctor
Paddy Kinnersley, spare captain

FLAG
Jasper Hyatt II, Commodore, Sound Yacht Club
Jasper Hyatt III, prospective Commodore, Sound Yacht
  Club
Wallace DuCane, sponsorship co-ordinator
Ellie DuCane, Wallace's wife

PRINCIPAL CREW MEMBERS

Art Schacker, Captain
Anne-Marie Schacker, Art's partner and wife
Pal Joey Greenhous, watch captain
George Hart, cook
Martin Hyatt, winch grinder
Mustapha Choudry, sail trimmer
Simon Lowell, winch grinder

TASMAN
Harry Redd, Chairman, Tasman Wine, chief sponsor
Tubes Murphy, Captain
Mo Stapleton, Financial Comptroller, Tasman Wine
Shar Stapleton, Mo's wife,
Sparko, cook/electrician
Dike Diggs, winch grinder
Horror Wilson, no. 2 watch captain

KELLY'S EYE
Dave Kelly, TV anchorman and supercargo
Bud Withers, Captain
Bennett, watch captain
Chuck Butz, cameraman
Hubert Carey, Kelly's agent
Omar Wohl, Network Manager, USTS, chief sponsor
Herb DeVito, sound man
Joppie Lawson, boatbuilder and surveyor

EPK ELECTRIC
Emily de Havilland, Captain
Harriet Agnew, executive, EPK
Lord Kimbolton, Chairman, EPK
Jack Asprey, sailor and Kimbolton's godson
Eric de Havilland, solo circumnavigator, Emily's
  husband

SILTEX-FRANCE
Jean-Luc Jarré, Captain
Comte Henri de Rochambaud, ship's doctor

ASSOCIATED MEAT
Sir Clement Jones, Captain
Sergeant Ernie Crystal, winch grinder

SIRÈNE
Georg Fischer, Viennese dentist
Anton Fischer, his brother and partner

CONTENTS

PRESS RELEASE

It is now exactly two years until the start of the first Lancaster Great Circle Race.

Notes on the Lancaster Great Circle

1 The race is sponsored by Lancaster PLC and administered by the Royal Yacht Racing Club.

2 The course shall be from Portsmouth, round the world, to Portsmouth, leaving the Cape of Good Hope and Cape Horn to port.

3 The race is open to any monohull sailing yacht with a rating (IOR) of 35–70', subject to survey for seaworthiness by the Committee's measurers.

4 Yachts rated 65–70' shall race level, i.e. without handicap. Other classes will race on handicaps determined by their ratings.

5 The Committee recognizes the great expense involved in entering a race of this nature. The rule against advertising on hulls and spinnakers is therefore waived.

6 All yachts shall carry automatic position and distress indicators, of a type to be approved by the Committee.

7 Dates: Start Portsmouth 12 noon, 5 September
            First boats ETA Cape Town 8 October
            Re-start Cape Town 6 November
            First boats ETA Sydney 5 December
            Re-start Sydney 16 January
            First boats ETA Rio de Janeiro 18 February
            Re-start Rio de Janeiro 15 March
            First boats ETA Portsmouth 9 April

ENDS

WORKUP

The Route des Voyageurs Tall Ships Race had started at noon on Sunday. It was the second Monday now; the procession of tall ships had moved across Lake Ontario, and down the length of the Saint Lawrence Seaway. The crowds had turned out to watch the stately piles of canvas wafting past the humped grey rocks of the Thousand Islands, the slime-green piers of Montreal, and the wooded cliffs of the Heights of Abraham.

As the Seaway widened and the shores fell away, the crowds diminished and the sails took on their traditional proportion, dwarfed by the grey sweep of the sea. The slow ships had already fallen well behind. Slowest of all were a couple of Polish sea cadet vessels, great white slabs of steel, barque rigged, wallowing in the first long rollers of the Atlantic. Slightly faster, and strung out over a hundred miles of sea, were a motley of French and Americans and British, leaned over under the fresh sou'westerlies spinning off the southern edge of an Arctic low. In the lead, accelerating in the freshening breezes of the open ocean, the Nova Scotia schooner *David Moss* slicing the long swells, and *Arpeggio*.

Arpeggio was a topsail schooner with steep-raked masts

and a fine clipper bow. The sun had set two hours previously, falling out of a sky wisped with mackerel cirrocumulus into the deep blue mid-June sea. The sunset position put her five hundred and forty miles off Cape Race, Newfoundland. It was Ed Cole, sailing master, navigator and first mate of *Arpeggio* who had taken the sight. Now he came on deck into the darkness, clasping his hands on his cup of coffee and thinking with regret of the recent warmth of his bunk. He squinted up at a sky from which the stars had disappeared. The wind had freshened, and there was a raw, wet edge to it. He found it unlikely that he would be able to use his sextant to take a dawn sight; it would have to be satnav, or nothing.

Cole stood on deck and shivered, waking up as the wind cut at his oilskins. The binnacle light was a dull glow that picked out the highlights of the famous features of Sir Clement Jones, KCVO, *Arpeggio*'s captain. Clement Jones had been knighted after his ascent of K2 in the Himalayas, without oxygen. He was on *Arpeggio* because he was chairman of Youth Venture. Youth Venture owned *Arpeggio*. It was a trust which believed in self-realization through violent exercise, of which *Arpeggio*'s mountains of canvas and archaic hull provided plenty.

'Hello there!' he boomed, and his strong white teeth gleamed in the binnacle light. 'Wind freshening. Forecast says veering westerly. Low coming up astern, with associated fronts. Course on the slate. We're doing bloody well, Ed. Bloody well.'

'Good,' said Cole, whose natural quietness was even more pronounced than usual in the half-hour after he woke up. 'If it goes westerly, I'll put the topsails on her.'

'It's a deep low,' said Sir Clement.

Cole shrugged invisibly, and said, 'I'll take her.' He stepped across to the wheel, and his hands closed round the brass-bound mahogany spokes. Sir Clement said, 'Well, then. I'll turn in.'

Cole did not answer. He was listening to the ship; with his ears, gauging the hum of the wind in the rigging; with his feet, measuring the lift of her deck as she drove up one slope of water and sank into the trough, sending spray to leeward in dim white clouds; and with his hands, feeling the weight on the rudder ease as the stern came over the crest, then the heavy push of the water resisting three hundred tons of timber and metal and canvas, and forty Youth Venture teenagers, all but ten asleep in the long, segregated cabins forward.

Cole glanced up at the schooner's spider's web of rigging, indistinct black strands against the lighter black of the sky. He knew the ship by heart. And he knew that *Arpeggio* would easily take topsails, even if the wind did freshen to force six. She needed her topsails to develop full power. Not for the first time, he was aware of the fleeting idea that Clement Jones was a hard man and a good mountaineer, but that he was a less than brilliant racing skipper on a tall ship. What Jones was really good at, he reflected with a wry twist to the mouth, was politics.

The wind freshened. Cole gave the wheel to the watch captain and sent the topmen aloft. The square topsails thundered down on the foremast yards, then quietened as they were braced and sheeted home. He stood at the knightheads, looking up, as the dark figures slid down from the tight billows of canvas. And he permitted himself

5

a secret grin of pleasure, feeling the presence of the sleeping crew in the deck under his feet, the tight run of the ship across the big seas with two thousand empty miles stretching ahead between him and Ireland.

He walked aft. Someone had left the doors of the crew cabins open; it got stuffy down there, and the young crews had not yet developed the seaman's taste for a fug. A stronger gust hit him, then another. The wind was veering, and freshening. But it did not stagger *Arpeggio*; she had fifty tons of pig iron in her bilges, and it would take more than a puff of force six to knock her down.

'Nice night,' he said to the helmsman.

The helmsman was surprised at being spoken to by Cole, whose taciturnity was legendary. He said, 'She's going well.'

Cole grunted at him.

'At this rate,' said the helmsman, 'we'll be home a week before that lot astern.'

'Shut up,' said Cole. His dark bulk was rigid, his head tilted as if he was listening. The helmsman lapsed into wounded silence. It had been too good to last. You thought he was opening up, and then he bit your bloody head off. Bloody brilliant sailor he might be, but he could try a bit harder to be civil.

'Give me that,' said Cole, shouldering him off the wheel. His face was hard as granite in the glow of the binnacle, the jaw opening to shout. 'All hands on deck!' he was roaring. 'Let go all sheets!'

There was a moment of stunned silence, in which it seemed to the helmsman that even the sky and the sea and the ship itself held their breath and waited for whatever would happen next. *Arpeggio* rocked up on to an even keel, sails flapping and booms swinging idly inboard. Out of the silence came a strange rustling. Cole roared, 'Hold tight!' The rustling became a roar that swept down on *Arpeggio* like an express train. A hill of water smashed into her starboard quarter and poured over her deck, and the rigging screamed a scream that climbed the scale as the deck tilted forty-five degrees, and then on and on until the yardarms dipped into the water. The roaring eased fractionally. The helmsman heard Cole's bellow, thin and remote: 'Liferafts!' He scrambled along the near-vertical deck and cut free the inflatables. The roar suddenly increased to a shriek, and the deck went from under him. Something huge and black rolled against the sky, and the helmsman realized with horror that it was the ship.

Then he was in icy water that burnt his mouth with its salt, kicking at the ropes that snaked at his ankles and tried to drag him down. He was going. The ropes had him. He thought: stop, all right, enough of this game. But it was not a game, because he very badly wanted to breathe, but his mouth was full of water.

He felt something grab at his hair and pull him up, away from the clutching ropes, and he was dragged over the side of a rubber raft. The roaring had stopped.

'This one's okay,' said Cole.

The helmsman dragged himself on to his hands and knees. His teeth were chattering. It was very dark. On a wave nearby, a white strobe flashed. 'There!' said a voice in the dark, Sir Clement Jones' voice.

They paddled across. The strobe was attached to a lifejacket, and the lifejacket was on one of the watch on deck.

7

They dragged him aboard, then went after the next strobe. The helmsman counted eight, in all. They picked them all up. Then they sat in the cold black and waited, straining their eyes into the rushing darkness that lay over the Atlantic. There were no more strobes. After perhaps half an hour, the questions in the helmsman's mind became too loud to ignore.

'The ship,' he said.

'Gone,' said Cole. 'White squall. Hatches open.'

'The watch below,' said the helmsman.

'Gone,' said Cole. His voice was a croak, cold and dry as the Gobi. Cold and dry as death.

'Gone,' said the helmsman, who was only nineteen and a computer trainee. Then he began to weep.

'You set topsails,' said Jones.

The room was large and painted cream, the ceiling with heavy, dust-grey mouldings that hung like storm clouds over the polished wooden benches facing the dais. Outside, the Plymouth mid-morning traffic hummed drowsily, like a swarm of distant bees. Inside, the chairman of the Inquiry lowered his bushy eyebrows towards the paper in front of him, ran the tip of his grey tongue round his wide, lipless mouth, and cleared his throat.

Cole concentrated on keeping still, bolt upright on his bench next to the black jacket of his solicitor. His suit was too heavy for the July weather, and he was hot. He swallowed to quiet the butterflies in his stomach, and his palms were wet. Across the courtroom – Inquiry room; there was a difference, but as far as Cole was concerned one of them could ruin him just as efficiently as the other – sat

8

Sir Clement Jones. He looked like a Roman Senator, relaxed but grave, his spade beard rock steady above his Royal Geographical Society tie. Next to him, the helmsman looked very young and pale. His tan had faded during the two months since what was now called the *Arpeggio* disaster, and sweat was rolling out of his hair. He had sweated throughout his evidence. Cole felt sorry for him.

The chairman squared his papers and began to speak. 'It is always disagreeable to have to apportion blame, in an Inquiry such as this.' His voice was dry and level, with only a trace of the quarterdeck delivery he had acquired during forty years in the Royal Navy. 'But thirty-one lives have been lost, and it appears from the evidence we have heard from three surveyors that *Arpeggio* was a well-found vessel. Regrettably, this means that the seamanship of her officers and crew is called into question.' Cole's stomach was so tight that it hurt. 'The Inquiry has established that no blame attaches to the Youth Venture Trust, the vessel's owners, nor her surveyors or builders. But the Inquiry has heard evidence that *Arpeggio* was over-canvassed for the squall that hit her. And that when the squall laid her on her beam ends, it was the fact that her hatches were open that allowed her to fill and sink within two minutes, with appalling loss of life.'

The voice droned on, mingling with the traffic's hum. Cole did not bother to listen as it chopped his career to ribbons. Instead he gazed, stony faced, across the room. In his mind, he was saying: *something wasn't right; she shouldn't have gone.* But he knew that it was no use saying it, because the evidence was a mile down, on the bottom of the North Atlantic. He could feel the eyes on him in the public gallery. The Inquiry might not technically be able to apportion blame, but the newspapers would have no such reservations.

The voice stopped. Another voice declared the Inquiry closed. There was a general shuffling of feet as the crowd rose. Cole turned to his solicitor and said, 'Is there a back way out of here?'

The lawyer looked at him for a moment, and Cole knew that his desperation was showing. Then he shook his head and said, 'Sorry, Ed. It's got to be the front steps.'

Cole sat for a moment taking a long breath, as if preparing for a swim in very cold water. Then he said, 'Let's do it,' and rose swiftly to his feet.

The lawyer followed him down the hall of brown marble, then hung back a little and let the small, square figure in the blue suit go out of the door on his own, into the electrical storm of flashbulbs. Then he went on and caught up with Cole, and took him down the steps, through the press of notebooks and miniature tape recorders and the blank eyes of the television cameras. The car was waiting, half buried in people. Voices were shouting questions. Cole kept his head down and his fists clenched, held tight to his sides. The lawyer grabbed the door handle and wrenched it open. 'Get in!' he shouted, his voice faint in the uproar. Then he turned, guarding the door with his back. The crowd stilled. He said, 'No comment, gentlemen,' and smiled. The crowd bayed its disappointment. To his right, the press of people heaved. A man in a dark suit was pushing his way through. 'Letter for Mr Cole,' he said.

The lawyer seized the envelope and dived into the car. Faces smeared against the windows, mouths framing inaudible questions. Flashbulbs popped, and a fist with a Rolex Oyster hammered on the window.

'Off we jolly well go,' said the solicitor clamly.

The driver pulled away, and the crowd fell behind. The lawyer handed Cole the envelope. 'A colleague gave me this,' he said.

Cole put it in his breast pocket unopened.

The lawyer said, 'Would you like some lunch?'

Cole shook his head. The lawyer thought he looked rather grey, but that was understandable in the circumstances. It was hard to think of this small man with bags under his eyes and receding sandy hair in charge of a giant sailing ship. Still, thought the lawyer, stranger things happen at sea. He laughed, inwardly, said, 'I'll drop you off at home,' and turned his mind to the afternoon's case, which was a nice, simple divorce, with no square topsails or pig iron or aspect ratios. Just good old dog eat dog.

When they reached Cole's home, he got out and trudged off up the long gravel track between the glasshouses.

'Poor sod,' said the lawyer to nobody in particular. 'He's finished. Come on, let's get me to the restaurant. I need a drink.'

Cole waited until the sound of the car had completely gone. Then he unlocked the door of the red-brick house at the far end of the glasshouses. The kitchen was cold and cheerless; a calendar from a winch firm hung on the white wall, and white crockery was ranged with Naval precision on the shelves of a chipped green dresser. He made a cup of tea. Then he sat down at the table, took a deep breath, and opened the letter.

> *Dear Ed,*
>
> *I'm very sorry to have to tell you that the directors of* Chinamite *feel we have a problem with regard to our sponsorship in the forthcoming Lancaster Great Circle Race. Frankly, we feel that we are in a difficulty with public relations here, and that we cannot continue under your captaincy though naturally we shall value your continuing co-operation and assistance. Please take this letter as signifying a termination of our contract with you, under Clause 21.*
>
> *Yours sincerely,*
> *Maurice Quain*
> *Marketing Manager*

'Sod it,' said Cole. He read the letter again. This time, his hands shook slightly. They must have had it ready written, to have got it to him so quickly.

Captaining *Chinamite* in the Lancaster Great Circle would have been the apex of his career. He had been at sea since he was sixteen; twenty years exactly. Merchant Service, delivery skipper, racing skipper. Solid and dependable Cole. Never had the time to get married. Wedded to the sea. Given it his youth. And now his hair was beginning to fall out, and he was on the bloody beach, with a house, a thousand square feet of greenhouse, and twenty thousand rare plants from New Zealand.

He filed the letter carefully, under *Chinamite*. Then he got up and went to the glass door of the kitchen and pulled back his fist and punched the glass out. The crash and jangle was very loud in the silent house. The telephone took up its tail end. Cole walked back into the room, bleeding a little. He pulled the telephone cable out of the wall, went to the first-aid cabinet, and bandaged his arm. After that, he changed into a blue boiler suit and went out to work in the greenhouse. The staff had missed out on the aphids while he had been away.

Control, thought Cole as he carefully measured thick brown Malathion into the sprayer. Keep it under control.

Gaston Rhys was very hot, and very proud. Beneath his chef's toque, his fat face glowed blood-red in the heat from the black coal range. It was not everyone (he hissed to himself, as he arranged the oysters round the last of the ramekins of lobster meat with corn, fennel and bourbon) who could manufacture ninety-eight servings of Lobster Hyatt in the oldest kitchens in Boston, and get them to the table sizzling hot and all at once, and expect a thousand dollars in tips. Gaston whirled, mopped his forehead with his red bandana, and screamed, *'Ou v'z êtes, gueules de con?'*

It was a rhetorical question, because the waiters were

right there, fourteen of them in line, and the commis chefs were already loading them with plates. The white-coated crocodile of men was indistinct in the drifts of steam that billowed among the sinks and tables and the cast-iron pillars that supported the sagging ceiling. Then it began to move, crunching underfoot fragments of lobster shell. The waiters filed up the spiral staircase, pursued by the shouts of Gaston Rhys as he ordered the new course, until his shouts were drowned by the thunder of the twenty-eight shoes.

In the room at the top of the stairs ninety-eight men sat round a huge oval table. In the centre of the table, a line of silver trophies reflected the lustres of a huge chandelier. The door on the inner wall opened. Ernest, the Sound Yacht Club's black butler, said, 'Gentlemen, the Lobster Hyatt is served.' The waiters' feet became silent as they passed on to the huge Turkey carpet. And the silence was absolute: it was one of the Sound Yacht Club's many traditions that nobody spoke from the announcement of the Lobster Hyatt to the clearing of the Commodore's plate.

So the Sound Yacht Club ate, at its oval table in the gigantic bow window on the first floor of the porticoed white building looking east over the Atlantic. The grey Atlantic light winked on the gilt buttons of the blazers. It shone on the bald head of Jasper Hyatt, the Commodore, a wizened gnome of a man shovelling chunks of lobster meat into the greedy slot set between his shrivelled cheeks. Hyatt was eighty-two, the third Hyatt to be president of the Sound Yacht Club. There were two other Hyatts at the table; his son Jasper III, paunchy in a dark business suit, and Jasper III's son Martin. Martin was on leave from the US Naval Academy at Annapolis. His skin shone pinkly through his cropped gold hair, and the gold on his stiff, narrow shoulders gleamed in the sun. The same sun also gleamed on the unnaturally white teeth of Wallace DuCane, the SYC's Vice-President, as he smiled between two of the heavy silver cups in the middle of the table. Martin did not return the smile. He might only be twenty-one, but he was a traditionalist. Like many of the club's traditionalists, from his grandfather down, he was made nervous by DuCane.

Farther from the bow window, George Hart was finding it difficult to believe his eyes and ears. He had arrived at the SYC's Summer Luncheon in place of his godfather, who ran the Boston law firm into which he would go when Princeton had finished with him. But looking round at the Sound Yacht Club, five billion dollars' worth of blue blood and big business munching its annual sacrament in complacent silence, George found himself wondering if he really wanted to spend the rest of his life with these people. He gulped deeply at the Sancerre in his glass, which was immediately refilled by a waiter. Then he re-applied himself to the Lobster Hyatt. The Lobster Hyatt was okay, thought George. It was fussy; more elaborate than he would have cooked himself. Okay for a ritual. A ritual in a nice restaurant, with a girl, maybe. But this was like a gourmet wax museum. He took another gulp of wine, and shuddered. At the end of the table, Jasper Hyatt, purple from swallowing, put his liver-spotted hands on either side of his empty plate and heaved himself to his feet.

'Gentlemen,' he said. 'I shall be brief.' He had said the

same thing every year for the past forty-three years and he was invariably as good as his word.

'The Lancaster Great Circle,' he said. 'After careful consideration, the committee has decided that the Sound Yacht Club will make an entry.' The clatter of knives and forks stilled. 'I should explain,' said Hyatt. 'The US has not until now been too involved in this type of race. But I have information that a strong American entry would bring about a US stopover on the race following such an entry. Which would be a highly desirable state of affairs, since this is the only important aspect of world racing in which the US is not pre-eminent.' He paused. The knives and forks went to work again. George Hart saw heads nodding into their plates; a popular suggestion.

'It won't be cheap,' he said. 'It is never cheap to be excellent, and the Sound Yacht Club is dedicated to the pursuit of excellence. We'll have to raise a supplementary subscription of, say, ten thousand dollars per member.' He looked down the table. Very few people looked back; it was a lot of money, though it was not a sum that SYC members would notice. Jasper paused, to let it sink in, and caught the eye of Wallace DuCane. DuCane's brown face was turned towards him, the white teeth brilliant in the square jaw, the pepper-and-salt hair in an immaculate brush-cut. Whippersnapper, thought Jasper Hyatt. Uppity. Pushy. But he made himself smile, feeling the unelastic skin of his thin cheeks fall into its deep creases. 'Wallace DuCane has agreed to co-ordinate sponsorships. I'm sure that many of you will wish corporate involvement. Please speak with Wallace.' He paused. He had not sold them yet. But he was not worried; he still had a shot in

16

his locker. 'By the way,' he said, 'I heard a rumour that the Australians are entering a boat.'

That got them. The eyes came up from the plates, and switched first to Jasper and then to an ebony pillar in the middle of the line of trophies in the centre of the table. The top of the pillar looked worn, as if by the rim of a cup. There was no cup.

'The prime mover in the Australian campaign is a Mr Harry Redd.'

Wallace DuCane said, 'Let's go get him.' It was a terrible breach of tradition for DuCane to have spoken, but the wave of anger that swept round the table blotted out the solecism. Jasper noticed, though. 'As you say,' he said. 'Let us, ah, go get him. Mr DuCane, ah, Wallace.'

The waiters began to clear. Apple pies appeared on the table, upper slopes waxy with melted cheese. Wallace said. 'Thank you, Jasper.' He set his knuckles on the table and leaned forward, meeting each eye in turn – as if, thought Jasper, he was addressing some damn sales convention. 'Harry Jackman, whose designs you all know, has submitted a set of plans to the Main Committee and the Race Committee,' he said. 'We have tested and modified these, with facilities provided by the US Navy among others.' Martin Hyatt looked smug, as if he had a controlling interest in the US Navy.

'We have sailed this baby three times round the world already on the Woods Hole mainframe,' said DuCane. 'She won the race the last two times. She'll rate seventy feet, built out of Kevlar and Nomex. She'll have on-board computers, radar, full comfort facilities.'

Next to Hart, a leathery banker in a dark-blue blazer

scribbled on his notepad, 'But will the goddamn thing float?' Hart grinned, then composed his face quickly. Nobody else seemed to think anything was funny. 'The drawings will be in the President's office,' said DuCane. 'Members only. No cameras.' He grinned. A warm pulse of excitement went round the table. 'Crew trials will start in two weeks. Nominations to the club secretary. And I would say that the word for nominees is dedication.' He paused and took a sip of water. His eyes were level and serious; the eyes that had brought him up from a corner employment agency to the head of the biggest management consultancy in America. 'We're going to win this one, for the SYC.' He paused, to let it sink in. 'Which brings me to our captain. We're going outside the club for the captain. The committee has a man in mind. We'll be contacting him this afternoon. He won't disappoint us.' He paused a beat. Then he grinned. 'He better not.'

And Hart, looking at the wink of the sunlight from those expensive teeth, found himself thinking: those teeth aren't just for grinning.

They're for biting.

In Quague Sound, it had started to rain again. The clouds were coming in long squalls from over the Head, which sheltered the Sound's maze of shoals and sand-flats from the turbulent Atlantic outside. Under the squalls the wind blew hard and nasty, raising a short chop that rocked a raft of goldeneye and whacked pettishly at the bow of the blue-painted lobster boat threading its way among the twisted channels of sand.

The boat smelt of weed and the half-rotten bluefish

used for baiting the traps. The man at the wheel had narrow grey eyes set at a slight tilt in a square face the colour of raw cedar. He looked hard and stocky. The hands on the brass-bound spokes were square. He was thinking about the bank loans that were keeping him afloat, him and the ten men and women who worked for him at Marblehead Clam and Lobster, in the green-painted buildings on the rain-whipped shore. And he was thinking that he should be out in hotels, explaining why expensive East Coast lobster was better than cheap Cuban lobster, not pounding through the short seas with a holdful of lobster with the rain in his eyes and the diesel up his nose. Fact was, he was a good lobsterman but a bad corporate president. His heart was not in being a president.

The little boat wound past the sticks marking the channel and came alongside the quay. The deckhands tied up, and the crane boom came across and started the unloading. Art Schacker stopped engines, ran up the iron ladder in the black oak pilings, and walked across the quay past the packing sheds. He squinted up at the roof as he passed. Then he went to a telephone and ordered maintenance to repaint two sheets of iron that were showing signs of rust. After that he went to the car park, climbed into the elderly but gleaming Bentley that he had rebuilt himself, and turned out of the factory entrance on to the highway.

Marblehead extended tentacles of steakhouses and gas stations, and drew him towards its old heart. He parked the Bentley in a garage and walked through a gate in a high clapboard fence. Inside was a yard, with a green lawn and a wide gravel path running under an avenue of snake-bark maples blood-pink with young leaf. At the end of the path was a house, two tall storeys with pilasters. Grapevines were beginning to shoot on the white clapboard walls. The racket of children came through an open window on the first floor. Schacker pushed open the door and walked through an oval hall with a sweeping staircase, and into a white room where a small, dark woman was painting a splashy picture of a whale. He kissed her. Four boys, the eldest eight, the youngest three, came in. They were all square and red faced, like Schacker. They said: 'Bonjour, Papa.'

The telephone began to ring. Schacker was tired, with the heavy, irritable tiredness that came of insoluble problems, time and money and bank loans. Anne-Marie looked at him and saw, and said, 'I'll get it.' She listened, said, 'He'll be right with you.' She put her hand over the mouthpiece. 'It's the Sound Yacht Club in Boston,' she said. 'They called earlier. They eat a hell of a lot of clams down there. It'd be nice to have their business.'

Art nodded, smiling as convincingly as he could. He lit a cigarette, took the telephone and said, 'Yes?'

She watched nervously as he listened. Finally he said, 'Well, thank you, Mr Hyatt, but I'm sorry.' There was more talk on the other end. 'Yes,' said Art, his flat East Coast voice going even flatter than usual, as it did when he was digging in his heels. 'I know it's a great race and a great opportunity, and I guess it will be a rather fine boat. But I gave up ocean racing when I turned forty.' He laughed. 'I have four kids, and I like to see them from time to time. Thanks for asking, but the answer is no.' The voice on the other end was agitated now. 'Okay,' said Art. 'Have him call. Goodbye.'

He put down the telephone, and crushed out his cigarette in an ashtray. 'They want me to go sailing for eight months,' he said. 'No clams.'

'Too bad,' said Anne-Marie, and put an arm round his wide waist. 'You wanted to go, didn't you?'

'I'm forty-three,' said Art. 'I have responsibilities. Some guy called DuCane's going to call. I'll see if I can sell him a clam.'

Jasper Hyatt II looked down the small table in the pannelled committee room off the big dining-room of the Sound Yacht Club. 'He said no,' he said to the four men with him.

Jasper Hyatt III said, 'Are we sure about him? His racing record's brilliant, of course. But he's been off the water for two years. And I've heard that . . . well, he can be a little independent in his thinking.'

Jasper Hyatt II laid his liver-spotted hands on the pile of papers in front of him. 'This is a big race,' he croaked. 'You need a man who's a seaman as well as a hard charger. And we want a good East Coast boy.'

'And if he gets too independent-minded, we'll reinforce his motivation,' said DuCane smoothly, smiling. 'The Sound Yacht Club will of course be proposing crew members of its own.' The telephone rang. DuCane picked it up, listened, and said, 'If you'll excuse me, it's my office. I'll take it outside.

He made his way into the office on the landing, and picked up the telephone from the eighteenth-century English mahogany partners' desk like an eighteenth-century statesman picking up a quill pen. 'Yeh?' he said. 'DuCane. Speak to me.'

The voice on the other end belonged to Arthur Somers, the Harvard Business School graduate in charge of DuCane's operations. 'Schacker,' he said. 'President, Marblehead Clam and Lobster. Assets, valuation one million two hundred thousand. Debts, five million dollars. Personal guarantees for the whole bunch. Turnover, six hundred thousand.'

'Hmm,' said DuCane. 'High gearing. Private money?'

'Private money, shit,' said Somers delicately. 'The bank's into him for most of his turnover. The man's a technical bankrupt, Wallace.'

'Yeah,' said DuCane. 'Well, Arthur, you get out and buy up his paper, and we'll turn this guy into a wholly owned subsidiary.'

'But –'

'You want to argue, go argue on somebody else's time,' said DuCane.

Back in the committee room, there was silence. DuCane leaned elegantly on the back of a Chippendale *fauteuil*. 'Well, gentlemen,' he said. 'That is all very satisfactory. I think that we can start drafting the press release.'

'But we don't have a captain,' said Jasper Hyatt III.

'Oh, yes, we do,' said Wallace DuCane, showing his sharp white teeth.

It was a sparkling hot day at Flemington Race Course, Melbourne. The State of Victoria had been at a standstill for five days; it was the first week of November, late spring, and the television cameras of Australia had been saturating the nation's viewers with horses and owners and women's hats and the cool gleam of big, expensive cars half-buried in champagne bottles under the shady trees behind the Members' Enclosures.

What the television cameras could not show was the heat; the glowing bars of sun that rested on the turf and the rose bushes and the top hats, gluing tailcoats to backs and muslin to breasts, and filling the air with the smell of horses and Chanel and green grass. In a month, the grass might be burnt sand yellow, and the racecourse deserted. But nobody was thinking a month ahead at two fifteen on Melbourne Cup day, with the jockeys in the weighing-in room before the big race and the bookies by the white enclosure rails besieged ten deep.

The weighing-in room is a spare, practical building that sits well away from the grandstand, which looks like a Mississippi riverboat stranded on a lawn. The door of the weighing-in room was the centre of a half-moon of journalists and touts and top-hatted owners. A little apart from the main crowd, a head crowned with furious red hair rose above the crush. Under the hair was a heavy, straight brow, a sun-blistered eagle's beak of a nose, and two deep-sunk green eyes that did not so much sparkle as glow. In the right hand dangled a magnum of Bollinger, holding about a cupful. In the left was a large silver tankard, bearing the inscription 'SOUTHERN OCEAN CHAMPIONSHIP – "Tubes" Murphy, skipper, *Vindaloo*'. The head was cocked to one side, so Murphy could hear what the very small man was saying.

The small man was wearing jockey's silks, and his wizened face looked faintly unhappy. Murphy slapped him on the back and made off at his usual rolling walk towards the bookies. It was noticeable that the trousers of his morning suit had been made for someone shorter than his six foot five, and that his coat came nowhere near accommodating his vast shoulders.

When he came within range of the bookies, he appeared to be looking for someone. After a couple of minutes' scrutiny, he found his quarry and beckoned. The man who pushed his way through the crowd was nondescript and brown, dressed in a tan suit and wearing a wide green tie, with drink stains. Murphy spoke to him quietly, and shoved his big hand forward. The man put out his own hands. Nobody saw the fat envelope that passed from Murphy's palm into the brown man's pocket.

Then Murphy turned away and ran up the steps on the side of the stand. Outside the door he paused, gazing over the suburbs of Melbourne and the people like bright ants on the green. The breeze cooled the sweat on his face. For a moment, he looked stone-cold sober. Then he shoved open the door, and went in.

The box was decorated with green-and-white striped bunting that billowed gently in the breeze. There was a bar along one side, covered with champagne bottles. On the white iron chairs, half a dozen men and women were sitting, talking. One of the men got up, and said, 'G'day, Tubes!' He was smoothly shaved and immaculately dressed in dark morning coat and dove-grey waistcoat. His head was close cropped, to disguise the fact that he had very little hair left on the top. His eyes were narrow and humorous and clever. 'Welcome aboard.'

'Honoured,' said Murphy, turning a brilliant white smile on the sitters, and pausing an extra second on a young woman in a white dress through which there shone golden gleams of skin.

The dapper man said, 'Have a drink?'

'Don't mind if I do,' said Murphy, and held out his tankard. A pretty girl in a maid's uniform filled it.

'Reddy, you old bastard,' he said. 'You got a horse?'

Harry Redd said, 'No.'

'Well, I have,' said Murphy. 'I was down the Enclosure, and I was talking to a bloke I know, a jock, and he says they're pulling the Antiquary to get Corkface Boy in.'

Harry Redd pulled a slender gold watch from the dove-grey waistcoat, consulted it, and replaced it. Then he said, 'What does the jock know?'

'It's him that's pulling Antiquary. Jacky Cullinane.'

'Guaranteed?'

Murphy's laugh fluttered the bunting. 'C'mon, Reddy,' he said. 'This is bloody horse-racing, not the bloody stock market. No certs here.'

'Who is it, then?'

'Corkface Boy. Who else?'

Redd said, 'Well, I'd better go out and do a little

business. I want to talk when I get back in. You've met Shar Stapleton, Mo's wife?' The woman in the white silk dress smiled at him. She had a wide red mouth and big blue eyes and black hair. The dress clung to the slopes of her high breasts.

Murphy said, 'Shar.'

'And you know Mo.'

'No,' said Murphy, and raised a spade-like hand to a tall, thin man with a hard face, sitting upright on a chair with a glass of Perrier in his hand.

'Come out and invest, Mo,' said Redd.

'I'll have ten dollars on,' said Mo, rising stiffly from his chair.

'Cheapskate,' said Redd. 'Still, I suppose it's a virtue in my financial comptroller. Coming, Shar?'

Shar said, 'Too hot. I'll stay.'

Mo Stapleton's hard eyes flicked at her, then at Murphy. 'Come on,' said Redd. The door closed behind them. Shar's eyes came up and held Murphy's. 'He's jealous,' she said quietly. Her eyes did not drop. 'Are you the bloke who sails boats?'

'That's right,' said Murphy. 'Can I get you a drink?' He thumbed open another bottle of champagne, poured her a glass, and splashed some more into his tankard. She came close to get it, and he could see little beads of sweat on her short upper lip, and damp curls of dark hair at her forehead.

'I'd like to hear about your boats,' she said.

Murphy was looking over her shoulder. It was a smooth, brown shoulder with a golden down, rising from breakers of white silk. 'Any time,' he said.

She smiled, and looked full into his eyes, and he saw that the gap between her two upper front teeth was wide. Sign of passion, thought Murphy, and grinned at her. Then he walked across to the front railings of the box.

Down below, a band was playing 'Waltzing Matilda'. The bookies crouched with their backs to their blackboards and grabbed in fistfuls of notes with both hands. Murphy saw Redd's gleaming brown head burrow through the crowd first to one bookie, then another. At the fourth bookie, the assistant started to rub out the chalked odds and substitute new ones. Corkface Boy came down from 6-1 to 5-1, then 4-1. Murphy gripped the rails and shook. Shar came alongside him and looked up. Tears were pouring from his eyes. She put her long-fingered hand next to his red paw. When she looked up at him, she saw that he was laughing.

'What's so funny?' she said.

He shook his head, and moved his hand to cover hers. She did not take hers away. Instead, he felt her nails lightly caress his palm. 'Tell you later,' he said. 'Corkface Boy's down to fours in the Members. And here come our lucky punters.' He stayed and watched as the bookies re-marked their odds. 'Strewth,' he said. 'The Antiquary's up to threes. Well, now.'

Redd looked extremely pleased with himself when he returned. 'Got ten thousand on at sixes before they realized what was going on,' he said. 'That donkey'd better win.'

'Yeah, yeah,' said Murphy.

'Sorry to leave you, Shar,' said Stapleton.

Mrs Stapleton sipped delicately at her champagne, a chaste vision in white and gold.

27

'C'm'ere, Murph,' said Redd. 'I've got a proposition for you.'

They went and sat in the corner. Redd said. 'You've been planning a round-the-world boat, but you haven't got any money.'

'Correct,' said Murphy. 'I'm having talks.'

'Bull,' said Redd. 'You're broke, mate, and you're not having talks with anybody. So I want you to build that boat; and I'll do you a total sponsorship. My blokes'll fix you up. Don't worry about it. What you have to worry about is getting the boat built and winning the race. Just send me the bills. You're sure it's a decent boat?'

Murphy said, 'Two hundred per.'

Redd said, 'If you say so. Shake, mate.' And his small, well-kept hand was engulfed by Murphy's scaffold-pipe fingers. 'Right,' said Redd. 'Let's have a glass of the old shampola.' While they had been talking, the box had filled with people. 'Ladies and gentlemen,' said Redd. 'I give you Tasman Wine's latest venture into the field of world sporting endeavour, a worthy successor to *Victoria* which you will remember blew the bloody Yanks out of the water in the Atlantic Cup last year. Our entry for the Lancaster Great Circle, designed by Joe Grimaldi, sails by Tubes Murphy, the world's greatest sailmaker, three times winner of the Southern Ocean Championship, who will also sail her. Ladies and gentlemen, *Tasman*!' They drained their glasses. Redd said, 'Now let's do some racing, eh, Murph?'

For a moment, Murphy looked almost pale. Then he said, 'Oh, yeah. Why not, Reddy?'

On the green turf beyond the white rails, the horses were

going down for the start. Corkface Boy was a big bay, moving easily in the heat. The Antiquary was a rawboned grey with an awkward action of the hind legs and a blistering turn of speed in the final furlongs. They were followed by Tertius, the favourite, a pretty, well-bred four-year-old. Tertius was not enjoying the heat. He shied at a fly, and capered sideways, and his jockey swore. The sun gleamed from the sweat on his flanks.

The horses went into the gates. The crowd hushed for a moment, so that the clang of the gates going up reached as far as the box. Shar Stapleton's hands clenched on the balcony rail. Her lips were parted, and her breath came fast. Tertius went for the rails, and stuck there. Corkface Boy glued his nose to Tertius' stirrup. After him came a couple of others, with the Antiquary lying fifth. They leaned into the first turn.

They held steady formation round the far side of the course. Redd trained his binoculars. Murphy said, 'He's going up!'

Redd grunted. Corkface Boy's nose had inched forward, and he was level with the root of Tertius's neck. An arm rose and fell. The jockey was using his whip.

'Six furlongs to go,' said the commentator. 'And it's . . . yes, it's Corkface Boy with his nose in front, then it's Tertius, dropping back, and Grasshopper and Harry's Kiss and Last Chance and after that it's the Antiquary, well back now, and the rest are nowhere with four furlongs to go . . .'

'He's making ground,' said Murphy. Corkface Boy was a toy horse, far away on the green, with daylight showing between his tail and the sheepskin noseband of

Grasshopper, who had come up second now that Tertius had shot his bolt. The bright group of horses and jockeys leaned into the far curve. 'He's using the whip,' said Redd. They rounded the curve and entered the home straight.

'And in the final furlong,' said the loudspeaker, 'it's Corkface Boy from Harry's Kiss, then Grasshopper, and good gracious it's the Antiquary coming up on the outside, and he's past Grasshopper and there goes Harry's Kiss and as they go down to the finish THE ANTIQUARY'S STILL COMING!'

The drumming of hooves on the hard ground drifted up into the box with the roar of the crowd. The big, raw-boned grey on the outside of the group seemed to slip into an extra gear. His stride lengthened and he drifted without apparent effort away from Corkface Boy, to go past the post an easy neck ahead.

'And it's the ANTIQUARY!' The loudspeaker's tinny voice was all but lost in the crowd's roar. 'The Antiquary wins the Melbourne Cup!'

Redd turned round and looked at Murphy. 'He wasn't supposed to win,' he said flatly.

Murphy said, 'You're right. But aren't you glad? He was the . . . popular favourite, eh?'

'Like some others I could mention,' said Redd. His small face was set, and his eyes glittered dangerously.

'Come on, Reddy,' said Murphy. 'This is horse-racing.'

Mo Stapleton was staring at him with dark, pouched eyes. A telephone in the corner rang. The maid answered it, and said something to Stapleton. Stapleton spoke for a moment, then said, 'We have the Metro meeting, Harry.'

'On my way,' snapped Redd. 'Murphy, you can tell that jockey I'm bloody displeased with him. Give Shar a lift home, would you?'

'C'mon,' said Murph. 'He nearly won.'

'Nearly's not enough,' said Redd. 'That's the last time I listen to you about a horse. Now get me my boat built, nice and quick. Mo'll sign the cheques.'

Mo smiled as if smiling hurt him physically, and followed Redd out of the door. Murph said, 'Phew,' went to the bar, thumbed the cork out of a fresh bottle of Bollinger. Now that Redd had gone the other guests left. It was cool and quiet in the box among the gently blowing green and white bunting. Shar said, 'You're sweating,'

'I have my reasons,' said Murphy. He drained his tankard, said, 'Better,' and winked at her.

'Why are you looking so pleased with yourself?' she said. 'You just lost Reddy ten thousand notes.'

Murphy nodded. 'True. But' – he fixed her with his bright blue eyes – 'can you be trusted, Shar?'

She lowered her lashes. 'Try me.'

'Only too delighted,' he said gallantly. 'Lookit, Reddy and I go back ages. We were neighbours on the Burma Road and my old man and his old man used to drink out of the same bottle and puke off the same dock. Reddy and I used to swipe lollies from the same shops. He got a scholarship to U of Sydney because he swiped my physics notes. I got my first job because I swiped his college diploma and took it to the interview. You have to give and take with your mates.' He walked to the balcony rail and scrutinized the crowd below. When he saw what he was looking for, he roared, 'Joe!'

Three minutes later, the man in the tan suit came in. His manner was nervous. He said, 'G'day, Murph,' accepted a glass of champagne, pushed a heavy paper bag into Murphy's hand, and fled. There was a distant clatter of rotors. A helicopter rose, tilted over the racecourse, and flew smoothly into the haze. On the side of the helicopter was written REDDY.

'So long, Mo,' said Shar. 'Don't hurry back.'

Murphy upended the bag. The floor of the box was suddenly ankle deep in money. Shar's hands had gone to her mouth. 'My *God*!' she said. 'That must be fifty grand!'

'Sixty,' said Murphy. He rushed to the cupboard in the corner of the box, pulled out a broom and began sweeping the notes into a pile. Shar helped him gather them up and stuff them back into the bag, laughing helplessly. He tucked the last note between her golden breasts.

'Oh,' she said. Her big blue eyes were suddenly serious, and she caught her lower lip between her teeth. She pushed him down in a chair, and sat on his knee. 'Tell me,' she said. 'How did you do it?'

Murphy was staring at her breasts as if hypnotized. 'The Antiquary's jock's a mate of mine,' he said. 'He told me his instructions were to take Corkface Boy in the final straight. But I only had fifteen grand to bet, so I wanted nice odds. And old Reddy goes at his bets like a bull at a gate, always has, so I thought I'd get him out there and get the odds down on Corkface Boy.'

'But you lost him ten grand. Is that a nice thing to do to your mate?'

'Nice?' For a second Murphy looked genuinely puzzled.

'Look, Shar, old Reddy's got fifty million in his budget account down the Commonwealth Bank. That was my last fifteen grand.'

'Yeah,' said Shar. Then, realizing what he meant, she said. 'You put your last fifteen grand on a *horse*? What if it had lost?'

'It won,' said Murphy, and laughed.

Shar turned round and put her arms around his neck and kissed him. It started as a mere touch of the lips. But somehow the lips, having touched, did not separate. Her mouth opened under his, and he could feel the length of her body against him.

'Let's go home,' she said.

'What about your old man?'

'He's off working. We've got eight hours.' She looked at him through her long lashes. 'Is that long enough?'

'We'll just have to rush it,' said Murphy.

'Two, one, *cue*,' said the director, squashing out her forty-fifth Kent since breakfast.

On the animation monitor, a computer-drawn American eagle spread its stylized wings and took to the stylized air. A man in a loud check jacket got up in front of the stage and made clapping movements, and the studio audience clapped and rocked and loosed a few rebel yells.

The director said, 'Cross fade.'

The eagle gave way to a bird's eye view of studio, audience and stage.

The director said, 'Give me the zoom.'

The bird's eye view centred on the chair in the middle of the stage, and its occupant. The chair's occupant grew until his face filled the screen. It was a finely boned face, with high cheekbones and a nose that was perhaps too slim and too short to be anything but pretty. The eyes, thanks to make-up, were deep set and so piercing as to be almost hypnotic. They were years older than the handsome face with its tight cap of dark curls and firm but delicately-chiselled jaw.

'Title,' said the director.

The screen filled with a picture of the eye socket of the man in the chair. The eye was huge and dark and still. Across it, in yellow capital letters, appeared the words: KELLY'S EYE.

'Close up,' said the director.

The man on the screen's voice rang out over the control room monitors. 'Welcome to Kelly's Eye, America's top-rated TV news show,' he said.

The director cut the volume and muttered, 'Bullshit.' The ratings had been nose diving for months. Then she swallowed a gulp of Maalox, for her ulcer, and wondered how she was going to avoid getting dragged under when Kelly sank.

Kelly read the news to camera off the autocue, and introduced the night's ten-minute documentary. It was a good, simple format; the documentary, followed by the ruthless dissection of the documentary's subject, live on camera. In the past, Kelly had among other things toppled a German government, reduced the leader of a Nicaraguan death squad to tears of remorse, and secured an admission of tax fraud from a Sun Belt senator. Tonight, the film was about suspect pipe joints in San Mateo de las Lagrimas nuclear power station.

Kelly slumped in his chair, watching it on the monitor, and wondering about getting another drink. A couple of production assistants were ushering on his guest, the power station manager; it was Kelly's policy to keep his guests moving about, distracted, while they saw the film that laid the charges they were to answer.

He had had dinner early, and a bottle and a half of wine because he had been feeling rough after lunch, at which he had drunk another bottle and a half to get rid of last night's hangover. As he watched the film, his stomach was queasy, and his mind was fuzzy at the edges. Even so, he could see it was bad. Well, thought Kelly, they can't all be great. He pushed away the knowledge that hardly any of his films had been even passable, lately, and consoled himself with the thought that the power station manager, who would be commenting on the film, was easy meat. Yeah, thought Kelly. This isn't television. This is Kelly's Eye. But then he remembered the ratings last week, and the week before, and what his agent had said: '*They're going to tell you it's time you took a holiday, Dave.*' And he strolled over to the hospitality trolley and poured himself a tumbler of cognac, drank it and hurried back.

The director lit another Kent and sighed the smoke into

the banks of switches. 'One of these days, he'll cut it too fine,' she said. 'Then we'll all be screwed.'

Kelly walked back to his chair with extreme deliberation. As he came down the step he stumbled slightly. The director drew in her breath, choking on the smoke.

No, she thought, he couldn't be drunk. Not with sixty million people watching. Things like that didn't happen. Through her mind there ran a series of pictures, as if through an editing machine; her house on the beach at Malibu, the perpetual smell of wintergreen on Kelly's breath, the ratings charts like Cannonball Alley at Aspen . . .

'Ah, shoot,' she said. There were things she was meant to be doing, and she wasn't doing them. Kelly was a professional. 'Get into the guest,' she said into the intercom.

She saw Kelly smile and shake hands with the dumpy, balding man in the dark suit, and she relaxed. The film was still running, and Kelly was talking hard, distracting the manager from the devastating conclusions of the film, so he wouldn't be able to defend himself later on. Kelly was a genius at putting people at their ease. The dark eyes sparkled, and the cheeks were pink above the smile, glowing with boyish charm. And he led them on, step by step, until they crucified themselves . . . Pure television, thought the director, with a surge of admiration. Her confidence renewed, she began setting up the next sequence.

The power station manager was arranging himself in his chair, his spectacles reflecting the monitor screen. He was smiling, bending his head towards Kelly to catch a joke. Another lamb to the slaughter; but as his nose entered the orbit of Kelly's breath he stiffened, and the smile weakened.

Kelly was watching him, and noticed the slight hesitation.

But the brandy was running hot and strong in his blood, and he dismissed it. 'So we'll just run the technical stuff by you, and then you can say your piece about the benefits of nuclear energy,' he said, turning on the charm. 'About which I for one am totally convinced. You can do it in your sleep, right?'

The manager smiled back at him, but Kelly thought he saw a coldness in the eyes, and they flicked quickly back to the monitor. The film was drawing to its conclusion, and Kelly tried desperately to think of something to distract the man. But the cognac was a fog in his head, and he couldn't think of anything. Things were going wrong. Kelly drew breath to speak, but the director's voice in his earphone cut him off. 'One minute,' it said.

Sweat broke in Kelly's palms. One minute wasn't nearly long enough. But he made himself smile and said, 'Okáy, ready to go.'

'Two, one, *go*,' said the director's voice in Kelly's ear. His heart was thudding. He'd lost guests before, and caught them again. He'd just have to wing it.

The lights came up. The audience clapped. Kelly pulled his famous wry grin, and uttered his famous catch line. 'Don't clap yet,' he said. 'Kelly's Eye tonight examines the proposition that Dr Parsons Klein here, of the San Mateo de las Lagrimas power station, is captain of a sinking ship which could take us all down with it.' He grinned conspiratorially at the manager. 'Well, Dr Klein?'

'The San Mateo is one hundred percent safe,' said Klein. His eyes were cold and direct, and Kelly's mouth became dry. *I've lost him*, he thought, for the first time in his career. *He could win this*. And he felt himself getting angry. As the brandy touched the anger, it began to burn. Jerk, he thought, hating the manager's pudgy cheeks and double chin; who do you think you are?

'Safe? That's not what we heard in the movie,' said Kelly.

'I am not responsible for your distortions,' said the manager.

Kelly stared at him, the smile frozen on his face. The audience were on the edges of their seats, eager for Kelly to start the forensic dismemberment of this public official who dared defy him. But the pause lasted fractionally too long. 'How do you explain the metallurgists' allegations of extensive cracking in coolant pipes?'

'Normal,' said Klein, with a precise, dismissive gesture of his podgy hand. 'As we saw in the film, they're replaced in rotation. Also, the cracks were insignificant.'

You bastard, thought Kelly. *You little bastard*.

The director said, 'Bring me Camera 2 on the big monitor.' Kelly's face loomed on the screen, huge in close up. Beads of sweat were forming on the hairline and tickling down into the eyes.

'Oh, my Jiminy Christmas!' said the director. 'He's corpsed!' She pressed the intercom switch with a shaking finger and said, keeping her voice as steady as she could, 'Trash him, Dave!'

Kelly could feel the muscles of his face locked tight as iron bars. The voice in his ear was a distant fly buzzing. He knew there was no way out but forward, and he tried to marshal facts, but the brandy kept them away. The anger was rising. Too early, too early, save it, said his inner voices. But the brandy spoke louder, with a droning that brought the blood up to his face and made his brain thud like an engine. 'Are you telling me,' he finally blurted, 'that you are happily running a nuclear power station that could at any time devastate the Western United States?' His voice was slurred, he knew, but at least he had said something. And the sixty million people hanging on his words would now be hanging on Klein's answer, and if Klein answered the question, he was screwed. He sat back and waited, a warm glow of relief spreading in him.

It did not last.

'My power station won't leak,' said Klein flatly. 'I refuse to answer a ludicrous question of that kind.'

'Answer it,' said Kelly, leaning forward in his chair and grinning. This time his voice was badly slurred.

'Oh, Christ,' said the director, with her face in her hands. 'Get the emergency film ready.'

'I will not be spoken to in this way,' said the manager. He got up to leave.

'Let him go!' yelled the director into Kelly's earphone mike. 'Let him go! You've won!'

But Kelly wasn't listening. He was on his feet, grabbing Klein's sleeve and yelling, 'Answer the goddamn question!'

Klein tugged away from him. Kelly shifted his grip and tried to push Klein back into the black leather chair, but he misjudged and Klein missed the chair and fell on the studio floor, pulling Kelly down on top of him.

'Run the film!' shouted the director, staring in horror at the tangle of limbs thrashing among the upturned chairs, live, nationwide, coast to coast, audience sixty million.

The horrid scene faded from the screens. The director lit

another cigarette, sat back and pressed her hands to her temples as pandemonium raged in the box.

Then the telephones started to ring.

The meeting after the show was not a pleasant one. On one side of the table in the windowless room were Kelly, and Hubert Carey his agent. On the other side of the table, bald and neckless and watching the unlit cigar he was rolling between his fat fingers, Omar Wohl, the network manager.

Wohl said, in his flat, reasonable voice. 'The ratings, David. And now this. My advice to you is take a holiday.'

'What does that mean?' said Kelly. 'You're tearing up the contract? Well, let me tell you that my lawyer –'

'Now hold on,' said Carey, who was English. 'Mr Wohl isn't even considering tearing up your contract, because he knows that would be terribly expensive for all concerned.' He crinkled his eyes at Wohl. 'Wouldn't it?'

Wohl shrugged and smiled with his wide, rubbery mouth. 'Of course,' he said. 'The network needs you, David. You've made sacrifices, I know. Overwork. What you need is a period of intellectual refreshment. Go sailing, take it easy, then come back, work good. Why not?'

'And the contract?' Kelly's face was dead white, the skin stretched tight so the skull showed underneath. His voice was edged with raw nerves.

'Who's talking contracts?' said Wohl. 'Now you go get yourself a nice dinner. I'd join you, only I have work.'

'Sure,' said Carey, shepherding Kelly out of the room.

Wohl waited until the door was shut. Then he picked up

the telephone, and dialled Leonard Krug of Krug, Bendix, the network's law firm. 'Leonard,' he said, when the lawyer answered. 'Did you see Kelly tonight?'

'Yeah,' said Krug.

'I want that fucker off the payroll,' said Wohl. 'Find me a way.'

There was a bar Kelly used on nights like this. It was off Sunset Strip, and it was dark. Also, it was not too fussy about checking IDs, so it was a good spot for finding seventeen-year-old girls with long thighs and firm breasts who were easy to take home when they realized you were a TV star, even if you were nearly forty years old and withered inside like an old leaf.

So Kelly parked his Porsche and went in and sat at the bar and tried to get the juices flowing. But the juices did not flow, so he tried brandy, and then some more brandy. At some point he must have moved off the bar stool, because there was a dark corner and a girl called Dolores, straddling his knees in shorts and a halter top, and the smooth skin of her breasts was against his face, and her nails in his neck. And he said, 'That bastard told me to go sailing.'

'I really like sailing,' said Dolores. 'It's real nice. Winning! Wow! You wanna buy me another Tequila Sunrise?'

Kelly waved at the waitress and placed the order, with another double Napoleon brandy for himself. Then he leaned back in his chair and looked at the blue neon bubbles that swept up the wall, and rested his hot head on Dolores' cool shoulder. And he thought of sailing; away from the thunder of the music and the darkness with its harsh points of light; cool and clear, on the swing of the big seas, lovely boats dipping like dancers gulls on the warm winds from Africa . . .

Dolores leaned over, and he felt her tongue in his ear like a hot snail, and her fingers walking towards his fly. He was tensed rigid. But it was nothing to do with Dolores. He pushed her off and jumped out of his seat and staggered across to the telephone and pulled a fistful of change out of his pocket, scattering coins on the floor until he found a dime. He dialled Carey's number.

'Dave?' said Carey. 'Do you know what the *time* is?'

'Listen,' shouted Kelly above the thunder of the juke box. 'I got an idea.'

Kelly woke to shattering noise. He rolled over in his bed and hit bare skin. Dolores, hot and sticky, her face fattish and grey without its make-up. The noise was the telephone. It hurt Kelly's head, but he was still enough of a journalist not to be able to resist picking it up. It said 'Hello?' in a small, tinny voice that was Carey's voice.

Muzzily, Kelly tried to piece together the night before. His belly sank as he remembered the studio. He did not recognize Dolores, but he knew the type. He felt not too terrible, which meant that he was still drunk.

'Hello?' said the telephone again.

'Yeah,' said Kelly. 'Wha'?'

'Wohl's agreed,' said Carey. 'He thinks it's a terrific idea.'

'He thinks what's a terrific idea?'

'Your idea.'

'Run it by me,' said Kelly. 'I was . . . upset last night.'

'I see,' said Carey, who knew his client extremely well. 'Hang on to your hat, then. We're signing a contract by which you agree to supervise the building of a boat for the Lancaster Great Circle, in California. You further agree that you'll compete in the Great Circle and send in reports, with a view to making four full-length features on the race. His only stipulation is that you stay with the boat and bring in the footage, and that the finished films are up to your usual high standard. Not counting last night, that is.

'You'll be backing the boat with a million dollars of your own money – don't worry, there's a tax break. The network will sponsor you for the rest, on condition that you call the boat *Kelly's Eye* USTS. I'll send you the contract.'

Kelly's mouth was hanging open. He shut it with a snap. 'Wait a minute,' he said. 'This is all . . . I mean . . .' Brandy was slopping around in his skull. 'You can't be serious.'

'I'm serious,' said Carey. There was a hardness in his voice. 'Listen to me, Dave. You screwed up in front of sixty million people last night. Then you called me at three a.m. to give me your idea. And you didn't wake me, because I was already awake, worrying about what the hell I was going to do with you. And I'd just worked out that you were a dead loss when you called with this boat suggestion, and it was the only exit from an elevator with a cable broken.'

'But the series,' said Kelly.

'Last night I got a call from a little dicky bird at Krug Bendix, USTS' law firm. They were looking at ways to end your contract, and they'd worked it out that it would cost

them three mill to get rid of you. Now they'll spend two on
your boat, and they'll get some shows, and you'll get some
shows. It's the only deal in town, Dave.'

'But eight months on a *boat*?'

'Bracing,' said Carey. 'You'll do it, and you'll make it
good, because if you don't, you've had it. Call me with
your final reply before lunch, okay?'

The telephone went down. Kelly lurched off to the pink
marble bathroom, and vomited into the onyx washbasin.
By ten o'clock he had thrown out Dolores and drunk two
brandy and sodas and read a few newspapers, whose TV
critics had by no means overlooked last night's lapse. He
had also managed to think a little. So he picked up the
telephone, dialled Carey's number, and said, 'Deal.'

It was a cold, clear dawn in February. Ice jingled by the
margins of the River Severn where it spread in a gleaming
black sheet between the mountains of Wales on one side
and the Cotswolds on the other. But at Sharpness in the
estuary, the water is salt, and the tide was high and on the
turn, and under the rotting pilings of the harbour there
was no ice.

Not that it was not cold. Emily de Havilland huddled

into her mink-lined Burberry and watched the man on the squat wooden yawl blow on his mittened fingers. There was a rime of ice on the yawl's rigging that made it crackle faintly as he pulled up the mainsail. Then he turned towards her and said, 'Well . . . er . . . goodbye.'

She said, rather stiffly, 'Goodbye.' The mainsail flapped idly in the small breeze as she cast off bow, stern, springs, for him. The small, cold crowd of press and friends – Eric's friends, mostly; outside their marriage, they led virtually separate lives – clapped and waved. The yawl crept out into the broad, gleaming river. The first swirls of the ebb caught it, and it began to shrink.

Emily turned and went back to her car, ignoring the greetings of the crowd.

She drove towards the dull green of the Cotswold scarp. Her square, short-nailed fingers drummed nervously on the wheel, and the tyres squealed as she hauled the big Peugeot 505 round the corners of the road as it snaked up Frocester Edge.

On the motorway, she turned on Radio 3, and caught the nine o'clock news. The dollar was up and the pound was down. Towards the end of the bulletin, the plummy voice said, 'Eric de Havilland, the yachtsman, today set out on a double circumnavigation in his yacht *Bran*. Mr de Havilland is not expected to return for two years –'

The voice disappeared as Emily twisted the knob. She was going down the fast lane, and the tears came up in her large, black-rimmed hazel eyes, and spilled into the little lines that were coming at the corners of eyes and mouth. She dried them, purposefully, with a red and white bandana handkerchief, and turned on the radio again. Baroque music tinkled.

45

'You bastard, Eric,' she said. 'Oh, you *lucky* bastard.'

It was exactly ten o'clock when she let herself into the flat in Hammersmith where she and Eric were meant to spend their time when they were in London. Actually Eric hated London, so the furniture and the things in the drawers were hers. There were no mementoes to miss him by, except one photograph, which she quickly took down from the bookcase and hid in the desk drawer.

She made herself Earl Grey tea, poured it into a thin Spode cup with a gold rim, and took it to her typewriter. Beside the typewriter was a list of companies. Almost all bore a tick and a cross. Two of them carried ticks only. The ticks meant she had written, requesting sponsorship for an entry into the Lancaster Great Circle. The crosses meant that sponsorship had been refused. Her stomach fluttered as she looked at the list. Time was running out.

The telephone rang. She picked it up. 'Harriet,' she said. 'How lovely to hear you.'

The voice on the telephone was young but firm. 'It must have been awful,' it said. 'Why don't we have some lunch next Tuesday. Au Poisson at one, all right?'

'Fine,' said Emily. Then she went back to her requests for sponsorship.

At two, the second post came, and she was able to put crosses against the last two names on the list.

Harriet Agnew was thirty-two. She had black hair cut en brosse, and the blue eyes of her Scottish ancestors. Her eyes were the only legacy they had passed on. Harriet's father had been a Naval officer whose twin enthusiasms for butterfly collecting and gin had meant that he had never risen above the rank of lieutenant-commander. Lieutenant-commanders do not make much money, so Harriet had received her education partly at St Columba's Grammar School in Edinburgh, and partly in the various hot and smelly corners of the world in which her father, commanding for most of her youth one of the Royal Navy's oilers, had been stationed.

Her mother had died when she had been eleven; a life divided between tough-minded feminist aunts in Blairgowrie Street and her hard-drinking father had given her a self-reliance unusual in a teenager. This independence had got her into St Hilda's College, Oxford, whence she had passed with the decade's best law first. Soon after this, her father died of cirrhosis of the liver and her aunts let her know that they considered it was time she led her own life, without reference to them. She was alone in the world, though this was not the fault of a succession of men (and several women) who had invited her to make up the other half of a duo. She occasionally wished that her breasts were less proud, and her waist less narrow, and her legs shorter. But only very occasionally. Most of the time, she rather enjoyed it.

She dressed like a barrister, in dark and sober colours, white silk shirts, and plain gold jewellery. But no matter how hard she tried, there was always what her grandmother would have called a hint of the tinker about her. It was this hint that the taxi driver recognized as she paid him off in Sloane Avenue the following Tuesday.

'Never mind the tip, love,' he said. 'What's your phone number?'

It was the tinker that made her reply, 'Too long for you

to remember,' and give him a smile that left him parked on the double yellow lines long after she had rung the bell and been admitted into the closed door of the Poisson.

The head waiter said, 'Bonjour, Mademoiselle Agnew,' as he led her between the tables to the one in the corner she always used. On the table was a bunch of Soleil d'or narcissi, from the Isles of Scilly *not* the Channel Islands, as Harriet had specified. 'Thank you, Alphonse,' she said.

The waiter showed white teeth beneath his large black moustache. She had a weakness for moustaches. 'Mademoiselle's usual aperitif?'

'Please.' Harriet leaned back in her chair. She liked the Poisson. It was somewhere between a restaurant and a club; you had to have booked a table to be admitted by the entryphone, and there were enough women there to make most male business lunchers feel distinctly uncomfortable. The restaurant's clientele was mostly successful women who wanted somewhere where they could eat seriously without having to bother about who was watching them or why. The fish was good, cooked by a talented but not megalomaniac Niçois chef. The round tables all bore white tablecloths that shone in the light from the big skylights above. There was a cut-glass vase of flowers in the middle of each table. The restaurant's only frill was that you ordered your flowers when you booked your table.

The aperitif was an Americano; Harriet had no scruples about having a maximum of two drinks at lunchtime. Her colleagues at EPK Electric stuck to Perrier; EPK was a large company, and internal competition was fierce. But Harriet was now head of the legal department, and the Americano was one of the small luxuries to which she considered herself entitled. She sighed. It was a strange set of priorities, to work eighteen hours a day for the privilege of drinking an Americano at lunchtime. Then the doors opened, and Emily came in.

It was six months since Harriet had seen her. She thought (as she always did with Emily) how well she seemed to fit, no matter where she was. Her presence made the Poisson seem a little precious, that was all. She was small and brown and dressed in beautifully cut fawn corduroy trousers, a heavy rust-coloured silk shirt cut like a lumberjack's mackinaw, and heavy silver earrings that swung as she showed her white teeth at Harriet. But Harriet noticed that she looked tired.

Emily sat down, quickly and gracefully. 'I've been having a ghastly time.'

Harriet smiled, a little amused by her. You never touched Emily when you greeted her, and she launched straight into what was on her mind.

Emily ordered a gin and tonic, put her square, beautiful brown hands on the table, and said, 'I can't find a main sponsor.'

'A boat?' said Harriet.

'Eric's gone off on a circumnavigation,' said Emily, as matter-of-factly as if she had said "a number eleven bus". 'And I want to go in for the Lancaster in a medium-sized boat, Swan 651. And they're holding the boat for me at the yard, but without a main sponsor I can't put the money together.' She smiled. 'Everybody's worried about women skippers.'

Harriet said, 'Do they know who you are?'

'Presumably,' said Emily, without vanity.

She would have been entitled to be vain, thought Harriet. She had sailed round the world single-handed, captained a boat in the Twostar and won the Sydney-Hobart race.

Alphonse was hovering. 'Let's order,' said Harriet.

'Yes. I love this place. It's so deeply sinful. So, lobster bisque, then Raie au Beurre Noir, I think,' said Emily.

Harriet ordered bass with fennel, and green salads, and a bottle of Sancerre, the Vacheron 1983, reflecting that one of the reasons she came to the Poisson was because it was the least sinful place she could think of.

Emily said, 'You do yourselves well, you industrialists.'

Harriet laughed. 'Not every day. It'll take hours in the gym to get rid of this lot.' Then she felt a little foolish; Emily would think gyms were a waste of time. She watched Emily deal with her soup, methodically and neatly, talking little until she had finished. That was Emily; total concentration on the matter in hand. Harriet waited until the wine would have warmed her. Then she said, 'What about this boat trouble?'

Emily said, 'The boat's all right. Available, I mean. But I've got no money, and nobody wants to give me any. You'd think someone would come up, wouldn't you? Half a million pounds, in return for which we call the boat anything the company wants, and the company gets at least twenty thousand mentions in the press? But nobody'll do it.'

Harriet concentrated for a moment on her bass, separating the crisp white flesh from the bones. She took a sip of Sancerre, feeling the delicate steeliness of it on her tongue. Then, without raising her eyes, she said, 'Why didn't you try us?'

Emily pursued a caper with her fork. 'Because you're sponsoring Jack Asprey's boat.'

'No, we're not,' said Harriet.

Emily's fork stopped half-way to her mouth.

'Jack's boat's no good,' said Harriet. 'He's been using some sort of laminate that isn't laminating. Nothing's been announced, but EPK are withdrawing sponsorship.'

'He'll be upset,' said Emily.

But Harriet wasn't listening. She had taken a notepad from her hand bag, and was scribbling on it with a gold Mont Blanc fountain pen. After a minute, she said, 'What's the least you'd need?'

'The least what?' said Emily.

'Money.'

'Quarter of a million. Plus bank guarantees for another quarter.'

'And we're saving three-quarters of a million by not using Jack.' Harriet took Emily's hand across the crisp white tablecloth. 'Emily, would you consider sailing as EPK *Electric*?'

Emily stood up and leaned forward and kissed Harriet on the cheek. Her hazel eyes were glittering with excitement. 'Yes,' she said.

Harriet was writing again. 'Okay,' she said. 'I'll put it to the board. We'll have to be careful. But we'll be saving a quarter of a million. The woman skipper bit will work to our advantage. We'll have to clear it with Jack, of course. But he won't be a problem.'

'I would be, if I were him,' said Emily.

'We'll fix him. Look, let's have coffee, and then you can give me a detailed breakdown of costs and contingencies.'

'I don't believe it,' said Emily.

'Well, you'd better start,' said Harriet. 'We are about to strike a mighty blow for womankind.' She raised her glass, and the gold bangles on her wrist jingled.

'To the Great Circle!' she said.

'To the Great Circle,' said Emily.

They drank. Emily thought for a moment. Then she said, 'Just as long as Jack Asprey doesn't want to come too.'

Jack Asprey had put on a grey pinstripe suit and an Old Harrovian tie for the meeting with Harriet. His long hatchet face was still and grim above his white collar, but he contrived a certain nonchalance in the crossing of his legs in the chintz armchair by the *sezession* coffee table in Harriet's office. Beyond the plate-glass window, St Paul's was deepening black against a deep blue, frosty sky. Harriet said, 'So the Board has decided to offer it to Emily.'

The skin around Asprey's watchful black eyes tightened momentarily, but his face remained still. 'Understandable, in the circumstances,' he said. He uncrossed his legs. 'Harriet, I want to come too.'

Harriet watched him carefully. There was a hard intensity about him that she had not seen before. 'Why?'

'Because I want to do it. And I'll never have the time again.'

Harriet said, 'I understand. I'll put it to Emily. But . . . I don't know if she'll co-operate. She's in an awkward position, you must see that.'

'I do,' said Asprey. 'But if you could . . . do your best?'

He got up, shook her hand. 'Thank you for presenting a ray of hope in a pretty dim situation,' he said. 'I'll show myself out.'

After he had gone, Harriet went to her desk and picked up the first of the two-foot pile of folders that she had to read, digest and initial before she could go home. Beyond the window, the stars were bright enough to penetrate the red glow of the street lamps. She felt suddenly weary to the marrow of her bones.

The green telephone rang.

It was Lord Kimbolton, the chairman of the EPK group.

'Harriet,' he said. His voice was deep, fruity and level. 'Congratulations on finding us a boat. One thing. Don't you think Jack Asprey would be a useful man to have aboard?'

'That's up to Emily de Havilland,' said Harriet, guardedly.

'Of course, of course,' said Kimbolton. 'But I think . . . to ensure everything goes smoothly, I'd like a personal connection with the boat.'

'A personal connection,' said Harriet. Her voice was wooden; she had a good idea of what was coming.

'Jack's my godson,' said the chairman. 'I'm rather keen.'

'I see,' said Harriet.

'So if you could make my view clear to Mrs de Havilland?'

'She will be hard to convince.'

'Surely not, when you remind her where the money's coming from? Anyway, I am assured by people who know that Jack's an excellent sailor.'

And an insufferable little prick, thought Harriet. She was almost weeping with frustration. Her shoulders drooped under the weight of that friendly, appallingly powerful voice. The pile of folders seemed to tower above her, threatening to crush her. The days stretched endlessly ahead, eighteen hours in this glass-walled box with its chirruping telephone and its mounds of paper and its Americanos at lunchtime that were the ultimate pathetic marks of power. And the voices that showed you exactly how much power you had. It was all too bloody stupid. So stupid that she laughed.

'I beg your pardon?' said Lord Kimbolton. 'Did you say something?'

'No,' said Harriet. Her heart was beating hard, and she could not believe that she had decided to do what she had decided to do – suddenly, off the top of her head, her, cautious Harriet. 'I was just going to say that you will get my letter of resignation in the morning.'

There was a silence on the line. Then Kimbolton's voice. 'Might one ask why?' he said coolly. 'You are a valuable part of the team, Harriet. A very valuable part. Surely you aren't going to let us down over a trifling matter of this kind? For of course I am absolutely committed to Jack's joining the, er, boat. Your resignation, though a blow, will make no difference to that.'

She let him finish, but she was not really listening. A wonderful, almost sexual glow of elation was spreading in her. She kicked off her shoes and dug her stockinged toes into the carpet. And she laughed again into the telephone, more loudly this time, and she said, 'No. I've made up my mind. I'm resigning because I'm going to sail in the

Lancaster Great Circle. I'm running away to sea, Mr Chairman.'

And she slammed the telephone into its cradle and sat there laughing and laughing until the tears ran down her face.

The peninsula of Ardnamurchan is a green toe that juts into the Atlantic above the Isle of Mull on the west coast of Scotland. The granite mountains that form its spine rise to a little more than three thousand feet – not a great height, as mountains go.

But as far as Nicholas Eason was concerned, three thousand feet was quite high enough.

He was lying on a rock with snow in his ear and his feet wet. At least, he assumed they were wet; he had lost touch with them four hours ago. There were twenty-five other men of about his age – between twenty-two and thirty – crouching in the patch of snow eight hundred feet above Loch Laga. Some were sitting, and some were lying. Three were lying face down. Eason felt a moment of quiet pride that at least he was lying on his ear. Alert and ready for anything, he thought, and heaved himself up and began to run clumsily on the spot to warm his notional feet.

There was an older man, sitting away from the rest. He looked neat and compact, with iron-grey hair. The skin under his chin was beginning to fall away. He caught Eason's eye, nodded, and rose. 'Let's go,' he called.

Groaning, the men got up. Three remained in the snow. Eason had got to know them all in the last two days of running up mountains in rainstorms, running down mountains in blizzards, and swimming across lochs in temperatures of 1°C. One of the men on the ground was the national Soling champion. Another had been a mastman on the previous year's Captain's Cup winner. The third was a weight-lifter, rated fourth best in Britain.

Eason ran a few more steps on the spot. It looked as if they weren't going to make the selection for *Chinamite*'s crew. The older man shouldered his pack, and said, 'We'll take it easy down the hill. Back to the boat, now.'

Still the three lying men did not move. Eason shouldered his own pack, and said to himself, *oof!* Then he went across to the Soling champion and said, 'Come on, cock. Don't want to get left behind, do we?'

The head rolled in the snow. The eyes were bloodshot and red-lidded. 'Don't care,' it said.

Eason grabbed one of the man's arms, and heaved. The man came up to his feet. He had been crying, Eason saw. Eason knew how he felt. 'Off,' he said. 'Look.'

He pointed. Far below, a shaft of sunlight blazed over the green arm of a sea loch. In the centre of the shaft was a long, lean yacht, painted turquoise with yellow letters on her side. The letters were invisible at this distance, but they read CHINAMITE UK.

'Ugh,' said the Soling man, at his side. 'What are you trying to prove?'

Eason fingered his stubbly chin. 'Same thing as you,' he said. 'Have a sweetie.' He handed him a glucose tablet.

'GO!' called the older man, and set off downhill at the trot. Eason began to jog, heavily, the pack bumping on his back.

Two hours later, the file of men came down the road to the harbour. This time, Eason could not get the pack off. He fell on his face on the sandy beach beside the quay, and stayed there.

He was woken by a hand shaking his shoulder. It was the older man, Henry Harper, Captain of *Chinamite*. Harper rolled him over, noticing the white, exhausted face, the eyelids that were even now trying to droop again in sleep. 'Nick,' said Harper, 'I'm happy to tell you that you've made the team. If you still want to come, that is.'

Eason croaked, 'Of course,' in a thick, gluey voice. Harper stumped up on to the quay, and stood on a bollard.

'Listen, please, all of you,' he said. 'Now you know who's coming, and who isn't. To the ones who aren't, I'm sorry. You're all good, otherwise you wouldn't be here. Now we're leaving. The minibus will take anyone who wants to Mallaig station. The rest of us will be sailing back to Plymouth.' He paused. 'Via Shetland.'

He waited for the groan. It didn't come. His eyes ran over the crew he had chosen to go round the world with him. They were a hard-looking bunch, mostly below average height; deep-sea racing demands big power from the shoulders and arms. The only exception was Nick Eason. Harper allowed his eyes to rest on the tall, gangling figure with the untidy shock of black hair, and the trace of a cynical grin hanging round his lantern jaw. He had taken a risk with Eason; of the whole crew, he was the only one who didn't fit the racing mould. He knew damn all about sailing, for a start. But there was something hungry about the man. And he was a journalist, by all accounts, and the sponsors wanted a writer aboard. As journalists went, Eason seemed a pretty good bloke. Also, he was going out with Harper's daughter – not, Harper assured himself hastily, that that had anything to do with anything.

Eason sat on the hard square stones of the quay and felt wretched. His fellow crewmen seemed unnecessarily brown and keen. He thought: what the hell have I done? The answer came fast enough. You've got your last chance, Nicko. Which is what you wanted. Yes, all right, don't be such a bloody prig, he said to himself. What I really want is half a bottle of whisky and some dangerous drugs, right sharp. Well, Nicko, said the inner voice, what you're going to get is seasick.

Harper watched them file down the quay to the tenders. Eason was looking almost solemn. He thought: it's a good crew. They're tough, and they can work together, and they've got the self-discipline to get on together. But at the back of it all, he knew there was something missing.

But then there would always be something missing as long as Ed Cole was on the beach at Plymouth.

Between Rhum and Eigg, the seas kicked up sharp and nasty, and *Chinamite*'s bows, built wide and flat for running in the longer seas of the Southern Ocean, slammed hard and monotonously. As they opened the Sound of Sleat, Eason was sick for the first time.

But not the last.

*

The pace was hotting up.

Chinamite sailed round the top of Scotland and ran before northerly gales down the east coast. She turned up the Thames estuary and moored in St Katharine's Dock, where Harper stood over her crew while they scrubbed her from pulpit to transom. Then he ran the *Chinamite* battle flag up her forestay and asked her public relations department to order a press conference.

At ten o'clock on the first Monday in December, eleven journalists clattered on to *Chinamite*'s aluminium decks and stood in a dispirited huddle, shoulders hunched against the drizzle. Henry Harper bounced up on deck, and began explaining.

'*Chinamite*. Seventy-three feet long overall, rates sixty-eight feet – that's her handicap, gentlemen. Built of aluminium by British craftsmen, the year before last. Aluminium is not a fashionable material, but it's a bloody good material. These drum-like objects are the winches with which we pull in the sheets, which are the ropes attached to the corners of the sails. As you will observe, the boat is a dirty great pontoon, with two dents in it. The dent at the back contains the steering wheel, and the people who are in charge of the sheets of the sails at the front. It is called the cockpit, do not ask me why. The dent at the front, just behind the mast there, is called the gorilla pit, because it is sat in by the crew, many of whom through no fault of their own resemble gorillas. There is a hatch in each of these two dents, providing access to the splendours below. It is now very wet. Shall we pop down?'

The group shuffled down the steep companion-ladder. 'We've got a crew of twenty-two who are at present, seeing that there is another nine months to go before the race, not living on board. You will see when you go below that I'm the only one with my own quarters, so the crew want to be here as little as possible unless they have to.'

The journalists peered suspiciously at the bunks arranged three high round the sides, the galley with its gas stove, the tiny saloon table. Some of them, the ones with imagination, shook their heads and seemed to be glad they were not going.

'Put on the coffee, Horace,' said Harper to the fat man in old corduroys who was fiddling with the innards of one of the heads. 'Wash your hands first, eh?'

'You're never this fussy when it's just us,' said Horace pettishly, and waddled to the galley.

'Horace is a Cordon Bleu cook,' said Harper. 'The most important man on the boat, but moody. Damned moody. Now come with me and I'll show you the other important bits.'

He took them round the navigation shack, showed them the radios and the radar and the weatherfax machine. Then Horace started singing snatches from *La Traviata*, and they went and sat on the bunks and asked questions. The sailing press asked knowledgeable questions. The tabloids had other things on what passed for their minds.

'Are you going to win?' said the man from the *Daily Mail*.

'We'll do our best,' said Harper patiently. 'There's a lot of luck involved. You need a good crew, and you have to be in the right weather at the right time.'

'How about you?' said the man from the *Mail*.

'Sorry?' Harper's smile had an edge of suspicion. 'I don't follow.'

'I was speaking to Sir Clement Jones. He's a competitor, is he not?'

'Yes.' Jones was driving a boat called *Associated Meat*, after its sponsors. The Commandoes had lent him a crew, and he had been trumpeting the fact remorselessly from the nation's front pages.

'Jones said he didn't think *Chinamite* was a threat.'

Harper was taken aback. 'Did he? *Associated Meat* is a heavy boat. Old.'

'He was talking about crew quality. He was saying . . . that is, how do you react to his comment on you personally that –' the *Mail* man referred to his notebook ' – you are "about ready to go out to grass"?'

Harper bit back the anger that rose in him. Clement Jones, you glib-tongued little politician, he thought. He took a deep breath, and felt the anger come under control. 'I'm fifty-five,' he said with a slow smile. 'And bloody artful, as Sir Clement will find out for himself.'

'You took the place of Ed Cole, didn't you?' said another journalist.

'Yes.'

'Is Mr Cole a friend of yours?'

'Yes.'

'Did it bother you, taking his place?'

'Of course it did,' said Harper. 'That Inquiry was –' He stopped himself. Everyone knew that the *Arpeggio* Inquiry had been an exercise in finding scapegoats. But that was not the kind of thing you said if you wanted to keep your job. 'Let's just say that I wish Mr Cole was aboard now,' he said. 'Now, if you'll excuse me, I've got work to do.'

Nick Eason was sitting in the Dickens Inn with a large gin and tonic in his hand, and the *Sporting Life* open in his lap. He watched the journalists file back up the jetty, and the small figure of Harper watching them depart. He looks properly pissed off, thought Eason, glancing at his watch. Ten to twelve. Ten minutes until the crew meeting. He drained his drink, went to the bar and ordered another double. No sense in wasting time.

He had managed two more doubles by one minute to noon, and the jetty felt pleasingly bouncy as he walked out to *Chinamite*, greeting a couple of other crew members as he went. He was wearing a blue pinstripe suit, rather shiny at seat and elbows; he looked like a slightly drunken cormorant, picking his way between the moored boats towards *Chinamite*'s towering mast.

The purpose of the crew meeting was for members of the crew to fill up their diaries for the next six months. They padded down the companionway and sprawled on the bunks while Horace called the roll. At the end of the roll-call he said, 'And still no Eddie Cole.'

Normally, Eason was a bit subdued aboard *Chinamite*. But today, the gin made him bold, and he said, 'Were we expecting him?'

Harper said, 'I asked him to come. I'll ask him to come to the next meeting.' He opened his diary. 'Now then.'

Chinamite had a busy nine months ahead. She was leaving for the US in a month, both as a shakedown cruise and to show herself to sponsors on the East Coast, where Chinamite Inc. had offices. On her return in April, there was more sponsor-stroking, then a summer's working-up and general racing, culminating with the Big Boat series at Cowes in July, and the Fastnet Race. 'And after the Fastnet, it's nearly September 5th, and we're on our own,' said Harper. 'Okay?'

Jason the helmsman said, 'What's the competition, so far?'

'Harry Redd in Australia, with Tubes Murphy. *Tasman*, she's called. And since Redd smashed the Sound Yacht Club in the Atlantic Cup last year, the SYC's spending eleven million on an entry. She should be all right, too, because they've got a great skipper and they don't like losing much. Clement Jones in *Kudu*, now called *Associated Meat*, with half the bloody Army to give him a hand. She's a heavy boat, and they've been making a right pig's ear of things in trials. Nearly lost a man off South Uist the other week, silly bugger wasn't strapped on. For keen fanciers of the fair sex, there's Emily de Havilland in a Swan 651, and in case you think she is a pushover I would like to tell you that she never, ever gives up, and that she will be a severe problem on handicap. And old Jean-Luc Jarré's building one in Marseilles, launching any day now. And there are a lot of other European bits and pieces, and something from California that sounds bloody odd; some telly glamour puss who is about to find out that water is wet. Though even he seems to be behaving in a serious manner, from what I hear.'

'Any more?' It was Noddy the grinder who asked, a stocky man with a badly broken nose.

'He wants more,' said Harper to the crew at large. 'Not content with the fact that Jarré's boats are always brilliant, if they don't fall to bits. Tubes Murphy doesn't know the meaning of the word "lose". And the SYC have got their unfortunate Atlantic Cup skipper washing dishes in Brooklyn, so there will be a bit of pressure on this Schacker bloke to do nicely. Nobody is entering this race to go cruising, my bully boys. It is going to be bloody murder out there, and you better believe it.'

After the meeting, Eason returned to the small room in Frith Street that he used as an office. Rhythmic gruntings came from the first-floor room with 'Model Within' scrawled on the door.

His office was small, and painted brown with years of other people's cigarette smoke. There was a message on the Ansafone from the editor of the *Sunday News*. With a slight chill of presentiment, Eason dialled.

The editor sounded even more shifty than usual, Eason thought. He turned on the enthusiasm. 'Going very well,' he said. 'You'll have my first piece tonight.'

'Oh,' said the editor. 'Well, actually, things have changed a bit. We've got a series on the conquest of, er, Nanga Parbat and on reflection we've decided to do that instead.'

'Oh,' said Eason. The chill had settled on his stomach. 'I suppose it's no use reminding you that we have a contract for me to supply you with dispatches from *Chinamite*'s foc'sle, monthly until the race and then weekly during?'

'Not signed, I don't believe,' said the editor. 'Save us both some time and trouble. Well, shall we leave it at that, then? Nice talking to you, Jack – er, Nick.'

'You sodding little weasel,' said Eason, but he was talking to the dialling tone.

After he had put the telephone down he pulled a bottle of

cheap gin from the chipped filing cabinet, poured himself three inches and added flat tonic. He drank it in two gulps. 'Thank you, Daddy,' he said.

For he knew that the *Sunday News*' change of mind was nothing to do with Nanga Parbat, whatever that was. It was simply that the old man was at it again.

Nicholas Eason's father was Sir Michael Eason, Privy Counsellor, Master of the Queen's Regalia and sometime Director of MI5. Sir Michael was a man of enormous distinction, universally respected by his contemporaries. He was also a man of enormous power in the secret avenues of influence that link the Monarch and Parliament, the Armed Forces and the City. As Sir Michael's son, Nicholas had been expected to go to Eton College and Christ Church, Oxford, and get a First; after which he would proceed into the Civil Service or a merchant bank, and learn to fine-tune the trim of the Ship of State.

What had actually happened was that Nicholas had gone to Durham University and emerged with a third, and then served a three-year apprenticeship on the kind of provincial newspapers that his father's friends owned, but never read. He had been good at it – so good that he had got a job as a reporter on the London *Morning News*. Then, one day, he had been fired.

He had not been able to understand it, at first. His stories were making the front page. He had excellent contacts, in and out of politics. But nobody had been prepared to give him an explanation – or a job. So he had gone freelance. And Lenny Sutton, editor of the *Politician*, had given it to him straight, while turning down a brilliant exposé of corruption in the Conservative Party over lunch in the Gay Hussar. 'I will tell you this because I have drunk five gins, two bottles of wine and a large Armagnac,' he said. 'Your papa leaks like a bleeding basket, Nick. And so do a lot of his friends. And your papa is so embarrassed by the stuff you put out that he and his pals, the ones I was talking about, ring up editors and say that he, I mean they, the friends I mean, not the editors, will never leak again if they print your stuff. You might as well give up, cocky.'

'I'm not going to,' said Eason, who had drunk the same amount as Lenny.

'You'll have to,' said Lenny.

After that lunch, Eason had gone to the Tatty Bogle under Golden Square and drunk steadily for the rest of the afternoon. That evening, at a party in Holland Park, someone had offered him a line of brown powder on a mirror, and he had thought, well, why the hell not? And from that evening on, he had sunk; not an alcoholic, but a heavy drinker. Not a junkie, but a frequent user. Not a dead loss, but as near as made no difference.

Until he had met Tean Harper at a party. She was blonde and blue-eyed and her friends called her strapping. She had taken him in hand. And almost before he knew what was happening, he was at her father's house in the outer suburbs of Plymouth, scratching because he had no heroin, signing on for *Chinamite*'s crew trials as prentice grinder and resident wordsmith. He had been accepted solely, as far as he knew, because the editor of the *Sunday News* had agreed to print stories from *Chinamite*'s gorilla pit – an idea that appealed greatly to the sponsors.

Nicholas Eason drank some more gin and wondered

what the hell he was going to tell Henry Harper. Nothing, he decided eventually. He would tough it out; and if necessary he would go down, uncomplaining, into the legion of the lost. He reached again for the gin bottle, but his hand stopped half-way. There was another member of the Legion whose fortunes were wrapped up with *Chinamite*.

Eason got a taxi to the lock-up garage where he kept his eight-year-old Ford Cortina. Half an hour later, he was hammering westward down the fast lane of the M4.

Ed Cole was still at the potting bench at midnight. He usually was, nowadays. He worked in a little pool of light, pulling the pot towards him, twitching the *metrosideros* twig from the stem, trimming the heel and spiking it into the pot. As he worked, his mind was far away in the warm drizzle of New Zealand's North Island, breathing the sulphurous smell of the hot volcanic springs, where the *pahutekawa* grew wild. The *pahutekawa*, midsummer blooming, flame of Christmas, Gauguin's tree –

'Who's that?' he said.

Down among the forest of growing plants, a pot had fallen. 'Me,' said a voice. 'Are you Ed Cole?'

'Who are you?' said Cole. His heart was beating fast; old woman, he said to himself. It was because he saw so few people, nowadays.

A tall, thin figure stepped into the pool of light. He was wearing a pinstripe suit and black shoes, and a crumpled shirt with the tie dangling and the top button undone. The face was long and thin, the eyes humorous but a little glassy, the straight black hair straggling over the collar. As he came closer, Cole smelt gin.

'Who are you?' he said.

'Nick Eason,' said the thin man. 'I'm sailing on *Chinamite* and we had a crew meeting this morning. You were supposed to be there, but you weren't, so I thought I'd pop down and see if you were all right.'

'Well, I am,' said Cole, harshly. 'Thanks.'

Eason sat down, and fingered a rejected cutting. 'I knocked something over back there,' he said. ''Fraid it bust. I'm a bit knackered. Long way from London.'

Cole said, 'Yes.' Privately, he was slightly impressed. It was a long time since anyone had come that far to see him. 'I was just packing up,' he said. 'Would you like a drink?'

'Yes,' said Eason. 'Please.'

He followed Cole back to the house. They sat in the kitchen, and Eason was oppressed by its bleakness. An empty baked beans tin stood beside the stove, and the days on the winch calendar were crossed off in black felt tip. He thought suddenly of scratched-out days on a cell wall.

Eason was exhausted. He watched Cole move around the kitchen, nervously, his eyes sunk in shadow on either side of his long nose.

He poured out two glasses from a dusty bottle. 'Hate drinking alone,' he said, by way of explanation, and ran his fingers through his sparse hair. Eason sipped. Now he was here, he didn't know what to say.

It was Cole who broke the silence. 'How's the boat?'

'*Chinamite*? Terrific. Very fast.'

'And the crew?'

'Great crew. Henry Harper had us running up and down mountains. I think he'd like you in it, though.'

Cole looked up sharply. 'Who told you to say that?'

'Nobody.' The whisky was interfering with his speech. He had the feeling that even though nothing had happened yet, things were going badly wrong. 'Look, Mr Cole. I'm pissed as a rat so I'll tell you straight that I think you're being a bloody fool. You've had a nasty time at that Inquiry. I don't know whether it was your fault that tall ship tipped up or not. I don't know any bloody thing about sailing. I just know that Henry Harper wants you aboard, and if you don't come, you're being a pig-headed git.'

Cole sat down and knocked back his drink at a gulp. 'Get out,' he said quietly.

Eason got up. 'I said what I came to say,' he said. 'Goodnight.' Lurching slightly, he walked into the night.

Two weeks later, Eason was at the end of his rope. He was greyish white, and he shook as he picked up the telephone and dialled the number of *This Week*. *This Week* was a new Sunday tabloid, so far down-market (as Lenny Sutton had said to him) that even the fish and chip shops turned their noses up at it. Eason had been having discussions with the editor.

He got through. 'Nicky boy,' said the editor. 'Yeah, we'd like some pieces from you. No women aboard, pity. But what about queers? Rum, bum and concertina. "I rode AIDS hell ship." Know what I mean?'

'Yes,' said Eason. 'I know. How often do you want pieces?'

'Oh, whenever you like,' said the editor. 'I don't believe in contracts. Tell you what, you keep sending stuff in, and if we like it, we'll print it. Two hundred quid a thousand.'

'But . . .' said Eason.

'Nice talking to you,' said the editor. 'Look forward to your stuff.'

Next morning, Eason went down to Torpoint Marine in Plymouth for a crew meeting. Harper was sitting in the cockpit, catching pale January sun on his small face.

'Ah!' said Harper. 'Here's the newsman!'

Eason smiled at him, rather weakly.

'Here,' said Harper. 'I want you to meet someone.' He stuck his head down the hatch and called, 'Ed!'

A head and shoulders appeared, the shoulders narrow and lightly built, the hair sandy and scanty.

'Ed,' said Harper, 'I want you to meet Nicholas Eason, our tame journalist.'

Cole's eyes turned to Eason. They were pale blue, and very unfriendly. 'I didn't know you were a journalist,' he said, and went back below.

Harper looked distressed. 'What's got into him?' he said. 'He just turned up this morning, God knows why.'

The sun does not often shine during a Massachusetts winter, and the eighth of January was no exception. Art Schacker stuck his hands into the velvet pockets of his peajacket, coughed Lucky Strike smoke into the fog, and watched the shadowy big shots and their detectives get out of the stretched Cadillac limousine and walk across the concrete to the dock.

They were a grey, indistinct group. They trailed wreaths of vapour as they arrived at the foot of the gantry rigged beside the main basin of Sound Marina. A female figure, booted and bulky in some kind of expensive fur, stepped forward. TV lights cast a sudden white nimbus in the fog, and there was the *pop* of a public address system being switched on. The PA magnified the sound of feet shuffling up steps.

'Did you see that mink?' said Anne-Marie Schacker, beside Art.

Art said, 'Is that what it is?'

'Expensive,' said Anne-Marie.

'You want one?' said Art. There was no bitterness in his voice. Anne-Marie was delighted the DuCane Management had both refinanced Marblehead Clam and Lobster, and was paying Art a good salary to run their Great Circle campaign. Art was pleased that she was pleased, and he would not have dreamed of letting her know his deep suspicion of the Sound Yacht Club and everything connected with it.

'No thanks, fur coats ain't *me*,' said Anne-Marie, and slipped her arm through his.

'Ladies and gentlemen and members of the Sound Yacht Club,' said an ancient male voice down the PA. 'If it wasn't for this fog, I'd say nice to see you here. As it is, I assume you're out there someplace.' A ripple of laughter touched the vague shapes in the fog beyond the dome of light. 'I'll now ask Annabel Stavros to launch this boat.'

There was another ripple, this time of applause. Annabel Stavros had been married to a senator from one of New England's royal families, who had been killed in a plane crash. She had then married a Greek shipping magnate who had died, leaving her one of the richest women in America. Art supposed that her launching of the boat was meant to confer the blessings of wealth, power, and privilege. He hoped it might also give her luck.

'I name this boat *Flag*,' came the voice from the dome of light. 'God bless her, and all who sail in her.' Art crossed his fingers, and spat, and looked down at Anne-Marie. She spat too, looked up at him with her wide-set, narrow dark eyes, and winked. He bent and kissed her, feeling her lips cool and fog-damp. The crane slings lowered, and *Flag* settled into the oily water of the dock and sat bobbing.

'Thank you, Annabel,' said the old voice; Jasper Hyatt's voice. 'Maybe the weather has let us down today, but I remember when I was eight, in the year nineteen-oh-two, we launched *Pocahontas* here in a fog that was thick as chowder. And she won the Atlantic Cup two times running. Yes,' he said musingly, 'she sailed the pants right off the British. In those days, they hadn't discovered Australia.' There was laughter, and applause from the little crowd on the gantry. 'Now then,' said Hyatt. 'Let's get us some lunch.'

Anne-Marie gently patted her husband on the arm and said, 'See you later, honey, I have to get back to collect the children from nursery school.'

A voice from the quay called, 'Schacker!' It was DuCane, his smile glistening white in the fog. 'Come and meet Mrs Stavros, Art. We'll give you a ride down to the club.' There was a woman with him, about thirty-five, lean and brown and wearing a sable coat and Cossack boots, and a sable hat beaded with the fog. She said, 'Hi, Mr Schacker. I'm Ellie DuCane.' Schacker said, 'Hi,' without paying much attention to her. Then he said, 'Sorry, Mr DuCane. I guess I'll just stay here and start work on the boat.'

DuCane's smile narrowed a millimetre. 'I think it would be nice for the club to meet its captain,' he said.

Art looked up at him. 'Sure,' he said. 'When there's time. Right now, I want to put some weight in this boat, and a mast, and then we can maybe get her sailing.'

DuCane was not smiling at all, now. 'The men at the yard can do that kind of thing,' he said.

Art pursed his lips. 'Done much sailing, Mr DuCane?'

DuCane smiled again, but this time it looked forced. 'Not as much as Ellie here, I have to admit.'

'That so,' said Art. 'Well, Mr DuCane, I'd love to eat a little lobster and meet the guys, but what I have to do now is get inside this boat and see what she can do. Eight months is not a long time for a complete work-up, and when that race starts, I have to know her real well.' He paused. 'That could sound ungrateful. But as far as I can see, your outfit can handle the PR, and I'm here to sail the boat. That's what I'm good at, right?'

The crowd was drifting up to the cars, a hundred people making the fog curl and writhe, each of them thinking of hot lobster and buttered rum and the fires blazing in the clubhouse hearths.

'It's a lot of work,' said Ellie DuCane to her husband.

'Mr Schacker is obviously a dedicated man. You should be grateful, Wallace.' She was looking at Schacker intently, her eyes fringed with sable. Art was glad that Anne-Marie had gone home.

DuCane looked at his wife as if for confirmation, and said, 'Okay, Art. If that's the way you want to play it.'

'Right,' said Schacker, and turned away.

When the Sound Yacht Club wanted something to happen, it happened fast. Even Schacker had to admit that, as during the next three weeks *Flag* acquired her sails and her fittings, the web of her rig and the fat winches to drive it, her sensors in air and water and the electronic minds that gave them intelligence.

DuCane left him alone. Once, Schacker saw him standing in the marina car park, watching. *Flag* had grown from a long, low hulk into a taut, elegant racing machine. Schacker got the feeling that DuCane was intimidated. It was as if the boat was growing away from DuCane and the Sound Yacht Club, and growing into Schacker. Which suited Schacker fine.

The boat had begun as an offer he could not refuse. But now it was getting to him. He started work on her at six o'clock most mornings, rising in the twilight, pushing the Bentley along the icy coast road, and getting down to work by the time the hooters went for the end of the night shift in the cannery across the dark water of the Sound. And he would keep at it all day, until the light failed and the yellow bulbs of the work-lamps stained the fog. His meals were sandwiches, snatched during pauses to talk to designers and suppliers on his car telephone. He got home around midnight, and did the day's paperwork sent up by the manager DuCane had made him install at Marblehead Clam and Lobster. He seldom got to bed before two, and he saw his sons only as sleeping dolls, open-mouthed among the covers in their room with the ocean liner murals. Anne-Marie was a shadow who brought him coffee in the morning and left notes for him at night, notes which he skimmed until he got through the affectionate messages and arrived at the parts that told him who had called and where the food was. And when he finally slept, *Flag* sailed through his dreams, red, white and blue, a slender package of innumerable details trailing arrowheads of foam.

On the evening of the twenty-first day after *Flag*'s launching, Art Schacker was walking past Ernest the black butler and up the grand staircase of the Sound Yacht Club. On the wall hung a vast canvas of the Massachusetts privateer *Revenge* engaging two British sloops in the War of Independence.

Schacker pulled at his collar with his finger. It was too tight. He hated wearing a tuxedo. Surreptitiously, he checked his hands. It had taken half an hour's scubbing to get them clean, and there were still traces of epoxy resin in the cracks in his broad fingers.

The reception line consisted of Jasper Hyatt and Wallace DuCane. He shook hands with both of them. Wallace said, 'You're familiar with the schedule?' and Art nodded and smiled to Jasper, and went over to the bar in the great saloon. As he pushed his way through the crowd of men in tuxedoes, acknowledging greetings, he wished that it was all over and done with, and he could get back to work.

'Hi,' said a voice. He turned, and saw Ellie DuCane, in a

long dress of blue velvet, with a necklace of fat lozenge-shaped diamonds hanging over the upper slopes of her breasts. 'How are you feeling?' she said.

Art grinned at her. 'Nervous,' he said. Her face seemed familiar. 'Excuse my asking, but do I know you?'

'Ellie Richter,' she said.

'National Flying Fifteen champion, maybe fifteen years ago,' said Art.

'Correct.'

'And you're married to Wallace DuCane.'

'Surprised?' said Mrs DuCane.

He was surprised. Ellie Richter had been a brilliant helmsman, with a reputation as a tough competitor and a hellion off the water. He felt her wary eyes boring into him, and grinned at her. 'Well, maybe I am,' he said.

'He's a powerful guy,' said Mrs DuCane. 'And he wants to buy me diamonds, and he bought himself a yacht club. We get on. Still surprised?' Her eyes were hard and ironic, now.

'Dinner is served,' boomed the voice of Ernest the black butler from the door.

'Looks like you're off the hook,' said Mrs DuCane disconcertingly. 'Now let's get one of those delicious young men to take me through.'

Dinner was round the big table in the bow window: soup, Lobster Hyatt, apple pie. Art ate without tasting it. After the waiters had cleared away the debris, and the SYC's special rum was circulating in Waterford decanters, Jasper Hyatt got up. 'Now then,' he said, in his old, rusty voice. 'Mr Art Schacker's going to explain what he's been doing with your money all this time. Is that right, Wallace?'

Wallace DuCane showed his dazzling teeth. 'Well, Art,' he said. 'Let's hear it.'

Art took a deep breath and rose.

'Thank you,' he said, looking at the circles of faces, eyes blurring in the glitter of silver from the trophies and cups in the middle of the table. 'Thank you for your support and confidence in making me captain of *Flag*.' There was a ripple of applause. 'I'm not much of a hand at speechifying,' he said. 'So I'll explain what kind of boat we've got, and why we got her.' He took a sip of water.

'This Great Circle has a lot of problems,' he said. 'You need a boat that's good in light airs, to get across the doldrums, so you want her light built. But you also want a boat that's powerful to windward, for the first and last legs in the Atlantic, so she doesn't want to be skittery. And legs two and three are right down there in the Southern Ocean, with the wind abaft the beam and a lot of very heavy water, so you want a boat that runs well and surfs well, and a strong boat, because if she cracks up down there it's going to be a long swim to Hawaii for some gaffer tape.' There was a ripple of nervous laughter. He was now talking about things he had been thinking about for eighteen months, and was gaining in confidence.

'Well, you've seen the plans,' said Art. 'We have a boat built out of Kevlar, light and strong. We have a boat with a good flare to her bow sections, so she'll stay pretty dry, and a nice surfing shape forward of the keel. She's got powerful sides and a nice broad stern so she doesn't roll badly or poop easily. Elliptical keel and rudder. And she's masthead rigged, so we can carry some nice big kites in heavy winds down there near the ice.

'Below, we have accommodation for eighteen. More about that later. Brains of the ship is the usual Brookes and Gatehouse equipment, plus an Apple Mackintosh for tactical analysis and a little bitty radar for close work. Usual radios and satnav stuff. And maybe most important, a weatherfax machine to keep us up to date with the state of the winds. I don't have to tell you that this race is won by the captain with the best organizational back-up who gets the weather right. We'll be trying hard with the weather. And now, ladies and gentlemen, if you turn to the window, there's your boat.'

Waiters drew the velvet curtains from the huge bow window. The chandeliers were extinguished, and the great panelled room plunged into darkness.

At first the window was filled with the blackness of the sea. Then a glimmer of light reflected from the waves. The glimmer grew until it was a glare from the searchlights in the upper windows of the Sound Yacht Club. And there, clean as a knife-blade, gleaming red, white and blue in a million candlepower of light, lay *Flag*. A *Flag* straight out of the bandbox, glowing against the complete blackness of the sky.

The room melted in a storm of clapping. The searchlights faded. The curtains were drawn, and the lights came on. To the members of the Sound Yacht Club it seemed that Schacker still had some of that candlepower in his tilted blue eyes. 'Tomorrow,' he said, 'we start crew selection. Goodnight.'

This time, the clapping lasted twenty minutes.

*

Next day, George Hart went down to the marina and parked his Volkswagen Rabbit convertible between two BMWs. His heart was thumping in his chest, because he had made a decision. He had put his name down for the crew trials originally more or less as a joke. But now he knew he was pissed off with law school and Boston and his nice orderly life. He wanted to crew a boat around the world.

Last night, seeing the boat from the club's bow window, it had all seemed pretty easy. Now, things were different. As he walked down the jetty towards *Flag*, his mouth was dry and his knees weak.

She was huge. Everything about her was huge; her mast was an aluminium tree trunk, the rod-rigging from her spreaders thick as a child's wrist. The whip aerials on her transom were like salmon rods, the hydraulic ram at the base of her backstay enough to buffer a train. Against the frost-grey hills of the Sound's encircling arms, she was a thing of beauty and terror. Hart swallowed and hesitated.

There were perhaps forty men on deck, talking edgily. A couple of them looked down at Hart, without interest. He grabbed a stanchion, and swung himself up. Schacker was aft, talking to DuCane in the cockpit. He glanced at Hart, and said, 'You're late.' Hart could feel himself go crimson. He said, 'Sorry,' and went away, making a show of examining the boat.

The deck arrangement was standard for a big, ocean-going boat. She had a cockpit aft, with a companionway leading below. Forward, there was a shallow gorilla pit with another hatch, crossed by three big rows of linked three-gear winch handles that ground the fat Lewmar winches on the cockpit's coaming.

'Okay if I look below?' said Hart to a large man in a New York Yacht Club blazer. The man in the blazer shrugged. 'Why not?' he said. Hart reddened again and slid down the padded ladder.

Her mid-section was open plan, with a galley and a lightweight saloon table that folded out to accommodate a 24-volt sewing-machine for sail repairs. There were lockers everywhere, and three cabins, each containing six bunks, jammed in hugger-mugger. She was divided at the mast by a bulkhead, forward of which was the sail locker, with three pipe cots. Right aft, at the bottom of the companionway from the cockpit, was the captain's bunk, partitioned with a repeater for the Brookes and Gatehouse and a compass. On the other side of the boat was the navigator's chart table, with the radios and the computer and the radar.

Flag might look big on deck. But below, you realized exactly how little room eighteen men could be spared, if they were sailing round the world. Hart shook his head. It was as exotic as a space capsule, down here. He wanted to be on the trip so badly his teeth hurt. He climbed up the after companionway and into the cockpit, and found himself face to face with Art Schacker.

Schacker said, 'Hi, there.' He was not used to crew like this. There were too many heavies; students from Annapolis, men who owned and sailed their own boats and won major races with them. They would be fighting dog and dog before he even got to the start line. He said to Hart, 'What can you do?'

'Not a lot,' said Hart.

Well, thought Schacker, that's a start. 'What's your name?' he said. 'I'll look up your notes.'

'Hart,' said Hart. 'I guess there won't be a lot on the notes.'

Schacker riffled over the papers on the clipboard DuCane had given him. *Hart, George*, it said. *No serious racing experience. Cruising. Sponsor connection – member club's law firm.* Holy cow, thought Schacker, they want a boat's lawyer. But Hart was broad-shouldered with blondish hair that came over his ears, a wide pleasant face with a short nose and reserved brown eyes. He did not look much like a lawyer, thought Schacker.

'Where did you do your cruising?' he said.

'Caribbean, mostly,' said Hart. 'And the Intracoastal Waterway.'

'Oh, yeah,' said Schacker, losing interest. 'Well, you come along for the trial, right? Trials are this afternoon.' And he turned away, wondering how the hell he was supposed to win a race with a collection of prima donnas and warm-water cruisers who were members of the boat's law firm.

'Okay,' said DuCane. 'You have the lists, Art. Have you made any decisions?'

'Nope,' said Schacker, wondering how he was supposed to make decisions without going sailing.

DuCane took the clipboard from his hand, cleared his throat and addressed the men on the deck. 'Your attention, please,' he said. His careful grey hair fluttered in the irreverent wind, and he smoothed it with a hand. 'Crew candidates will be divided into two crews, the A crew and the B crew. Each will get a preliminary outing this afternoon.'

They divided. Schacker said, 'Okay. A crew, report for cast off at two p.m.'

'Better make that two thirty,' said DuCane. 'There's a club lunch, with sponsors, and you'll need to be there.'

Schacker said, 'The tide's at two.'

DuCane said, 'Can't it wait? Oh, I see, yeah. Okay, we'll get you back by two.'

'I have to stay,' said Art.

DuCane shook his head. 'Uh-uh. The sponsors want to meet you. You have a duty, Art.'

'I have a duty to win the Great Circle.'

DuCane leaned close to him. 'And to keep your company afloat. Eh, Art?'

Schacker's fists clenched. He said, 'I forgot you'd bought me.'

DuCane laughed, showing his teeth. 'And you got a great price. Come on, Art, I'll give you a ride.'

When Art came back from lunch, he parked next to a very old Ford pickup truck, with Florida plates and more rust than paint. It was by no means the manner of vehicle usual in the car park of the Sound Marina. 'My *God*,' said Martin Hyatt, the sun gleaming on his crewcut scalp. 'Whose is that thing?'

Art Schacker noticed the truck and noticed the reaction. He was feeling tired and bored, without having done anything. The truck seemed to lift his spirits, though his face did not change. He went quickly down the jetty towards *Flag*, lying slim and predatory at its end. A ragged-haired head rose above the level of the cockpit, looked incuriously at the approaching procession, and returned below eye level.

'Who's *that*?' said Martin Hyatt, his smooth face crinkling superciliously.

Schacker did not answer, but swung himself up on a stanchion and said, 'Joey.'

The lean blond man in the cockpit looked up. He had a big scar down his left cheek and no front teeth. He was wearing scuffed blue topsiders, tattered navy-blue trousers with paint specks, a White House Drinking Team T-shirt and a denim jacket that might once have belonged to a stock car driver. 'Art,' he said, and went back to the midships spoke of *Flag*'s wheel, on which he was putting the final touches to a Turk's head knot of great beauty and complication.

Art turned to Jasper Hyatt III, who had come along to (as he put it) maintain a watching brief. 'This is Pal Joey Greenhous,' he said. 'I asked him to sail with us as a watch captain.'

Jasper Hyatt's pudgy face was blank. 'Watch captain?' he said. 'You asked him?'

'He asked me,' said Pal Joey, without looking up. 'Izzat a problem?'

Art watched the skilful movements of Joey's flat-ended fingers with a cord. 'Tell him about yourself, Joey. Then we'll get some sail on, if you wouldn't mind.' He turned away, and began organizing his recruits.

'Okay,' said Joey. He finished the Turk's head, got up, and leaned on the boom. 'Well, I worked tuna boats out of Oregon. Bitch of a job, so I stopped. Then I was cruising in the West Indies, out of Jamaica. Then Jamaica went independent, and my boss went out of business –'

'Independent?' said Hyatt. 'But that was in 1962.'

'Yeah,' said Joey. 'I was eleven at the time. Well, after that my dad died and I kind of drifted up to Florida, and I did some crewing here and there, sailed the Onion Patch, and a few Transpacs and nobody made no fuss. Then old Art asked me along and here I am.' Pal Joey spat accurately over the side. 'Nice sled,' he said. 'If she sails.'

Hyatt's face was a purplish red. 'Kindly control your spitting on the club's premises,' he said. 'I have to tell you that Mr Schacker was exceeding his authority when he asked you to join.'

Joey looked at him and then at the Sound Yacht Club's nominees, smart in their navy-blue sweaters and white duck trousers. The shore lines were off, and *Flag* was motoring. The cold wind rippled the open cuffs of his denim jacket. He contemplated Hyatt's bulging, red-veined eyes for a long twenty seconds. Then he said, 'Who exactly the fuck are you?'

Schacker shouted from the wheel, 'Joey! Take charge at the mast!'

'Excuse me,' said Pal Joey politely, and trotted forward to the mast, where five SYC heavies were struggling with the mainsail. Joey thought for a moment. Then he gave a couple of orders Hyatt could not hear, in a conversational tone of voice. The SYC men looked at him, not recognizing him.

'*Heave*,' he said, almost apologetically.

They heaved. The mainsail went up.

Schacker went aft, to take the wheel. He called, 'Number two genoa, please.'

Hart was one of the triallists on the foredeck. He looked down the hatch into the sail locker, where the big bags nestled up to each other; like sleeping walruses, he thought, and about the same weight. He braced himself for some heavy lifting. But Joey said, 'I shifted 'em around before you come. Number two's on top.'

Hart looked at him in amazement; the scrawny arms, the skinny chest, the flapping T-shirt under the thin denim jacket. Two Captain's Cup types went down after the sail. Joey said, 'Christ, you surely ain't going to *lift* that thing?' And he sent down the end of a halyard and swung it up himself, with one hand.

Art cut the engine. The sudden hush was so complete it left a ring in the ears. He said, 'Foresail.'

The genoa went up. There was a ragged burst of clapping from round the deck. The cockpit sole tilted under Schacker's feet, and for the first time he felt that the boat was a living thing, heard the musical bubble of the water at her transom. Ahead, past the mast and the forestay and the blue backs coiling away ropes, the gap of clear water at the Sound's mouth grew by the minute. For the first time in weeks, Schacker smiled.

The cameras started going in the escort boats; the club had invited its favourite journalists to the luncheon, and now they were dogging *Flag*'s every tack. George Hart sat on the weather deck and tried to look useful. It was not easy; there was nothing to do that was not already being done. The genoa winches were manned by grinders who had worked in Captain's Cup triallists. The foredeck was being patrolled by the foredeck men from one of the year-before-last's Atlantic Cup contenders. Three men from Cloake's, the world's biggest sailmakers, were trimming genoa and main and mast, fighting for the last ounce of speed. George had a sudden gloomy presentiment that among all this talent, he was wasting his time.

Martin Hyatt was sitting next to him, looking keen and alert and slightly disapproving. 'I could do with some coffee,' said George. Hyatt paid no attention. 'Why don't you make some?' said George.

Hyatt smiled faintly at the absurdity of the idea.

Hart got up and began to trot off just as Schacker, in the cockpit, shouted, 'Helm's a-lee!'

Flag came on an even keel. Hart ducked as the boom came over, then got up and started aft again. Someone was shouting, 'Lazy!' He kept going.

'LAZY!' roared four or five voices. Something hit him on the leg, and he fell heavily on to a winch. His leg hurt, agonizingly. When he looked up, he saw Schacker. Schacker was pointing at him. 'This is an eighty-foot boat,' he was saying. 'You have to treat it with respect, not go straight through the middle of a lazy sheet. You're lucky you didn't break your leg, boy.'

Hart got up. His leg felt as if it was broken, at that. He could feel the eyes of the crew on him. Well, he thought: I'm finished. He limped aft to Schacker and said, 'How about I make some coffee?'

Schacker looked at him and said, 'You may be a clumsy bastard, but you got good priorities.'

George went below to the galley.

It was peaceful down here, with no sound but the crunch as *Flag* stuck her nose into a wave and the booming of feet on the deck. George made the coffee and wiped the flat electric hob, and put the cups on a tray with a box of cookies he found in a locker. The pain in his leg was subsiding. For the first time since that morning, George felt relaxed. It seemed he was being useful.

He reappeared on deck with twenty-three mugs on a tray. The SYC men gathered round him and took their mugs, and a couple of them even thanked him. He sat on the weather deck, keeping out of the way of stray sheets, and watched the photography boats. They were well out at sea now, perhaps four miles off the coast. There was a long swell running, and a cold easterly blowing out of a sky full of big grey clouds. A Cessna, chartered by the sponsors, came low overhead. 'He's filming,' said Art. 'Let's try her with the 2.2 kite, Joey.'

Joey and the foredeck party flew the kite in a creditably short time. The red, white and blue spinnaker bearing the Stars and Stripes swelled huge against the low grey clouds as *Flag*'s nose turned for the land. Pal Joey made his way back to the cockpit at his peculiar rapid shuffle, buttoning the fly of his paint-stained pants as he came.

George Hart collected up the coffee cups. When the boat came alongside to take off the first team of triallists and put on the second he climbed across the narrow gap of water, and looked back at *Flag*, dipping and gliding away across the slate-coloured sea, with a virtual certainty he would never set foot on her again.

Now that he was off her, he was cold. And it was not just a physical cold. He wanted to be part of that boat, and the feeling that he wasn't going to be was like leaving a beautiful woman and then finding you had lost her telephone number with no way of finding it again. So he drove his Volkswagen Rabbit convertible back to Boston and went to the apartment he had in back of his father's house and showered, and then wondered what he was going to do with himself that evening, or for that matter ever.

He drank a beer and debated whether he should ring up a girl. He did not want to talk, but he hated to eat alone. So he rang Iris down the road, and told her to get over. Iris liked to eat, and she didn't talk much.

Then he went into the kitchen and took a beef fillet out of the refrigerator. He made some puff pastry, carefully cutting little pieces of butter into the flour, adding a little water, rolling it out, folding it, turning the pastry and doing it all over again and again. As he manufactured his *filet en croûte*, the frustrations faded into the background, and he was totally absorbed. He rolled out the pastry, spread a layer of smooth pâté on it and carefully wrapped it round the meat. Then he put it in the oven: eleven minutes, he told himself: no more. Iris would be here.

Nine minutes later the telephone rang.

'Hello,' said the voice on the other end. 'Schacker.'

Hart's heart banged, once.

'Thank you for sailing the trial today,' said Schacker. 'I called to say –'

'Could you hold it a moment?' said Hart. 'Only I have something in the oven, it's very precise. Hold it.' He ran back to the oven, pulled out the *filet en croûte*, and ran back to the telephone. 'Sorry,' he said. 'I have a girlfriend coming over. I was cooking.'

'Okay,' said Schacker. 'Look, I'll make this quick. I guess we need a highly trained crew, and I'm sorry, but – Hey. Did you say cooking?'

'Yeah,' said Hart, dully. No sailing. Just the law firm.

'You know how to cook?'

'Sure,' said Hart, wishing he would say what he had to say.

'Could you cook for eighteen guys in a barrel going over Niagara Falls?'

'I never tried,' said Hart. 'I guess so.'

'Well, you'd better come to the main trial tomorrow,' said Schacker. 'And bring your chef's hat.'

The doorbell rang. It was Iris. 'Kiss me, Iris,' said Hart. 'I'm Vasco da Gama!'

Art sat at home, eating dinner with the family for the first time in weeks. As on all important occasions in the Schacker household the children were there too, and the heavy silver candlesticks burned in the middle of the big Vermont pine table. They were eating chicken, and the children were drinking Coca-Cola, which was a treat for them and was making them unnaturally quiet. Anne-Marie sat at the opposite end of the table from Art. She was thinking that his broad, brown face looked older and tireder than it should. Art looked back at her, the dark wings of her hair shading the high, almost Red Indian bones of her face, and he was thinking that he must be insane to throw up all this to sail round the world at the bidding of a snake like DuCane.

He tried to push the race from his mind. 'What have you all been doing?'

'We went skiing,' said his eldest son, George.

'George fell over,' said his second son, Abraham.

'And so did Abie,' said his third son, Jesse.

'And so did I. And Jesse,' said his fourth son, Nathaniel.

Then they started to kick each other under the table. 'QUIET!' said Art. 'I'll tell you what I did.'

'Yeah,' they all said.

'I went sailing in a racing boat.'

'Oh yeah?' said George. 'Well, I am pissed off with your racing boat –'

'George!' said Anne-Marie. 'Language! Leave the room!'

'Not fair,' said George. 'I heard you saying it to someone on the telephone.'

'Okay,' said Schacker. 'You can leave the table, all of you.' They got down, and left, squabbling. Schacker said, 'Sorry.'

Anne-Marie came and sat next to him and said, 'Not your fault, honey.' She took his hand. 'It hasn't been easy for any of us,' she said. 'Is it going well?'

Art said, 'I'm in the middle of getting a crew who think they're God's gift to ocean-racing.'

'They'll settle down,' said Anne-Marie. 'You pick good people, they'll win you the race.'

The telephone started to ring. Art went into the living-room, where the telephone sat under a portrait of the first Nathaniel Schacker, who had been Marblehead's most successful whaling captain in 1847.

It was Wallace DuCane. His voice was hard and angry. 'See here, Schacker,' he said. 'You are acting outside your terms of reference. This Joey Greenhous character. What is he doing on board our yacht?'

Art had expected this, and he knew how to handle it. 'Making it go faster than anyone else can,' he said. 'I want him as a watch captain because he is a genius. He will work your college boys till they want to die, but he will also sail *Flag* faster than you will believe. Understand?'

'But the club –'

'I appreciate that due to an oversight his name has been

omitted from the Social Register,' said Art, drily. 'You want to win this race?'

'Of course,' snapped DuCane. 'But next time –'

'Look, Mr DuCane, you run my company and I'll sail your boat,' said Schacker.

There was a long silence.

'Okay,' said DuCane finally. 'But next time, could he piss in the can, not off the front of the boat? We were filming, and he spoilt the picture. They'll be out again tomorrow, so ask him to wave his hand, not his dick.'

The previous May, Murphy had travelled in Harry Redd's helicopter to a boatyard in Port Melbourne.

'Is she cooked?' said Murphy.

The man in overalls looked at his watch and wiped the sweat from his forehead with a sopping rag. 'To a turn,' he said. He pulled the walkie-talkie radio from his belt and said, 'Doors open, please.'

Murphy's hands tightened on the warm iron of the gantry railing. Below, on the floor of the enormous corrugated-iron shed, men in heat-resistant suits and visors moved painfully around a long, shrouded shape. Two of them went to the end of the long shape and pulled open double doors.

'We'll leave her to cool slowly,' said the boatbuilder.

'Not too slowly,' said Murphy. 'I want a look.'

'Nip down, then,' said the builder. 'Then we'll have a cup of tea in the office. The heat's killing me.'

Murphy slid quickly down the steel ladder that plunged down the wall of the shed. The builder watched him walk across the floor to the doors and peer inside. He said, 'Christ, he'll burn his ass off.'

Harry Redd was standing further along the gallery. He was wearing a neat tan suit and a Panama hat, and he seemed entirely unaffected by the heat that rose from the long oven below and beat against the corrugated iron roof overhead.

'He knows what he's doing,' he said.

From above, Murphy was foreshortened until he looked like a tremendous ape. He stood for a moment, arms swinging, at the entrance to the oven. Then he darted forward through the doors. He came out a second later, running backwards, bellowing with laughter. The builder said, 'What's he playing at?'

Murphy was shinning up the ladder again. 'She's beautiful!' he roared, and ran down the gallery towards them.

Redd said, 'What have you done to your face, you steaming drongo?'

The builder peered at Murphy's mouth. He was a tall man, but it was still slightly above his eye-level. 'Burnt,' he said.

'I had to kiss the baby,' said Murphy. 'Tell you what. When you put on the gelcoat, you might paint that spot a lovely luscious red. In the shape of my succulent lips. Right, sport?'

'If you insist,' said the boatbuilder. 'Where did you kiss it?'

'Right on the bum,' said Murphy. 'Most of me skin's still on it.'

They went into the builder's office, and drank tea out of thick white mugs. The office had a plate-glass wall. Beyond the wall, on the shed floor, a fork-lift truck reversed up to the doors of the structure, and drew forth the long, knife-like shape of a boat. It looked like the chrysalis of a butterfly; matt grey, anonymous, the shape hinting at the beauty to come. *Tasman*.

Redd's helicopter was racing its shadow over the gum forests on the slopes of the Snowies, heading back for Melbourne. Redd said, 'You'd better put some stuff on your mouth for the burns.'

'No,' said Murphy. 'I'll suffer. She's worth it.'

'Suffer, then,' said Redd. 'And I hope she bloody is worth it. I can't tell you how much she's cost.'

'I can guess,' said Murphy. 'I dunno how you do it, Harry.'

Redd looked at him, dead straight, and passed a hand over his cropped skull. 'I went to the bank,' he said. 'I had a set of drawings, and I said, hey, you bastards, I want to build a distillery. Well, all good Poms know we're a bunch of alkies down here in Oz. So they gave me the money, and I gave it to the *Tasman* fund. So when you're sloshing around in that thing, you better realize that you are up to your neck in whisky.'

The gear for putting *Tasman* together was already waiting in a pile in the sheds at Sydney Harbour Building, and the yard worked on her twenty-four hours a day. She was using as many standard parts as possible, so spares would be available anywhere in the world. Tubes Murphy believed in running a gypsy campaign, not dependent on shore squads to shadow him all over the globe, but carrying his spares and his skilled men with him, as far as possible.

To this end, he chose a crew of experienced racing sailors who doubled as skilled tradesmen. His spare helmsman was a plumber. His trimmers were experienced riggers. He took on a full-time cook who was also an electrician, and a sailmaker who was also a doctor.

All over the world, big boats were thrashing through the winter weather, trying to find out weaknesses in crew and hull and rig and gear. *Tasman* did her share, in the late months of the year following Tubes' win in the Melbourne Cup. On Boxing Day, she took the windward end of the line at the start of the Sydney–Hobart race, and sailed straight into the arms of a Southern Buster. For almost a week she had disappeared in huge seas and blankets of fog coughed out by the Bass Strait. The race fleet had been hard hit; there were four dismastings, and a lot of retirements. As it turned out, *Tasman* had disappeared simply because nobody had been able to believe she was as far ahead of the fleet as it transpired she was. She rollicked over the line a day ahead of her closest competitor. That night, Harry Redd sent a photograph of *Tasman*'s stern to the Committee of the Sound Yacht Club, Boston, Mass, USA. On the back of the photograph was written *Kiss my ass, Flag. It's the only part of me you're going to see.*

There was no reply.

*

On 15 January, *Tasman* was on the move again. The damage caused by her drive through the appalling weather of the Sydney–Hobart had been repaired. Her racing sails were in their bags, sealed and stowed in the aisles below. Most of Sydney had come to see their entry off on the delivery trip to Portsmouth and the start of the Great Circle. As she hit open water, Murphy set a Dacron cruising mainsail, and popped out a cruising spinnaker bearing the Redd trademark, a Tasmanian tiger's face, black with a red tongue lolling between white teeth.

The engine stopped. The roars of the crowds on the quay floated across the water. People were hanging on to cranes and perched in the crosstrees of yachts. *Tasman* heeled to the westerly blowing across her starboard quarter, and the brilliant summer sun struck ruby glints from the Cabernet Shiraz splashing from the fountains Harry Redd's people had laid out to quench the thirst of his guests.

'You'll be glad of some peace and quiet,' said Harry Redd, who was standing beside Murphy in *Tasman*'s cockpit. He had jumped aboard at the last minute for the first part of the ride.

Murphy looked down at him with an eye that had lost none of its clarity, despite the fact that he had not been to bed for two nights. 'You bet,' he said. 'Sea air, no booze, I'll be living like a monk.'

They passed the Sydney Harbour fireship, all water cannon firing. The Australian Navy was dressed overall with bright bunting. Further down towards the bridge, someone in a giant ChrisCraft was letting off distress rockets. Nobody was paying any attention, which was just as well, because the ChrisCraft was surrounded by a raft of empty champagne bottles, and if the owner was in distress he seemed blissfully unaware of the fact.

Tasman ploughed through the crowd of spectators, sounding her foghorns. Every ship in the harbour sounded its siren. The sound boomed round the white towers of the great city as they fell astern, blinding in the sun. The flotilla passed on, into the choppy waters of the Heads and into the Tasman Sea.

Off the land, the wind freshened, and *Tasman*'s tall sails drew away from the lesser ones of her accompanying yachts. The sea out here was lumpy, and the motor boats fell astern one by one. At about four p.m., *Tasman* leaned alone on a great blue sheet of sea. Redd said, 'Let's get the chopper,' and went down the aft companionway to the radio shack.

Murphy hung on to the wheel, watching the trimmers work. Far away to windward, a boat was approaching. It was a power boat, and a fast one; sometimes it came right out of the water, and landed with a crash and a bloom of spray on the next wave. By the time Redd came on deck, the power boat was near enough for the snarl of its engines to be audible, and closing fast. Murphy looked slightly embarrassed. He said, 'Er, Reddy. What you are about to see is a bit, er, confidential.'

The power boat came alongside. There were only two seats. They both held anonymous figures in goggles and red-and-white crash helmets that matched the boat. The figure in the right-hand seat stood up and took off its helmet. A flag of black hair rippled down the wind, and the blue eyes sparkled in the sun. She tossed across a sea-bag, waited for the power boat to come up on a wave and jumped across the gap of water, grabbing Murphy's hand to steady herself. The throaty gurgle of the power boat's exhausts deepened to a roar. It threw up a sweeping fan of spray as it turned and headed for the low line of the land.

'Evening, Shar,' said Murphy, and caught her by the waist and kissed her on the mouth.

'Tut, bleeding tut,' said Redd. Far away to landward, a silver dot glittered in the heat-hazed sky. 'Here comes the chopper. Reckon I'd better make an excuse and leave.'

'I'm on my auntie's sheep station for a couple of weeks,' said Shar. 'Just think, all that peace and quiet, and no telephone.'

'Of course you are,' said Redd. 'But you bloody watch out. If anything happens to me, your old man's mister money bags for this crate, and your sheep-farming activities might make him none too generous.'

Murphy grinned, and the downdraught of the chopper whitened the water to port. Redd caught the bosun's chair it lowered, climbed in, and gave the dispatcher the high sign. *Tasman* shrank below.

He watched her go from the co-pilot's seat of the chopper. The wrinkled sea wheeled beneath him, cut by the arrow of her wake. The waving figures in the cockpit were tiny. The high road. Tahiti, Panama, Portsmouth, he thought. Then he sighed. Someone had to earn the money to support Murphy in his dalliance. He picked up the radio telephone.

'Right,' he said to his secretary when she answered. 'Let's write some letters.'

The sun was setting over Moorea, the small rocky island off Papeete, capital of Tahiti. The air was full of *tiare Tahiti*, the South Sea gardenia; the sky was violet and yellow and green, with gold-rimmed battleships of cloud sailing down the Trades to the shores of Heaven. Darkness had fallen over the sea, mercifully concealing the shoebox lines of Papeete's hotels, and the upperworks of the cruise liners in the harbour.

Tasman was anchored in the lagoon, as far off as Murphy could manage; he had been to Papeete before. The crew were ashore, drinking beer that tasted of coconut oil, and probably meeting natives from well-known South Sea Islands like Des Moines and Wagga Wagga. Murphy was not at all keen on civilization when it meant what the tourists had done to Tahiti.

Shar Stapleton stirred beside him on the cushions in the cockpit, and the point of her naked breast brushed against his chest.

'Murph,' she said. 'I've got to go tomorrow.'

'Go?'

'There's an airport here. I want to radio home.'

'Okay,' said Murphy. He wrapped a towel round his waist, went down to the radio shack, and got himself patched in. Shar came and stood behind him, rubbing the big muscles of his neck with her slender fingers. After fifteen minutes, he gave her the handset. 'Live from your auntie's sheep station,' he said.

She brushed against him, and he felt the smoothness of her body and the fur of her groin as she said, 'Mo? Shar here.'

The handset chattered angrily. 'Yes,' she said. 'Sorry no call, we've been riding the fences. I'm ever so brown, though.'

More chattering.

'That's what I was ringing for,' purred Shar. 'I'm coming back tomorrow or the next day. It's real nice out here, but kind of lonely, with just the sheep.'

'Baa,' said Murphy, quietly.

'Gotta dash,' said Shar. 'So long, then.' She dropped the handset on the deck and swept the towel from Murphy's waist, and then it was skin on skin, and those pointed breasts digging into his chest as she drew his head down to her open mouth.

He reached across and clicked off the radio. Then he knelt on the pale sailbags spread on the deck, and plunged into the hot, tropical darkness of her body.

In his penthouse apartment on the forty-eighth floor of Sydney's Frazer building, Mo Stapleton held the receiver to his ear as it clicked into silence and stared across his cluttered desk at the Sydney Nolan painting of Joshua trees in the Nullarbor Desert. If he had been a man whose facial expressions gave anything away, he would have frowned. As it was, his eyes were cold and absent.

If Shar was up country with her aunt, what was that voice, crackling with the static, that had come in after the link had been cut and said, '*Tahiti terminée*?

'*Les voilà*,' said the reporter in the brown raincoat and the Gauloise.

'Ah,' said the photographer. Actually he had seen them some five minutes ago, but he had kept quiet about it because the journalist liked to see things first and he wished the journalist to be in a good humour, and take him to lunch at Freddy's in Riec-sur-Belon, oyster capital of Brittany. He took his Nikon from under his anorak, where he had been holding it to protect it from the sand the wind was lashing off the Quiberon Peninsula. In the viewfinder, a line of eighteen men straggled down the face of a grass-topped white dune. Even at this range, he could tell they were near exhaustion.

'*Extra*,' he muttered; brilliant images. Perhaps one of them would throw up, and he would win an award.

He shot assiduously, wiping the drizzle from the lens between pictures. This was about the only chance he had to explain the characters of the crew of *Siltex-France*, before the race. The French public was passionate to understand its nautical heroes. Once they were at sea, they were lost as humans; merely a boat, and the personality of the captain, Jean-Luc Jarré. And perhaps, later, a disaster. The photographer smiled, remembering the shots he had got of the last Great Circle race, off Tierra del Fuego, from the cargo door of a Chilean Air Force Boeing. They had made his reputation, those shots: *Vins Arnaud II*, sinking while her captain broadcast live on radio. And the captain's quote they had used as the caption: *J'ai les pieds mouillés pour la France*: I have got my feet wet for France.

One of the figures in the dunes stumbled and fell. The photographer zoomed in, then said, '*Chut!*' disappointedly as the man got up again and stumbled after the file. But he got a good shot, of a face glistening with sweat and rain and a sweeping Gascon moustache caked with sand.

The owner of the moustache spat and coughed and kept running, staring grimly at the shoulders in front of him. The breath rasped in his throat and the sweat stung his eyes, and the soft sand sucked at his legs. It was eleven o'clock on the twelfth of April, and he should have been sitting in his consulting rooms in the Boulevard Raspail, speaking soothingly to one of his ulcer patients, who would then write him a large cheque and leave him alone, so he could go to a long lunch with Madeleine, or Sylvie, or Magrit. Instead, he was running like a Foreign Legionnaire across a desert, and he thought he was going to be sick.

'*Allons-y!*' shouted Jarré, the captain, whose sinewy legs were pounding the sand at the front of the file. '*Dernier kilomètre!*'

The shapes of the dunes blurred before de Rochambaud's eyes. His legs pumped, left, right, left, right. The sea was a blue line, cut at its centre by the vertical of a boat's mast. The mast of *Siltex-France*, eighty feet overall, rating seventy feet, built of carbon fibre and exotic foams, titanium rod rigging, ten million francs' worth of sails. A midnight-black shark, snubbing at her anchor line in Quiberon Bay, impatient for the first of September and the beginning of her glory.

The runners halted by the crowd of reporters. De Rochambaud staggered to one side, cannoning into a reporter in a fawn raincoat and a brown slouch hat, 'Excuse me,' he said.

'Not at all,' said the reporter. 'Evidently, you are tired. You are Docteur le Comte Henri di Rochambaud, are you not?'

'Yes,' said de Rochambaud curtly. He needed all his breath for panting.

'Tell me, M. le Comte. What is it that makes one of France's leading gastric specialists, a man famous as an escort of beautiful women, wish to go on an uncomfortable race such as this?'

De Rochambaud had got most of the sand out of his moustache. He looked up, and this time there was that hint of amusement in his brown eyes that had made him and his female companions some of *Paris-Dimanche*'s favourite victims. 'God knows,' he said. The photographer clicked at him.

'*Allons-y!*' cried Jarré again.

Wearily, de Rochambaud rose to his feet and began plodding towards the rain-pocked beach. In September, there would be the *vendange* at St-Roch, his little château in Gascony where the foothills of the Pyrénées joined the pine-clad dunes of the Landes. There would be singing, and Mère Hermine's rôti de veau, and warm nights, and warm women. So why was he going to lock himself up, him, a man of thirty-nine, with a lot of people ten years younger than himself, in a plastic jail on the high seas?

The photographer snapped them as they trotted on to the beach, with *Siltex-France* in the background. Next to him, he could hear the reporter muttering into his tape recorder. 'They jogged away towards *Siltex*,' he was saying, 'and towards the start of the race, four months away, five hundred kilometres over the cold sea; towards Portsmouth. And Destiny.'

Quel con, thought the photographer. What a berk.

'Summer,' said Anton Fischer, 'is in the air. Is it not, Trixi?'

'*Ja, Herr Doktor*,' said Trixi. She was a pretty girl, but her eyes were red, for she had been crying.

'Find yourself a pleasant young man,' said Fischer. 'Eat. Drink a little too much. Make love.'

'*Ja, Herr Doktor*,' said Trixi. It was a Tuesday, mid-July. The sunlight was bouncing round the tall, beautiful room on the *piano nobile*, the first storey of the Baroque house in the Singerstrasse. It bounced from the little steel hooks and mirrors she was packing into the slotted drawer. It winked on the chromed fittings of the dentist's chair in the middle of the floor, and it gleamed on the perfect porcelain caps on Trixi's front teeth as she tried a brave smile.

'So,' said Fischer, who had fitted the caps himself. 'All is prepared. Kiss me, Trixi.'

'*Ja, Herr Doktor*,' said Trixi. She buried her face in Anton's white coat and sobbed a little. There was a knock on the door.

'That will be Herr Georg,' said Anton, disengaging himself. 'Enter, dear brother.'

Ten minutes later, the brothers Anton and Georg Fischer knocked on the window of the receptionist's lodge at the bottom of the wide helical staircase. The receptionist, a stout woman past middle age, said, 'So you're off.'

'We are,' said the brothers, together.

'God spare your lives, then,' said the receptionist. 'I wish I had your money, but I don't envy you.'

The brothers laughed, again together. They said, 'Until a year from now,' and walked out into the hum of Vienna.

'Coffee, Anton?'

'Coffee, Georg.'

They proceeded towards the graceful loom of the State Opera House, two dark, dumpy little men in dark suits, talking deliberately but with animation, bowing from time to time to passing acquaintances. Opposite the Opera House at the Hotel Sacher they ordered coffee, *mit schlag*.

'*Sachertorte?*' said Anton.

Georg looked doubtful, and patted his convex worsted waistcoat. 'A little large,' he said.

'But one must prepare for salt horse and biscuits with weevils,' said Anton. 'As your dentist, I authorize it.'

'And as your dentist, *I* authorize it,' said Georg.

Twenty minutes later the brothers rose, paid their bill, shook hands with Axel, their waiter, and boarded the taxi that drew up at the kerb. The taxi took them to the airport, where they boarded the flight for Lisbon. At Lisbon they changed planes, landing at ten p.m. in Faro. They stayed the night at a hotel, and in the morning drove down the coast to a blue marina hedged in by the tall white buildings of Vilamoura, behind an endless beach of white sand. Here, their Nicolson 48, *Sirène*, lay waiting.

They spent a busy three hours taking deliveries: cases marked Springli, Fortnum and Mason, Fundalor, Fonseca, Montecristo piled on the jetty and were stowed.

At last, the jetty was clear. 'Ah!' said Anton, filling a bucket with ice cubes from the ice machine in the galley and slotting a Pavarotti *Bohème* into the compact disc player. 'Back to basics! The adventure begins!'

During the next forty-eight hours, the minibus travelled to and from Faro airport another four times, and *Sirène* took on her full complement of eight. On the Monday morning, they motored out into the wide, blue-grey Atlantic. *Sirène*'s nose turned for Cape St Vincent; and beyond the Cape, the Bay of Biscay, the Western Approaches, Portsmouth, and the start of the Great Circle.

Dave Kelly's British researcher had a face like a horse and a touching belief that everything in the United States was the equivalent of something in Britain. 'I always think that Southampton's a bit like Los Angeles,' she said as the rented limousine turned off the M27. 'All those freeways.'

'Yeah,' said Kelly. 'Sure.' It was eleven in the morning, and it was raining. The motorway was crowded with little British cars, roof racks piled with suitcases, going on their holidays. It was August, after all. In Kelly's view, they were all insane. 'Is there a cocktail cabinet in this heap?'

The researcher opened a walnut door in the partition

dividing them from the driver. 'Sherry,' she said, 'gin, whisky.'

'Sherry,' said Kelly. 'It's the middle ages.'

The researcher had misunderstood his scorn as a request, and handed him a small crystal glass of brownish fluid. Kelly opened his mouth to protest, then thought, what the hell, and tipped it down his throat. 'Yeh,' he said. But the truth was that when you had a hangover like this, it did not much matter what you drank, as long as it had alcohol in it.

Kelly's Eye had arrived two weeks ago, after a transatlantic work-up cruise. She had had good weather and only minor teething troubles, and her crew had worked together well. This was not only good news, but unexpected news.

For *Kelly's Eye* had given rise to a good deal of debate in ocean-racing circles. Her designer, Norbert Widmark, had done a lot of work on boats for the Transpac, the West Coast-Hawaii race. He had never designed for the North Atlantic or the Southern Ocean before, and in the opinion of the pundits, it showed. They said *Kelly's Eye* was built too light for the conditions she was going to meet; that she was too much of a racer, and not enough of a sea boat; that her fractional rig was too complicated, with too many things that could go wrong; and that one transatlantic cruise was not enough work-up time.

This had pleased Kelly. It had pointed up *Eye*'s state-of-the-art technology, and emphasized the fact that she was a death-or-glory racing machine. Bud Withers, the captain, was a Transpac veteran with a reputation for absolute dedication to his race campaigns. All in all, *Eye* was a pretty glamorous proposition, and even Carey, Kelly's agent, had to admit that so far she had done Kelly's somewhat battered image a lot of good.

He opened the wad of newspapers on the seat in front of him, and began to strip his way methodically through the pages, as he had done every day since he had got his first job as a disc jockey on radio CXFM, Oakland, California, at the age of eighteen. It was reading the newspapers, and providing his own mean slant on the news, that had brought him to the attention of his first agent, who had seen that he was wasted on radio and brought him to TV. His first assignment had been a live interview with a suspected homosexual mass murderer. Kelly had extracted a confession from him. Afterwards the guy had blown his brains out, live to camera, and soon after that Kelly had got his own show.

He drank another glass of sherry to the memory. Then he went back to the papers, concentrating on the sports sections.

The East Coast papers were mainly occupied with the South Yacht Club's entry. *Flag* had performed well in trials, and was reckoned to have an expert, highly disciplined and well-financed crew. The further you got from Boston, the more pleasure the yachting correspondents took in the fact that the SYC's campaign was the most expensive ever staged, and was known to be an attempt to avenge its humiliation by Harry Redd's Australian syndicate in the Atlantic Cup. Harry Redd, for his part, had recently sent Jasper Hyatt II of the SYC a pair of oars, small size, one bearing the word 'left' and the other the word 'right'.

The London *Times* made little copy of the controversy. It was the first day of Cowes Week, and the paper's Great

Circle story was well down the list of events. It agreed with the *New York Times* that *Flag* and *Tasman* were the obvious front runners. But it also pointed out that the English entry, *Chinamite*, had trained long, hard and well, and that the boat, while by no means new, was a proven performer. Trouble could also be expected from *Siltex-France*; Jean-Luc Jarré was a formidable seaman, backed by immensely rich sponsors and carrying the goodwill of most of France. *Siltex* herself came from a designer and a yard that had been producing Captain's Cup winners for France for five years. In fact, *The Times* was inclined to regard *Siltex* as an extremely strong contender, though there were doubts about her new keel, which seemed likely to cause disputes with the rating authority, which determined the yacht's handicaps. *Kelly's Eye* was described as a dark horse. The writer pointed out that she was undoubtedly fast, as evinced by her commanding lead in the Big Boats Championships, but that the race was a test of endurance as well as speed. It repeated the view that *Eye* might be too lightly built for the punishment handed out by circumnavigation.

'Hah!' said Kelly, and scored through the line of type with a yellow felt tip. It would sound nice in the list of prophecies of doom that he meant to voice-over on a shot of *Kelly's Eye* at the race start.

The article went on to discuss the subtleties of the race. It pointed out that the two main prizes were for the quickest boat round the world, irrespective of rating, and the first boat round on corrected time. One of the maxis – *Flag, Siltex, Tasman, Chinamite, Kelly's Eye* – was bound to take the time elapsed prize. But the corrected time was different. It had been shown that big boats could seldom save their time, and very small boats, while advantageously handicapped, were usually too weighed down with supplies to perform their best. There was a magic middle zone in the rating bands, into which fitted EPK *Electric*, the stripped-out Swan 651 skippered by Emily de Havilland which had performed exceptionally well during trials.

It pointed out that many boats competed for the honour of taking part, without much hope of winning. It added that the Great Circle was also known as the Sailor's Everest, and drew a link with the fact that Sir Clement Jones and the Commando crew of *Associated Meat* were better known as mountaineers than as sailors.

Finally, it went through the smaller boats: two Dutchmen, a Spaniard, three Frenchmen, one Brazilian, and (rather to the amusement of *The Times*) the Austrian entry, *Sirène*. *Sirène* had the distinction of being the only unsponsored boat in the race, and the only boat with a wine cellar. *The Times* described the attitude of the Fischer brothers, her owners, as 'relaxed'.

Outside the darkened windows of the limousine, lines of semi-detached houses flowed up the A27 back towards London. Soon the limousine turned right between the wire gates that separate Port Hamble's forest of masts from the suburbs outside. Kelly climbed out and looked around him. There were boats everywhere: boats on chocks, flying big flags with FOR SALE written on them. Boats shrouded in polythene from which came showers of sparks and the whine of sanders. Boats on cranes, ready to be dropped into the water after their bottoms had been hosed off. And boats moored at jetties; hundreds, thousands of them, stretching away into the grey drizzle as far as the eye could see.

Among the boats, people moved with the purposefulness of hurrying ants, sure-footed on the wavering jetties, dressed in yellow oilskins and rubber boots and sou'westers and yachting caps. Each of them knew where he was going and why.

Kelly suddenly felt that he was the only person in the yard who did not know exactly why he was there. Until now, everything had followed plans that he had laid out. Now for the first time, he realized that he was doomed for the next eight months to be part of a world in which he was a participant, not an observer. It was a nasty, cold, panicky feeling.

'Where's the yacht?' said the researcher.

He turned his dazed eyes on her. She was amazed to see that the delicate bones of his face were blurred with beads of sweat, and his skin was grey. 'What?' he said.

'The yacht,' she said.

He shook his head slowly.

He looked completely lost, the researcher thought. The chauffeur brought Kelly's two crocodile-skin Louis Vuitton suitcases from the car, and said, 'Where to, sir?'

'Hey!' said a woman's voice. 'You David Kelly?'

Kelly turned. The speaker was six feet tall, wearing short white shorts. He said, 'Yes.'

'Boat's over here,' she said. 'I'm Bennett.' She held out her hand. Kelly shook it. It was like gripping an oak plank.

The researcher held out her hand, and smiled with her big teeth. 'Goodbye, Mr Kelly,' she said. 'And good luck.'

Kelly ignored her. The drizzle had stopped. He was looking down a jetty at a mast so tall it seemed to touch the sky. On the forestay, a huge flag flapped in the light breeze. 'KELLY'S EYE USTS', it said.

'Bring the cases,' he said to the chauffeur, and began to follow Bennett towards that mast.

At the end of the jetty, *Eye*'s hull blocked the way, black, with the name in gold crackle-finish. The chauffeur lifted his cases up to Bennett. 'Shee-yit,' she said. 'What you *got* in here? Rocks?'

Kelly scrambled clumsily over the lifelines, and stood up. 'Just my stuff,' he said, slightly ruffled. 'So this is the boat.' He ran his eye over the incomprehensible tangles of rope that cluttered the deck. Then he came back to Bennett, and noticed that she was beautiful. She had wide shoulders and deep breasts, a short nose with freckles, and blue eyes.

Kelly decided it was time to get back on top. 'What's your first name?' he said, crinkling his eyes.

'Bennett,' she said. 'Here's Bud.' She went off forward to inspect the work of two young men who were painting an aircraft identification number on the foredeck.

Out of the corner of his eye, Kelly saw the limousine pull out of the main gate and into the traffic.

Bud Withers was small and wiry, with well-brushed chestnut hair that came over his ears and a well-brushed chestnut beard. He looked busy. When he saw Kelly, he said, 'Dave! Welcome aboard.' He looked at the Rolex Oyster on his brown, hairy wrist. 'Five minutes,' he said. 'Then we're off on the water and across to Cowes.'

'Great,' said Kelly. 'Where can I change?'

Withers looked faintly puzzled. 'Below, I guess.'

Kelly carried his cases gingerly down the companionway, and found himself in a white plastic vault, its walls lined with tiers of bunks. He began to feel apprehensive. He had been cruising, and he knew the importance of privacy on boats. But down here, there were no partitions. He pulled canvas trousers, a windbreaker and a white-topped yachting cap from a suitcase and tossed the case on a convenient bunk. 'I hope that doesn't belong to anybody,' he said to a man reading a Judith Krantz novel in a bunk nearby.

'Sure,' said the man, grinning.

'She's stripped out for the Big Boat series, eh?' said Kelly.

'Sure,' said the man. 'Hey, you're Kelly, huh?'

'Right,' said Kelly.

'Well, think of that,' said the man, and returned to his book.

Kelly's feeling of disorientation became more intense. He went up on deck. Soon, Chuck the cameraman and Herb the sound man arrived. Kelly greeted them like long-lost friends. They were both young and tough, and they looked browner than he remembered. 'How's it going, boys?' he said.

'Terrific,' said Chuck. It was always hard to tell whether Chuck was on the level.

'Nice boat,' said Kelly. 'Had some fun sailing?'

'Terrific,' said Chuck again.

Eye was slipping past the end of the quay.

'Dave,' said Herb. 'Pardon my asking, but have you ever done this before?'

'You mean sailing? Sure,' said Kelly. 'Well, a little. In San Francisco Bay, mostly.'

'Right,' said Herb. 'Dave, I have to tell you that this isn't quite like that.'

Kelly laughed. 'It's all water. They're only boats.' A grey

Royal Navy frigate loomed over the deck. 'Come on, let's do a piece at the wheel.'

They went aft, to the cockpit. Bennett was at the helm. Kelly said, 'Could I drive for a while?'

Bennett shrugged, 'Be my guest.'

Kelly gripped the leather-sheathed wheel. *Eye* was carrying mainsail and spinnaker, leaning gently to the force three breeze pushing at her quarter. He composed his features into the mould familiar to sixty million Americans. 'Well,' he said to camera. 'This is it. We're sailing over the Solent to Cowes, Isle of Wight. Cowes Week is in full swing, which means the cream of the world's yachtspeople are meeting the cream of society, and the high spot of the week is . . . us. *Kelly's Eye* and the other fourteen entrants for the –' The wheel twitched in his hands. He looked down. Bud Withers' head was sticking out of the companion hatch, and his hand was gripping the lower rim of the wheel. Withers said, 'You were letting her come up a little high.'

Kelly said, 'Oh, Christ.' The spinnaker was slapping and billowing. 'Cut that, Chuck. We'll do it again.'

'Must be hard to concentrate,' said Bud. 'We don't want to blow out the kite. Why not you rest your hands on it, and say your piece, and I'll steer from down here.'

Kelly said his piece again. But even as he said it, a foreboding came over him and the cold panic returned. He was right out of his element. Other people were in control of him. It was a new experience. And a terrifying one.

The Fastnet race is sailed from the Solent, round the Fastnet Rock Lighthouse off the southwest tip of Ireland, and back to Plymouth. In 1925, when it was inaugurated, the old school of yachtsmen maintained that such a long race in open water was asking for trouble. But the expected disaster failed to happen, and the gaff-rigged fleet straggled home, led by the converted French pilot cutter *Jolie Brise*.

Jolie Brise took 6 days, 14 hours and 45 minutes to complete the course. *Flag* and *Kelly's Eye* sailed into Plymouth Sound neck and neck in about half *Jolie Brise*'s time, and the rest of the fleet straggled in over the next two days – except *Sirène*, which withdrew in order to visit an excellent seafood restaurant in Clonakilty, County Cork, and arrived three days later.

It was, as Art Schacker commented to the London *Times*, a little light exercise before the main event. As *The Times* also observed, it was not much of a work-out for Schacker, because his chief rival *Tasman* was sitting in Padmore and Bayliss's marina at Gosport, waiting for a new forestay.

Here, during the following week, all the Great Circle entrants joined her. Padmores roped off a jetty for their use. Crowds of sightseers trooped down the dreary road from Southampton, and crammed the ferries across from Portsmouth Harbour railway station to stare at the huge metal trunks of the masts and brown, fit-looking men and women – surprisingly young, many of them – who walked the jetties in groups, talking hard about subjects that had no meaning for the tourists. Parties proliferated along the South Coast, each with its Great Circle lion. But as the week wore on, the lions more often than not failed to turn up at the parties, because they had work to do.

Inside the ropes, piles of stores accumulated on jetties beside the yachts, and chains of crewmen passed them in hand over hand. The crews were edgy. There was no privacy, and there was also the Official Measurer.

It was the Official Measurer's job to satisfy himself that the boats were equipped for the race; that they conformed to their stated ratings; and that they carried the regulation amount of food and water and safety gear; that they were seaworthy, and that they carried VHF and SSB radios and automatic position indicators, and that the crews knew how to use them. The Official Measurers were worthy men, doing their jobs. But in the charged atmosphere of the final fortnight before the start, their hair-splitting had made them about as welcome as hornets on a bathing beach, and by the Thursday of the last week in August, tempers on both sides were at breaking point.

On the afternoon of that Thursday, Dave Kelly arrived at Padmores, ducked through the ropes, and strolled down the jetty, picking his way among piles of cardboard boxes. He was wearing white ducks, a Versace jacket in heavy beige silk, and a blue and red spotted bow-tie from Charvet.

Eye was lying astern of *EPK Electric*. *EPK*'s crew were tossing boxes of lavatory paper from hand to hand on to her deck, where a pretty dark-haired woman was checking them off on a clipboard. Kelly tried to catch her eye, and failed. He went on to *Eye* and swung himself up on the stanchions. Bud Withers was arguing with a Measurer, growling, his beard jutting forward, banging his fist in his palm to emphasize a point. Kelly went below.

What he saw took the bottom out of his stomach. His mouth fell open, and for a second he gaped. Then he shouted 'WITHERS!'

Bud Withers caught the urgency in his voice, and said, 'Wait a minute', to the Measurer. He walked quickly to the hatch and slid down the padded companion ladder, landing lightly on the deck below.

'What the hell *is* this?' said Kelly.

Withers looked about him. The bunks were strewn with stores and equipment, and the trunking was off the cables, revealing a many-coloured spaghetti of wires. 'Gettin' set,' he said. 'I guess it is kind of untidy.'

'How,' said Kelly in a low, dangerous voice. 'How are you going to get the partitions up in the time left before the goddamn race starts?'

'Partitions?' said Withers. 'What partitions?'

'To divide up the cabins,' said Kelly. 'You had her stripped out for the Fastnet. Right?'

'The cabins,' said Withers, bemused. Then light dawned. 'You were expecting like a *cabin*?' He laughed. 'We don't use cabins on a racing boat, Dave. Just one big, happy family, that's us. If somebody said stripped out I guess he meant stores, equipment, you know.'

Kelly looked round the low, white vault lined with bunks. His tongue was dry in his mouth, and his brain refused to register. Finally he said, 'Oh. Right. Well . . . can I pick a bunk? And where do I put my stuff?'

Withers looked at him with a new understanding. He said, 'Pick any bunk. But I guess we'll be switching about some. You keep your gear in your locker.' He pointed to a little door set in the bunk wall. It was a foot square. Inside, it was a cube, one foot each side. 'Okay?' said Withers. 'That's your space, from now on.'

'Okay,' croaked Kelly.

'Excuse me,' said Withers, and returned on deck.

Kelly stayed below, gazing at his locker. On the jetty outside, his two Louis Vuitton suitcases gleamed in the August sunshine. His mind said, over and over: *Twenty-nine thousand miles. Twenty-nine thousand miles.*

The Official Measurer was a retired lieutenant-commander with a thick skin, a perpetually pleased expression and a love of archaic American slang. On the Friday morning he was making his final checks. He looked at his list, frowned and bustled off to the closed shed where the French had hidden away *Siltex-France* from the prying eyes of the competition.

Jean-Luc Jarré was sitting high on the scaffolding tower by *Siltex*'s keel, with a Gauloise hanging out of the corner of his thin mouth and his big dark eyes narrowed against the sunlight that streamed in through the crack in the shed door. A figure stood at the door, said, 'Jeepers!' and paused, to allow its eyes to adjust to the gloom. Jarré pitched his cigarette into an empty paint tin, and started down the ladder to greet the Official Measurer.

De Rochambaud was deep inside the radio, his surgeon's hands busy with voltmeter and soldering iron, concentrating entirely on the circuit board before him. He was connecting the final board into the pre-amp when a sudden burst of loud speech filtered up from the echoing depths below the cockpit. The voice was Jarré's, but the words were indistinguishable. Carefully, de Rochambaud finished the connection he was soldering and put his head over the side.

The Official Measurer was standing with his head bowed, tapping his chin with his measuring stick. Jarré was facing him, shoulders thrust forward, making short stabbing movements with his hands. 'I assure you,' he was saying, 'my designer has told me these keel modifications do not make a change with the rating.'

The Measurer nodded pacifically. 'But I think we'd better measure her up all the same, eh? I mean I'm sure you see my position.'

Jarré's hands tugged at thin air, like a parachutist manipulating his webbing. 'It is more delay,' he said. 'I must load my stores. I refuse.'

The Measurer appeared not to hear him. He looked at his watch and said, 'Jimmy! I'd better go and get my stuff right now.' His footsteps echoed in the corrugated shed and the door slammed with a great hollow clang.

Jarré snarled, 'You crazy pig!' at the closed door. Then he shouted, 'Okay. Let's get the scaffolding down and this boat in the water now, because if these sons of bitches start we'll be here for weeks.'

The shed doors rolled back. The tow-truck arrived and the dockyard men hitched it to the cradles. De Rochambaud went into the August glare with Jarré. 'But if you don't get your rating certificate, you can't compete in the race.'

Behind them *Siltex-France*'s matt black nose rumbled

from the shadows of the shed into the bright sunlight of the yard. Jarré turned and grinned at him, his white teeth gleaming, black pirate's eyes glittering in their web of wrinkles. 'Listen, my friend,' he said. 'If they measure us, we will not be ready for the start. Also, I know our rating will not change. But if this fool of a Measurer manages to increase it to more than seventy feet, we can't start anyway. So they can measure us in Cape Town, and if we don't like what they find, we appeal.'

Siltex's snout was going downhill now, as the cradle approached the slipway. 'But what about the Race Committee?' said De Rochambaud, helplessly. 'Will they not object?'

'Hah!' said Jarré, with scorn. 'The Race Committee!'

As *Siltex* entered the water, the Official Measurer returned with a hand-trolley full of equipment. He stood staring at *Siltex* as she floated free of the cradles. Jarré, small, spidery and intensely energetic, jumped on to the boat's coach-roof and bowed deeply.

'Ah, nerts!' said the Official Measurer, who knew when he was beaten. 'Looks like I'll have to take this to the committee , Mr Jarré.'

'Please do,' said Jarré.

'Tch,' said the Measurer, and stumped off towards the telephone.

That Friday morning, the committee room was a chaos of ringing telephones. The wooden-faced admiral who was chairman picked up his telephone, and listened. The colour of his face darkened from mahogany to redwood. Then he said to the five men at the round table, 'That damn Frog's relaunched his boat without a rating. Deliberate defiance. We'll have to disqualify him.'

There was a brief silence, except for the telephones. Then the man on the admiral's right said, 'I don't see that that's necessary.' He was smooth faced and wavy haired, and he looked tired – as well he might, for he was Charles Cunliffe, head of Public Relations, Lancaster. 'Look,' he said. 'They're all under pressure, from their sponsors, from the race. Of course Jarré has to have a rating, but I think we could stretch a point here and rate him retrospectively. In Cape Town, say.'

He did not outline the circumstances, because everybody knew. A good Great Circle was a Great Circle in which as many maxi-rated yachts started as possible, even if it meant bending the rules. The more maxis in the race, the more publicity the race would get.

'It's not ocean racing,' grumbled the admiral.

'Carried that we re-measure in Cape Town?' said Cunliffe.

'Carried,' said four voices.

'Tchah!' said the admiral.

Associated Meat had not bothered with the Fastnet. Instead, she had been sailing around Britain. Innumerable civic dignitaries had stood on her decks and basked in the buccaneering grin of Sir Clement Jones. Countless school children had left their ice-creams in the bin by the gangway and trooped through her gloomy bowels. Now she lay full, dark and heavy, sunk to her marks at her jetty in Gosport.

On her big silver mast, her halyards slapped. The ropes on her deck lay coiled into flat mats. She gleamed with a high, military polish in the light of the red sun hanging low in the dirty Portsmouth sky. The water slopped at her sides, full of red glints that looked like blood. One man sat in her cockpit, left to mind the ship. Sir Clement was in London, lecturing a group of industrialists on the benefits of deep-sea sailing to an under-achieving workforce.

Under the plastic cut-glass chandelier of a pub in a grimy street near the Portsmouth Naval Dockyard, a very large man with a broken nose and mean, narrow eyes sat at a Formica table with a single chair. His large arms lay on the table like two slabs of butcher's meat. In the right hand was a pint of bitter, and in the left a treble rum. The man was Sergeant Ernie Crystal, of *Associated Meat*. Sergeant Crystal was talking, to nobody in particular.

'Tomorrow night,' he said, 'I will be at a reception given by the mayor and bleeding corporation of Portsmouth.

And you will still be here. Which is because you have not joined the army, like I did.'

Portsmouth is a Naval town. The other men in the bar looked unimpressed. A youth with a shaved head, Doc Martin boots, and an anchor tattooed on each bicep pointedly turned his back on the speaker and ordered a pint of Pompey.

'We are going to sail round the bleeding world,' said Sergeant Crystal. 'Just us, in a little boat. And you know why? Because we are the real men, and you are a bunch of brown hatters.'

The silence became complete and awful, except for the tick of the Babycham clock above the bar. Sergeant Crystal placed his hands flat on the table and listened to the singing of his muscles after the half-marathon he had run with the rest of *Meat*'s crew that morning. He sipped delicately at his rum. 'Bunch of poofs,' he said.

The skinhead at the bar paid for his pint, the jingle of the change loud in the silence. Then he said, 'Fucking pongoes.'

Sergeant Crystal rose to his feet. 'Did you speak?' he said.

'Gentlemen, gentlemen –' said the landlord.

But the skinhead had turned round, 'What if I did?' he said.

Sergeant Crystal went closer. 'I thought you might like a spanking.'

The skinhead was nearly as big as him. 'Who from?' he said. The men at the bar edged away. The skinhead worked as a riveter down the Navy dockyard, and he was well fancied as a light heavyweight.

Sergeant Crystal watched the anchors on the biceps

twitch as the hands came up to grab his jersey and the shaved head came forward to smash his nose. Then he put his own head down, so the skinhead's skull met hard bone instead of yielding face. The men at the bar saw him move, very fast, and the skinhead went limp and was sailing across the room, and his face hit the dartboard with a wet thump.

'Double tops,' said Sergeant Crystal. He walked over to the skinhead and kicked him once very hard on the upper thigh of his left leg. The bone broke with the sound of a dry branch snapping. Sergeant Crystal drained first his rum, then his pint, and walked out into the darkening street.

He was two blocks away when the sirens started; no police, just an ambulance. Sergeant Crystal felt a warm satisfaction in the pit of his hard belly. His life streamed ambulance sirens like a comet's tail. He broke into a jog. *Associated Meat* was only five miles away. He felt like stretching his legs, and then getting an early night.

The sun was shining. Gulls screamed high above the grey winding of the river and the forest of masts in Padmore's basin, and a small breeze made the wavelets sparkle and glitter.

Nicholas Eason was enjoying himself. He was sitting in *Chinamite*'s cockpit, covered in dried-out sweat, sipping a can of a sub-sponsor's beer and watching the jetty. *Chinamite*'s stores were abroad, except for last-minute fresh food. She was ready to go.

He took a sip of his beer, and went back to watching the brand names on the boxes going aboard *Flag*, moored ahead of *Chinamite* on the jetty. 'Diet Coke,' he said to Slicer the grinder, sitting beside him. 'Ma Prudhoe's

Homebake Kookie Rolls. What the hell are they? Busch's Hi-Energy Pretzels. Sail thread.'

'Yuk,' said Slicer. 'Bit peckish myself.' He slid below. Slicer was a short, broad rugby player. He was usually eating when he was not talking, and he talked very little.

The sail thread was followed by Vaseline. Eason was just wondering what use they could find for a whole case of the stuff when his attention was caught by a burst of laughter from *Tasman*, moored astern. *Tasman* had finished loading, and her crew were eating sandwiches on deck in the sun that illuminated the large battle flag high on her forestay. The flag said 'LAST YEAR THE CUP – THIS YEAR THE WORLD', and *Flag*'s crew were making a big point of not noticing it.

A couple of Australians had jumped on to the jetty, and were walking past *Chinamite*. Eason lifted a hand in greeting. One of the Australians said, 'G'day. Just nipping up the pub.'

Eason recognized him as Sparko, the cook. The boats' crews had mixed on and off throughout the summer – some more than others. The Australians had been relaxed and friendly. The *Flag* people and the French had kept themselves to themselves.

'Must get a snap of those Yanks before they go,' said Sparko's companion. He lifted his Nikon and shot.

An American on deck looked up and shouted. 'Hey!' He was tall, with a brown face peeled pink at the nose. His hair was yellow, cut short enough to show the pink scalp beneath. He vaulted the lifelines and landed face to face with the Australian. 'What are you photographing, sir?' he said.

The Australian said, 'You, beautiful.'

'It's against the rules to take photographs, what do you want them for?'

'To show the folks back home the silly bastards they have on American boats.'

'Okay, sir.' The American's face was red. Eason thought he looked very young. 'I'll have that film, please.'

The Australian's face became very still. 'Get your paws off, Yank,' he said.

Eason watched, fascinated, as the American's big hand crept forward and made a grab at the camera. The Australian whipped it back. The American went for his arm.

'Get it, Sparks,' said the Australian. Sparko took the camera and stepped back up the dock.

A wide, solid man had appeared on *Flag*'s deck. Eason recognized him as Art Schacker. 'Hey!' said Schacker. 'Hyatt!'

But it was too late. Hyatt had not seen the Australian pass the camera over. He was trying to get the Australian's arm into a half-nelson, but Hyatt was young, and the Australian had been grinding winches for ten years. The Australian's arm was not bending. The two men staggered to the edge of the jetty.

'Hup!' said the Australian.

Hyatt hit the dirty water with a big brown splash, and vanished. He came up, his face bright red, and thrashed back to the jetty.

Schacker jumped down from the deck. 'Okay, you guys,' he said. 'Let's break it up.' He bent down and pulled Hyatt out of the water. A crowd began to gather behind the ropes, and telephoto lenses stared with empty eyes. 'Get some dry clothes,' he said to Hyatt. 'Move.' His voice was

125

hard and authoritative. 'And as for you lot,' he said to the Australians, 'maybe you could stick to racing, not aggravating my crew?'

The Australian shrugged. 'Roll on Sunday,' he said.

Schacker's face was suddenly haggard. 'Like you say, roll on Sunday,' he said. The Australians turned and headed for the ramps off the jetties and on to the land.

Schacker sighed heavily, and went back aboard.

Eason finished his beer, threw the tin into the gash bag, and went back to the pile of sheets whose ends he had been whipping. Silly idiots, he said to himself. The sun was warm on his neck and he whistled as he worked. There was a feeling of great peace in the gently moving air and the soft ping of the halyards; the calm before the storm. He looped flat waxed sail thread along the Terylene genoa sheet, and seized it with a couple of turns.

A shadow fell across his work, and he looked up.

Ed Cole was standing by the rail, running his fingers nervously through his sparse, sandy hair. 'Skipper aboard?' he said.

'Back at six,' said Eason.

Cole nodded, then looked at Eason for the first time.

'Have a beer,' said Eason.

Cole came and sat down. Eason handed him a can, and went back to work. He wanted to know more about Cole. But Cole sat in silence.

Finally, Eason said, 'So you're coming on the race.'

Cole's shadow nodded.

'You moving aboard?'

The shadow nodded again.

'What have you been up to?' said Eason.

Both men had sailed the final work-up in dribs and drabs. Unlike some of the other boats, *Chinamite*'s sponsorship did not extend to paying her crew a salary.

'Working,' said Cole. His voice was tight and stiff.

'Me, too,' said Eason. It was a lie, of course. He had been doing some petty freelancing, going to parties, living for his time on *Chinamite*. Cole had hardly coincided with him on the boat. It suddenly occurred to Eason that Cole might have been avoiding him. He said, 'Working in the greenhouse?'

Cole said. 'Just working. Look, Eason. I don't talk to bloody journalists.'

'Why not?' said Eason.

'Does the fox talk to the hounds?' said Cole, and dived down the companion-ladder.

Eason pushed the end of the whipping through the running loop, and drew it snug. He pulled the thread harder than was strictly necessary. Touchy bastard, he thought. One of life's victims.

Like Nicholas Eason, only different.

Even stripped out for racing, Swan 651s like *EPK Electric* are luxury liners compared to the maxis. Harriet Agnew was in the head, applying kohl to her upper eyelids by the strip light in the mirror above the washbasin. She had changed, in the four months since she had left EPK's legal department. Her skin was firmer and browner and the whites of her eyes were whiter, which made the blue bluer. She had lost perhaps seven pounds. As she wrapped a towel around her breasts she thought that she was looking none too bad, for a deckhand with three law degrees. She grinned, picked up her washing bag and opened the door.

Jack Asprey was outside, thin and elegant in a guernsey and dark-blue canvas trousers. His hatchet face was sardonic as his eyes crawled from Harriet's toes to her face. She felt a tremor of disgust.

'We ought to take off the head doors,' he said. 'Save weight,' and leered.

'Suggest it to Emily,' said Harriet, turning her back on him to put her washing bag in her locker. She padded quickly forward to her bunk above the padded banquette in the saloon.

The bunk was six feet long and three feet wide. It had a skylight with a blind, a reading light, and a shelf above her head. She could sit up, just. For privacy, there was a curtain that drew all the way along, but when the curtain was drawn, the ventilation was bad. Harriet had used the bunk for about thirty nights on and off, during the work-up. She still wasn't sure she was ever going to get used to it, but at least she had come to grips with the basic manoeuvres. She drew the curtains, not so much for privacy as to hide the ridiculous contortions necessary for putting on her underwear. She writhed on the bed like a butterfly shedding its chrysalis.

Tonight was the crew reception at Portsmouth Town Hall. In her previous life, she would have confronted the mayor and corporation in a frilled shirt and tailored suit. But tailored suits could not be kept in two-by-one lockers, so she pulled on a pair of dark-green rough silk Kenzo pedal-pushers and a cream silk sweater top. Round her neck she fastened the heavy turquoise and gold necklace from Cartier that had been her one big extravagance on leaving EPK. She squinted at herself in the tiny mirror. She looked five years younger than her thirty-two. She laughed, and dabbed a little Givenchy behind her ears and in the hollow of her throat.

'Christ,' said Jack Asprey's voice from outside the curtain. 'Smells like a brothel in Cairo.'

How long had he been waiting there, she wondered. She pulled the curtain back. He had changed into a blazer with gilt Royal Ocean Racing Club buttons, navy-blue trousers and a white Turnbull and Asser shirt with a Royal Corinthian Yacht Club tie. His eyes crawled over her again. 'Come on,' he said. 'The others have already left. We'll be late. I'll give you a lift.'

She said, 'Thank you.' After all, it would have been ridiculous to catch the bus. As his silver BMW 735 snaked into the centre of town, she smiled at him sweetly and asked after his wife. 'Safely elsewhere,' he said. His practised white smile came back like a searchlight. *Ugh*, she thought. As they went up the steps of the town hall, he took her arm, and flashbulbs popped. She drew her arm away, but he took it again, and she let it lie, not wanting to play tug o'war. Inside, they were alone as they walked up the stairs, and she pulled away.

'I can climb up steps on my own,' she said. He laughed and made elaborate way for her to join the receiving line. The toastmaster hooted her name, and she shook hands with various dazed-looking notables, moving as fast as she could to distance herself from Asprey. She was flustered, overpowered by dislike, telling herself that she had to be sensible, if she and Emily were going round the world with this man. Perhaps it would be better when they were at sea. Under the high grey ceiling, the crowd roared and surged like a whirlpool. Taking a deep breath, she plunged in.

She knew the faces. It was impossible not to know them, not only from sitting by the jetty, but from reading newspapers and watching television. But even on the jetty, all the boats had things they wished their competitors not to see. Now, in Portsmouth Town Hall, for the first time Harriet got the idea that all the members of all the crews were a race apart, setting out on a common quest. She felt the beginning of a bond.

Tubes Murphy was watching four of his crew having a picnic of canapés and champagne, sitting on the floor by one of the mayor's pillars. Schacker went up to him and said, 'I see your boat's still afloat. Did you hear one of your guys put one of mine in the harbour?'

'I chewed his bum for him,' said Murphy. 'Served 'em both right, I reckon.' He sucked hard at his drink. 'Which end of the line you starting, tomorrow?'

'I dunno,' said Schacker, disingenuously.

'Well,' said Murphy, 'see you in Cape Town, if the rowing lessons were any good.'

'You want a tow, say the word,' said Schacker, and his oaken face split in a rare grin. Hyatt watched from a distance, his face as acid as the glass of orange juice in his hand.

After three glasses of champagne, Nicholas Eason was beginning to recover from Ed Cole's rebuff. In fact, his confidence was burgeoning. He surveyed the crowd with benevolence. Beside him, Slicer said, 'Cor. Look at that bird.'

'I am looking,' said Eason. Harriet Agnew was talking to a stout, florid man whom he recognized as Lord Kimbolton, Chairman of EPK Electric and a friend of his father's. Eason knew that if he went anywhere near them, he would get cornered. He looked around, and saw the famous features of Dave Kelly, near the bar.

Eason went over to get some more champagne. He said to Kelly, 'Hi. I'm Nick Eason.'

Kelly looked at him and said, 'Oh, really?' Close up, his cheekbones were webbed with little veins, and his eyes had a boiled, glassy look. He was wearing a buff silk suit, an open-necked shirt, and co-respondent shoes. Fleetingly, Eason wondered if it was the first time anyone had worn a silk suit in Portsmouth Town Hall.

'I'm a journalist,' said Eason.

Kelly said, 'Oh? Look, I have no comments to make at this time.'

'No, no,' said Eason. 'I'm sailing in the race. On *Chinamite*.'

'That right,' said Kelly, looking down at his platinum Rolex.

'Do you think you'll get a good story out of this race?' said Eason. 'You're making a movie, right?'

'I have no problem with stories,' said Kelly. 'They're all

around.' He leaned over to the bar, swept up a fresh Scotch, and said, 'Let me give you some advice, kid. You want a good story, follow your nose, find your angle, get the facts. Now if you'll excuse me I have some important people to see.' He smiled a quick stretch of his thin mouth over his well-capped teeth. Eason thought: follow your own nose, you pompous jerk. He picked up another glass of champagne. Follow your nose, he thought. Well, what about Ed Cole? Something smelt funny about Cole.

He could see Sir Clement Jones' grey beard wagging sagely at the Lord Mayor. Draining his glass of champagne, Eason marched across, joined the pair of them, and waited for a pause in the conversation. 'Nicholas Eason,' he said. 'Grinder on *Chinamite*.'

The Lord Mayor said, 'What's a grinder?'

'Chap who winds a winch handle,' said Sir Clement, urbanely. 'Jolly hard work, too.'

'I should think so,' said the Lord Mayor, his eyes glazing over. 'Excuse me, Sir Clement.' He moved away.

Eason said, 'Sorry to break things up. I wanted to ask you some questions.'

Sir Clement's hearty smile did not change, but his eyes took on a slight wariness. 'About what?'

'Well, we've got Ed Cole as a watch captain, and my skipper Henry Harper said you've worked with him in the past.'

The wariness was definite now. 'What about him?'

Eason summoned up reserves of Dutch courage. 'He seems to feel he's been hounded by the press,' he said. 'Have you any idea why that might be?'

Sir Clement said, 'The man was found negligent at a

Court of Inquiry into the sinking of the *Arpeggio*. Effectively, he killed thirty people. Frankly, I'm amazed Harper will have him aboard *Chinamite*.'

Eason was taken aback by the violence of his reaction. 'I heard about *Arpeggio*,' he said. 'Weren't you the captain?'

Sir Clement said, 'Look here, I suggest you read the findings of the Inquiry. I've got a lot of people to speak to. No time for gossip behind a chap's back.' He turned away. Eason stood and looked at his retreating figure, and thought: you and Ed Cole are two touchy bastards, and I wonder why. Then he went back towards the bar.

On the way, he saw the tall, slim woman with the black hair and the eyes that matched the turquoises in her necklace. She was detached from Lord Kimbolton. He started towards her just as a small man with a huge black moustache, immaculately dressed in a double-breasted grey flannel suit, stepped up to her and bowed.

Sod it, thought Eason; can't compete with handlebar moustaches, don't know how to bow. He turned back to the bar.

The small man said, 'Good evening,' to Harriet and handed her a glass. 'Permit me to introduce myself. I am Henri de Rochambaud, ship's doctor, *Siltex-France*, and I think this is a most disgusting party.'

Harriet was surprised for a moment. Then she laughed at the small man's solemnity, and he laughed in return, and she introduced herself. 'Look at this old pig in a gold chain,' he said, indicating the Lady Mayoress. 'And this Englishman with the tie of one club and the buttons of another.' He indicated Jack Asprey. Harriet warmed to him immediately. 'We all have better things to do. Everybody wishes to sail, not to stand here and drink this champagne of a German brothel.'

Harriet smiled, 'You're being very nasty to the poor Mayor. I'm sure he's doing his best.' There was a crackle of electronics, and an amplified voice began to squawk: *Pray silence for His Worship the Lord Mayor.* Harriet looked around for Emily, but she was nowhere to be seen. A stout man in a chain walked on to a makeshift stage and started talking about Great Adventures, from a prepared text. De Rochambaud made a sound like a beer-can opening, and said, 'Come on. Let us go.'

'With pleasure,' said Harriet, with an enthusiasm that surprised her. Then she caught Asprey's eye. He was staring at her. She smiled, and waved, and turned to follow de Rochambaud.

Eason looked regretfully at Harriet's straight shoulders as she picked her way through the crowd towards the exit. 'Maybe in Cape Town,' he said to himself.

De Rochambaud trotted down the town hall steps beside Harriet, speaking with animation of his hatred of civic occasions. It was just as well; to tell the truth, Harriet was somewhat surprised at herself for leaving with this, well, rather attractive little man, having only exchanged a couple of words.

'Now,' he said. 'It is a warm night, and I shall take you sailing.' She started to protest, but he held up a hand. 'No, I insist; leave it to me.'

And bizarrely, she trusted him.

His Alfa Romeo Spider was parked on a double yellow line nearby. He opened the door for her, and drove her very fast and precisely to Padmore and Bayliss. At the marina, he took her not to the reserved area where the Great Circle boats lay, but to a jetty where a dockyard man in blue overalls was waiting by a small, cabinless yacht, built of wood and gleaming with varnish. Her mainsail was already up, fluttering in the light breeze.

'And now,' said de Rochambaud, 'shall we sail in my Dragon?'

The sun was low, but still warm. The breeze was a zephyr that caressed Harriet's cheeks.

'I should be delighted,' she said gravely. 'A turn before dinner.'

'During dinner,' corrected de Rochambaud, handing her down. They hoisted the jib, the dockyard man cast off, and they slipped discreetly into Portsmouth Harbour.

The channel widened into a grey sheet of water. From a hamper, de Rochambaud produced cold grouse, bread, and a bottle of red wine. They ate off the hamper lid, while wharves and mud-flats and the distant buildings slid by.

'This is delicious wine,' said Harriet.

'I am glad you like it,' said de Rochambaud, 'I make it myself.'

De Rochambaud picked up the bottle, and pointed to a house with pepperpot towers drawn on the label. 'My house,' he said. He poured the big glasses full again, and tossed the bottle over his shoulder. It fell astern quickly; Harriet watched it bob away. 'But it is goodbye to all that,' said de Rochambaud. 'Tomorrow, we go to sea.'

Harriet stared at him. The wind ruffled his moustache. 'Why are you going to sea?' she asked.

He shrugged. 'Why are you?'

She said, 'I was bored. Getting bogged down in my job.

And it's partly to be with a friend.' He looked up sharply, and she said quickly, 'Oh, not that sort of friend,' and felt an idiot. It was the wine, and being keyed up for the race. . . .

But Henri de Rochambaud was looking at her with his soft, humourous eyes, and he said, 'I am glad that it is not that sort of friend.'

She felt the blood rising in her cheeks and herself smiling in acknowledgement that she was glad, too. And the critic returned; it was too silly, with someone you had met for the first time ninety minutes ago. She looked away.

They were passing under the high, grey sides of a warship. A frigate, by the look of it. On the quay beyond, tiny figures in dark-blue uniforms and white helmets stood ramrod-stiff in a square. The low sun winked from brass instruments. One of the figures raised a white glove, and a thin, harmonious blare drifted among the grey gun-turrets and on to the water. 'Anchors aweigh'; Harriet recognized it.

'Why are they playing?' said de Rochambaud.

'They're beating the retreat. My father was in the navy.' Harriet suddenly knew she was going to cry: exactly the same feeling she had had all those years ago, every time her father went off somewhere and she would not be seeing him again for months. 'I often used to . . .' It was no good. The tears choked her.

'I am sorry,' said de Rochambaud.

'Not your fault,' she said, feeling suddenly gauche. 'We'd better get back.'

They sailed back in silence, the sky deepening, the lights of the city dirty ropes of jewels against the dark land. When they climbed on to the jetty, de Rochambaud said softly. 'I hope you are not sad.'

Harriet took a deep breath. 'Of course not. It is just that the band . . . well, I suppose I associate it with separation from . . . men who are dear to me.' She became still, appalled.

De Rochambaud said, 'That is kind.' He paused. When he spoke again, his voice was quiet as a thought, almost lost in the slop of water and the pinging of halyards on metal masts. 'And me, I have found the reason to be in this race. To see you in Cape Town.'

They held hands as they walked back along the jetty. When they reached the floodlit enclosure, they separated without another word.

Harriet walked on past the boats. The piles of stores had gone now, except for the odd crate and cardboard box on deck. Expectancy hummed like an electric current from mooring line to mooring line. *EPK*'s crew were up in the cockpit, drinking beer and talking nervously. Harriet stayed a moment, then went below.

The door of Emily's cabin was closed. Harriet wondered if she should knock. Emily was under more pressure than anyone. But Harriet's blood was bubbling like champagne, and she knew that she had to confide in someone. Emily was the only possibility.

She tapped on the door and pushed it open. 'Emily?' she said.

Emily de Havilland was sitting on the edge of her bunk. Her face was in her hands. She did not look up.

'Emily?' said Harriet again. 'Is something wrong?'

Emily's hands came down. Harriet was shocked at the

change in her. Her neat brown face was blurred and haggard. The cobwebby lines around her eyes and mouth looked suddenly deep-etched, as if she had aged five years. 'Eric,' she said in a small, distant voice. 'He's in the southern Pacific. It's been blowing like hell down there. He's missed two radio sign-ons.'

It was the first time Harriet had seen Emily out of control. It was frightening. But she made herself smile. 'His radio must be bust,' she said.

Emily's eyes widened with hope. 'Do you think so?' she said. 'Do you really think so?'

'It happens,' said Harriet.

Emily took a deep breath. 'Of course it does,' she added. Her voice was firmer already. 'Goodness, I am a fool to make such a fuss.'

'Don't be silly,' said Harriet, with affection.

Emily looked at her, eyes wide open. She said, 'I can't tell you how glad I am that you're aboard.' Embarrassed, she turned away to the mirror and began to repair her tear-ravaged make-up. 'Look, I'd rather nobody knew about this. I mean nobody does know, yet.'

'Of course,' said Harriet. She put her arm round the older woman's narrow shoulders. 'Now you get some sleep, because tomorrow we're racing round the world.'

LEG 1 · PORTSMOUTH ~ CAPE TOWN

FROM THE NOTICE OF RACE

6.1.2. The start will be at noon, Sunday, 5 September.

6.1.3. All competitors will take part in a Parade of Sail while proceeding to the Start Line.

'Up main,' said Henry Harper.

Eason put his back into the winch and set his teeth and ground. *Chinamite*'s mainsail, buff and white Kevlar strong enough to make bullet-proof waistcoats, swept smoothly up the silver mast and into the piled cumulus of the sky.

'Okay,' called Henry Harper.

Eason looked aft along the cluttered hogback of the deck. Harper was brown and calm. He showed none of the tension that was loosening Eason's bowels and making his stomach feel as if he had swallowed a butterfly farm. Beyond Harper, the grey sea was whitened with the wakes of cabin cruisers, cruising yachts, rowing boats, kayaks, windsurfers, chartered ferries. Overhead, the air vibrated to the buzz of light aircraft and the clatter of helicopter rotors.

The Parade of Sail was beginning.

The VHF squawked, and Harper went below. Cole took the wheel, squinting up at the mainsail, and the trimmer gave him some more mainsheet. The deck tilted. Harper's head appeared through the after hatch. He said, 'Stop the donkey,' and ducked back to the VHF.

Cole bent down and twisted the key. The vibration in Eason's feet stopped abruptly, and *Chinamite*'s motion smoothed. Eason thought: that's it. We're on our way. He would have taken a note of it, but Cole's voice forestalled him.

'Genoa!' he shouted. Eason bent over the halyard winch, and began to grind.

The genoa dug her shoulder in and moved her hard towards the green loom of the Isle of Wight. Harper's head came out of the hatch, and said, 'We're astern of *Flag*, ahead of *Tasman*. Stop them fighting, I suppose.' There was nervous laughter round the deck, and Cole eased off to let *Flag* by, gleaming red, white and blue with a moustache of silver foam.

So they moved down to the start, led off by *Wings*, winner of the last Great Circle, fifteen yachts dipping in the confused wakes of the spectator boats, heading for an invisible line marked at its southern end by the squat concrete of Fort Gilkicker, and at the other by a Royal Navy minesweeper.

'Let's gather round,' said Henry Harper. The crew, eighteen men, went aft, and sat on the weather deck while he spoke. 'Keep it clean and tidy, no smoking below decks, and listen to the watch captains. You know it all already. If you can do it, we'll all live happily ever after.' He gestured ahead. 'I'm going for the right-hand end of the line at the start. There'll be a hell of a scrum and the bloody spectators will be in the way, but don't worry. If we get foul, we've got seven and a half thousand miles to get sorted. Wind's due south, so we'll dodge around a bit and begin on starboard, which will make it a close reach to a beat until we get clear. Any questions?'

They sat and cradled the hot mugs; there was a depression coming in from the west, and the breeze had a cool, almost autumnal edge. Nobody said anything. The silence was apprehensive. It was as if the switching off of the engine had propelled them into free fall.

'Yeah,' said Horace the cook, finally. 'Anyone want more tea?'

The Parade of Sail was set to last half an hour. After ten minutes, a huge orange spinnaker bloomed over *Tasman*'s foredeck, and she ran out of the line to starboard, shadowed by the Margate paddle steamer Harry Redd had chartered for the occasion. Her sails shrank in the general direction of Cowes.

'Wonder what he thinks he's playing at, pissing off so early? Most illegal,' said Harper, mildly. 'Watch that Yank's backstay.'

And sure enough, there was a movement of figures aft of *Flag*'s cockpit, and up fluttered the little red protest flag.

'Blimey,' said Harper. 'We haven't even started yet.' He yawned. 'But I suppose we'd better give it some thought.'

On board *Tasman*, Tubes Murphy was below in the navigatorium, and his crew were sitting up to weather. The radio was tuned to the race commentary on Radio Solent, and the commentator was wondering aloud why *Tasman* had broken out of the Parade of Sail.

On the chartered steamer a hundred yards to windward, Redd was wondering the same thing. 'What the blazes,' he said on VHF, 'are you playing at, over?'

144

Murphy's face was uncharacteristically solemn. 'Tactics,' he said. 'There is a reason for everything. Also, do not interfere with your bloody skipper, out.' He climbed up the aft ladder, stuck his head out of the hatch, and said, 'Dike, go and turn on some taps.'

Dike was five feet five inches tall, and about the same across. He did as he was told.

Horror, the number two watch captain, was an intelligent person. He said, 'This is all very illegal, Tubes.'

Murphy did not bother to answer. Thirty seconds later, jets of water began spurting out from *Tasman*'s sides. 'Har, har, har,' said Murphy, and his nose and his chin almost met over his grin.

A couple of miles to the eastward, the other boats were sailing out of line-ahead formation. Foresails came down as crews rested and tried to talk away the tension. Tubes drank a cup of coffee, and put in a couple of tacks. *Tasman* was running like a Swiss watch, her crew doing what they had to do with the precision of long practice.

After twenty minutes, Dike came up and said, 'All done.' Murphy glanced down at the digital repeater by the hatch coming forward of the wheel and pushed the button. Wind southerly, three to four. Boat speed, eight knots. Time to start, eighteen minutes. 'Okay,' he said. 'Let's have the number two genny and see if we can make some trouble.'

Tasman's nose came round and steadied on the white triangles by the distant grey loom of the Gilkicker. The headsails were going up over there, the white triangles beginning to lean as the long stalk of the prestart manoeuvres began.

*

'Six minutes,' said Pal Joey.

'Ready to tack!' called Art Schacker. The blue jerseys and white trousers were crouching ready at their stations. He waited for a dark shadow of breeze racing across the water from Bembridge, and wound the wheel hard over to starboard. The big genoa bulged back; the boom came across, and the winchmen behind his right shoulder grunted over the ratcheting of winch drum and windlass as the sheet came in.

'Okay,' he said. 'Trim her, now.'

The trimmers sighted at the luffs and tell-tales, inching the 16 mm Kevlar sheets off the drums. Schacker handed the wheel to Pal Joey.

'I'll call,' he said. 'There's rubberneckers everywhere.' He stood high on the weather deck.

Over to port, the Gilkicker and the mineswepper at opposite ends of the start line were almost obscured by the huge crowd of small boats. He called, 'Martin!'

The young Hyatt trotted aft, his well-scrubbed face pink and eager below the yellow hair. 'Yessir!' he said, snapping to attention.

'You stand up like that, the boom'll have your head off,' said Schacker. 'Get up in the pulpit and clear the way, huh?'

'Aye, aye, sir,' said Hyatt, and stepped briskly forward.

Christ, thought Art. Then he said to Joey, 'We'll run up to the minesweeper, tack, and do it on starboard, along with everybody else. Watch that yacht, blue sail.'

'I see him.'

A Westerly with at least a dozen people grinning and waving on the deck swept by ten feet to starboard. *Flag*'s

main rippled as the Westerly tickled its wind, and Joey
spat to leeward. George Hart, on the weather deck, waved
politely to the helmsman, a fat man in a nylon shirt and a
straw hat, drinking Long Life beer from a tin.

'White ChrisCraft on your starboard bow,' said
Schacker.

'EXCUSE ME, SIR!' cried Martin Hyatt, in the pulpit,
'YOU ARE OBSTRUCTING MY COURSE!'

Drunken cheers came from the ChrisCraft, and *Flag*
staggered as the power boat accelerated away from her
gleaming red, white and blue port side.

'Dickhead Brits,' muttered Joey.

Flag ran on for the start, converging with the other sails
on the knot of surging pleasure boats that surrounded the
minesweeper.

'Three minutes,' said Ed Cole. 'Give that Yank a hail.'

Chinamite was on starboard tack, close-reaching, the
water hissing past her lee stanchions as she dug in her side.
Ahead, *Kelly's Eye* was close-hauled on port, on a cover-
ing course. Cole hardened on to the wind, and the trimmers cranked.

'STARBOARD!' the man in the bow yelled.

From *Chinamite*'s gorilla pit, Eason looked under the
boom. He saw Bud Withers' face, eyes narrowed, yelling;
but the racket of the power boats and choppers drowned
him out. Blimey, thought Eason, we're going to hit. He
looked astern, to where Cole had his eyes firmly fixed on
the minesweeper, ignoring the twenty-eight tons of hurtling boat bearing down on his right. Eason opened his
mouth to shout.

But at the last moment the black bow of *Kelly's Eye* sheered away, and her sails clapped briefly as she tacked. Eason laughed, a great guffaw of relief, and looked back at Cole. Cole's face was still grey and set; locked up tight.

The boats were only five feet apart, now, *Eye*'s side a shining black and gold wall. At the top of the wall, legs in waterproof trousers dangled, surmounted by a line of heads. Between two of the heads, the black eye of a camera glared down on Eason. Dave Kelly stood beside it, dressed in immaculate red wet-gear, talking into a microphone. High up there, somebody shouted 'LAZY!'

The heads turned, and the camera vanished. The only one who did not move was Kelly. Eason watched entranced as a woman with blonde hair got up and began to run along the weather deck. When she came to Kelly, she lowered her shoulder and barged him hard in the middle of the back. He went down like a poled ox. She freed the knot in the lazy genoa sheet with a skilful one-handed flick and disappeared from sight.

On *Eye*, Bud Withers said, 'Bastard.' The mainsail was shivering, and the trimmers were having trouble with the genoa. 'He's got us covered.' He turned the wheel to port, and the gap between the two boats widened.

Dave Kelly was picking himself up from the deck. Bennett was in the gorilla pit. 'Your nose is bleeding,' she said.

'What did you do that for?' said Kelly, almost whimpering.

'I'm a watch captain, not a movie star,' said Bennett.

'Ninety seconds,' said Bud Withers. 'Eighty.'

*

'*Ach, du lieber Gott*,' said Georg Fischer. *Sirène* was far down at the left-hand end of the line, with several other small entrants who had decided to leave the right-hand end to the maxis. 'Look at those crazy fools.'

His brother Anton shook his head. Up at the far end, *Tasman* had just attempted to luff *Flag* over the line, lost her wind, and bounced upright so suddenly that it seemed inevitable they would lock spreaders and lose a mast. For a moment, the Fischers stood gazing. Then Ilse said, 'Forty seconds.'

'Good,' said Georg, nodding. 'We are in an excellent position.' Ahead, there was empty grey water, cut by the invisible line that would stop *Sirène* being a cruiser and topple her into the Lancaster Great Circle. There were boats close to starboard, but they were all on starboard tack, set to cross the line after the gun. It would, thought Georg, be a nice, tidy start, the kind that gave him immense satisfaction.

'That's a nice one,' said Mrs Eve Norris, wife of Mr Daniel Norris, Manager of the Midland Bank, Stanbridge, Dorset.

Mr Norris twitched the tiller of *Evedan*, his twenty-one-foot bilge keel cruiser, to bring *Sirène* on to his starboard quarter. 'Yes,' said Mr Norris, who though a great messer about in boats knew less about them than he liked people to think. 'A Swan, I believe.'

'Can we go closer?' said Mrs Norris.

'Certainly,' said Mr Norris. 'Ready about, Rudge.'

Rudge, the bank's assistant manager, was plying the jib sheet. He was a fiercely ambitious man, who knew nothing about sailing, but had agreed to accompany Mr Norris in the hope that it would favourably affect his Annual Assessment. 'Ready about,' he said.

'Lee-oh,' said Mr Norris, and pushed the tiller away.

So far, Rudge had not been faced with a tack, having limited himself to hauling in the jib sheet or letting it out, according to Mr Norris's instructions. As *Evedan* came round, however, Rudge hauled in briskly on the other sheet. Too briskly; the sail backed, pushing *Evedan*'s nose back as it came across the wind.

'Let go!' shouted Mr Norris.

Rudge let go, just in time to trap *Evedan* in irons, head to wind, everything flapping. 'Oh, dear,' said Mrs Norris, her voice rising nervously. 'That one's getting a bit close.'

Mr Norris cast an agonized glance over his shoulder. Twenty yards away, *Sirène*'s bottle-green bow cut the water. It looked huge and sharp, and it was coming straight for him. The back of his neck crawled. He reached forward, pulled the jib sheet out of Rudge's hand, and yanked. *Evedan*'s nose came off the wind, and she fell away towards the shore.

So, unfortunately, did *Sirène*.

Mr Norris was livid with Rudge. He was shouting, 'Silly, silly, silly, silly, *silly*,' when *Sirène*'s side crunched into his rail abaft the mast. *Sirène* rounded up and stopped dead. On her deck, two men with red faces were shouting in a foreign language. The yachts locked rails. There were white splinters of fibreglass where they had made contact. Mr Norris had never been so embarrassed in his life. Making a mental note to deal with Rudge later, he said, in the slow English he used when refusing to cash travellers' cheques without identification: 'Please give me your name and address, and that of your insurance company.'

Another boat was bearing down. The name on her bow was *Associated Meat*. 'Oh, Dan!' cried Mrs Norris.

Clement Jones, at *Associated Meat*'s wheel, had three options. He could turn downwind, and go aground. He could carry straight on, and ram the two locked boats. Or he could go about, straight across the bows of the Belgian entry on his starboard quarter. The choice was obvious. As he swung the wheel to starboard, he could hear Ernie Crystal bellowing a string of obscenities at the obstructors. Despite his irritation at the messiness of the start, Jones could not help smiling. Spirited lads, spirited lads, he thought.

On *Chinamite*, Cole saw the chaos developing to leeward, and sheered hard off to port. The extra speed off the wind took him out of the chain reaction. The boat to his right went about, then, further up the line, *Flag* and *Kelly's Eye* and *Tasman*.

'Now,' said Harper, as smoke blossomed from the squat barrels of the minesweeper's forward six-pounder, followed by the thud of the gun. 'Hard on the wind till we open Bembridge Ledge.'

All over the harbour, the sirens sounded: tankers and rowing boats, liners and dinghies, all found something to let off, and let it off. *Chinamite*'s rail dug into the grey water, and her nose turned up for the green corner of the Isle of Wight. Behind her, the rest of the fleet disentangled itself. As they set off in pursuit, the protest flags flicked out at the backstays.

'Well!' said Daniel Norris, in disgust. 'Imagine! They would not furnish names and addresses. This is all most irregular, and no good will come of it, I shouldn't wonder.'

Rudge, disgraced, did not reply.

After Bembridge Ledge, the fleet tacked and sailed hard on the wind down the southeast coast of the Isle of Wight. Overhead, piles of grey and white cumulus raced northward, cut with deep blue canyons of sky. The Channel seas were short and steep, jabbing out of the eye of the wind, and the spray of smashed waves whizzed aft in curtains, washing away the pent-up nerves of the weeks of waiting. *Chinamite* hung grimly on to her early lead, trailed by the other big boats.

The sailing members of the spectator fleet soon fell behind. The motor boats went soon after; the wind was freshening, and off St Catherine's Point the waves were black and lumpy under a sky whose clouds had closed up, squeezing out the blue and bellying low over the sea.

Chinamite's crew were divided into two watches. Technically, Nicholas Eason was off watch until four p.m. But he stayed on deck anyway, watching the high cliffs and hills slide by, and thinking: the last of England.

It grew cold. *Chinamite* freed off for a while, close-reaching for an invisible spot to the north of Ushant. But the depression was moving in, and the wind headed, forcing her to harden up. Eason tried to feel happy that he was away on his adventures beyond the reach of his father and his father's friends. But what he really felt was cold; so cold that he could not bring himself to stagger below and into his dry-suit. He was also feeling slightly queasy, and thoroughly depressed.

Chinamite stuck her nose into a grey-bearded roller, and a sheet of water hissed aft. It caught Eason in the face and chest, and soaked him. He said, 'Bloody hell,' and avoided the eyes of Noddy and Slicer in the gorilla pit, experienced men who had had their dry-suits on from the start. They would be laughing at him, and quite right too. He needed a drink, but there was no all-day drinking on *Chinamite*.

He went below and scrambled into the narrow zipper that ran between the shoulder blades of his dry-suit. Immediately, he was warmer. The watch bell rang as he returned on deck.

'Ready for the fray, is it?' said Henry Harper, who was taking duty as captain of one watch while Cole looked after the other. 'Where's that bloody cook, then?'

They drank tea, and ate bread and jam and sponge cake provided as a leaving present by Henry Harper's village WI. *Chinamite* was pounding monotonously; they had been going five hours. No land was in sight. Squalls of rain trailed over the horizon. *Flag* was half a mile upwind, and *Tasman* perhaps a mile to port and slightly ahead. Far down to port were two other sails: *Kelly's Eye* and *Siltex-France*, noses well off the wind, sailing freer.

'Wind's freshening,' said Harper after a while. *Chinamite* was lumbering now, mast pressed down towards the horizon, water sluicing through her lee stanchions in the gusts. 'Let's have the number four.'

So Eason went forward to his halyard winch, and the foredeck men wrestled the new sail from the forehatch, shoved its luff into the track, and hauled it up inside the number three genoa. The number three came down, a mass of wet Mylar, and the foredeck men pummelled it flat along the rail and folded it into its bag.

'Bloody slow,' said Henry Harper. 'We'll have to do better than that. Now let's get the sails aft and to windward.' So for the next hour, Eason and the eight men on his watch struggled with two-hundredweight sailbags on the thrashing foredeck, dropped them down the hatch in the gorilla pit, and hauled them into position in the windward gangway. Then Henry Harper decided she would take the number three genoa, so it was down with the number four and up with the number three again, and Eason was panting like a steam engine, running sweat as he bent over his winch.

At eight o'clock, change watches, he went below, and what had been a dry haven from the shrieking wind and flying spray was a shambles of sails that tripped you up as you clambered along the wildly jerking hull. And the sails and open hatches made everything soaking wet.

Eason stared miserably at the roast lamb, cabbage and potatoes that Horace the cook slapped down on the saloon table, and thought: if I eat that, I will puke.

'Not hungry?' said Slicer, with offensive glee. 'I'll eat it.' And he did, noisily.

Eason sat and looked at the strip light illuminating the grey plastic lining of the hull, and wished he was allowed to smoke. Slicer finished his lamb and said, 'More protein. Got any liver?'

Horace wiped sweat from his fat forehead. At thirty-six, he was the third oldest man on *Chinamite*. He said, 'Yeah. Cook it yourself.'

Slicer grinned, went to the galley and constructed a sandwich of bread, butter and raw liver. As he bit into it, blood ran down his chin. Eason averted his eyes, got up and worked his way aft to the navigator's bench next to the captain's cabin.

'Okay if I use this?' he said.

' 'Course,' said Harper. Eason had taken a radio operator's course, but it seemed temporarily to have deserted him. There was a bad, stuffy smell, and back here at the stern, far from the centre of effort, the motion of the boat was generally exaggerated. 'Okay?' said Harper.

'Okay,' said Eason.

'If you puke, puke overboard,' said Harper. 'Tell 'em we're lovely.'

It took twenty minutes to get a telephone line through Portishead, the great radio clearing house on the southern side of the Bristol Channel. During that time, Eason flicked on the radar. The green screen flooded the chart table with a sickly light, by which Eason wrote sparse notes. Eventually, there was a ringing tone, and a voice said, '*This Week*, newsdesk.'

'Nicholas Eason. Copy-taker, please.'

'Who?'

'On board *Chinamite*. On the Great Circle Race.'

'Oh yeah,' said the voice, unimpressed.

When the copy-taker answered, Eason dictated an account of the start, told them it was wet, and gave them the dinner menu. Then he outlined the boats' positions as far as he could.

'Oh,' said the copy-taker. 'I've just 'ad it from Charlie Mukler, in a pub in Portsmouth. He was in a plane. You ought to try it, you get a proper look. You big boats is all pretty close together, and there's a couple of medium-sized ones behind you. That *EPK Electric*'s well up with *Associated Meat*, the rest nowhere. Anything else you want to know?'

'You seem to be better informed than me,' said Eason.

' 'Course I am,' said the copy-taker. 'Frankly, mate, this lot'll go straight on the spike. If I was you, I'd look for a few angles. And if you can't find 'em, make 'em up.'

'Thanks,' said Eason.

'Don't mensh,' said the copy-taker. 'Well, over and out, Commodore.'

After they had disconnected, Eason sat for a while and watched the nameless dots on the radar. Then he went back on deck.

Chinamite was corkscrewing through a heaving grey sea. To the east, the sky was darkening. Far to the west, the clouds were tinged with sick orange. Ahead to port and in line to starboard were the white dots of two sails. Eason did not care whose they were. He gulped the raw air. It did him no good. He lurched to the lee rail and was sick into the sea.

When he had finished, he crawled back into the gorilla pit, where the watch on deck were huddled. After a while, he felt at least partially alive. He noticed that somebody was whistling, 'The Sailor's Hornpipe', with vigour and cheerfulness. He looked around. It was none of the crew. Then he looked aft. Ed Cole was at the wheel. It was him.

The world rolled on to the east, and the shadow of night spread over the cold seas of the Western Channel. On

Tasman, the watch below was laughing hysterically, at nothing. On *Kelly's Eye,* Dave Kelly was asleep, and Bud Withers was on the radio, with a detailed list of protests which he ticked off as he passed them to the Race Committee. On *Sirène*, the Fischers and their party were cooking fillet steaks in the beautifully equipped galley. On *Flag*, Martin Hyatt had banged his head on the deckhead while leaping to attention. On EPK *Electric*, Harriet was feeling faintly nauseous and wishing she was going to Cape Town to meet de Rochambaud some easier way; then, thinking of de Rochambaud, the nausea went, and a delicious warmth followed.

And in the flight-decks and chart-rooms and navigatoria, the tacticians who had radars crouched over their screens, their faces lit green like wizards conjuring visions from mystic bowls. And the wind wailed in taut steel, and sails darkened against the rushing skies. And the fleet corkscrewed southward, for Ushant.

The wind rose all night; by six o'clock, it was force seven. *Siltex*'s long, narrow hull burrowed through the waves like a submarine, swept every sixty seconds by the white beam of Ushant. De Rochambaud was on deck, muffled in his wet-gear. Exhaustion was leaving spots in front of his eyes; soon, he thought, I shall get into the rhythm of this four hours' watch, four hours' sleep, and then I shall be a useful citizen of the republic of *Siltex-France*. He went below. The air was already warm and humid, full of the rank smell of sweat and black tobacco, with a sour overtone of wine. He wrinkled his nose. It would most certainly become worse, he thought, as he made *café filtre* for eight.

While he waited for it to drip through, he looked up at the little Plexiglas skylights in the deck. They were greying with the dawn, flickering with the lighthouse's glow. De Rochambaud found an indescribable desolation in the sight; other humans so close, and to leave them behind, wilfully. Courage, he thought; your blood sugar is low. He took the coffee on deck.

Jarré lit another Gauloise, and warmed his hands on the mug. It was very clear and cold. The land was low and grey in the early light, the lighthouse a mere speck. There were several merchant ships plugging up-Channel in the eastward lane under the coast. A low grey gunboat, patrolling for ships out of place in the busy lanes, moved among them like a sheepdog among the sheep of the hill-land above de Rochambaud's château.

'Farewell, France,' said de Rochambaud, self-mocking, but half meaning it despite himself. 'I wonder when we shall see you again?'

'It had better be before the rest of these people, or the sponsors will kill me,' said Jarré. And he gave the wheel to de Rochambaud, lit another Gauloise, and went below to get an update from the weatherfax.

*

When Kelly awoke, he kept his eyes shut. He had a terrible hangover, with a burning head and a queasy stomach. Also, he was being rolled and buffeted as if he was in the boot of a car travelling on a bad country road. It took him perhaps a minute to remember where he was. Then he opened his eyes.

Daylight from the skylights in the deck stabbed fingers of pain into his brain. *Eye*'s flat bow sections lifted out of a wave and slammed downwards into a trough with a huge, unmusical *crunch*. Kelly sat up and pulled his watch and a packet of Stugeron anti-nausea pills from his trousers, folded under his head.

The hands of the gold Rolex pointed to nine a.m. On the other side of the boat, uphill, he could see the sleeping figures of three other crewmen.

Kelly crawled out of his bunk, pulled his clothes on and clambered aft to the galley, where he remembered seeing thermos flasks of coffee in racks yesterday.

The flasks were still there. He poured with a trembling hand, drank two cups fast, and felt ready for the first drink of the day. But there was no drink to be seen, and he had finished his private bottle yesterday.

That and the location of the flasks was about all he remembered from yesterday. It had been cold and wet and rough, and he had got some good footage. Today, he was going to get organized.

He put his coffee cup in the sink, and started up the companion-ladder. A voice said, 'Hey.' He turned. It was Bennett, propped on her elbows in a bunk. Despite his hangover, Kelly thought she looked good enough to eat. 'That coffee's for watch on deck,' said Bennett. 'You drink it, you make some more and fill her up. And you wash your own cup, and put it back in the rack, or some other guy'll have to.'

Kelly hated washing up. 'I have to speak with Bud,' he said. 'Excuse me.'

'It don't take long to clean up,' said Bennett. 'And it's six weeks to Cape Town. So wash that sucker now, eh?'

Kelly turned his back on her, and went on deck, clinging to the companion steps against the motion of the yacht. *Eye* was heeled steeply to port on a long, black swell running under grey clouds. There was no rain in sight. There was nothing in sight. *Eye* suddenly seemed small. Bud Withers was in the cockpit, sweeping the horizon with a pair of rubber-cased Steiner binoculars, his chestnut beard fluttering in the wind.

'Hi,' said Kelly to Withers. 'Do you have a minute?'

Withers said, 'Sure,' without dropping his binoculars.

'What's the position?' said Kelly.

'We're past Ushant. That's the Bay of Biscay to port. If the wind holds, we'll make Cape Finisterre tomorrow.'

'Great,' said Kelly.

Withers lowered his glasses. His eyes were red and sleepless. 'What's great?' he said. 'We're lying third. And the Race Committee's disallowed my protests.'

'What protests?' said Kelly.

'The protest against *Siltex* for goddamn near ramming us at the start. And against *Tasman* for dropping out of the goddamn parade. And *Sirène* and *Associated Meat*, for fouling the course.'

'Why?'

'They said that the parade was semi-voluntary, and

Siltex was fouled by *Associated Meat*, and was taking evasive action when she fouled us.'

'What if that's true?'

'Matter a damn, this is a race, not flotilla cruising,' said Withers. 'Look, I have to go navigate. What is it?'

Kelly felt nobility and self-sacrifice surge through him. 'I'd like to be a fully functioning crew-member,' he said. 'Nobody called me to stand watch last night. I'd like that to change.'

Withers looked at him with sceptical eyes. 'Yeah?' he said. 'Okay. In Bennett's watch.'

Down the hatch, Bennett called, 'How about starting by doing your own fully functioning dishes?'

Kelly ignored her. He said, 'And I ordered a few cases of cognac. Where are you storing them?'

Withers said, 'I sent them back. I run dry boats to win races. Oh, and Dave. You should do what your watch captain asks. That's what she's there for.'

Kelly said, 'But –'

'The cook does the dinner dishes,' said Withers. 'The rest of it we do ourselves.'

Kelly said, 'I can't believe we're arguing about dishes.'

'Who's arguing?' said Withers, and turned away to resume his searching of the horizon.

Kelly went down.

Bennett was at the galley sink, rinsing out the coffee pot she had used to top up the thermos flask. 'You want to clean portside or starboard?' she said.

'What?'

'Watch below cleans up, right?' She pulled open a locker and threw him a mop.

'Clean up?'

'The maid went swimming, and we ain't seen her since,' said Bennett. There was a ripple of laughter from the men in the bunks. 'You want technical advice, I'll be mopping portside. You can take starboard.'

'I have a movie to make,' said Kelly.

'So get one of your guys to film you,' said Bennett.

Kelly's nerves were screaming for a drink, and he felt ready to be sick. He stood holding the mop, hatred for Bennett boiling in him like lava. But he knew there was only one way out: forward.

'Nice idea,' he said, with a grin that hurt his face. 'Pass that bucket, and let's go. Right, Chuck?'

'Right, Dave,' said the cameraman. And the faces in the bunks turned away, losing interest, as Kelly took his first swabbing lesson from Bennett, live to camera.

'*That's* better,' said Bennett.

Wait for it, you bitch, thought Kelly. Wait for it.

For the rest of that day he shuddered by the lee rail. All his raw nerves were channelled into a black hatred of Bennett. By the time he came off watch, he was exhausted. He made it to one of the weather bunks, crawled into someone else's still-warm sleeping-bag, and fell asleep immediately.

Someone was shouting in his ear. He was being shaken violently by the shoulder. 'Gerroff,' he muttered.

'Up!' shouted the voice. 'Shake a leg!'

There were noises now. A flogging of sails, and a crash, and a terrible whirring that seemed to go on for ever.

Fear went through him like an electric shock. He sat bolt

upright, banging his head on the bunk above. 'What is it?' he said, his voice high with panic. 'What's happened?'

The deck lurched, and tilted the other way, so his bunk was at the bottom of a steep hill of deck. Figures were lumbering about in the dim yellow twilight, dragging things like huge bolsters.

'Liferaft,' said Kelly. 'Where's the liferaft?'

'We just took a tack,' said the man who had woken him. 'Get out of there and put your bag in a bunk to weather, and then give me a hand dragging these sails across.'

Kelly whimpered as he staggered across the wet and icy deck. Someone trod on his toe.

At last, it was all done. He climbed shivering into his new bunk, and slept immediately.

They tacked again twenty minutes later, and twice more during the watch below. The last time, Kelly sat on his bunk and wept. But he did not have long to weep, because it was time to climb into clammy foul-weather gear and clamber on deck, into the pitch-black and icy spray.

He was still snivelling when the dawn came up over the rugged granite cliffs of Finisterre.

Three days later, Kelly knew that he had to get a drink, because he was going crazy. He was trusting to instinct to make his film, but otherwise he was crawling into corners for privacy, his mind rolling over lurid schemes for the disgrace and misery of Bennett. And when he was not filming or plotting, he stared between the lifelines looking for land.

Of course, there was no land to see. Only the heave of the waves, a uniform blackish-blue, and the monotonous

163

gurgle and roar of *Eye* punching through the swell. He grew to hate that gurgle and roar. It made his head sore, and he would wait for the roar, his nerves shrieking, and it never came quite when it should.

On the sixth day, there were no sails in sight. The radar showed *Flag, Tasman* and *Chinamite* in a bunch, perhaps thirty miles ahead and fifty miles to westward. Withers was silent and snappy. He was not sleeping much. Somewhere to the east lay the Straits of Gibraltar. The air had become warmer, but the wind was cool, from the northwest.

It was Bennett's birthday. The cook made a cake. Kelly stayed on a bunk, claiming an upset stomach, twitching with hate. The thoughts swam like hot fish in his head as they sang 'Groovin', with out-of-time doowops, their brown faces flushed with pleasure. *Kids*, thought Kelly scornfully. *Brats*. Then his fingers clenched suddenly on the down-filled nylon of the sleeping-bag.

Bud Withers was looking more relaxed, the mean competitive lines round his small eyes smoothed with laughter. Now, he bent quickly to the locker under his bunk, pulled out a bottole of Jim Beam bourbon, sloshed a measure into Bennett's mug and returned the bottle to the locker.

Saliva filled Kelly's mouth, and his heart hammered in his chest.

The winds fell light that night, the seventh, and the boat was hurdling the waves gently, digging in with a *sploosh* once in a while, then pressing ahead. Kelly lay awake in his bunk, his muscles locked rigid, his eyes straining into the pitch-dark where Withers' bunk was. Withers was on his bunk, but Kelly had watched his man, and he knew that

the race had made him restless. He saw the grey square of
the hatch obscured as Withers passed through it en route
for the deck. Then he had climbed on to the non-slip
decking, and was inching his way aft.

He knew exactly where he was going.

The locker was closed with a press-latch. He pushed the
button. The door opened smoothly. He ran a dry tongue
round salt-cracked lips. Just a sip. Two sips, maybe. His
hand groped among the shapes in the locker. There it was,
square, cool, heavy. His hand shook, and knocked something hard. Objects clattered sharply in the locker. Kelly's
heart boomed in the quiet. But the silence descended
again, except for the hollow sounds of *Eye*'s passage
through the water.

He took the bottle by the neck.

A blinding light held him in its eye. A voice said quickly,
'Hey, Kelly! You got a drink?'

The voice was Bennett's

Kelly's heart began to pound again.

'Hand it over,' said Bennett. 'I could do with a drop.'
She sounded husky and alluring. Suddenly, Kelly realized
that this was his chance to share a conspiracy with Bennett,
to get on her side. Then he would be able to use her, the way
she had been using him. He peeled his dry lips apart.

'Be my guest,' he said, and passed it into the dark.

Their hands touched. He waited for the glug-glug of the
bottle. It did not come. Instead, the darkness shifted, and
Bennett's bare feet padded to the head. Then the glug-glug
came, accompanied by a smell of whiskey. The glugging
went on for a long time. Kelly jumped to his feet.

'Hey!' he said. 'What are you doing?'

'Tipping this shit down the john,' said Bennett. 'You don't need it.'

'WHAT!' roared Kelly. 'Who – you can't do this!'

'Keep quiet,' said Bennett. The head door clunked as she came out.

'You bitch!' screamed Kelly.

Bunk lights were coming on. 'Ah, shut up,' said a drowsy voice from the darkness.

Kelly was beside himself with rage and disappointment. 'You're fired!' he screamed. 'You've been riding me since the day I stepped on this goddamn boat. Well, I've had a bellyful –'

Bennett said, 'So fire me. I ain't swimming nowhere. You want to explain how you stole the captain's booze? It won't look too good, Dave. I'm doing my job as watch captain, is all.'

Kelly's head felt as if it would burst. He said, 'Maybe you are forgetting that I am the owner of this boat.'

'Part owner,' said Bennett.

'Okay,' said Kelly. 'If that's how you want it, I'm putting a call through.'

He lurched aft to the radio shack, colliding with Bud Withers, who had come below to enquire about the noise. Withers watched him as he sat down in the radio operator's seat and began twisting knobs. Then he sat down himself.

Kelly stared at the banks of olive-green boxes. His nerves were jumping. He had no idea how to use a radio. Next to him, Withers was punching buttons on the weather-fax machine.

'Get me the US,' snapped Kelly. 'I have to make a call.'

'Hold it,' said Withers slowly. The weatherfax machine rolled a map from its slot. He studied it. 'Nice wind,' he said. 'Moving right into the trades, here.'

'A call,' said Kelly. His fingers were crawling on the chart table.

Withers laid the map aside. 'Dave,' he said. 'I have to remind you that you gave me a contract to sail this boat, and I aim to sail her. We have a good crew, and they're right behind me. There's only one problem on this boat, and it's called David Kelly.' He picked up the map again, and sat stroking his beard.

Kelly said, 'I don't give a good goddamn about your contract, I want Bennett off this boat.'

The light from the radar screen turned Withers' face lime green and emphasized the grain of the skin over his cheekbones. He looked dwarfish and mean. Finally, he said, 'We have a deal. You had the boat built. You make the movie. I sail the boat round the world with a crew I pick, a camera crew and you. And I sail her as fast as she'll go. Bennett is the best go-fast person I know. I have to tell you, Dave, that you go before she does.'

Kelly said, 'I don't think you get me, Withers –'

Withers turned round to face him. His eyes were slits in which the radar's reflections burned with green fire. 'I get you, all right,' he said. 'Your ass is on the line. Well, buddy, so's mine. They said I was crazy to take this on. Maybe they were right.' He leaned forward and grabbed Kelly by his shirt. 'So you smarten up, and stop acting like a goddamn kid.' He loosened his hold. 'And maybe I'll tell Bennett to get off your back, because you can't take it. That what you want?'

Kelly stared at Withers' face. The veins were standing out on his temples. 'I can take it,' he said. 'I can take it.'

'You'll have to,' said Withers. 'Now get out of here.'

After Kelly had gone, Bennett came through. Withers raised his hands. 'Don't talk to me,' he said. 'Just keep that asshole quiet, and I don't mean gag him.'

'But –'

'We're racing,' said Withers coldly. The subject was closed.

He pushed the weather map towards her. 'The other boats are well out towards the Azores. They're going to catch the middle of the high. Flat calm.'

'And us?'

'Here come the trades,' said Withers.

The crew of *Associated Meat* had just finished the morning PE session with a hundred press-ups. Sergeant Ernie Crystal was face down on the deck, feeling the good sting of the sun in the sweat on his wide back. This was the life, thought Crystal; him and the boys, bloody miles away from anywhere, with some good hard sweating to do, and a load of beer that nobody had to pay for except the sponsors.

Pity about not winning, though. Crystal felt a moment's

anger against the poofs in some of those other boats. *Flag* and *Tasman* and *Chinamite*, and that *Kelly's Eye*. All bloody equipment and no guts. *Associated Meat* might be a bit light in the equipment department, but she certainly had guts.

By the starboard rail, something made a noise like blowing a candle out. Crystal raised his head from the deck and cocked an eye.

The sea was like moving blue-black glass. As Crystal watched, green torpedo shapes shot to the surface, glowing like neon signs in the night sky. Rubbery backs rolled, each one dimpled with a blowhole. The porpoises said *whoomp* and streaked down again into their green and ink-black world.

They played like children, prance, spin, leapfrog and rollover, dived deep, whizzed up from the darkness trailing green bubbles and breathed gusty sighs, grinning all over their long, bottlenosed faces. Then, again like children, they came along *Associated Meat*'s lee rail where it dipped to the water, and cruised behind her bow-wave as if waiting for applause.

Sergeant Crystal watched, rapt. The dolphins came up to breathe in a regular rhythm. The nearest was five feet away from him.

Sergeant Crystal pulled the boathook from its clips. The closest of the porpoises came up to breathe. It was small, about half-grown. Crystal rammed the boathook home, hook and all, in the creature's blowhole, and heaved it on to the deck.

'Bastard,' said Crystal, his big shoulders juddering to the thrashing of the porpoise. 'Get a knife.'

The man next to him went to the mast, where a big diver's knife was strapped in its sheath. He jammed it several times into the dolphin's body. Blood bubbled from its blowhole. It seemed to die fairly quickly.

When it had stopped moving, Crystal picked it up on the boathook and stood in the attitude of a big game hunter displaying his trophy, while his crewmates photographed him. It took him five minutes to get tired of the game. After that, he kicked it overboard.

'Look what you've done to my deck!' said Sir Clement Jones, who was at the wheel. But he grinned as he said it, to show that he knew blokes had to have a bit of fun, from time to time. And as he watched them scrub up the blood and the lung-froth and the bits of blubber, he thought: good lads, ready for anything.

Jaw-jaw was something to look forward to. It was the hour in the evening when, by prescription of the Race Committee, all Great Circle boats called the duty radio boat, and each other. It also coincided with Happy Hour, when the non-dry boats observed cocktail time. The whole Great Circle fleet used jaw-jaw as an electronic parish pump, swopping news and information, which the duty radio boat concentrated and relayed to Portishead, whence it was seized avidly by the wives and families of crews, and the public relations managers of sponsors, and the world's press. Like most parish pumps, jaw-jaw was also an excellent vehicle for the spreading of rumours and the telling of lies. If you could convince your opposition one hundred miles west of you and in winds of force three that you were sailing hard in winds of force five abaft the beam, when actually you were slopping about in force two, dead on the nose, your opponent was liable to change course to get a share of your wind, and slow down accordingly.

Tonight, however, truth seemed to prevail – at least as far as Jack Asprey, wedged in the padded chair by *EPK*'s radio, could tell. As an accomplished liar himself, he was a good judge. *Tasman* was in the doldrums, and had blown out two spinnakers in squalls that had shifted direction. *Associated Meat* seemed to have been fishing. *Chinamite* had claimed generator trouble, and had merely signified that she was alive and kicking; Asprey seemed to detect some forced reticence there. The only real news came from *Flag*, hove-to in the doldrums with stay trouble. She reckoned she could fix it on the spot. At this point Bud Withers broke in, from *Eye*.

'The rules state that shrouds will not be detached from chainplates while racing,' he said. 'Change that shroud and I'll protest you.'

Art Schacker's voice was level. 'So what would you like me to do?' he said.

'Your problem,' said Withers. 'Motor to the Cape Verdes, maybe.'

Art Schacker said, 'Bud, as far as I am concerned this is a

stay, and I am fixing my stay at sea. It's necessary repairs and you can look that up in the rules and then you can go eat dick.'

'Okay,' said Withers. 'I'm protesting. Duty boat please relay to the committee.'

'Acknowledge,' said Asprey.

'Prick,' said Schacker. Thunder crackled the ether.

Jack Asprey grinned. It was nice to hear a couple of men who seriously disliked each other. He switched the radio to stand-by, in case anyone else called in. Then he got up and got a glass of orange juice from the galley and sat at the saloon table, dealing out cards for a clock patience.

He was pleased with the way things were going, on all levels. Emily de Havilland, stringy little bitch, still hadn't heard about her ghastly husband. She was beginning to look tired and unsure of herself. The rest of the crew were – well, not exactly intellectuals. They wouldn't mind who was running the show. Except Harriet.

Looking up, he could see Harriet's lower legs and ankles as she stood by the wheel, talking to Emily. Her legs were golden brown, the ankles delicate as a gazelle's. In his imagination, he followed them up, past the dimpled knees to the smooth brown thighs, up the thighs into the dark secrets of the white canvas shorts . . .

Harriet held other possibilities, thought Asprey, swallowing dry-mouthed. But it would not do to let himself get over-enthusiastic. Not yet. Not until he had made quite certain that Lord Kimbolton, Chairman of EPK, realized whose was the credit for *EPK Electric*'s fine performance.

For Jack was resolved to win the race. And he was also

resolved that everyone should understand that it was Jack Asprey who had brought it about.

Later that evening, the wind fell light, and in the west the sun was sinking low towards the sea. Around it, huge towers and anvils of cloud stretched up into the deepening blue. They were like a great industrial city, black with soot, red-lit from within by furnace fires. It had none of the glory of a tropical sunset. It looked dirty and menacing, and powerful.

'There you are,' said Jack Asprey, leaning so close to Harriet that she could smell his aftershave. 'The bloody doldrums.'

Daylight coming through the skylight above his face woke Art Schacker. His eyes were heavy; it was the first full four hours of sleep he had had since the start, twenty-three days ago. He lay for a second, and prayed: one, that the mast repairs he had done yesterday would hold; two, that none of those little jerks from the Yacht Club would get into arguments with Joey today; and three, that they got a wind to blow them out of the doldrums and level with *Tasman* and *Siltex* and *Chinamite*, who must be way down towards the Equator by now. *Eye* had made good a lot of ground. She was light, and she would make yet more ground in the doldrums.

He put a foot out of his bunk. The deck was gritty underfoot with a brown, sandy dust. Part of Africa, descending with the dew. He poured coffee in the galley, took his cup to the head and washed his face in desalinated water. There were two bug carcasses in the lavatory pan, big African moths, five hundred miles from home. Then he walked aft to the radio shack, settled on the padded bench, and punched the buttons on the satnav. 10°16′N 21°52′W. He stabbed more buttons on the repeaters. Wind speed, 0.5 knots. Direction variable. Boat speed not registering. Night's run 23 miles.

Art pulled a Lucky Strike out of his packet, then changed his mind and laid it on the chart. The pencil line connecting the crosses came straight as a die down the Moroccan coast and inside the Cape Verde islands. Today's cross would be painfully close to yesterday's, when he marked it at noon. Becalmed.

On the chart, the cigarette rolled six inches left, then six inches right, as *Flag* slopped in the swell. The mainsail flapped and banged. Wearily, Art stuck the cigarette in his mouth, climbed the companion-ladder, and planted his feet on the deck. He stood short and stocky on his short, thick legs and scowled around him.

The sky was overcast, the horizon lost in a brownish haze. Far to starboard, rain trailed on the water. The air was still and hot. *Flag* heaved restlessly, her boom crashing. She was not wearing a headsail. Pal Joey said, 'Hi.'

'She's doing some banging,' said Art. 'You better go up and take a look at that stay.'

The watch on deck ground Joey up on the genoa halyard. The new stay looked good. A sudden lurch slammed him into the rod rigging. His eyes travelled down the flapping mainsail, eighty feet to the deck, littered with men and ropes. It looked small, small as a boat in a kid's bathtub. He stood on the spreader a moment, sniffing for wind. There was none; they had a dirty smell, these doldrums. The sea was a metal dish, its sides obscured by a brown haze. They were a long, long ways back, thought Joey. Those straw-hat bastards in Marblehead would be after Art's ass right enough. It was hot, and his hands were slipping with sweat.

Far to westward, a shadow caught his eye, as if someone had breathed on the steel of the water. Wind. And in that shadow, something white. The voices of the gorillas on the deck below came up clear in the dead air.

'Hey!' shouted Pal Joey. 'We got company!'

The smudge blotted out the white sail. 'And we got wind! Stand by, below!'

Art watched Joel come down the mast, spider on its thread, as he shouted, 'Number two genoa.' The SYC's men jumped to it. Christ, they can move to orders, he thought, but it was only a fleeting thought, because a curtain of rain was lashing across the sea under a pregnant blue-black belly of cloud. The genoa climbed up. The squall hit. And the world was full of water.

It roared as it fell. Art squinted through a whipping screen of the stuff that blotted out everything forward of the gorilla pit. After five minutes the wind veered one hundred and eighty degrees. He could hear the genoa grinders' angry shouting above the roar of the water. The genoa went out the other side. The wind freshened. Joey, in wet-gear that streamed water, shouted, 'You want a spinnaker?'

'No!' said Art.

As if in reply, the wind dropped dead. Flat calm, with roaring rain. And then, fifteen minutes later, the rain stopped. The sea heaved like moving glass. A steam rose from it.

'*Shit*,' said Joey, in disgust. The deck was crawling with big cockroaches.

'Sweep 'em overboard,' said Art.

Two hundred yards across the water, a voice called, 'Hi.'

A sail slatted, high and white and narrow above tendrils of mist that hid the hull. Art could tell it was a Swan 651. It did not surprise him. Anything could happen, in a place where it rained cockroaches.

'Shit,' said Joey, as the mist blew away. 'That there's *EPK Electric*. Now I wonder if those guys are carrying such a thing as a *beer*?'

The mist cleared from the water as the air warmed. There were no more squalls. The sea slopped nastily, and the sails crashed.

'Well, we're not planning on going anywhere for a while,' said Art. 'Why not try your luck?'

Joey nodded. He dived into the lazarette, pulled out the small tender, and began to inflate it with the footpump.

Forward, Martin Hyatt was writing in his private log. He was always writing in his private log, when he was not crouching on the deck waiting to spring to his allotted task. He looked up, his pencil hovering above the page. Then he folded away his notebook and padded aft.

'Where are you going in that?' he said.

'Get some beer,' said Joey, without breaking rhythm.

'Beer?' said Martin, as if the word was in a foreign language.

'Beer,' said Joey. 'Listen, boy. We are sponsored by Pershing Chocolates, remember? And they are sponsored by Smiles Ales. And I intend to fill this sucker up with candy bars and do a little trade.'

'But we're a dry ship,' said Hyatt.

'And we're coming up for the Equator,' said Joey. 'You'll need a beer on the Equator. There's Father Neptune and all.'

'It has been decided between the club and the captain that *Flag* shall carry no alcohol of any description,' said Hyatt. 'I am quoting from the contract. Also, under race rules such an exchange could be construed as accepting outside assistance and render us liable to protest and disqualification.'

'Construed, eh?' said Joey, still pumping. 'Ah had one of them thangs, but the wheels fell off.'

Martin Hyatt stood looking at him for a moment. His hair had grown, and his scalp was no longer visible. But it was neat and slicked back, and his face was keen and pink and square-chinned, and the anger practically glowed behind his stupid blue eyes. 'We'll see about that,' he said, and turned to Art. 'Are you giving your permission?'

Art lit a cigarette. 'Yes,' he said, and his face was the colour and hardness of teak. 'Get going, Joey, or we'll get a wind and you'll get left.'

Martin Hyatt was sweating. 'I guess I should tell you that there are some of us here in the watch who consider the attitude of this ship is, well . . . casual. And I have to say that we shall be making a report to this effect to the owners.'

Art looked at him for a while from opaque, slanted eyes. 'Not working hard enough, eh?'

'We have no complaint about the work. It is a matter of *attitude*.'

Art said, 'You want to explain?'

Martin Hyatt said, 'Well, there's him,' pointing at Joey.

Joey winked. Schacker's slant eyes were bleak. 'He isn't the problem,' he said. 'The problem is –' He swallowed. 'Listen, Martin, we've had bad winds. Also, it's hot, and we're all frustrated. So this is men from boys time, and right now I know which side Joey's on, but I'm not certain which side you're on. Do you read me?'

Hyatt's eyes narrowed. 'Loud and clear,' he said. 'Request permission to make a call via ship's radio.'

'Permission denied,' said Art. 'Try me this evening.'

'One final request,' said Joey, dropping the tender over the side, 'is that should I fail to return, y'all win the race in memory of me.'

Joey came back with two twenty-four packs of beer, grinning his gap-toothed grin. Art gave out one can per man. He noticed that Hyatt took one. He also noticed that Hyatt drank it with a will, and joined in the laughing and shouting that even a tiny dose of booze will produce in young, fit men at sea in the tropics. The time for sending radio messages came and went. Hyatt did not come aft to the radio shack.

So Art went below, and studied the chart and the repeaters and the weatherfax, and drew no comfort from any of them. The doldrums were beyond the predictive skills of science. At jaw-jaw, he heard that the other maxis were drawing near the Equator. And he was two days' sailing behind, if he got a wind. There was no guarantee of getting one.

So he sat and he thought of the Sound Yacht Club, and Anne-Marie and his children, and wondered what they were doing. It was easy enough to work out what the SYC would be doing: finding some excuse to get dressed up and eat lobsters and explaining to each other what they would do with the hired hands if the hired hands didn't win. But what about Anne-Marie?

Art sat and dripped sweat on to the chart, and for the first time in a year, worried. He worried about the company and the children, the house, Anne-Marie, debt, and the revenge of the SYC for his getting their boat stuck in the doldrums. Then feet pounded on the deck above his head, and Joey slid down the companion ladder.

'Squall coming,' he said.

The squall struck. *Flag* came alive and shot forward. Schacker went on deck, to feel the breeze, while it lasted. It blew from the east, twenty knots.

'Pity it won't last,' he said to Joey.

Joey grinned, toothlessly, and crossed his fingers.

Twelve hours later, the wind was still blowing, and Art was still on deck.

When he went below for coffee, the radio operator was sitting at the table.

'Any positions?' said Art.

'Yeah,' said the operator. '*Kelly's Eye* becalmed, a hundred and fifty miles southeast. *Chinamite* fifty miles behind her. *Siltex* about level with *Chinamite*, I guess.'

'And *Tasman*?'

The radio operator was an SYC man. He grinned, suddenly, his teeth very white in the tan of his face. 'Becalmed,' he said. 'One hundred miles, due south.'

Schacker sat down. 'Well, well, *well*,' he said. 'Not *bad*.'

And the wind stayed with them all through the night, and into the following day. In jaw-jaw the following night, they all spoke of calms. But *Flag*, sails full, marched on south.

Georg Fischer woke from a deep, well-fed sleep, donned a pair of candy-striped bathing trunks, and went topsides. He greeted his brother, who was sitting at the wheel with a steaming beaker of coffee and a plate bearing the remains of a raspberry sorbet – all he could face eating in the great heat. Then he said, 'I shall swim.'

So he swam, plunging into the clear blue water in a shoal of bubbles, fat and sleek as any porpoise. It was good to taste the salt, to feel the cool water on his bald patch. Then he had the disturbing idea of himself kicking in the top skin of a five-mile-deep sea, and he felt a little touch of vertigo, so he went up the ladder and dried himself, and then went below and showered in fresh water from *Sirène*'s double-sized desalinator tanks.

As he was coming out of the shower, he was surprised to be seized by five pairs of hands. The owners of the hands wore astonishing face paint. The women seemed to be wearing only scales painted on their bodies with some kind of make-up. Georg protested slightly as they pulled him on deck and sat him up against the mast.

A fearful apparition rose from the centre hatch. It wore a golden crown draggled with seaweed, and its beard was a brilliant green. In its right hand was a trident.

So it was that the mermaids covered him from head to foot in whipped cream, which was then shaved off with a huge wooden model of a cut-throat razor. After that, champagne bottles began to pop.

'So,' said Anton, removing the crown and whiskers. 'Actually we crossed the Equator while you were in the water. So it is not everybody who has swum across the line. Congratulations, dear brother. Perhaps you will like a shower again, now.'

Anton drained his glass of champagne. 'A good idea,' he said.

But his mind was not really on showers. He was thinking of his dental nurse in far-off Vienna. She was very partial to whipped cream as a form of dress, also. He thought of the seas that separated them, and felt perhaps a little sad. But when he was thoroughly clean and shaved, properly this time, with soap and a razor, he lit a Montecristo, blew fragrant smoke at the gun-metal horizon, and thought: after all, this is a great adventure. One cannot have everything.

Tasman was moving across the water under her biggest, lightest spinnaker, to a freakish north wind. A long swell was running from the southeast, and it made her dip and curtsey with the elegance of an Elizabethan court lady.

In the flight deck, surrounded by a litter of used weather-fax maps, Tubes Murphy was not appreciating the beauties of the situation. He was very hot, for one thing, and the sweat was smudging the lines on his chart. For another thing, he had just plotted the tracks of the opposition and his conclusions were very unsettling.

Over to the east were three blips: *Siltex*, *Chinamite*, and *Kelly's Eye*. *Eye* was trailing now, still more or less becalmed. *Tasman* had spent two days becalmed herself; the northerly was a recent arrival. The big problem was dead level and slightly to the west; according to last night's jaw-jaw, that was *Flag*, busting along for all she was worth. And if she kept her weather, she was going to be well ahead of *Tasman* in twelve hours. Tubes punched the computer keyboard. His heavy red eyebrows came down as he scowled at the map of the Atlantic that appeared on the screen.

On the Great Circle, the Equator marks more than entry into the Southern Hemisphere. It is here, at the gates of the Gulf of Guinea and with the unpredictable doldrums safely astern, that the navigators have to make a choice.

South of the Equator, the southeast trades blow hard

and steady, spinning anti-clockwise off the top of the
South Atlantic high, located about a thousand miles west
of Cape Town. The traditional route took the clipper ships
of the last century across almost to Cape San Roque, the
easternmost elbow of South America. From there they
would go south on a reach, with the trades on their beam,
until they arrived southwest of the South Atlantic high, in
the heavy westerlies of the Roaring Forties. And with the
Forties flat astern, they could be sure of a fast and furious
run for the Cape.

The traditional route is a huge curve. The tea clippers
that used it were outward bound, and therefore had time
on their hands. The problem of the Great Circle was different.

The shortest route from *Tasman* to Cape Town would
bring the yacht hard on the wind, starboard tack. But the
southeast trades would veer southerly down the coast of
Africa. In practice, that meant a long tack on starboard
into the Gulf of Guinea, followed by a long beat down to
Cape Town. The winner would be the boat who timed that
crucial change of tacks exactly right – always assuming
that it got the weather right, too.

Tubes Murphy did not even consider the traditional
route. Nor would any of the other big boats.

He took a final squint at the computer screen, which
showed a tacking point three hundred miles south of Cape
Palmas, on the Ivory Coast. It would change, he thought.
Everything changed. He scrambled on deck and breathed
in the evening air. The sun had fallen into the sea and a
quick dusk had passed, leaving the sky a high blue bowl,
traversed by the broad silver band of the Milky Way. He

strained his eyes southward across the glittering waves at the black horizon. The stars were winking out, dropsical in the gently moving air. He trained his binoculars.

Low on the horizon, he saw it. Four stars, two brighter than the others, on the very rim of the world. The Southern Cross.

'Right!' he roared. 'We're on our way! Let's have a beer!'

A couple of hours later, the wind dropped dead. *Tasman*'s big chute collapsed, and came down. The foredeck philosophers propped themselves against the mast and began dissecting the Bodyline crisis of 1932-3. Below, someone put Paul Simon on the stereo. Make and mend began: ropes to whip, sails to sew, gear to grease; the doldrums routine, anything to make sure you didn't go mad with boredom.

But the doldrums should have been miles astern. There was catching up to do, and the maintenance had been done already, and it didn't need doing again.

So at bang on midnight, with a gibbous moon over the flat calm sea, Sparko the cook and electrician decided to celebrate his birthday. He got himself a case of beer from Murphy, and handed cans round to his watchmates. They sat in the gorilla pit, sipping, the stars hanging like drops of white fire in the black velvet sky. It was hot and clammy. The beer tasted metallic. Nobody wanted it, but Sparko knew his duty, so he forced it down anyway. By the time his watchmates were half-way through their first cans, he had drunk five, and was reminiscing about a night in Newport, when he had drunk thirty-six –

'Shut it,' said the helmsman.

'Wha'?' said Sparko.

'Here we go,' said the helmsman.

To port, the moon's reflection in the wavering mirror of the water was frosted with ripples.

'Wind,' said Murphy, and threw his half-full beer can overboard.

The breeze hit with a solid *bump. Tasman* leaned over to port, and began to march. The wind blew firm, and it blew cool, and Murphy was out to get everything he could from it. It blew twenty knots steady out of the east, with a touch of south in it. *Tasman*'s deck, which in the doldrums had been a wide, flat platform for sun-bathing and games of imaginary polo, became a hard, treacherous slope. Sparko was frankly indignant, but nobody would listen to him. So he took himself below.

On the way down, he caught a wave in the left ear. The cold water heightened his indignation, and he demanded rum, to soothe his hurts. Murphy said, 'If you want rum, you can make your own.'

Sparko drew himself up to his full five feet two. 'Right,' he said. 'I think I will.' He went below, and tried to read *The Cruel Sea* by his bunk light. But he found it tough going, and after five minutes he tossed it aside and went to get a tool kit from the tool locker.

Half an hour later, Noddy the grinder, who was snoring in the bunk nearest the central equipment console, rolled over in his sleep and said 'Wha's burning? I can smell smoke.'

'Nothing,' said Sparko, and hastily replaced the cover on the piece of equipment with which he had been tinkering. He put the tools back in the locker, opened himself another beer, and wedged himself in the galley against *Tasman*'s bucking. As he made coffee for the watch on deck, he yawned. Bed, he thought, after the tray.

He took it up to the watch on deck, then went to his bunk. He slept uneasily, jolted by the new movement of the boat, and conscious of the running of the engine to charge the batteries. It was cool when he rolled out, with a grey, dewy feeling that would not survive the rapid ascent of the sun. He made more coffee, took it to the watch on deck, and went back below to make breakfast.

As he was opening a tin of bacon grill, a head appeared in the hatch. 'Hey!' it said. 'Did you get the sugar box or the salt cellar this morning?'

'Sugar,' said Sparko, through his headache.

'I'd check, if I was you,' said the head, and disappeared.

Sparko checked. Then he ran the galley tap, and tasted the water. After he had tasted, he stood very still for a moment, his face white. Then he turned off the stove and walked aft, to Murphy's bunk.

Murphy was reading the *South Africa Pilot*.

'Murph,' said Sparko. 'I gotta talk to you.'

'Yeah?' said Murphy, not looking up.

'The desalinator,' said Sparko. 'She's bust.'

'Let's mend her, then,' said Murphy calmly. But he was looking up now, and there was a glitter in his blue eyes.

'It'll be hard,' said Sparko. 'I burnt her out, last night. We've got no spares.'

'*You* burned her out?' said Murphy.

'I was trying to . . . distil beer,' said Sparko. 'I . . . cripes, Tubes, I'm sorry. I'll leave in Cape Town.'

'Distil *beer*?' said Tubes.

186

'But we've got the emergency tanks, right?' said Sparko.

It was Murphy's turn to become completely still. Then he swung his legs out of his sleeping-bag, and said, 'I think we'd better have a crew meet about this one.'

'Sorry,' said Sparko miserably.

'What's done's done,' said Murphy, and looked grim. Then he punched Sparko on the arm, and said, 'Well, don't do it again, you silly bastard. And you can thank the Lord you're not the only silly bastard aboard.'

'What do you mean?' said Sparko.

'You'll find out,' said Tubes. 'Now see what you can do with that machine and report back.'

Two hours later, both *Tasman*'s watches were clustered on the weather deck. They were ragged and dirty, and their hair was matted over their dark-brown faces. Tubes stood in the pushpit and said, 'Right. Listen to me, you blokes. The bloody water machine's gone U/S. So we've got no more drinking water, except what's in the tanks. Two bits of news, now. First, the good news. As you know, race rules specify that we carry one and a half litres per man per day in permanent tanks. Second, the bad news. You will remember that we got a good fast start. That's because I told Horror and Dike to pump out the tanks before we went into the area, so we were a ton and a half underweight by the time we began. So, gentlemen, there's nothing to drink on this boat but beer and Perrier water, and I'm rationing that to a pint a man a day. But of course the beer comes from our sponsor's brewery, so there'll be no worries for the sponsor. Nice bit of publicity for the old bastard.

'I did positions on the way up. You'll be glad to hear we're now forty miles in front. Anybody who doesn't like being thirsty can swim to Angola; it's only five or six hundred miles. Anyone else can stick around and help win. It won't be much fun. But who said this was meant to be fun, anyway?'

As they drew south, the winds freshened and the seas increased. *Tasman* became a quiet ship, because talking dried your mouth. Sparko was quieter than anyone. He collected as much as he could from rain showers and spent a lot of his time with an apparatus of pipes and pans on the galley stove distilling seawater. He grew gaunt and blackened, for he would never touch any himself.

And *Tasman* plunged on, converging with the rest of the fleet on the northeast corner of the South Atlantic high.

The Tasman Tower is one of the newer and gaudier landmarks in the city of Sydney. It is topped by a broken pediment and faced with reflective wine-red glass; its architect was once heard to admit that it symbolized the triumph of drink over good taste.

On the forty-fifth floor, in a battleship-grey boardroom

full of Georgian furniture, Harry Redd was at war. He sat at the head of the walnut Sheraton boardroom table. On the left-hand side were ranged Mo Stapleton and three lawyers. On the other side were Gary Hobday, Chief Executive of Garden Life Pensions, Joe Whalley, a large shareholder in Tasman Wine, and their legal advisors.

'What we require as major shareholders,' said Hobday, distilling the morning's discussions into one sentence, 'is a whole lot more openness from the company.'

'And what I'm telling you is that I can't play poker without hole cards,' said Harry Redd. 'So if you want to make the decisions, get on the board.'

'As you know, you've made that very difficult for us,' said Hobday patiently. 'That's why we're here this morning.'

Redd smiled seraphically, a compact, crop-haired buc-caneer in a tan linen suit. There was a faint sheen of sweat at his temples, despite the air-conditioning.

'Listen,' said Hobday. 'This one-man-and-his-boat stuff went out with Henry Ford. What would happen if you . . . went?'

'You'd fight like bastards,' said Redd cheerfully. 'Only way I go is if I die.'

Hobday looked at Joe Whalley's seamed and leathery face, and knew it was true. Then he looked across at Mo Stapleton. The comptroller's face was saturnine as ever. But he held Hobday's eye, and nodded, almost imper-ceptibly. And Hobday, who had not been a fund manager for twenty years without learning this and that, thought: hello, trouble at head office.

'So,' said Harry Redd, looking at his Patek watch.

'Time for a bite, eh? Hold on, though. Got ten minutes? Let's hear the news from the boat.' He called his secretary and told her to put in a call to *Tasman*. While they waited, he said, 'Now I wouldn't get *Tasman* past you bastards if you were on the board. Would I, Mo?'

Stapleton smiled, his usual pained, lipless widening of the mouth.

'Where *did* you find the money, Harry?' said Hobday.

Redd winked, his little cheeks red as apples, his eyes sparkling with mischief. 'From our budgets. And our allocations. Right, Mo?'

'I don't recall seeing the figures,' said Stapleton. There was an ugly hush.

The secretary said, '*Tasman*'s on, Mr Redd.'

Redd pushed buttons on his console with neatly mani-cured brown fingers. 'Hello,' he said to the loudspeaker in the middle of the table.

'Reddy,' said Murphy. 'How're you doing, you old bastard?'

'Not so bad,' said Redd. 'What gives?'

'Hacking along,' said Murphy's voice, fading with dis-tance. 'No water. Boiled beer for breakfast. Fizzy cola for tea. But we're bearing up.'

'Yeah?' said Redd. 'Well, you're causing a bit of a disturbance back home, I can tell you. The whole coun-try's right behind you. Provided you beat those Yanks, that is.'

'We're fifty miles behind,' said Tubes. 'We can catch them.' Even through the distortion of the ether, his voice sounded tired. 'Listen, Reddy, it's blowing up out here and I gotta do things.' He laughed. 'It's bloody amazing to be on a boat with the distilling apparatus broken down when the boat itself is a distillery, on paper. I bet you never thought of that –'

'Thanks a lot for talking to us,' said Redd smoothly. 'Me and the board and the principal shareholders have enjoyed sitting here in the boardroom and listening to your report. See you in Cape Town.'

'Yeah.' There was a click, and the room filled with static. Otherwise, there was silence, which lasted perhaps a minute. Then Hobday said, 'What was that about a distillery?' His normally jovial face was set and grim.

'Private joke,' said Redd, smiling. 'He didn't know you were all here.'

'So it seems,' said Hobday. 'Well, Mr Redd, I'll await the auditors' report with interest. Come, gentlemen.' He walked quickly from the room, without shaking hands.

Redd dismissed his own lawyers. When he was alone with Stapleton, he walked to the floor-to-ceiling window. Beyond, Sydney Harbour stretched away blue to the Bridge. He leaned his forehead against the glass, looking straight down on the ant-sized people on Martin Plaza, far below.

Stapleton said, 'Redd. What's this about distilleries?'

Redd shrugged. 'Relax, Mo. If it was important, I'd have told you.' He sighed. 'It's a shame. Simple bugger like me works hard to set up a little company. Then a lot of flaming pen-pushers want to take it to bits and make it just like all the other companies they've learned about in Business School.' He signed again. 'It's hard to understand.'

Mo Stapleton stared at him, his mouth a thin line. 'Are you saying that the money Reef Bank lent us for Snowy Distilleries went on that boat?'

'For Chrissakes, Mo,' said Redd, throwing his hands in the air. 'At the last count, Tasman owned two chains of movie houses, a bank, four trucking fleets, an airline, four thousand acres of vine, a brewery, six canneries, and that's only in Australia. How am I supposed to remember what happended to a poxy little distillery?' He grinned at Stapleton. 'Anyway, you're the comptroller. You ought to know.'

'But it's fraud,' said Stapleton.

'Like I said, you're the comptroller,' said Redd. 'Now cheer up, and we'll win the Great Circle and we'll be a household name.'

'Yeah,' said Stapleton, his mouth stretching in an approximation of a smile. 'Of course we will.' His eyes shifted. 'But I wouldn't trust Murphy, if I were you.'

After he had left, Redd ran his fingers across his bald patch and said, 'Bloody hell.' Then he rang up Shar Stapleton.

'Harry,' said Shar in her amused, smoky voice. 'How are you?'

'Still kicking,' said Redd. 'Look, Shar, I'm calling to tell you that I reckon Mo's on to you and Tubes, so watch out.'

Flag's navigatorium was an electric womb of green liquid-crystal displays, red lights and white bar-indicators swimming in the dark as Art Schacker corkscrewed over the waves in the padded navigator's chair. It was peaceful in there, sound-proofed; and warm. Outside it was cold, and the Brookes and Gatehouse repeaters explained why. Position, eight hundred miles northwest of Cape Town. Wind speed, twenty-three knots. Boat speed, eleven point three knots. Wind direction, southeast. Angle of heel, twenty-one degrees. Close hauled indicator reading, hard on the wind, port tack. Compass course, 178°.

There were other statistics available beyond even the powers of Brookes and Gatehouse. These had come from jaw-jaw, which had just ended. Art knew that he was three or four days' sailing out of Cape Town, with the right wind. He also knew that *Tasman, Siltex,* and *Chinamite* were behind him in a bunch. He suspected, but was not positive, that *Kelly's Eye* was closer; she had given a false position on the radio, which should have put her within radar range of the rest of the fleet, but she was not showing on the screen. Giving false positions was a favourite Withers trick. Schacker was not worried. What mattered was that he was out in front, with his boat sailing nicely, not at the outside of her performance envelope, and maintaining her lead. It was a contented Schacker who climbed out of the deep cushions, pulled on a jersey and went on deck.

Not all the crew were contented. Martin Hyatt watched Schacker's stocky shoulders square against the backdrop of a grey wave as he sniffed the air, then hunched to light a Lucky Strike. The wind was beginning to wail in the shrouds now; rising. In Hyatt's view, *Flag* was under-canvassed. He sat in the gorilla pit, and said, 'He could put on the number two.'

'Sure he could,' said Simon Lowell, who had been elected to the SYC thanks to his pull with the Hyatt family. 'But he won't. He sails like a dam clam-dredger, not a racing skipper.'

Mustapha Choudry, crouching with them in the gorilla pit, was brown-skinned and black-haired. His forefathers were Lebanese and Omani, and he had crewed winning yachts up and down the East Coast of the States. He said, 'If we're sailing round the world, I'd rather have a clam-dredger than some twelve-metre cowboy.'

Hyatt looked at him with arrogance curdling his smooth pink face. 'Oh, yeah?' he said. 'And what would you know about seamanship?'

'Camels, maybe,' said Lowell. 'The ship of the desert, right?'

Choudry smiled at them and got up and went aft, to talk to George Hart, the cook. Lowell said, 'Black bastard.'

'For Chrissakes,' said Hyatt, pretending to be shocked. '*Aye*-rab bastard.' They laughed unpleasantly. The wind howled. 'But seriously,' said Hyatt. 'Schacker better cut this day-cruising crap; we're paying him to *sail* this baby.'

Schacker's mood soured as he took in the two figures crouched in the gorilla pit. He shouted, 'Bring up the number four genoa, eh?'

Hyatt's face faced towards him, black and sullen. 'The number two?' he shouted.

'Number four,' said Art. 'Hustle.'

It was gusting up now, and the stronger gusts were taking the tops right off the waves and blowing them across the deck in grey clouds that seemed almost lazy until they were on you, when they stung like birdshot.

A gust beat *Flag* steeply over to starboard and buried her lee stanchions in green water. At the wheel Art struggled to get her nose off the wind. The pressure on the wheel eased. When he looked over Choudry had the other wheel, heaving.

Hyatt was on the foredeck, hitching the number four into the track.

'Get her up!' roared Art.

The number three roared and sank to the deck, and the number four appeared in its place. Under Art's hands, the wheel tugged violently as *Flag*'s snout groped up to weather, unbalanced by the smaller headsail.

'Now get aft and let's have a slab out of the main!'

Hyatt trotted bent-kneed along the deck. He shouted something at Art from a dull, angry face.

'What?' shouted Art.

'We're racing, right?' shouted Hyatt. 'So what's all this crap about reefing?'

'You see how you feel in a couple of hours!' shouted Art. 'Now button your lip, boy, or you can spend the rest of the race cooking.'

Hyatt's mouth opened, then closed. His lips curled, and he turned back to join the other figures in their red, white and blue dry-suits gathered along the boom.

Schacker looked at his watch and went below, to where Pal Joey's watch was flaked out in the windward bunks. He went into the navigatorium, and put in a call to Cape Town.

Jasper Hyatt and Wallace DuCane had established themselves in a suite of offices at the Transvaal Credit Bank, in which the Hyatts maintained an interest via a string of companies in Israel. Jasper Hyatt was out; he was dining with English acquaintances from the Table Mountain Yacht Club, who were offering hospitality to *Flag*'s crew when they arrived.

Wallace DuCane was pretty well pleased with himself. He had been profiting by his visit to set up a few business deals with trade-hungry South Africans, and he had made some good ones. *Flag* was another deal, and he was looking forward to getting her sorted out. Now, he sat with a glass of Perrier water at his elbow, making notes with a gold pencil and from time to time gazing out of the window at the sea of white buildings lapping against the grey cliffs of Table Mountain.

The pale blonde secretary said, 'We have a radio call for you. It's the boat.'

The telephone crackled. Schacker's voice, tinny and distant, said, 'We're ahead, Mr DuCane.'

'Great,' said DuCane. 'I'm very glad to hear that. And I'm sure Mr Hyatt will be, too.'

'How's the weather with you?' said Art.

DuCane felt a moment of irritation that Schacker should want to talk about the weather. 'Fine,' he said. 'Just fine. Listen, we have to plan your reception. When are you going to get in? Do we put on a lunch or a dinner?'

There was a pause. Then Schacker said, 'It's kind of hard to tell, right now,' in a voice in which strained patience was mingled with disbelief. 'How about Table Mountain?' he said. 'Any cloud up there?'

'You really want to know?' said DuCane.

'Yeah,' said Schacker.

'Hold on,' said DuCane irritably, and got up and went to look out of the window. The flat top of the mountain bore a blanket of thick white cloud.

'Yeah,' said DuCane. 'The secretary said it had its tablecloth on. Now about this reception –'

'What colour?' said Art.

'White,' said DuCane.

'See you in a couple of days,' said Schacker. 'I have to go.' And the line went dead.

DuCane put the telephone down and shook his head. His wife understood people who went sailing. But he never would.

He sat down at his desk, and took a sip of Perrier. Still, he was not mixed up with the SYC for fun. The SYC was all part of DuCane's business, though it did not know it yet. He smiled, showing his sharp white teeth. It would find out soon enough, if things worked out according to plan.

Schacker got the full crew of *Flag* at the saloon table. They sat jammed together, greasy-haired and brown, with grey, sleepless circles under their eyes, cradling plastic mugs of coffee. 'We're in for a blow,' he said. 'Since it's the first real one, I guess I have to remind you to keep your lifelines on and stay cautious. We're over the African continental shelf, now, and I guess you are aware that we can experience some pretty strange conditions here. I don't want to lose a man, and I don't want to lose a mast.' He looked at Martin Hyatt, who was looking bored and staring ostentatiously at his fingernails. 'And I have to tell you that the wave that blows you away doesn't give a pinch of coonshit what yacht club you belong to.' Hyatt's eyes flicked up and caught Schacker's.

'Well,' said Hyatt. 'I declare ah'm *terrified*.'

Mustapha Choudry took a swig of his coffee and directed a dark, level stare at Hyatt. He muttered 'Asshole' under his breath. Art could smell the dislike in the cluttered cabin. He said, 'Watch on deck, let's go. Watch below, let's get it all shipshape, right?'

As darkness fell, the wind continued to rise. Schacker reduced sail still further, until *Flag* was moving through the big seas under a mere rag. But the log still read between eight and ten knots.

At about 2000 hours, the seas began to change. Hitherto, they had been perhaps twenty feet, but with the usual long intervals, and *Flag* had ridden them well. Now Schacker, at the wheel, noticed an increase in height and frequency. It was a disturbing sight. *Flag* would be diving down into a trough, and the next wave would rise like the side of a house until it came level with the first spreaders, and *Flag*'s nose would arrow at the flat, gleaming wall of water until it seemed that she had to burrow into it, into the tons of wet blackness, and be overcome. But at the last minute the bow would come up until she was almost standing on her tail, and the crest of the wave would topple, but she would be through, water from the crest running off her decks.

Then her nose would come free and she would hang suspended, and down she would go into the trough with a huge *bang* and a giant bloom of spray, and it would all happen again.

It was unnerving, and uncomfortable. But *Flag* was a strong boat, and she could take the slamming; she was making headway, and she was under control, and that wall all that mattered.

By 2100 hours, Schacker's head was aching, and his shoulder muscles were sore from the wrenching of the wheel. *Flag* rose on a wave bigger than all the rest. Schacker's legs started to prepare themselves for the trough. The trough did not come. Instead, the deck under his feet continued pushing at his knee joints like an elevator. It went on and on. Then it stopped, and to Art it seemed as if there was a split second of deadly silence, and he heard himself shouting, 'Hang on!' And then the deck was falling free underneath him, and he knew that *Flag* had sailed up the front of a wave that had no back.

She hit the trough beam-on. Schacker hugged the wheel as white water eddied round him. When he could see again, he saw *Flag* was lying on her beam ends, mast-tip in the water. His mind was working very clearly. Hatches closed, he thought. She'll come. She'll come.

Another wave came under as she wallowed. The wind shrieked triumphantly. Her mast began to rise, was beaten down into the trough. Someone was roaring on the foredeck. Schacker spat out water and shouted, 'SHEETS!' He clambered along the side of the cockpit, normally vertical but now a horizontal floor, and yanked the mainsheet out of the self-tailer.

Another wave came under. This time, Schacker felt the deck stir. Come *on*, he said. Come *on*.

And slowly, the great white shadow of *Flag*'s mainsail lifted towards the vertical, crackling and flapping, and her deck shed tons of water.

'Main!' roared Schacker.

Shadowy figures ground the sheet winch. The booming of the sail stopped, and she was sailing again.

'Names on the foredeck!' roared Schacker.

He counted them. All there. And suddenly, despite the chill of the water that had crept into his suit, he was sweating with relief. Someone came aft and said. 'Bill's broken his arm, seems like.' And he was so pleased that Bill was even alive that he said, 'Great. *Great.*'

It was a bad night. George Hart wedged himself into the galley and tried conscientiously to make up freeze-dried beef curry with rice.

But not a lot of the food got eaten. Half a dozen men were being seasick again. And the slamming had a bad psychological effect, as well as a physical one. From where he was edged in the galley, George could see Simon Lowell's face. Every time the boat went up a wave, the thin lips pressed together and the eyes screwed up, waiting for the *bang*. When it came, he would jump convulsively, laugh nervously and tense again.

The night wore on. The wind strengthened; force nine, severe gale. The slamming was constant now, monotonous, as if a giant were banging the hull with an enormous sledge-hammer.

Everyone on board could imagine vividly that half-mile

of black water underneath. Nobody said anything. Most tried to sleep, rattling in their leaping bunks. Everyone dealt with it as best he could, in his own way.

Martin Hyatt lay in a bunk and seethed with anger. This had to be someone's fault. Schacker's fault. Through one of the eyelets of his lee cloth, he could see the zig-zag stitching on a sailbag. He followed it up to the limit of vision, then down again; up, down; his mind drifting back to the crisp parades of Annapolis, far from this untidy, disorganized hell.

Flag went into free-fall again, stopped dead on her lee side. Hyatt felt himself plucked from his bunk and slammed into the wet fabric of the sailbag. Something heavy crashed into him, making his head ring. When he looked up, he saw Mustapha Choudry scrambling up the deck to weather. Choudry said, 'Sorry,' and smiled. In that smile, Hyatt read superiority, arrogance, disrespect, and contempt. Hyatt said viciously, 'Why don't you piss off back to your mud hut, boy, you got no idea how to act on a boat.'

Choudry grabbed a handrail and braced himself against the wild lurching of the deck. 'My ancestors were sailing dhows in the Gulf when yours were shovelling horseshit in Hoboken,' he said.

Hyatt saw red. 'You little bastard,' he said. His right arm came back, his fist clenching. His frustration with Schacker, and Joey, and Choudry, and all the rest of them who didn't measure up to the ideals of the SYC, overflowed. Choudry's face smiled at him infuriatingly.

'Grow up,' said Choudry. 'It's a storm, we all got problems.'

Hyatt knew that he was going to hit him. He could feel the anger building up in his arm –

Someone grabbed his elbow from behind, thumb and finger digging deep into the nerves above the joint. A voice said in his ear, 'C'mon, pull yourself together.' The voice was calm and reasonable. Art Schacker's. Hyatt tried to wrench his arm free, but the thumb and fingers were like a steel clamp. Sobbing with pain, he sat down on a bunk.

'Right,' said Schacker. 'Now you cool down, you hear?'

And to his acute misery, Hyatt recognized the authority in the voice, knew he was wrong and Schacker was right. And he turned his face to the wall and vowed vengeance. Then he began to weep.

When DuCane awoke the next morning, he climbed out of bed carefully so as not to wake Ellie, sleeping at his side. He showered, shaved and looked out of the window of the rented house. Yesterday, there had been a garden of *proteas* and tree heath and giant, brilliant daisies. Today, there was grey mist, and the faces of the daisies were closed, awaiting the return of the sun.

When he went down to breakfast, the air was clammy and cold. The black servant brought him guava juice, hot white rolls and biltong. 'Goddamn weather,' said DuCane.

'Black southeastah, sah,' said the servant. 'Big wind, strong as hurricane.'

'Okay, okay,' said DuCane dismissively. 'Bring me the phone, will you?' He dialled the race information office as he ate. 'They're experiencing winds force nine and ten,' said the girl on the other end. '*Flag*'s dropped back in the night.'

'What?' said DuCane.

'There's very little to choose between the leaders,' said the girl. 'Not a nice day for sailing.'

'Yeah,' said DuCane, and put the telephone down.

Beyond the picture windows, Table Mountain had vanished in black fog.

The telephone rang. It was Jasper Hyatt. 'Just had a call from Martin, on the boat,' said the old, creaking voice. 'They're under storm canvas in winds of sixty to eighty knots. The Australians have caught up.' Hyatt paused. 'I hope you're sure you chose the right skipper,' he said.

DuCane sat there and smiled his sharp smile, trying to relax. Beyond the huge dining-room window, the fogs writhed on Table Mountain. In the garden, the Canary Island palms blew inside out. And in DuCane's ambitious soul, anger and uncertainty quarrelled for dominance.

Ellie DuCane came into the room. She was wearing a cream silk dress, with a lot of gold chains around her tanned throat. The fingernails on her long, powerful hands were varnished blood-red.

'What's happening out there?' she said.

DuCane told her.

'Poor guys,' she said.

'Their job's to *win*,' said DuCane savagely.

'Oh,' said Mrs DuCane. 'So Wallace is in one of his little rages, is he? But I forget. Wallace knows absolute zip about sailing.' She picked up an apricot from the breakfast table and bit into it. 'But you'd better learn soon – especially if you want to take over this yacht club.'

'Who says I do?' said DuCane sharply.

Ellie smiled, a slow, narrow smile. 'Wallace, you know I love you. But we've been married five years now and I have no illusions. You married me because I was rich and because I knew the right people. So let's not have any silly secrets. If you want to take over this yacht club, you'll have to get into yachts as well as politics.'

DuCane looked at her. The lined face under the perfect iron-grey hair was solemn, the eyes detached. 'Perhaps you're right,' he said. 'Ellie, if this is truth-telling time, tell me, why did you marry *me*?'

'I didn't have much choice,' said Ellie, with her smile. 'You always get what you want, don't you, Wallace?'

'Helm's a-lee!' said Ed Cole.

Chinamite's nose pointed at the dark clouds as she went up through a wave. Then, responding to the bite of the rudder, the sky began to turn. Nicholas Eason uncleated the genoa sheet, and kept four turns on the winch drum until the sail trembled on the brink of backing. Then he let go the lazy end and jumped up to the big handle of the coffee grinder pedestal in the gorilla pit. Slicer was already there. The winch began its long jingle as the tailer pulled up the slack. The genoa came over as Eason slapped his hands on to the double handles, one either side of Slicer's.

'Go!' shouted the tailer.

Eason put his head next to Slicer's hood and set his teeth and wound. The deck bucked under his feet. The pressure on the handles increased as the sheet came on to the winch.

'Change!' shouted Slicer.

Eason reversed direction. The winch handles sped up again as the gearing relieved the grinders of the sail's weight.

'Fast!' shouted the tailer.

And *Chinamite* was heeled sharply over on the starboard tack, ploughing across the steep waves rather than taking them nose-on.

'Better,' said Slicer.

'Yeah,' said Eason. His voice sounded loud, because of the tight foul-weather hood round his face. 'Hitler,' he said.

'Hitler? Ah,' said Slicer. 'We were playing Botticelli. No. Not Hitler.'

'Was this person a US Presidential candidate in the 1984 election?'

Slicer said, 'Shucks. You got it. Gary Hart.'

'Thank you,' said Eason. 'That will be another chocolate digestive biscuit you owe me. Making twenty-three in all, if I am not mistaken.'

'Correct,' said Slicer. A sheet of water hit him in the face. He did not appear to notice. 'But you've got an education.'

'First bit of good it's ever done me,' said Eason.

If anyone had told him, three months ago, that he would be playing Botticelli for chocolate biscuits in a force nine gale four hundred miles northwest of Cape Town, he would have thought they were completely mad. But here he was. And it was not only Botticelli. 'Slicer,' said Eason, 'I have learned many things. I have crossed the Equator, and father Neptune has soaked me in crankcase oil. I can whip a sheet. I can steer. I can trim. Peeling a spinnaker holds no secrets from me, I have slept in a wet bunk for five weeks, and I have not been seasick for a month. I am Renaissance Man.'

Slicer screwed his eyes up against a drift of spray. 'WHAT?' he roared.

Eason sighed. 'Nothing,' he said.

'Oh,' said Slicer. 'I was just thinking. When you get to Cape Town, will you bother with champagne or do you reckon it'll be better straight into the brandy?'

'Requires thought,' said Eason. It was an important question, and one which was increasingly occupying the minds of *Chinamite*'s crew. It made being strapped to a near-vertical deck and deluged with icy water almost tolerable.

'Rum might be the thing,' said Eason. His eyes travelled bow to stern; it had become a habit, the constant checking. Shrouds, lee chainplates under water. Gorilla pit, two men in, lifelines secure, jib sheet secure. Mainsail, three slabs out, all lines secure, nothing fraying or flapping. Aft, backstay good, Ed Cole in the cockpit, silent, face shrouded by the hood of his gleaming red wet-gear, as if he was part of the boat.

Eason frowned. Cole was the only problem. He was still tight shut. And the tighter he was, the more he tickled Eason's curiosity.

'I dunno about rum,' said Slicer. 'It's not bad stuff, cham –'

The deck they were sitting on suddenly twanged like a bass viol.

'Wha –?' Eason did not have time to finish saying it, because he was up and running, on to the foredeck. Slicer was already there, hanging on to the halyards taut on the mast, his head thrown back.

'FORESTAY!' he yelled. There was a crack high above, and something like a black snake carrying the number six genoa coiled down out of the clouds, smacked viciously into the rail, and went over the side.

'Get it!' shouted Slicer. The foredeck went up fifteen feet on a new wave, then hammered down into the next trough, rolling violently to port. Eason clung to the mast a moment. His heart was beating too hard. He clipped himself on to the jackstay, and ran forward across the streaming triangle of non-slip fibreglass. He jammed his backside into the pulpit and twisted his feet into the rail as the bow went down and into the next wave. Green water closed over his head, and he thought: this is it. But the yacht shuddered and came up, and then the nose was moving away from the waves as Cole dragged it off the wind.

Eason and Slicer began to pull the forestay and the sopping cloth of the genoa. It was heavy, only semi-flexible. More hands arrived. *Chinamite* was well off the wind now, and the seas were at least not coming aboard green.

The end rattled over the toe-rail. The toggle that fitted into the eye of the mainsail casting was gone.

'Watch the babystay,' shouted Slicer.

The babystay springs from the deck half-way between the pulpit and the mast, joining the mast three-quarters of the way up. It is there to support the middle sections. Now, it was taking the full weight.

'Gawd,' said Slicer. 'Look at the top.'

Unsupported, the top thirty feet of the mast was waving like the top of a fishing rod. The babystay was emitting an ominous twanging.

'MAIN!' came the voice from the cockpit.

The deck was suddenly full of men as the watch below spilled up from the hatches. The mainsail came down until its headfoil reached the part of the mast still supported by the runners and the babystay. The top of the mast still whipped nastily, with an evil whistle as *Chinamite*'s roll took it through the air. The foredeck group fell quiet, breathing hard and clammy with cooling sweat.

Then a figure in red came up the deck at a shambling half-run, balancing against *Chinamite*'s dreadful roll. It was Ed Cole. Eason found his heartbeat slowing as he started work under Cole's confident stream of orders. They got a spare genoa halyard, and ground it up taut. That stopped the whipping of the mast. Eason wiped the spray from his face and thought: okay, but the halyard won't last long under this punishment, and there's no way of getting sail up. As if in answer, Cole said, 'I've got a spare toggle. I'll go up on the spinnaker halyard, and you can haul the forestay up to me on the genoa halyard, and I'll fix her up, and then we can pull the new forestay up tight, and bob's your uncle.' Somebody handed him the bosun's chair. He clipped it to the genoa halyard. 'Give way,' he said.

Eason looked up at the racing sky and the lashing hounds a hundred feet above his head, where Cole was going to sit and put a toggle through an eye, and delicately insert split-pins. He shivered.

The bosun's chair tightened under Cole's buttocks. He had given his orders fast, so none of the gale-shocked crew had time to offer to go up the mast themselves. Cole knew that he was doing something bloody dangerous, and if anyone was going to do dangerous things on *Chinamite*, it was going to be him. The mast moved past his face. He fended himself off. Even though he had run the last spare halyard through the bosun's chair shackle, the aluminium was leaping out at him to butt him with its hard metal forehead. The sweat broke and ran inside his dry-suit.

First spreader. Time for a rest, he thought. He shouted, 'Avast hauling!' and stood with a foot on each side of the mast. *Chinamite* plunged into a trough. He felt his feet yanked away from under him and heard the shout below as he swung suddenly away from the mast, pulling the halyard out like a bowstring over a void of deck and water. He clenched his fingers over the spreader shroud, swearing viciously at the pain. Oh, no, he thought; no more rests. 'Heave!' he roared.

The motion was getting worse. He clung to the mast with his arms as it swept across the sky. From the pain at the end of his fingers he assumed that he had torn out at least part of his nails. A line from a song went through his mind: *If you're dead already, you don't have to die*.

Second spreader. His face was stiff in a grimace. The wind buffeted at him, clear of the wave crests now, seventy feet above the grey-white ocean. He came to the headfoil of the mainsail. Up here, the mast waved horribly. He looked down between his feet. *Chinamite* stuck her nose into a wave, and it came over the deck, green and white, swirling round the legs of the tiny red figures with the white faces looking up at him. And for a moment Cole felt that the boat was gone, and that he was suspended between heaven and earth, pulled towards heaven by the remorseless pressure of the halyard. And so he arrived at the hounds.

He took two turns of his lifeline round the mast, lashing himself tight. Then he examined the screw.

He roared between his feet. The stay came up to him on the spinnaker halyard, one hundred and twenty feet of black Indian rope trick above the needle-nosed triangle of the foredeck. Gripping the toggle in his left hand, he steered it through the eye. Then, clutching the mast with his legs, he rammed in the first pin and the second pin. It seemed so easy that he found himself grinning, a grin that stiffened his face.

The sweat was streaming off him now. The wind battered at the back of his neck, and the disc of sea around was a grey chaos streaked with white foam. He detached his lifeline from the mast, feeling rising mists of spray wet his face even up here. And for some reason there came to him the hot, dusty smell of the Inquiry room in Plymouth, the heavy drone of bluebottles under the thick plaster mouldings of the ceiling. And he suddenly felt completely free, and laughed aloud. As he laughed, *Chinamite* slid sideways off a wave with a peculiar twisting wrench, and this time he flew all the way into space, and hung there. Suspended, he thought, 'This is going to hurt.' Then he was sailing in again, and the mast slammed into his chest, and he felt something give: rib, he thought, and before the pain could take over, he shouted, 'Quick!' Then the pain burst through his head. But now he could laugh at it. Because for the first time, he had seen past the dull ache of that courtroom in Plymouth, and had felt what it was like to be free again.

On deck, Eason unclipped him and helped him aft, down the bucking deck and into a bunk. They took the dry-suit off him and lowered him back on to the pillow. Eason could see the muscles of his jaw corrugate under the skin as the pain tore at him. But when he lay back, and the pain had stopped, Eason was amazed by the change in him. Under the yellow glow of the bunklight, the pinched face was suddenly relaxed, and the tight-slitted eyes opened, and the down-turned corners of the mouth turned up.

'So,' said Bones, the ship's doctor. 'What we got here?'

Eason turned away. Henry Harper was standing behind him, braced against the lurching of the deck. He looked dazed, a little surprised. 'Now that's what he used to look like,' he said to Eason.

'You mean before the *Arpeggio* business?' said Eason, at a venture.

'Yes.' Harper paused and shook his head. 'I never will believe all that.' Then his eyes suddenly focused, and his tired face jerked up. 'Can't stand here gossiping,' he said. 'Let's get some sail on.'

And Eason had the feeling that he had had a glimpse, through carelessly opened gates, into another world.

During the remainder of the watch, Eason alternately

211

fought the number five genoa, shrugged water out of the neck of his dry-suit, and thought about Cole. It was a good story, there was no getting away from that. Going up that mast in these seas had been more than brave; it had been the act of a man who had little left to live for. And when he had come down, the relaxation in him had not been the relief of a man who had screwed himself up to sticking point, but simple satisfaction in a job well done. Eason heard Harper's words echoing in his mind. 'I never will believe all that.'

Eason found himself more than ever wanting to talk to Cole about *Arpeggio*.

Meanwhile, there was his own career to consider. He had to file, this evening. He knew the headline that ought to go over the piece: ARPEGGIO 'KILLER' IS HURRICANE HERO. But when he went below and got through to the newsdesk, he filed a piece about the difficulty of eating soup in rough seas. 'Oh dear, oh dear,' said the static-crusted voice of the copy-taker, who now seemed to regard himself as his best friend and severest critic. 'That one's on the spike for sure. I dunno why you bother, mate. Wet out there?'

Eason looked at the deck between his feet. Jets of water were sloshing out of the finger holes in the cabin sole, and a smell of burnt grease wafted aft from the galley. 'Oh, no,' he said. 'I'm on the pool deck and chef's just called us for the caviare pasties. Must dash.'

'Lucky sod,' said the copy-taker.

Seasickness had returned to Dave Kelly with the onset of the bad weather. For two days now he had been lying in a bunk, wedged against the pounding with bundles of stores, refusing to budge except to crawl to the head and vomit green bile into the bowl. Chuck the sound man brought him dry biscuits from time to time. The crumbs got into his sleeping bag and he was miserably uncomfortable. But nobody was sympathetic. At best, he was ignored. At worst, he could feel active dislike. Which was unfair, he felt. It wasn't his fault he was ill. It was the unfairness that rankled so terribly.

Inside, *Kelly's Eye* was a slum. Somehow, water had seeped into the fuel, so the generator only charged the batteries for an hour each day. The lighting was now two yellow bulbs which raised reflections from the film of water that covered the plastic surfaces. Sails coming down the hatch brought gallons of water with them, and anyway, *Eye*'s lean lines made her a wet boat in a seaway. Also, she stank; the food debris that had found its way into her bilges had mixed with water and fermented, and the hammering of the hull had prevented anyone from cleaning up the mess.

Kelly was writing in his notebook, trying to arrange the footage he had shot into scenes that would show him in a creditable light. He could feel the pressure of the bunk's base on his spine as *Eye* climbed a long, long hill of water. *Wdeshot of dolph*, he wrote.

His pencil lifted without finishing the word. *Eye* was still going up. And there was the sound of confused shouting on deck. Kelly opened his mouth, then, and the sound that came out was a howl of terror.

For everything inside *Eye*'s plastic coffin of a cabin had suddenly floated into the air, weightless. Kelly felt himself rise. Then there was a terrible crash and things whirled round his head as he flew forward down the cabin and slammed into the door of the compartment forward of the mast. The door burst open under his weight, and he plunged through, screaming with pain, and landed on the deck by the sailmaker's sewing machine. He lay winded, his mouth open, gasping like a fish.

At last, his breath came back. *Eye* struggled in the trough, then began to rise to the next wave. Kelly waited for the pain to subside, whimpering to himself. He was braced between a sailbag and one of the ribs supporting the hull. Suddenly, someone nudged him violently in the back. He shifted peevishly, clambering to his hands and knees, bracing himself as the nose went down into the next trough. As he did so he looked round for whoever it was had kicked him in the ribs.

There was nobody there.

Kelly opened his mouth. His face was the colour of a dead fish's belly. He meant to yell, but days of vomiting had made his throat raw, and the best he could manage was a croaking bellow.

The rib had broken. As he watched, *Eye* stuck her nose into a trough, and a section of her side six feet long and three feet high bulged inwards like a great white blister. Kelly scuttled on hands and knees through the leaping hull, and stuck his head out of the hatch into the shrieking wind. 'Quick!' he screamed. 'That boat's bust! We're sinking!'

Bud Withers handed the wheel to the crewman at his side, squinted at the grey wave blotting out the horizon and said calmly, 'Okay, Dave. I'm coming.'

Kelly, by now shaking uncontrollably, followed him through the crew cabin. Withers braced himself against the door and eyed the bulge for a while. Then he said, 'Yeah,' and lapsed into silence.

The noise of water rushing past the bow filled the forepeak. The nose lifted and fell with a deafening *boom*. The blister on the side bulged horribly. 'Oilcanning,' said Withers. 'What we got here is a little core separation.'

BOOM, went the bow.

'And she sure as hell ain't going to take much more of that,' said Withers. 'Let's get out of here.'

Kelly searched his face for encouragement. Bud Withers' eyes were hooded, and the beard hid the line of his mouth. 'Are we going to sink?' he said.

'Sure hope not,' said Withers. 'Let's get on the other tack, then we'll take a look.'

Kelly sat down on his bunk and listened to the racing feet on the deck, the roar of the winches. Then he climbed into his wet-gear and went on deck.

After they had tacked, Withers took a work party below. They cut up the galley worktops to make a pad for the blister. While the carpenter was fitting them, Bennett and two men brought the spinnaker jockey poles through, cut them to length and jammed them into place across the forepeak.

It took two hours, and Chuck filmed the whole thing. When it was finished, Withers said, 'Let's tack back on course and get back in the race.'

'You sure?' said Chuck. 'Isn't it kind of dangerous to tack back on to the bad side?'

Withers did not bother to answer. But Bennett said, 'We keep on this heading, we'll hit Antarctica in about a month. That what you want?'

Chuck's viewfinder was full of Bennett's face, her eyes and cheeks hollow with exhaustion, sweaty tendrils of hair sticking to her forehead, and in the background the ramshackle cross-bracing of the forepeak.

'Screw you,' said Bennett, and turned away.

'Yeah,' said Chuck, still filming. He knew a Pulitzer when it stared him in the face.

When Bennett came on deck, she went aft and made sure the liferafts were free. Automatically she made her usual check to see that everything was in place. *Eye* was forging across a hill of water, heeled sharply to starboard. We are going to die, if this wind keeps up, she thought as her eye quartered the deck. Up by the gorilla pit, a figure in white wet-gear sat hunched, knees under chin, hood far down over his eyes. Dave Kelly.

Bennett clambered along the weather deck, her ears full of the scream of the wind in the rigging. Kelly turned a white, terrifed face up at her.

'Is it okay, now?' he said.

Bennett bared her white teeth in a laugh that had no

216

humour in it. 'Hard to say,' she said. 'You've got a hull made for harbour-racing in a sea made for armour-plating. So if the bracing holds, the delaminating might not spread. Then again, the whole goddamn works may split right open, and then we are all off to Davy Jones, me hearty.' *Eye* lay over into a wave. The sound of groaning timber came from the forepeak. 'That could be it now,' said Bennett, and ran below. Aft, Withers shouted, 'Get those headsails off!' The foredeck men ran at their curious deep-sea shamble towards the cloud of spray shrouding the foredeck.

Kelly took a deep breath. Five minutes passed. The ship did not sink. The knot of fear in his belly made him feel horribly sick and his heart was ticking like a time-bomb. He had to do something. Unsteadily, he crept aft.

Withers said, 'Yeah?'

'Are we going to make it?'

'Who knows?' said Withers.

Kelly's trembling hand went out to touch him, then drew back. Chuck's head was sticking out of the after hatch. Kelly said, 'I have to know.'

'What the hell do you mean, you have to know?' snarled Withers. 'Listen, Kelly, she's about as strong as a paper bag. So, if you want to prepare to die, prepare to die. Me, I was hired to race.'

Kelly had expected consolation. He staggered back, as if he had taken a slap in the face. Then he said, 'At least tell me the odds, Bud.'

'Who knows?' said Withers. 'Now, piss off, I'm busy.' Then he bellowed, 'All braced below? Stand by to tack!'

Kelly knew that this was the moment between dying or

not. He found himself staring at Chuck, in the hatch. Chuck was filming.

Chuck was filming.

'Helm's-a-lee!' shouted Withers. Kelly wanted to fall on the deck and scream and blubber and beg for mercy. But the eye of the camera had hynotized him. The will of the camera sapped his own. Now, his terror was dulled by the greater terror of looking like a coward. He turned and spoke directly to the camera's eye. 'The hull is collapsing. But we're still racing. We're turning for Cape Town and damn the consequences.' The deck lurched under his feet. 'You may never see this footage,' he said. 'But I have to tell you that it will all have been worthwhile.'

'Okay, Bud,' he said to Withers. 'Let's go for it.'

'Go for what?' said Withers, narrowing his eyes at a crumbling crest of grey water rolling down on the bow.

'The race,' said Kelly.

Eye's genoa filled, and the bracing in her forepeak groaned as she dug her blistered hull into the sea.

It was the noise that woke Wallace DuCane: a noise like the howling of thousands of wolves. For a moment he lay and stared at the ceiling, hearing his wife's breathing long and steady, and sweated with terror. There were many things that terrified DuCane as he lay alone in the night watches. But he had always managed to analyse his terrors, treating them with the same contempt as he treated heads he hunted in the course of his work. Now, he analysed the noise.

The noise was the noise of ships' sirens, dozens of them, all blowing at once. There was only one reason for sirens to be blowing all at once at – he squinted at his Cartier alarm clock – at five thirteen a.m.

DuCane rolled out of bed and ran into the living-room of the house. He pulled back the heavy curtains and picked up a pair of binoculars.

To the east, a big red sun was heaving itself up above the rim of a gun-metal ocean. Its rays spread streaks of blood across the water and pinkened the cliffs and screes of Table Mountain, picking out each individual pebble and gleaming in the silver leaves of the *leucodendrons*. The smoke of early fires drifted up from the suburbs, and wisped away on the southwest breeze.

Ellie came to stand beside him, and looked out into the crystal air that bathed the sea and the city and the mountain.

In the circle of DuCane's binoculars was a yacht. She was carrying a spinnaker, but she was too far away for him to be able to read its logo. Boats were swarming round her, obscuring her hull.

The telephone rang. It was Jasper Hyatt, his old voice even rustier than usual with the early morning. 'Wallace,' he said, 'do you see what I see?'

DuCane said, 'I do,' without detaching his glasses from the crowd of small boats in the harbour. As he watched, the grey minesweeper masking the yacht's hull moved aside. 'You bastard,' said DuCane.

'What?' said Hyatt sharply.

'That boat. It's *Siltex-France*,' said DuCane, and put the phone down. He put his small, deeply tanned hands into his black silk pyjama pockets. His head sank into his neck. 'I'll ruin the bastard,' he said.

His wife looked at him. Without make-up, her face was harder and older, and there was a puffiness to the copper-brown skin. 'Oh, no,' she said. 'Please don't. Or anyway give him to me first.'

DuCane suddenly smiled. His teeth flashed in the growing light. 'You wouldn't want him,' he said. 'There won't be hardly anything left.' He stumped into the bedroom, shrugged into a tracksuit and trainers, and trotted out into the fresh early air.

DuCane ran along the wide pavement under the jacarandas. Black servants on their way to work stood aside as he passed; he paid them no attention. As he ran, he thought. It was his moment for thinking about business matters, and this morning he thought about *Flag* and the new age about to dawn on the Sound Yacht Club.

He ran up on to the lower slopes of Table Mountain, where the houses began to thin out among the faces of rock. Policemen were scrubbing at big paint inscriptions: ANC, TAMBO. What a mess, he thought, and turned back for home and breakfast.

The home route took him along a shallow terrace overlooking Table Bay. The day was heating up now, and the sun blazed a glittering track across the water. Already, small pleasure boats were crawling out into the sparkling blue, towards the place where, to seaward, a spinnaker bulged against the horizon. It bore the Stars and Stripes. *Flag*.

As the day went on, the harbour filled with sightseers. They cheered in *Flag*, and escorted her to the dock next to the one where *Siltex* was lying. At two p.m., five hours and twenty-one minutes and fifteen seconds after *Flag*, *Tasman* crossed the line. Champagne bottles tumbled through the air like little Indians clubs, and Tubes Murphy roared with joy as the white fountains gushed skywards. But some of his crew took a single sip of champagne, for luck, and then begged water. And only when they had soaked up a quart or two did they go back to the champagne. Art Schacker went over and shook Tubes Murphy's hand, under the hot eyes of Martin Hyatt. The day began to vanish in a haze of flying corks and the blare of hooters. Someone came down from the mountains with an enormous grape vine in the back of a pickup and winched it up *Siltex*'s backstay. And there were the women, hundreds of women, and all they seemed to want was to go somewhere quiet for a little while with a hero who had come all the way from England in a boat.

Chinamite came in as the sun was setting, and again the champagne bottles tumbled across the gap as she came alongside, and the parties under the lights on the docks spread from deck to deck. It was very late, well past midnight, and Eason was singing the Marseillaise with a mixed group from *Siltex* and *Tasman*, with George Hart from *Flag*, when *Kelly's Eye* came in, the last of the maxis. The singers looked at her running lights ghosting across the water, a ruby and an emerald in the centre of a knot of brilliantly lit pleasure boats. They cheered as she came alongside the dock. Two men jumped down with mooring lines. But once they had made fast, they did not jump back aboard. Instead they remained on the jetty, chatting to spectators, not looking back at the boat, and as far as Eason could determine, trying to keep their eyes off her.

As soon as the lines were ashore, a thin, dark man came on deck with an expensive suitcase, climbed on to the jetty, and walked fast for the darkness beyond the lights. 'Hey,' said George Hart. 'That's Dave Kelly.'

A stretched Mercedes materialized out of the darkness. Kelly got in, and the Mercedes whispered away. 'Looks like a nice chap,' said Eason. 'Mucking in with his crew, sharing the salt horse and hardtack.' He watched *Eye* as the crew tidied up. Television cameras came aboard, and hard lights glared below decks. Then he hopped down to the jetty and went round for a closer look.

There was no party: a case of champagne, and a lot of journalists, but not the mass of eager well-wishers that surged round *Flag* and *Siltex, Tasman* and *Chinamite*. A tall blonde woman was sitting with her legs through the lifelines, gazing at the lights of the town. 'Hi,' said Eason. He held out his bottle of champagne. 'Have a drink?'

'Sure,' said the blonde woman, and drank deeply. Then she stuck out her hand. 'Bennett,' she said.

'Eason,' said Eason. 'I heard you had a little trouble.'

'Boat collapsed,' said Bennett. 'I'd show you, only there's some guys from Lloyds down there right now.'

'That's okay,' said Eason. 'Why don't you come over and eat a few lobsters?'

'Sure,' said Bennett. She jumped down from the jetty. Eason said, 'Have a nice trip?'

Bennett turned her head, 'Are you *kidding*?' she said. 'With that jerk Kelly acting like a spoilt brat and the goddamn boat cracking up?' She paused. 'That guy is a monster. And I guess maybe the boat's not seaworthy.' The singing had started again. It was loud, even raucous. In the floodlights on *Tasman*'s deck, Sparko could be seen conducting a choir of mixed nationalities with a rum bottle. Bennett ran her arm through Eason's. 'Anyway, it's real nice to be ashore.' And Eason, looking across at her, saw her white teeth and the lights of the town glittering in her narrow blue eyes below the thick fringe of blonde hair, and thought: hello, this is a beautiful woman.

The Race Committee met the following day, in Lymington. It was raining, and blowing hard from the northwest. Gusts sent icy rain rattling against the windows. The wooden-faced admiral was not amused.

'Lucky beggars,' he said. 'I suppose they're sunbathing. Late October, it's spring down there. What's on the agenda?'

'*Siltex* first,' said the secretary. 'No rating. She wouldn't be measured, if you remember.'

'Of course I remember,' snapped the wooden-faced admiral, on whose liver envy had a bad effect. 'Ought to be disqualified.'

'We-ell,' said Cunliffe, Lancaster's PR man. 'We agreed that a time penalty would do as well.'

'Twenty-four hours,' said the admiral.

Cunliffe smiled. Lancaster had just bought a large bakery chain in France, and was anxious for a good press there. 'Four,' he said. 'Surely four would be enough. And of course re-measuring.'

'Tchah!' said the admiral.

The debate continued. Eventually the committee decided that a six-hour penalty would suffice, since it would deprive *Siltex* of her win.

'Cable tomorrow,' said the admiral. 'Any other business?'

'*Kelly's Eye*,' said the secretary. 'We're insisting on a full survey.'

'Then get one done,' said the admiral. 'Now for God's sake can we please go and have some dinner?'

CAPE TOWN

The Sound Yacht Club had not stinted on the arrangements for accommodating its crews. Wallace DuCane had had his people organize billets for those members who had no connections in Cape Town. Art Schacker, by virtue of his captaincy, had an apartment to himself. George Hart was staying with an accountant who had fourteen black servants and two beautiful daughters. Mustapha Choudry, had, however, been a problem.

The problem was that Mustapha Choudry, while not actually *black*, was by no means white, either. And the Table Mountain Yacht Club, through which DuCane's people had made the arrangements, had no coloured members. This was, the committee were at pains to explain, purely a matter of accident. So there had been a slight crisis until the Rev. Angus Hoyt had agreed to open his doors to Choudry. But the minister was an elderly man given to grim silences, and his Afrikaner wife spent most of her time on the tennis court and ostentatiously kept her distance from Choudry, who rapidly became lonely and depressed in their forbidding red-brick house with its smell of disinfectant and old Bibles.

On the third day after their arrival, he spent seven hours

hosing the debris of the past six weeks from *Flag*'s interior. Afterwards, reluctant to return to the Hoyts, he went up to the Race Club on the quay, got an orange juice from the bar and went and sat in a corner by the window.

Outside, crews were straggling up from the docks. He recognized Eason, the journalist from *Chinamite*, with a blonde woman from *Kelly's Eye*. They looked as if they were having fun. Seeing them only made him more conscious that he was in the wrong place in this beautiful, revolting country.

Three other men came up the dock, with a gaggle of women. Martin Hyatt, Simon Lowell; Lowell laughing sycophantically at something Hyatt had said, his wizened monkey-face creased with mirth; Hyatt pink and smug; and George Hart, looking faintly uneasy, though Choudry did not know whether that was because of the girls, or because of Hyatt and Lowell. Choudry knew them all pretty well after six weeks at sea, and he suspected it would be because of Hyatt and Lowell.

They came into the club, and got beers at the bar. Choudry finished his orange juice; after the incident at sea, he felt uncomfortable in their presence, and he meant to leave. But then George Hart, big and broad-faced and good-natured as ever, waved. And the others noticed him, including the girls, and brought their beers over to his table.

'I was just going,' said Choudry.

'Don't,' said Lowell, whose glittering, pinkish eyes said he had been drinking. 'Hang about, meet the girls.' He started to introduce them. Choudry smiled at the freckled faces and the appraising eyes. One of them was darker than the others, with brown eyes and olive skin and a vaguely Semitic beauty. She was called Rachel. Choudry suddenly realized how lonely he was. They began to talk.

Rachel was not very interesting; she worked for a travel agent and she lived with her parents, and seemed to do little but go to parties. But it was good to talk to somebody, and she seemed keen to listen. At one point, one of the girls suggested they go on to a bar, and they did, though Choudry did not notice where they were going, because dusk was falling and Rachel was getting more sympathetic, and actually she had her hand on his knee under the table. They drove in someone else's station wagon down a wide street lined with palm trees and then into a white building with ceiling fans, more like a club than a bar. There was a black porter behind a desk in the hall, and he gave Choudry a look of some astonishment as the party walked in over the black and white geometric tiling.

They sat down in cane chairs. Choudry wondered, not for the first time that evening, what he was doing sharing a table with two men who despised him. Rachel's hand stealing under the table reminded him. A black waiter brought yellow beer. Choudry drank orange juice. Rachel's fingers were a tarantula of pink flesh on his upper thigh. He talked to her of a whale that had surfaced alongside *Flag*; her brown eyes turned to melting toffee, while across the table the others shouted, their red faces beginning to take on a wild-eyed and sweaty look – except George Hart. George was silent, his face still, as if he were somewhere else.

The whale had come up like a great black dream in the

open space of the ocean. When he had seen it, Choudry felt he had known it all his life. He was explaining this to Rachel when her eyes focused on somebody behind him, and the blood flushed under the clear olive skin of her cheeks. Choudry looked round.

'Hi there,' said the man who had walked up behind his chair. He was six feet six inches tall, and his shoulders sloped from the junction of jaw and neck to hands the size of legs of lamb. He was wearing a white short-sleeved shirt, a tie, and khaki slacks. His eyes were slits of metal under his low forehead.

'Hello,' said Rachel, in a small voice.

'Nice to see you,' said the big man, in a thick Afrikaner accent. 'What are you doing here?'

'Let me introduce you –' said Rachel.

The big man laughed. 'That's okay,' he said. 'I'm not staying long.' He allowed one of his big hands to fall on Choudry's shoulder. 'And anyway, I can never remember the names of these black bastards.'

It took a second for it to sink in. Choudry could feel the smile freeze on his face. His stomach turned over with shock. Then the anger came, and he got up. As he rose to his feet, the grip on his shoulder tightened. 'She's a great little groper, Rachel, eh? Now say goodbye, because you're leaving.' The hand continued to tighten.

Choudry said, 'Let go of me.'

The big man picked him up until their eyes were level. Choudry's feet were seven inches off the floor. He said, 'Okay.' And he began to carry Choudry towards the door. Choudry took a swing at him. His fist hit muscle toughened like rubber, and the big man paid no attention. The sound of laughter came from the table. He looked round, and saw Hyatt and Lowell raise their glasses, grinning all over their red faces. *They fixed this*, he suddenly thought. He saw George Hart pushing back his chair, pale-faced, coming towards them. Then everything happened at once.

The big man dropped him. Hart's fist came round in a wide, clumsy arc. The big man parried with his forearm, His other fist came forward and crashed up against Hart's skull. Choudry was scrambling to his feet, his eyes fogged with rage. He pulled back his fist and let fly again. It hit the big man in the nose. Choudry felt the boneless squash of it. *Bone removed*, he thought. He knew what that meant. Then the hands had him again, and he was travelling across the black and white tiles of the hall floor. '*Voetsak*,' said the big man.

He saw the hall porter's eyes white in his black skin, the palm trees, the street. They whirled around his head. Then his skull hit the pavement, and the air filled with bright specks. A red face in a peaked cap was bending over him. 'Look at this,' he said. 'Pissed as a rat.'

'Yeah.' A boot prodded him in the ribs.

Choudry got to his knees. 'No,' he said. 'I don't drink. I'd like to report –'

The boot slammed into his shoulder. He lay on the ground and looked up at the two men in their peaked caps and bluish uniforms. 'Shut up and get in the van,' they said. 'You're under arrest. Drunk and disorderly.' And one of them flexed a whip between his hands.

Choudry had seen the whip on TV in the States, rising and falling on the bodies in Soweto. The *sjambok*. He became quiet. From the open doors of the club tinkled the sound of laughter.

The desk sergeant's eyes were light blue, and very eager. 'Sign here,' he said, pushing the book across to Schacker. Schacker signed. 'It certainly is a privilege to get your autograph,' said the desk sergeant.

'Where's my man?' said Schacker. His square brown face was still, his eyes bleak as he took in the green-painted room, the shabby desks, the rack of shotguns in the corner.

'They're bringing him,' said the desk sergeant. 'Heard you had a hard time in that southeaster, eh?'

Schacker ignored him. The barred door behind the desk slid back. Choudry appeared between two konstabels. His eyes were swollen, his left cheek grazed. The konstabels were helping him walk.

'We cleaned him up,' said the policeman. 'Terrible state. Dead drunk. Bit of luck we discovered who he was.'

'He's a Muslim,' said Schacker. 'He doesn't drink.'

The taxi drove slowly past large suburban houses. Black sweepers dabbed languidly at the street, and through the high green hedges, turquoise swimming-pools glittered in the early morning sun.

'What happened?' said Schacker.

Choudry told him: 'And then they took me to a cell and kicked me around a bit,' he said. 'When I told them I was with the boat, they must have called a high-up, because soon after a doctor arrived.'

'You okay?'

'Bruises and abrasions,' said Choudry. His eyes were

swollen slits, his mouth crusted with dried blood where his lips had been driven on to his teeth.

'You fight a wing forward with the national rugby team, that's what you get.'

'The boyfriend?'

'The boyfriend.'

'Ugh,' said Choudry.

'I'm sorry,' said Art.

'Sorry you're white and sorry I'm black?' Choudry let his head rest on the cab's seat back.

'Take it easy,' said Art. Choudry did not reply. 'We have to see the Club Committee.'

'Oh yeah?'

'Bringing the ship into disrepute,' said Art. A policeman with a shotgun lounged on a corner under a jacaranda tree. 'Do you want a doctor?'

'Let's get it over with,' said Choudry.

Jasper Hyatt was in a room at the Rand Credit Bank. He was seated behind a desk. Wallace DuCane was beside him, standing, with his back to the window. Both men wore SYC ties, blue blazers, white flannels. Their straw boaters lay on the desk which with two hard chairs was the only furniture in the room.

Hyatt cleared his throat. 'Choudry,' he said. 'I'm sure you're aware that we can't have crew-members arrested for being drunk.'

Choudry said, 'I was arrested for being black.'

Schacker said, 'I can confirm that.'

Hyatt fell silent, his old, seamed face completely still. DuCane stepped foward from the window. 'You have caused us grave embarrassment with our South African hosts.'

'You're an ambassador for your club and your country,' rasped Hyatt, stabbing his finger on the desk.

Choudry sat down. His brown face was grey, and his swollen lips were open as he panted for breath.

'With respect,' said Schacker, 'you have this wrong.'

Hyatt's eyes rose slowly towards him. 'Listen here, Schacker,' he said. 'My grandson is a fine young man, and I know what took place last evening. Further, there is independent corroboration from Mr Lowell.'

Choudry said. 'How about George Hart?'

'In hospital,' said DuCane. 'Concussion. He'll face disciplinary charges when he comes out.'

'No he will not,' said Schacker quietly. 'Mr Hyatt, Mr DuCane, we have things to discuss.' He put his hand on Choudry's shoulder. 'Mustapha, maybe you had better wait outside.'

Choudry shrugged, got up and left, without looking at him.

'No disciplinary charges,' said Schacker, after Choudry shut the door. 'Not on my boat.'

'The club's boat,' croaked Hyatt. 'Now see here, Schacker, you're in no position to bargain with me.'

'Us,' said DuCane.

'Us,' said Hyatt. 'I may be old, but I' not stupid. You were hired to win, and you aren't winning. My sources tell me you're not driving that boat. You're not carrying sail, and there's slackness and inefficiency in the crew. This case is another example of that slackness. On a well-run boat, it would never have happened.'

'Okay,' said Schacker. At the back of his mind, he could see Anne-Marie and Marblehead Clam and Lobster, and the white house, and he knew it was all riding on what he said next. But in the front of his mind he saw Choudry's battered face, and the toadying grin of the desk sergeant who had one set of assumptions about whites and another about non-whites. Just as Jasper Hyatt had one set about the SYC, and another about the rest of the world. 'I guess we have a central difference of opinion here. You have two weeks to find a new skipper who'll beat the Australians. Because I resign.'

There was a silence, broken by the secretary's voice on the intercom. 'A telex has just come through,' she said.

'Wait,' said DuCane. 'Later.'

'I think you'll want to see it,' said the secretary.

'Okay,' said DuCane, irritably. 'Bring it in.'

The secretary came in with a slip of paper. DuCane took it and read it. Schacker rose and said, 'Since our discussion is over –'

'You might be interested in this,' interrupted DuCane. 'Yeah?'

'Yeah,' said DuCane. He was smiling now, holding the flimsy in front of Hyatt's face. 'Don't you think so, Jasper?'

'I do,' said Hyatt. He rost stiffly from his chair. 'Mr Schacker, my felicitaions on a good race. This is from the committee. The French take a six-hour time penalty; we have won. And I cannot accept your resignation.'

Art stared at him, taking in the turtle-like striations of the old neck, the watery blue eyes glittering with excitement. 'Great,' he said. 'I'll withdraw it, on condition you take no action against Choudry and Hart. And another thing. Martin Hyatt and Simon Lowell are disruptive. They go.'

'Now wait a minute,' said DuCane. 'Martin Hyatt is a fine young man.'

'And my grandson, damn it,' said Hyatt. His eyes were narrow, angry slits.

'If I might . . .' said DuCane. He looked like a small Roman emperor on a coin. 'Sure, we can solve the discipline problem. You're the captain, and I think it's fair you should deal with Choudry and Hart as you see fit.' His voice was quiet and sensible, so reasonable that Art found himself nodding. Wait a minute, he said to himself; you're being hypnotized. DuCane went on. 'Lowell may be a problem,' he said. 'Disruptive. If you feel he's out of place on board . . . well, you're the man out there. But both of us think it would be a mistake to be hasty in the case of Martin Hyatt. He's young, remember. Headstrong, maybe. I suggest that his grandfather have a word with him, and that you give him another chance. Call up a reserve, but keep Martin on. We'll review the situation in Sydney.'

'Wait a minute,' said Art. There were currents in the room he could not identify, and DuCane's voice was hideously persuasive. 'I'm not about to make any deals here –'

'Nobody's asking you to,' said DuCane, smoothly. 'Martin Hyatt will be disciplined.'

'I said my conditions were that Hart and Choudry stay, Hyatt and Lowell go.' Schacker picked up his briefcase. His teak-coloured face was entirely expressionless. 'You can get in touch with me at my apartment.' He turned and left the room.

Outside, the secretary was sitting at a desk. She smiled at Schacker and said 'Congratulations,' and handed him a note.

It was from Choudry.

> *Thank you for trying*, it read. *I can't take any more of this country. I've left, and I'm not coming back.*
> *Mustapha*

'Give me that phone,' said Schacker, and dialled the number of Choudry's host.

The voice on the other end was a woman's thickly accented and somewhat muffled. 'Mr Choudry? He's gone. Twenty minutes ago. He told the maid he was going to the airport. He'll be there by now.' She sniffed. 'He left so quickly he didn't even say thank you. Still, I suppose one has to make allowances for . . . them.'

Schacker put the telephone down, and dialled the airport. He tracked Choudry to the boarding gate of a flight to New York, and asked the ground hostess to call him to the telephone. There was a pause.

'I'm afraid Mr Choudry won't speak with anyone,' said the hostess. 'Now if you'll excuse me, we're boarding.'

The line went dead. Schacker slammed back the receiver and sat down with his square brown hands on his knees and stared at the carpet. 'Oh, Christ,' he said. He heard the outer door open.

'Art?' said a familiar voice. 'Surprise.' He looked up. It was a woman, dark-haired and slight, wearing a bright red linen dress, with a flight bag over one shoulder and a heavy padded coat over the other. The kind of coat you might wear in Marblehead in late October, if you were on your way to the airport.

Art stood up and opened his arms. 'Anne-Marie,' he said. The woman ran into them. 'Honey.' He hung on to her for a long time. Then he said, 'Thank God you came. Leave that stuff here and let's go and get us a drink right now.'

The secretary said, 'He won the leg, did you hear?'

'Oh, *Art*,' said Anne-Marie, her eyes dazzled with joy.

Later, in the darkened bar of a small restaurant, Anne-Marie told him the news. His initial euphoria had worn off, and he couldn't help feeling oddly disconnected as he listened to her. She was glowing, and the news from home bubbled out of her like clear water from a spring; the children, the business, her painting; everything was just perfect. And it was perfect because for the first time in years, the threat of bankruptcy had been lifted, and the sun was shining. And all this was due to Wallace DuCane, who had re-hired and rationalized and re-financed at giveway rates . . .

Art sipped his beer, and felt the chill of it spread through his veins. In his mind's eye, he looked at the lobster boats moored at the quay. He could see his children playing in the garden, the house standing as it had always stood, full of Schackers. And he looked at Anne-Marie, her deep, dark painter's eyes for once unshadowed by worry. And he knew what he had to do. He took her hand across the table and held it for a moment. 'Honey,

I've got a little meeting. It won't take long.'

'Sure,' said Anne-Marie and smiled at him.

He went out into the blinding sunlight of the busy street and walked back to the office. DuCane and Hyatt were still there. DuCane looked up as he walked into the room. He didn't look surprised to see him. Hyatt sat stiffly at his desk and waited for him to speak. 'Lowell goes. Hyatt stays. Choudry's gone. Hart stays. We review in Sydney. I withdraw my resignation. Right?'

DuCane beamed. '*Right*,' he said. 'I knew we'd sort things out.'

'Sure,' said Jasper Hyatt. 'Sure.'

'Bastard', said Harry Redd.

'What do you mean, bastard?' said Tubes Murphy.

'I mean bastard, you bastard,' said Redd. He was bullet-headed as ever, wearing one of his perpetual tan linen suits. His hands were curled like a wrestler's on the white damask tablecloth. 'You've damn near fixed me,' he said.

'Ah,' said Murphy, with scorn. 'Take more than me to fix you.'

'Not when you tell the whole bloody board that I fiddled

the money to buy you a new boat,' said Redd. He drank deeply of his glass of Perrier, and mopped the sweat from his close-cropped temples.

'Sorry, mate,' said Tubes. He drank the beer in front of him, then called for another. 'You got a problem?'

Redd said, 'Climatic change. I'm hanging in there and there's a bloody ice age on. It used to be you could keep moving fast and stay a couple of jumps ahead, but now it's all shared responsibility and full disclosure and it's bloody difficult to turn a crooked note, let me tell you, mate. Anyway, enough about that. How's the bloody race?'

'I'm starving,' said Tubes. 'Let's order. Steak and red wine, eh?'

'Fair enough,' said Redd. 'I suppose we're celebrating.'

'Too right,' said Tubes. 'Okay. The race. We came third, mostly becaue the bloody desalinator broke down and we were getting, well, pretty dry. But Schacker's good and Jarré's got a tough bunch of bastards and a lot of support back home. Never fear, though. We'll beat 'em down there in the big breezes.' He paused, and poured most of a bottle of red wine into his enormous glass. 'Reddy,' he said. 'Drink up. You're looking pale.'

Redd looked doubtful. Then he said, 'Sod it,' and filled his glass. 'How about us winning on corrected time?'

Tubes said, 'Well, you know how it is. We've got problems. *EPK Electric*'s due in this evening, and she'll save her time.'

'Yeah,' said Redd.

The food arrived. Redd watched in fascination as Murphy demolished his steak and a vast pile of fresh vegetables. Another bottle of wine came, and another. The wine waiter was black, and wore white gloves. Around them, prosperous-looking white men and their wives and secretaries talked in low, comfortable tones. As they ate, Redd cross-examined Murphy about schedules: sail repairs, a new desalinator, the hundreds of minute details that made the difference between a seriously organized race campaign and a joy-ride. The first course was cleared away. There was a long pause, while they drank and talked and finished the administrative details. Finally, Redd said, 'Okay. Want some dessert?'

The waiter, who had been hovering, came up and whispered in Redd's ear. His small face stilled, then creased into a monkey-like grin. 'Chef's made you a special afters,' he said. 'In honour of our being Australian sailors.'

Tubes was deeply moved. He stood up, his red head seeming to brush the ceiling, and bowed deeply. 'Too kind,' he said. 'Let's have a bottle of brandy, and give the chef a good belt out of it.'

The waiter's white teeth showed a little nervously in his black face as he turned away. A silence passed over the restaurant; then the low buzz of talk resumed.

'Listen, mate,' said Redd, leaning over the table. His eyes had a slightly boiled look, but Murphy did not notice, because he was not much better himself. 'One last thing. Shar Stapleton. Tubes, you gotta lay off that woman.'

'Oh yeah?' said Tubes, 'I don't think so.' A sober man, watching the narrowing of his eyes, would have changed the subject. But Harry Redd was not sober.

'Oh yeah?' said Harry Redd. 'Well, Mo Stapleton has his suspicions about what she was up to when she said she was on that sheep farm. So old Mo is not greatly in favour of you at the moment. Which is part of what's making my life difficult with the board just now.'

'Issat right?' said Tubes. 'Well, you can go and tell Mo to take a long walk off a short pier.'

'Get a grip, Tubes,' said Redd. 'Be reasonable.'

'No,' said Tubes. Redd looked at his enormous face and eagle nose and narrowed eyes, and realized that he was extremely drunk, drunk as he got about once a year, usually with fatal results to the interior decoration of his immediate surroundings. Tubes banged his fist down on the table. 'Reddy, you and me came up from the Burma Road. Don't you tell me to lay off any sheila because it's losing you money.'

A trolley came up alongside the table, propelled by a chef in white apron and toque. On its top shelf was an enormous dome of whipped cream, on which cunning hands had emblazoned in cherries, chocolate and kiwi fruit the Tasmanian tiger. 'Look,' said Redd. 'Isn't that beautiful?'

But Tubes was still stuck on Mo Stapleton, and the injustice of it all. 'True love,' he said, ignoring the chef, who was clearing his throat expectantly. 'True love, and my oldest mate stands in the way. There's no justice.' The chef coughed again. Tubes turned to look at him. 'Frog in yer throat, mate? Oh. *Really* beautiful. Much too good to eat.' He stood up and examined it. '*Much* too good,' he said.

Only Redd, who knew him very well, caught the inflection in the last sentence. And even Redd did not get its sense for a moment, but sat there, grinning.

'My oldest mate,' muttered Tubes. Then, confidentially

to the chef, 'I think I'll give him the lot.' Picking up the Pavlova from the trolley, he inverted it like a giant custard pie on Harry Redd's small, gleaming head.

Redd sat for a moment perfectly still. Then he leaped to his feet, clawed the cream from his eyes, and flung it at Murphy. But the cream was interfering with his vision, and he missed. Behind Murphy, a woman wearing an off-the-shoulder Balenciaga screamed as white goo enveloped her neck. Murphy looked round, and started to laugh hysterically. Redd said, politely, 'Sorry, madam.' Across the tables, the manager began bustling towards them. Redd, looking as if sea birds had been perching on him for hundreds of years, sized up his options. There was only one thing to do, and he did it. Lowering his head, he butted Murphy in the stomach. The big man went back into the dessert trolley, and lay there. Redd picked up a mango flan and dropped it gently on his face. Then he turned to face the manager. 'Ah,' he said. 'A little local diffculty. Garçon, the check. Chef, that was one of the best Pavlovas I have ever consumed. Would someone help my friend out to his car, if you please?'

Tubes clambered to his feet. Glass from the trolley had nicked his cheek, and the blood running down his face mixed festively with the cream and kiwi fruit. The two men shook hands. Then, bowing to left and right, they made their exit from the restaurant and stood, arms round each other's shoulders, on the steps.

Somewhere out in the darknes, a flashbulb popped.

A week later, Harry Redd was twelve miles southeast of Jerez de la Frontera, on one of the dun-coloured *fincas* that surround the village of Quintillo de Rojas. All morning, he had paced the *bodega*, his Gucci shoes echoing between the rows of the wooden barrels, rank on rank, stacked five high in cool caverns under the hot earth of Andalusia. Now he was discussing the final terms with the Duque de la Vega. The vines of de la Vega greened Andalusia's chalky hills by the square kilometre, and the sherries they produced were as august as the Duque himself.

Harry Redd had been in negotiation for the de la Vega empire for two years. It had been a business slow as a Holy Week procession: breaking down the reserve that shrouded the de la Vegas like the concentric walls of a convent, using the wiles of a courtier on the one hand, while holding out an adventurer's promise of new worlds with the other. Harry Redd had staked his poker-player's reputation on it.

The final moment was at hand. The Duque's long, paper-white fingers had removed the gold cap from his gold Mont Blanc fountain pen. The company secretary had passed the transfer papers into the strip of light that fell from the Gothic windows of the study on to the blackened oak writing-table.

The door opened. Nobody turned his head. A woman came to the Duque's side. He looked up, and said, 'Teresa, my dear.'

The woman was about fifty, beautifully dressed in boots and a dove-grey riding habit, with a face as thin and ascetic as her husband's. Slung on her back was a flat-topped Andalusian horseman's hat. In one hand was a riding-switch, in the other a copy of *Paris-Match*.

'*Mira,*' she said, and thrust it under her husband's aquiline nose.

The Duque looked. Then he raised his eyes, sad and remote and hardly visible under the long, papery lids, and pushed the magazine across the table with tips of his fingers as if it was something dirty he could scarcely bring himself to touch.

Redd looked. It was a black and white picture, half a page. Himself and Murphy, leaning up against each other, covered in cream and jam. A bottle dangled from Murphy's hand, the label towards the camera. The caption read: LE MILLIONNAIRE ET LE PIRATE PRENNENT LE DESSERT.

The Duque shrugged his shoulders in their Savile Row worsted. He capped his pen and replaced it in his pocket. Then he pushed the papers, unsigned, back to the lawyer, rose and left the room. The lawyer also shrugged. 'It looks as if there will be no deal,' he said.

'Another day, maybe,' said Harry Redd.

Later, as the helicopter's shadow flicked across the black fighting bulls grazing on the marshes of the Guadalquivir delta, he turned to Mo Stapleton. 'Mo,' he said. 'Let's get a print of that photo from the bloke who did it.'

'Will you sue?' said Stapleton. His face was white and still and full of hollows above his white collar and dark-blue tie.

'Nah,' said Redd. 'But you'll notice that Murphy's showing the label on that brandy bottle very nicely, and it's one of our brands. I reckon that picture's worth a million dollars to us.'

Stapleton stared with his blank, dark eyes. 'The de la Vega estates were worth twenty-five million to us,' he said.

Redd laughed, his small face creasing in his monkey grin. 'Bird in the hand's worth two in the bush, sport.'

'Let's hope the board sees it like that,' said Stapleton, and folded his hands on his black briefcase.

Sparko stuck his head down the hatch and shouted. 'Telephone, Skip!'

Murphy wiped the oil from his hands on to a filthy rag, and picked his way across the litter of timber and wire and toolboxes to the companionway. 'Harry Redd,' said Sparko.

Murphy pulled the aerial all the way out.

'Are you private?' said Redd.

Murphy looked around. Forward, two men were touching up the aircraft identification number on the deck. Forty people were watching from the quay. From the edge of a diesel slick a couple of harbour seals eyed him suspiciously. 'More or less,' he said.

'Then listen. You might like to know that I've got a few worries, which means you have, too. The banks did an audit, and I had to start building that distillery. You saw the picture. Well, so did they, and they weren't too amused. Specially Mo Stapleton, because he's been putting the private dicks on his missus and he is getting a lot of answers with your name in them.'

'Is that all?' said Murphy.

'No,' said Redd. 'They got so pissed off at us that I've had to file assault charges against you.'

'You *what*?'

'Ah, jeez, I'll pay for the lawyers. It's just to look good. But there's something else.'

'I'm still listening.'

'Mo's been at work on some of my shareholders. He reckons that *Tasman*'s no good for the corporate identity, that you're a load of galahs who cost money and lose races. Now it is my heart's desire that you lot get around the world, and that you do it faster than any other bloke. But if you don't show a result next leg, we're in trouble.'

'What kind of trouble?'

'Empty pockets trouble.'

'Great,' said Tubes. 'Win or bust, eh?'

'Literally,' said Redd. 'So long, sport.'

The line went dead. Murphy stared at the receiver a moment. It looked the size of a matchbox in his enormous hand. Then he flung it as far as he could into the harbour and went below.

A harbour seal sniffed the strange plastic box as it sank, bubbling, through the dirty water. Then it turned and swam away from the clatter of the shore where the high-masted sailing boats rocked at their jetties. There was too much noise and fuss for its liking. It preferred the clear, cool waters of the ocean.

The invitation was a gilt-edged card. The copper-plate had said that the directors of EPK Electric invited Harriet Agnew to a *braaivleis* in the Drakensberg to celebrate the victory on handicap of the yacht of the same name in the Lancaster Great Circle. Harriet, arriving in a taxi and walking towards the floodlit trees round the pool, observed that it was Jack Asprey who was doing the meeting and greeting. It was the Jack Asprey Harriet had known in London: immaculately dressed in Royal Yacht Squadron blazer and white flannels, his hair brilliantined in waves back from his narrow forehead, his elegant but manly hand lightly clasping the upper arm of a pretty woman as he whispered a confidence, or throwing his head back in frank male laughter at a joke made by a solid Boer.

Harriet felt a stab of dislike. But then she told herself to take it easy. Jack Asprey was only doing what the chairman's godson had to do. Besides, the *braaivleis* was good.

It was good because the steaks were thick and tender and juicy and perfumed with woodsmoke. It was good because the wine was the legendary and virtually unobtainable Rozendal Farm '83. It was good because in the firelight the lines round Emily de Havilland's eyes were smoothed away with the satisfaction of winning and the glow of wine. But there was another, more important reason.

248

Harriet had spent the last days of the leg in what she had to describe as a complete tizz. Nobody had noticed; all EPK's crew had been excited as it became more and more obvious that they were going to win on handicap. As soon as was decent after they had docked, she had gone to look for Henri de Rochambaud. But he had been outside Cape Town, staying with friends. She had got their number, but she had found herself trembling in front of the telephone, unable to make herself call him. After all, they had met for a total of three hours six weeks ago. A lot could change in that time. She had not rung. And Emily, with whom she was having lunch, had looked at her with her clear hazel eyes and said, 'Something's wrong.'

'No,' said Harriet.

'Look,' said Emily. 'My husband's disappeared. But even I'm feeling good, because we won. So why aren't you?'

Harriet had taken a forkful of avocado salad – she had eaten three salads at every meal, since coming ashore. She had told nobody about de Rochambaud. Perhaps there was nothing to tell. It had been easy to keep quiet in the strange world of watchkeeping, where the interruption of sleep blurred the distinction between dream and reality. But now she had to tell somebody. So she told Emily.

Emily had said almost off-handedly, 'Why don't you invite him to this party? Have some more shrimps.' She had been quite surprised when Harriet had hugged her and ordered champagne.

The reason the *braaivleis* was good was because Henri de Rochambaud was there, and soon she was dancing with him, slowly, on the floor by the swimming-pool, while the

Zulu band played a long, winding tune and the moon hung in a net of stars slung between the mountains. She could feel him breathe in her ear, the firm grip of his arm at her waist, the slight scratch of his moustache on her cheek. When the tune had finished, they walked to a table in a sort of arbour, honey-scented with a tree heath that grew beside it, ghostly in the moonlight. Someone from *Chinamite* had fallen fully clothed into the pool, and was swimming. Some Australians were baying at the moon in four-part harmony. Harriet sat in a bubble of joy, her feet scarcely seeming to touch the ground.

Come *on*, part of her said. This is standard boat-deck stuff: a lunar aberration of the libido. Six months ago, she would have believed this part of herself, and got up and walked away, proud of her control. That was what you did as head of the legal department at EPK Electric, allowing yourself an Americano at lunchtime on Friday, on condition that you worked all night when you got home. She saw Jack Asprey, an impeccable marionette, bobbing and grinning to a rhino-necked Boer on the verandah.

'Harriet,' said de Rochambaud. 'We must go on a journey.'

'A journey?' she said.

'I want to take you to Botswana,' he said. 'I have a cousin, a poor man with a nice wife. He lives in the desert. It is a good place.'

'Of course,' she said. His face was in shadow except for two little orange glints the cooking-fire made in his eyes. The scent of the tree heath was heavy. She wanted to kiss him. No, she thought; I'll wait until he kisses me.

But he did not.

That night he drove her down from the mountains to the apartment EPK had rented for her. Outside the door, he kissed her three times, once on each cheek, and once again. Then he said, '*A demain*.'

She turned as she went in, aching to ask him across the threshold. He stood there with his hands in his pockets, his eyes grave above the great moustache. Harriet's knees were weak, and she could not catch her breath. She opened her mouth to ask him in, but instead she said, 'Goodnight, Henri. And thank you.'

He bowed. She was seeing him with almost microscopic clarity; the skin around his eyes tightened faintly with amusement. She thought it was the most beautiful thing she had ever seen. 'I will come at nine thirty tomorrow,' said Henri. He turned, and went down the stairs.

Harriet shut the door.

All night, Henri's face hung before her eyes. She hardly slept a wink.

The Kalahari stretched on all sides to the horizon: yellow dust, broken here and there by patches of scrub on which grazed humped cattle with pelvises like coat-hangers. De Rochambaud drove the rented Land Rover fast, and with precision. But the road was a corduroy of ridge and pot-hole, and the dust rose behind in a long brown plume. Harriet had subsided into a sort of coma, gritty with dust, battered and exhausted by the South African Airways flight to Gaborone, and the buffeting of the Piper Cub that had brought them to the Land Rover.

'Here!' shouted de Rochambaud above the roar of the engine.

They had breasted a ridge. Below, a valley lay spread; a sinuous line of boulders and gravel that must be a water-course, and beside it, perched on an outcrop of yellow rock and shaded by a grove of apparently dead trees, a wooden bungalow surrounded by a thatched verandah. The bungalow was the same colour as the sand and the rock; except for the piercing blue of the sky, it looked like a painting roughed out in ochre and abandoned by the artist.

De Rochambaud's cousin Jack Schneider was a doctor turned farmer turned doctor again. He was a tall, dried-up man with a professional stoop and kind blue eyes. His wife Edie was small, plump and untidy, dressed in a dashiki of native cotton and exuding energy like a dynamo. Both of them welcomed de Rochambaud in voluble French, and then switched without effort into English, for Harriet's sake. Jack immediately took de Rochambaud off in a Land Rover, to accompany him on his rounds. Edie said, 'I'm so glad Henri has brought you. He talked about you very much, on the radio telephone.'

Harriet flushed with pleasure. 'Really?'

'Come on,' said Edie. 'Let's have a drink, and then you can have a bath. Oh, Henri, yes, it's about time he met someone special.' Edie looked hard into Harriet's eyes. Her own eyes were grey, gentle but shrewd. 'I think you just might do.' She laughed, managing to give the impression that she found herself ridiculous and Harriet adorable. They drank gin and tonic, and sat in the shade of the verandah, looking at the low, yellow hills. 'It is the most beautiful place in the world,' said Edie.

Harriet agreed, insincerely. She thought it hot and

unpleasant and dusty. Edie spoke of the bushmen, one of the oldest peoples in the world. Many of Jack's patients were bushmen – Asian-looking, copper-skinned, nomads of the dry places who could smell water at a depth of ten feet. After a couple of hours, the men came back. There was something different about Jack Schneider, a repressed excitement. 'We met that party of bushmen,' he said. 'They said it will rain.'

Harriet went and bathed in strongly mineralized water from the ranch's artesian well. The ceiling of the bathroom was of stretched canvas. She lay and watched the little dents the mice made as they ran across it, and thought about Edie's warning to check her clothes and shoes for snakes and scorpions.

Her room was simple, with plank walls and a high, cool ceiling of thatch. She sat on the bed and dried herself carefully. Then she dressed; indigo Chinese silk pyjamas with a heavy gold chain for her neck. The gold gleamed dully againt the smooth tan of her skin. She felt almost shy of herself; the desert seemed to strip away illusions, and she was suddenly a lawyer half-way round the world from home, doing something foolish in a hot, smelly place; and perhaps about to do something more foolish still. Resolutely, she pushed the thoughts away. She dabbed a little sandalwood oil in the hollow of her throat, and went out on to the verandah.

There was nobody there. She wandered into the big living-room, where pot-bellied French provincial furniture sat oddly alongside a big freestone fireplace and deep modern sofas, their feet in little bowls of water to keep the ants away. The air was thick and heavy, and weighted down on the scrubby hills. Somewhere behind the house, a woman was singing in a strange, high voice. The song rose into the silence like the smoke of a single fire in a deserted landscape.

Jack came on to the verandah. 'You can feel the rain,' he said. 'Look.' He pointed to the south, where the sky had a muddy, yellowish tinge. 'She'll come,' he said. 'Champagne's on ice. I'll get it.'

'How often does it rain?' said Harriet, when he returned.

'Oh, we're pretty lucky here,' he said, filling her glass. 'More often than further east. About once every five years, maybe.'

And Harriet laughed. The laughter broke the mood, and she knew what she was doing: being alive, for the first time in years.

They ate on the verandah, some sort of buck, with vegetables from the laboriously tended garden behind the bungalow, and an excellent claret; Jack seemed to have a share in a vineyard in France. Thunder muttered on the horizon. 'Come *on*, Jack,' said Edie. 'Make it happen. More champagne.'

'I suppose,' he said. He went to get another bottle of Bollinger. This time the pop of the cork found an echo high above as the sky was suddenly split from end to end by a blue blade of lightning, and the clap of thunder that followed shivered the floor.

They sat and watched the forks of lightning striding across the hills. De Rochambaud's hand sought Harriet's under the table. She looked towards him. His lips said, 'To bed,' but the thunder was too loud for her to hear the words. She did not remember saying goodnight to the Schneiders. All she remembered was being in de Rochambaud's room, and the feel of her silk shirt as it slid down her arms and to the floor, and of de Rochambaud's fingers as they unfastened the last button; and then being naked, skin to skin, the hard muscles of his body, the kiss of sheets against her back. And laughing, opening up to receive him; and her own body moving wild as the lightning that flashed in the sweat on his shoulders, powerful as the rain slamming into the soft dust of the desert outside.

Much later, they lay drowsing, entangled. A new roaring came; the floor was shaking.

'The river,' whispered de Rochambaud. 'The river is running.'

Next morning, when she awoke, the sun was pouring in at the window. Where there had been a dry gully, a brown river roared. And the low yellow hills beyond had turned a young green.

Nicholas Eason's arm hurt. So did his pride. They both hurt for the same reason, which was that he had been Indian wrestling with Bennett, and he had lost. But it was hard to stay hurt for long on an evening when the wind was cool from the southwest, and the ripples glittered red under the sun setting across the yacht basin.

'You're buying,' said Bennett. There was a row of seven empty lager glasses in front of her, and a similar row in front of Eason. They had been sitting in the Race Club for two hours now, talking. Eason was fascinated by Bennett, who had spent her life within arm's reach of a boat. And Bennett seemed fascinated by Eason, rather as a professional fisherman might have been fascinated by a parrotfish which swam into his net instead of a cod.

'So tell me about this school of your yours,' said Bennett. 'They dressed you up in clawhammer coats and stiff collars and they locked you up in a middle-ages-type dungeon, right. What did you do for parties?'

'Parties,' said Eason, musing. 'Well, we didn't really have parties. Except when we were older, in the Library, prefects, you know, we used to have our own room and sing along to, well, Supremes records and stuff.'

'*Supremes* records?' said Bennett. '*Weird*.'

A man in a dirty blue boiler suit had come in at the door. It was Ed Cole: he had scarcely been off the boat the ten days since *Chinamite* had touched the Cape Town dock. Nor, for that matter, had Nick Eason, except to go to a few parties, where he had disgraced himself by making political remarks. Nick Eason was finding South Africa hard to take.

Eason called his name. Cole looked round quickly, with his old wariness. When he saw who was calling, he came over. 'Have a beer,' said Eason.

'Yes, please,' said Cole. His sandy hair was matted with

grease. 'Been repacking the rudder gland,' he said. 'Messy job. Thirsty, too.'

Eason grinned at him. He had discovered that as long as he stuck to boat subjects, Cole and he got on. Anything else, and he clammed up tight. 'And this is Bennett,' he said.

'Hello, Bennett,' said Cole. 'My hand's too dirty to shake.' He gulped thirstily at his beer. Then his eyes narrowed. 'I've met someone who looked incredibly like you,' he said. 'Where?'

Bennett grinned, her blue eyes lazy, her teeth white and even in her wide red mouth. 'I couldn't say,' she purred. 'Well, I have to go. You want to go out tonight, Nick?'

'Yes.'

'See you in a couple of hours?'

'Right,' said Eason.

They watched her as she walked away with her long, swinging stride.

'Pretty girl,' said Cole.

'Who was it that looked incredibly like her?' said Eason.

The eyes Cole turned to him were hooded, as they always were when Eason spoke of the past. 'God knows,' he said. 'Got a terrible memory for faces. You want another beer?' And from then on, they talked of the perpetually fascinating details of the boat.

But Eason's mind was not altogether on the conversation. It wasn't like Bennett to leave a beer unfinished. Could it be that Cole was not the only one reluctant to talk about the past?

Later that evening, they were in a cellar on Constitution Street, drinking more beer and listening to a black man and a white man playing an arrangement of Charlie Byrd's 'Foggy

Day in London Town' for two guitars. The audience was mixed, about a quarter white, the rest black and coloured, and Eason felt easy as he seldom did in this country. Their host, a journalist Eason knew who had been freelance since his sacking from the Rand *Daily Mail*, was off at another table, talking shop. Eason said, 'So what's all this about Cole thinking you look like somebody?'

'Who knows?' said Bennett. Her face was almost touching his. He could see her tongue, held lightly between her teeth. He could smell the smell of her, light and lemony; verbena, perhaps. She took his face between her hands, no longer hands that could crack nuts, but smooth fingered, sensuous. 'Nicky,' she said. 'Too much talk and not enough action. Your place or mine?'

'What for?' said Eason.

'Catch up on some partying you missed out on when you were singing along to Supremes records,' said Bennett. 'My place. C'mon.'

They started in the back of the taxi, and left a trail of clothes up the stairs to Bennett's hotel room. It was not until ten o'clock the following morning, when he woke up in the wrecked bed, that Eason thought again: last night was useful timing for someone who didn't want to talk about the past. But Bennett turned over, and he saw her blue eyes dangerous under thick lashes. 'Come here,' she said, and pulled him down with her strong, strong arms. And he felt the softness of her breasts and her thighs, steel and velvet on each of his hip bones, and he forgot about Cole's lapse of memory.

For the time being.

*

'Watch him,' muttered Chuck the cameraman to Herb the sound man. 'Here he goes.'

They were sitting in black leather swivel chairs in a viewing room at the South African Television Corporation. The lights were going up, and Dave Kelly's famous features were emerging from the darkness on the far side of the coffee table. It was noticeable that the features had lost their hollowness. Under the influence of a couple of weeks ashore, they were once more tanned and delicate, the broad forehead balanced by the large, sympathetic eyes and the chiselled jaw.

Beside Kelly in another black swivel chair sat Eli Chance, Omar Wohl's personal assistant. He was roundish and baldish, and his pudgy hands clasped a briefcase while his gleaming dome wagged from side to side. 'Brilliant,' he said. 'Brilliant, Dave.'

Kelly sat back, sipped his brandy and said, 'I thought you'd like it, Eli.'

Chance said, 'Of course, we never expected anything else. You're a genius, Dave.'

Chuck the camerman caught the eye of Herb the sound man and moved his head in the direction of outdoors. 'Yeah,' said Chuck. 'Great, Dave.' He knew there was no object in pointing out that most of the film had been made by him and Herb, while Kelly sulked in whatever corner he could find. 'I guess we'll go get some lunch.'

'Sure,' said Kelly. 'See you tomorrow. We'll begin on the run-up to the re-start.' He laughed, showing the famous Kelly teeth. 'Have a good time while you can, right, guys?'

'Sure, Dave,' said Eli, shaking his shiny dome as if

awestruck. 'I have to tell you that Stateside, this will attract a lot of attention.' He looked shy for a moment. 'Maybe things weren't so good for a while there . . . But, well, Kelly's back. Provided you finish the race and turn in the movie, of course.' He chuckled, as if the idea of such a thing not happening was too ridiculous to entertain.

'Of course,' said Kelly, easily. 'You know, Eli, this is some assignment. The men from the boys, and all that.'

'Bullshit,' muttered Herb under his breath. He had worked with Kelly for fifteen years, and it never ceased to amaze him that Kelly believed the stories he told. Particularly the ones about himself.

Kelly had lunch with Eli Chance at the Kruger Hotel. Half-way through the Rioja, his bleeper went, and he had a telephone brought to the table.

It was Joppie Lawson, proprietor of the boatyard where *Kelly's Eye* was awaiting survey and repairs. He sounded agitated. 'Mr Kelly,' he said. 'Could you get down here right after lunch?'

'Sure,' said Kelly, mellow with wine. 'I'll bring the crew, we'll do a little shooting.'

'I wouldn't if I were you,' said Lawson. There was something in his voice that made Kelly's heart beat unpleasantly fast. He put the telephone down.

'Everything okay?' said Chance.

'Sure, sure,' said Kelly abstractedly. He finished lunch as quickly as was decent, and had his chauffeur-driven Mercedes take him down to the yard.

The sun was beating down on the boats moored in the basin, and a cool breeze from the sea set the halyards pinging against the metal masts. Lawson, a short, florid man in khaki shorts and a Lacoste shirt, shook his hand, unsmiling.

'Problems?' said Kelly, smoothly. 'I'm not a great authority on boats.'

'You're the owner,' said Lawson, and the way he said it chilled Kelly's stomach. 'Come here.'

Kelly's Eye was propped on enormous baulks of timber. She towered into the sky; Kelly remembered how small and frail she had seemed at sea, and was amazed by the colossal bulk of her now. Lawson ran up the scaffolding and went along the deck from the cockpit. She was silent and still, like the skeleton of a dead animal.

'Why aren't you working on her?' said Kelly.

Instead of replying, Lawson handed him a sheet of brown cardboard-like material, about the thickness of a paperback book. Its surfaces, the covers of the book, were hard and shiny. The middle, the pages of the book, was a foam. 'Know what that is?' said Lawson.

'Tell me,' said Kelly.

'That's part of your boat's hull,' said Lawson. 'Look at this.' He put his thumbnail under one of the shiny surfaces and pulled upwards. The shiny part came away from the foam part. 'Just like taking an egg sandwich to bits,' said Lawson.

Kelly was looking at him hard, his face completely still. 'What does that mean?'

'It means that you've got a composite hull that's gone unstable. It means that if you come off the side of a wave down there in the South Atlantic and you get a sudden impact loading, the whole bloody boat's going to come apart.'

Kelly looked at the piece of brown composite in the man's hard, square fingers, then at his face, 'So?' he said.

'So the surveyor's report is going to say she's not fit to race,' said Lawson.

A muscle under Kelly's eye twitched fiercely. 'When's the survey?' he said.

'I submit my report day after tomorrow,' said Lawson.

'Oh,' said Kelly. 'Pity.'

Lawson shrugged.

Later that afternoon, Kelly contacted a researcher whose name he had got from a member of the Stock Exchange at Johannesburg. He talked to him for some time. The following day at noon, a sheaf of typescript landed on his desk at the hotel where he had a suite. The papers rattled in Kelly's hand as he read them. When he had finished, he smiled, drank a glass of brandy and went to the Transvaal Bank, from which he emerged three-quarters of an hour later with a briefcase that seemed heavy. The manager offered him a bodyguard. Kelly smiled and shook his head. The manager thought he looked ill; his eyes were surrounded by dark shadows and his face was pinched. Funny how different people are when you see them in the flesh, thought the manager, as the stretched Mercedes disappeared in the direction of Lawson Boats, yacht-builders and repairers.

Lawson was in the office when Kelly arrived. He was wearing long trousers and a tie and white jacket that emphasized the bloodshot tan of his face. He stood up when Kelly came in, and put out his hand. He had blue eyes, rather popped. Today they looked good-natured, but worried.

'So,' said Kelly, when the secretary had brought coffee. 'What's in the report?'

Lawson put his thick hands on the vinyl-covered desk. 'I've had to recommend that your boat withdraw from the race.' He patted a slim pile of handwritten notes in front of him. 'It'll be typed up tonight. I'm sorry, Mr Kelly.'

'Me, too,' said Kelly. 'I hate to see a good man go down.'

'Go where?' said Lawson, frowning.

Kelly reached into his breast pocket and brought out the researcher's report. His hands were trembling again. 'Things aren't looking so good, are they, Mr Lawson? I hear that you've been losing some international contracts, eh? And the domestic market's kind of depressed. And you're pretty heavily borrowed. In fact you're technically bankrupt.' He tossed his papers in front of Lawson. 'Chapter and verse, right here.' Lawson started to say something, then read.

When he had finished, he shrugged. 'Times are hard,' he said. 'For everybody.'

'Yup,' said Kelly. 'True. But not everybody has a way out, huh?'

'A way out?' The bulging blue eyes were puzzled. Looking at them from the standpoint of years of experience, Kelly knew what he was about to do would work.

'A bolt-hole,' said Kelly. 'A nest egg. A little pot of gold.' He reached down, put his black briefcase on the desk, and opened it. 'It's worth a lot to me, to carry on in this race. I'd like you to tear up your report to the surveyor and effect any repairs you deem necessary.'

'Tear up my report?' said Lawson. 'But –' His eyes had been on the contents of the briefcase for perhaps thirty seconds. Now he registered what it contained. The colour faded from his cheeks, leaving them the greyish white of unbleached paper.

'A hundred thousand dollars US,' said Kelly. 'Yours, if you put in a report that says local failures only on the hull, which can be taken care of by repairs.' Lawson's eyes had come back to him. 'Yes,' said Kelly. 'Finishing this race is the one thing I really want to do. Everyone has a dream. I guess you might have a dream about tucking a little away in a Swiss bank. It's not too useful holding rand nowadays, eh? Not a fair reward for a life's work. Much better to have dollars. Those are dollars in that case, Mr Lawson. If you feel bad, ask your wife. She'll tell you. She'll tell you that when old Sambo comes running down that road with a meat cleaver, she wants to be far, far away, and a hundred grand will help. It's not a lot to ask, for a hundred grand. The boat stayed together so far, right? She'll stay together a while further. Go on. Take it. It's yours.'

For a moment they sat there, Kelly pale, eyes glittering, hunched forward in his chair; and Lawson, red and suddenly soft, slumped back with his blue eyes fixed on Kelly's, contemplating his personal apocalypse. Then his hand stretched out and closed the lid of the briefcase. Kelly got up, grinned, and left.

Later that evening, the telephone rang in his hotel. He picked it up with a hand damp and slippery with sweat. It was Bud Withers. 'Hey,' said Bud. 'Thought you'd like to know, the boat got a clear survey. We're in there racing, Dave.'

'Great,' said Kelly. 'That's just great.'

As he put the receiver down, his hand shook so badly it

took him three tries to get it in the cradle.

He sat for a while staring at himself in the mirror. The mirror was a television. Television was the only thing that was real; you had a problem, bail out, on to the next project, leave the researchers to clear up the mess. But this time, he was locked in. Make or break, no bailing out.

The curtains were drawn; the room smelt of flowers and brandy, and there was no air. Outside the sun shone and the traffic boomed, and people went about their lives, not even thinking about their apocalypses. Kelly sat and drank brandy and thought about his. When he had drunk three-quarters of the bottle, he dialled the airport. The film was what they wanted, not him. He had ben overworking, he decided. What he needed was a holiday.

The Norwegian Antarctic survey ship *Bent Larssen* was sailing due south at latitude 67°, across the vast black swells of the Southern Ocean. There was ice in sight; a large berg, bluish white and spiked with pinnacles, to the southeast; and another, of tabular form, surrounded by a cream of breaking water due west. Her captain was by no means worried; the *Bent Larssen* had been designated for work in the ice, and was even now on a supply voyage to a Norwegian research station on the shores of the Ross Sea. Here she would spend the Antarctic summer and the long, dark winter.

The captain's light-blue eyes travelled slowly and methodically across the sea ahead, quartering the waves for bergy-bits, flat shards of ice from the Antarctic floes. Suddenly his eyes stopped, and he reached for the binoculars clipped to the bulkhead.

On the front of a wave was a small cluster of something whitish. Wreckage of some kind. The captain spoke to the helmsman, and then through the intercom to the watch on deck. The *Larssen* slowed, turned head to sea, tiny against the long sweep of the swell. A man with a boathook went down into her waist as the helmsman brought her smoothly alongside the little patch of wreckage. Five minutes later, the wreckage was piled on the deck; a hatch cover, varnished mahogany; the vane of a self-steering gear; and a horseshoe lifebelt of the kind carried on the transoms of yachts.

The captain stepped out of the warm bridge and into the cold wind. The lifebelt's cover was orange. Black letters said *BRAN RCC*.

'Royal Cruising Club,' said the captain. A devout Lutheran, he remained silent for a moment with his head bowed in prayer. Then he went back to the bridge and got on the radio.

The hangovers of coming ashore had disappeared now. The crews had done their travelling; for ten days they had been drifting back into Cape Town. Once again the cardboard boxes had mounded the quays, and the sanders had howled in the yards, and the bogeys had squeaked in the rails as the big boats rolled ponderously back into the water. Now, the stores were all stowed, and the masts were stepped, and the trials had been sailed. They were as good as they were ever going to be. The night before they were to sail, all the crews went to the GCB.

The Great Circle Ball was in a big warehouse on the outskirts of the city. The captains had arranged it between them; Cape Town had had that effect. The overwhelming attentions of the South Africans, the parties, the barbecues, the ever-present policemen, had driven the crews in on each other. They were beginning to be a community of their own.

The warehouse had once been used to store tobacco. Now, it was festooned with bunting and plants and flowers, and someone had got a lot of theatrical flats painted with pillars and arches and Arcadian vistas, and nailed them up against the walls. Lancaster had provided the champagne and two or three bands had appeared from somewhere. By eleven o'clock, the timber floor was shivering under the onslaught of an electric rhythm section and four hundred dancing feet.

Eason was sitting at the *Chinamite* table, surrounded by women. Henry Harper was sitting at the far side. Like all the captains, he had been working hard, and his tough, middle-aged face looked tired and pouchy. He got up, bent over and said in Eason's ear, 'I'm off. Got indigestion. If anybody wants me, I'm on the boat.'

'Fine,' said Eason. He drank another glass of champagne. The girl next to him had beautiful dark eyes and wanted him to go sailing with her next time he was in Cape Town. He agreed, politely, his eyes searching the dancers. Bennett was in there somewhere. Since their night out, she had been avoiding him; not because she didn't like him – actually there had been another night, after a barbecue, but he had had other things on his mind then. It seemed she did not like answering questions, and he couldn't help asking them. So she had suddenly got busy, and he couldn't track her down any more. Which depressed him, because he was beginning to like her quite a lot. And he was also becoming extremely curious as to why Cole thought he recognized her, and whether her reluctance to talk about the past had anything to do with Cole's reluctance to talk about the past.

The sound of male laughter cut across the music. Eason looked across the room. It was coming from the *Associated Meat* table. In the middle of the table, a large man was doing a one-handed handstand. He was wearing a singlet and studded wristbands and the muscles of his arm shone with sweat. The other arm held a bottle of champagne, which he was still drinking.

'Wow,' said Eason's brown-eyed companion. 'That's *fantastic*.'

268

'Totally,' said Eason. He was watching Sir Clement Jones, who was grinning and clapping, his spade beard giving him a devilish, faintly Elizabethan look.

'Come on,' said Eason. 'Let's be a journalist.'

'What?' said the girl.

'Nothing,' said Eason. He shoved his shock of black hair back out of his eyes and said, 'Back in a minute.' Then he went across to the *Associated Meat* table.

The man with the wristbands had come down from the table and was leaning back in his chair, eyes glazed, dangling his champagne bottle by the neck. 'Hello,' said Eason, sitting down next to Jones.

'Hello,' said Jones, without much enthusiasm.

'Nicholas Eason,' said Eason, with all the gung-ho he could muster. 'Off *Chinamite*.'

Jones nodded. The lines of his face were genial, but his eyes were hard and calculating. 'Doing a good job, you lot,' he said. 'Didn't we meet before?'

'Oh,' said Eason. 'Yes. Briefly, at the reception in Portsmouth. Before the race began.'

'Yes,' said Jones. 'I remember now.' There were new lines in his face, unfriendly ones. He looked, thought Eason, like Sir Francis Drake about to hang a mutineer.

'I'm researching the *Arpeggio* incident,' said Eason. This was not going to get anywhere, he realized. But it was his last chance to get across for another six weeks. 'I've been talking to Ed Cole. Do you agree that it's hard to imagine him being negligent?'

'I only know what the Inquiry found,' said Jones, curtly. 'We all slip up, sometimes.'

'Yes,' said Eason. It was, after all, the longest sentence

Jones had ever addressed to him. 'But I keep getting the impression that, well, nobody seems at all anxious to discuss the whole business. I mean, are they trying to hide something, or what?'

'You'd better ask them,' said Jones. 'What did you say you were? A journalist? Or just a bit of a Nosey Parker?'

'Curious,' said Eason. 'That's all.'

'I don't see why I should rake up painful memories to satisfy your curiosity,' said Jones.

Eason was encouraged. 'Because I don't think the truth –'

He was trying to say that he thought the Inquiry had been incomplete. But at that moment he felt hands under his armpits, one on each side. Large, powerful hands that lifted him out of his seat and carried him without apparent effort across the hall. The hands belonged to two of *Associated Meat*'s crew. One of them was the man who had been standing on his hand on the table. There was drink on his breath, and a red glint in his eye.

'Why don't you leave the skipper alone?' said the man in a quiet, reasonable voice. 'He's got a lot on his mind without brown hatters like you creeping round him.'

They went out of the door and on to a sort of gallery that hung twenty feet above a stretch of waste ground. The night air was cool, but Eason was sweating. One of the man said to the other, 'Leave him here, Ernie.'

'Okay,' said Ernie, who was the one with studded wristbands. 'You go back. I'll have a slash.'

The other one went back into the light and the music, laughing. Eason made to go after him.

'Hold on,' said the one called Ernie. His face was very

wide, and his neck was even wider. His hands came up, and grabbed Eason by the shirt front. Eason felt his feet leave the ground. He saw the gallery railing pass his eyes, the moon and the stars spin in the sky. Then he knew what Ernie was going to do, and he tried to shout. But it was already happening, and the fear stopped his voice working.

Ernie Crystal heard the *thump* as the body hit the ground below, dusted his hands and went inside. He fancied a drink.

Ten minutes later, the ambulance sirens sounded.

'TIED UP FILMING MAURITIUSWISE PROCEED WITHOUT SELF GOOD LUCK KELLY. Is that right, Mister Kelly?'

'Sure,' said Kelly, clinging to the edges of the telegraph desk for support, and scowling drunkenly at the telegraph girl. She was worth looking at, like all the women in Mauritius. Nice coffee-coloured skin, nice straight black hair from Indian ancestors, nice body. Kelly wondered vaguely if she would be as good in bed as the one waiting in his cabana in the hotel garden.

She turned to her keyboard, and was tapping out the message, care of the *Kelly's Eye* campaign office in Cape Town. And for a moment, panic drove out the thoughts of women, and Kelly saw clearly what he was doing; sending sixteen men and Bennett to their deaths. He shivered in the air-conditioning of the reception area, then lurched out of the doors. But it made sense, he reasoned through his fog of brandy. Chuck could make the movie. The main thing was for him, Kelly, not to take any chances with himself. Didn't Eli Chance say his public were waiting for him back in the States? If the boat survived, he could deliver the film, which was what mattered. If not . . . well, there would be some publicity mileage in that, too.

Outside, the sun beat down from a dazzling blue sky. It was hot, even where the palms cast their black spiders of shade across the glare of the white sand paths. Kelly went to his cabana. The building seemed suffocating. He said, 'C'mon. We're going to the beach.'

The girl on the bed scissored her long brown legs to the floor. 'Okay,' she said. 'I show you somewhere really pretty.' She smiled, and her eyes were deep and lascivious. 'And real private.'

'Okay, okay,' said Kelly, shoving two bottles of Martell into a Vuitton flight bag. 'Let's go.'

On the beach, he lay in the sand while the girl swam in the pale turquoise water. From time to time he sipped brandy. Back there in Cape Town they were getting up, reading his telex. The bands would be playing down by the harbour, the wind wailing in the rigging, the jokes nervous as the shore lines were cast off and the big yachts moved ponderously into the harbour for the warmup. No. He looked at his gold Rolex. Not yet. Mauritius was three hours ahead of Cape Town. They'd only just have got up, over there. They would be looking greedily at the land, the last time they'd see it for six weeks. His mind slid to that piece of biscuity composite in the hand of Joppie Lawson. Maybe the last time the people on *Kelly's Eye* would ever see it.

He reached for the bottle and took a big, fiery gulp to warm the chill under his breastbone. I ought to be there with them, he thought. Like the time at Khe Sanh, standing up against a backdrop of exploding NVA shells, with Marines yelling at me to get down. Or on the roof of the World Trade Centre, on the ledge, persuading a Polish would-be suicide to come inside. The Pole's breath had smelt of onions, and a cold, sour wind had blown vertically from the abyss. But you could ignore that; you couldn't show it on TV. You couldn't show the death of *Eye* on TV either; not the cold, wet collapse thousands of miles from anywhere. Chuck and Herb would work until they died, sure. But they were technicians. Kelly *understood* TV. He owed it to people who watched TV to stay out of anything that wasn't TV.

Kelly felt a hand on his thigh. He looked down at the girl's long, brown fingers as if they were a noxious insect, and brushed them away. She made a *moue*. *Christ*, thought Kelly, digging his fingers into the sand. *They're all going to die*. He took another swig at the brandy.

He was doomed. With the clarity of a man who has drunk more than a bottle of brandy since breakfast, he knew the film was not enough. He had to be there himself, even if he was doomed. Tears ran down his face as the brandy drove hot gusts of emotion through his brain. He had to be aboard. It was ten o'clock. He could make the eleven o'clock flight, connect in Botswana, charter a chopper and get aboard. Yes. He jumped to his feet, grabbed a new bottle of brandy, and ran up the beach to the jeep. The wheels spun on the sandy track. The roar of the engine drowned the cries of the girl on the beach. Kelly took another swig of brandy, the glass knocking against his even white teeth as the vehicle jounced over the bumps. Green jungle flashed by on either side, then a corrugated roof; then he was on the road, the ribbon of patched tarmac weaving down the hairpins through the lush green sugar cane. Kelly grinned ferociously, and tramped on the throttle.

The tyres screamed on the first hairpin, then on the next. The jeep accelerated for the third. Kelly chose his line, cutting off the corner. There would be nobody coming; there was practically no traffic this end of the island.

He was drifting for the inside of the corner at fifty miles an hour when he saw the big yellow shape of the bus coming up the other side.

He knew he yanked the wheel to the left. He knew the tyres were wailing, and the steering wouldn't answer. He knew he'd missed the bus. And finally he knew he was in mid-air, sailing over the trees and bushes of the slope with the jeep banging and crashing behind and to the side of him. Then he touched down, and hit something unimaginably hard, and lay there, with his face in green leaves, not wanting to move.

He knew he had missed his aeroplane. And slowly, through the pain, there drifted a new knowledge. He knew he had missed the plane for the only reason everybody would have to accept. Including him, and Omar Wohl.

The vision of a drowned *Kelly's Eye* drifted away. In its place, despite the pain in his leg and his ribs, came a feeling of pure satisfaction. Great work, Dave, he thought, and lay in perfect composure listening to the crashing of the rescuers hacking their way down the hill towards him.

LEG 2 · CAPE TOWN ~ SYDNEY

'I need hardly tell you,' said Tubes Murphy, 'that we are now on the home run, destined for dear old Sydney, Steak and Kidney. Like we have all been telling the men from the newspapers, we are entering the waters the boat was built for. And this time, the desalinator is going to work. So all we have to do is win.'

The crew was spread over *Tasman*'s deck forward of the mainsheet track. She was jogging along with her genoa down, taking it easy before the run up to the start, under a sky full of little white clouds. Cape Town was out in force, the blue waters of Table Bay creamed with the wakes of the spectator fleet. Across a hundred yards of water, *Chinamite* was pulling up her genoa. Sparko watched her idly, tasting the delight of a last moment of idleness. He had sailed the Southern Ocean before, and he knew that in the weeks to come such moments would be few and far between. Most of the figures on *Chinamite*'s deck were familiar, since the last month. Sparko checked them off. One of them was tall and thin, moving rather stiffly as he went to his winch. Then he sat up, suddenly. 'Hey,' he said. 'That's Nick Eason!'

'Yeah?' said Murphy, with an eye on the stopwatch.

'Genoa up in a couple of minutes, right?'

'Right,' said Sparko. 'He fell right off a balcony at that dance. Twenty feet. They reckon he cracked a couple of ribs. He must be as sore as a flagpole sitter's fundament.'

'Genoa,' said Murphy. 'Let's go.'

The triangle of heavy Mylar climbed her forestay. She dug her wine-red shoulder hard into the blue water, and started down for the distant line.

Sparko leaned over the winch handles that crossed the hull from one side to the other, and ground. A month's soft living and hard drinking had stolen his wind. The muscles of his arms screamed in agony.

'Poor bloody Eason,' he said to himself.

Eason was indeed sore. His ribs hurt so much that he needed all his strength to keep his face straight, let alone work *Chinamite*'s big winches. He sprawled down the side of the cockpit, keeping as still as he could to quiet the stab of pain every time he breathed. The doctor at the hospital had told him to take it easy for a week after he got out. Eason had discharged himself immediately after the doctor's visit. He had taken it easy during the twenty-minute taxi ride to the yacht basin; that would have to do.

Now he was heading for the Southern Ocean, a spot not notorious for its restfulness. Perhaps the Southern Ocean would be full of stories for *This Week*. So far he had got in four and a half column inches.

But now he was pretty sure he was on to a big story. What had happened last night was attempted murder. And if he had not landed in a thorn bush, it might have been murder. You needed a big motive for murder.

Eason set his teeth and fed the genoa sheet off the winch drum as Henry Harper brought *Chinamite* to the edge of the start area.

'Spinnaker,' said Harper, easing *Chinamite* off the wind so her bow came on to the windward committee boat. As the nylon ribbon went up and cracked full against the clouds, he squinted at the competition. It would be a reaching start; not much scope for battles, unless somebody wanted to get clever. And there didn't seem much point in getting clever at the beginning of a seven-thousand-mile leg. He rubbed his upper belly. Horace the cook, frowning out of the hatchway, said, 'You in pain?'

'Nah,' said Harper. 'Indigestion. It's your bloody cooking.'

Cruel, cruel, cruel, thought Harriet Agnew. Down towards the tankers moored on the quay to shoreward, *Siltex-France* was changing foresails. She could see Henri de Rochambaud at the mast. Nobody but her would have recognized him; but she new from the set of the shoulders, the turn of his head, the way his right arm went up in a gesture that meant wait a minute, take it easy. Harriet knew every inch of de Rochambaud. She knew him as well as she knew herself – as if he were another half of her, missing since birth, with which she had just been reunited.

And now they were to be separated for a month. Cruel.

Harriet took a deep breath and concentrated on not blinking, in case the tears blurring her vision ran down her face. For Jack Asprey was alongside her, on the big grinder that controlled the spinnaker sheet.

'Oh, well,' said Asprey, with his dark, artificial grin.

'There goes the boyfriend.' She managed a minute smile, though the corners of her mouth felt stiff, and wanted to turn down, not up. Asprey put his hand on her shoulder. 'Cheer up,' he said. 'It's only six weeks.'

Her flesh crawled at his touch. He wasn't consoling, and he wasn't a big brother. What he wanted was a quick feel. She let six feet of spinnaker sheet off the drum with a jerk. He took his hand off her shoulder to grind.

'Concentrate!' said Emily de Havilland, at the wheel. Her face was a white mask, the eyes slitted against the sun's glare on the water.

'Whoops!' said Asprey quietly, for Harriet's benefit. 'What's got into the skipper?' He was breathing hard from the grinding.

'Eric's disappeared. They picked up wreckage from his boat,' said Harriet.

'My God!' said Asprey. 'How *terrible*.'

On *Siltex*, de Rochambaud had finished at the mast. His small figure turned; he stood high above the black wall of the yacht's side, and lifted an arm in salute. Harriet lifted hers, too. Then she turned away, to hide the tears which had begun to slide unstoppably down her cheeks.

Emily de Havilland ran grim-faced for the start line, four hundred yards away.

Chuck the cameraman was out on the end of *Kelly's Eye*'s spinnaker pole. His viewfinder was filled by a wide-angle shot of spinnakers blooming like big, bulbous flowers in front of the white houses and the enormous cliffs of Table Mountain. It was a beautiful shot, and he held it for a long, long moment before he panned to the start line, three hundred yards off the nose.

Eye was moving down with the fleet. It was a fine sight, and a rare one; the entire Lancaster Great Circle entry in line abreast, with the sun sparkling from the white water that sprang from under their canted bows. But few of the knot of people in *Eye's* cockpit were admiring the spectacle. They were looking up, at the sky, where light aircraft and helicopters buzzed and clattered.

Bud Withers said, 'Doesn't look like he's going to make it.' His bearded face was still, his eyes worried.

Bennett, trimming the mainsheet, her long blonde hair tied back in a pony tail, said, 'We should worry.' She squinted up at the swarm of aircraft, and said, 'Stay away, you hear?'

'What about the movie?' said Withers.

Herb the sound man said, 'We can make the movie. You keep us afloat.'

Withers did not smile. 'Better than that,' he said. 'We have a clean survey. So this time, we're going to win.'

Herb the sound man let his eye rove over the crew. Some of them didn't look too happy. Sure, the boat had come through the survey. But . . . well, once bitten, twice shy.

'Going for the line,' said Withers. 'He won't make it now.'

Moving in line abreast, the fleet bore down.

Georg Fischer crossed the line downwind of all the other boats. He saw the maxis *Tasman* and *Flag* elbowing one another to windward. There was a protest flag at *Flag's* backstay. Fischer frowned, and sipped the glass of champagne in the hand that was not holding the wheel. A puff of smoke burst from the low grey gunboat at the windward end of the line. Georg raised his glass. 'To a fruitful voyage,' he said.

His brother Anton smiled back at him from a face plumpened by good living in Cape Town. 'And no jostling,' he said, waving his glass at the maxis.

As the day wore on the wind rose and shifted southerly. The spinnakers came down and the boats spread out, moving in single file under the mighty shoulders of the Twelve Apostles, hugging the shore to stay out of the tide. Night fell. The Cape of Good Hope light blinked to port as the fleet moved southward with the land, rolling in the first big waves from the South Atlantic.

The meeting of the warm Agulhas current with the cold waters of the Benguela has given the Cape a dirty reputation. The temperature of the sea jumps from thirty-seven to sixty-five degrees within a few miles, and the air that overlies this seam can be twisted and flung into sudden storms and impenetrable fogs. A couple of hours after dark, the wind fell patchy. *Chinamite* caught the best of it, and moved out ahead of the pack. After another hour squalls began, hard, mixed with patches of fog. Then the wind settled in strong and dirty from the northwest, and the big seas rolling in on the starboard quarter stood upright and began to break.

It was the kind of weather in which the watch below stayed below. Eason was sitting at the saloon table with four other crew. He looked pale and greenish, and his black hair lay flat and despondent on his head. He was reading the London *Times* airmail edition to his watchmates.

'We aren't even fancied,' he said. 'The odds are *Flag*

7–5 on, *Tasman* evens, *Siltex* evens, us 2–1, *Eye* 3–1. It also says, and I quote, "The next two legs are a prospect to make the strongest quail. In the Southern Ocean, waves, uninterrupted by land on their circuit of the globe, can reach enormous heights. In addition, the fastest route from Cape Town to New Zealand, the so-called Great Circle, passes through the Antarctic ice. Tacticians will have to compromise between this and the fact that the westerly winds they will need blow north of the ring of low-pressure areas that roll round the Antarctic High. Sea temperature hovers around freezing. Winds of forty knots and upwards are the rule rather than the exception. And there is a constant threat of icebergs." '

'Did you get any money on, then?' said Slicer, between mouthfuls of a chocolate cake donated for his personal use by a motherly inhabitant of Cape Town.

Eason shook his head. Reading was making him feel sicker.

'Nor me,' said Slicer, spraying crumbs. 'But I bet you a packet of chocky bix we are going to get bloody cold and bloody wet.'

Eason did not take the bet. He discovered the wisdom of this an hour later, on watch, sitting in the cockpit with Cole. It was black as pitch, except for the glimmer of the crests as they passed under *Chinamite*'s bottom with a roar. Cole had set a flat reaching kite. From time to time Eason had to give him a hand on the wheel as *Chinamite* tried to run her nose up into the wind, lying over so her boom raked furrows of foam from the invisible sea.

'Nasty,' said Eason, breathing as gently as possible in an attempt to still the throb in his ribs.

'Hah,' said Cole. 'Wait till we get into the real stuff, boy.' He spun the wheel as a wave went under, and *Chinamite* skidded into the trough. 'How high d'you reckon that wave was?'

'Thirty feet?' said Eason. 'I dunno.'

'Fifteen feet,' said Cole. 'They've seen them fifty-five feet high down where we're going.'

Half an hour later, Harper came on deck. 'There's a nice big low coming in down there,' he said. 'Sooner we get below forty degrees the better. Won't be long at this rate.' The black bulk of his hood turned towards Eason. 'Having fun?' he said.

'Terrific,' said Eason. He had been sick once, and he was pretty sure he would be sick again.

'You get icicles on the spreaders,' said Harper. 'Very picturesque.'

'Can't wait,' said Eason. Harper's face was a white glimmer, and the compass light blackened the leaden bags under his eyes. He laughed. It was a hollow sound, Eason thought; unconvinced. He looked towards Cole, to see if he had noticed anything. But the dim shape of Cole's head was cocked to one side, as if he was listening. 'Hello,' he said. 'What's that?'

Eason could not hear anything. Then, a couple of minutes later, he thought he saw a light in the murk to port.

Cole had seen it too. 'Bloody hell,' he said.

For the light was a three-colour masthead light, and it cast an unearthly glow over an unreefed mainsail and a huge running spinnaker over a gleaming hull. As Eason watched, the hull crested a wave and slid down the front slope, wings of spray whizzing thirty feet on either side.

He could hear the groans of the sheets, taut as iron bars as the wind pressed into the tower of sail. *Tasman*.

'Christ,' said Cole. 'That's his big kite. And not a single slab out of the mainsail. Are we undercanvassed, Henry?'

It was a rhetorical question. Harper shook his head.

'Well, she's coming through.'

Ten minutes later, *Tasman* was abreast. Just before the blackness and the fog swallowed her, Eason saw the mast-head light glowing in the copper-coloured hair of the figure at the wheel, saw the helmsman raise a hand in salute, the open mouth of a black O. And he heard a new sound above the roar and crunch of the spray. The sound of Tubes Murphy, laughing.

'Christ,' said Cole. 'The Flying bloody Dutchman.'

The Westerlies proper began at 44° south, blowing over a dirty grey sea streaked with lines of dishwater foam. Murphy was sitting at the chart table, studying the Southern Ocean Chart. It showed few intrusions of land; merely widely-spaced soundings, the amoebic squiggles of the Kerguelen and Bouvet Islands, and the hatchings that marked the limit of the ice. On a day-to-day basis, the chart was just about useless. But Murphy was marking on it his personal compromise between the rhumb-line – the straight line on the chart – and the Great Circle route. The compromise was a line that headed southeast to the vicinity of the Prince Edward Islands, and then curved eastward, rising towards the rhumb-line, passing the Kerguelen Islands.

Tasman lifted to a wave. Her stern went up, and her nose went down, and she began to sing a loud, complicated song, shuddering and bubbling as she surged into the trough. Murphy's lips stretched back from his teeth in a tight, violent grin. This was what *Tasman* had been built for. Her big, powerful stern would bear up on rollers that might have pooped a yacht with less buoyancy in her aft sections. Her wide, flat sections forward of the keel would let her surf down the waves, and bring her up before she buried her noise in the wave in front. At least, that was the theory. Tubes grinned again, and took the weight off the chart, which sprang back into a roll. He was going to make bloody good and sure it worked.

He pressed the buttons to the right of the radar screen. The green line swept round; there was one echo, far back on the screen at the limit of its range. That would be *Flag*. The radar was handy for iceberg-spotting, and close tactics. But the only certain way of knowing the whereabouts of the competition was to check the positions relayed back to the Race Committee by the Automatic Position Indicators installed at the start of the race by order of the Race Committee. The API also had a panic button, which issued a distress call in case of emergency. It had made racing around the world as safe as it would ever be.

But Tubes Murphy, hammering southeast before a force

six westerly under all plain sail, was not much bothered with safety. In fact, he decided, the API was an unwarranted invasion of his privacy.

Pulling a screwdriver from the rack under the stack of radios, Murphy climbed into his wet-gear and scrambled up the companion-ladder.

The watch on deck were huddled on the weather side. There were two men at the wheel, one the main helmsman, the other there to apply auxiliary power in case *Tasman* took it into her head to broach. But Murphy paid no attention to the hard, heavy movements of the boat. He went aft, to where the aerial of the API jutted from the transom, and started to unscrew the cover.

'She crook?' shouted the helmsman.

'Too right!' yelled Murphy over the roar of the wake. 'She's letting every other bastard on the ocean know where we are!' With his screwdriver, he loosened the retaining ring, pulled the unit out of the deck, and flung it into the railway-lines of white foam whizzing from *Tasman's* transom. Then he slid down to the navigatorium, picked up the radio mike and called the radio duty boat. 'Had a bit of an accident,' he said. 'The API got wet, and I don't think it's working. Okay?'

'Okay,' said the duty boat, which was *Flag*. The scepticism in the operator's voice was audible even over the static.

'And we're having power trouble,' said Murphy. 'Emergency sign-ons only from now on.' Murphy disconnected. Then he went on deck. 'Right,' he said. 'I think that from now on, we will preserve total radio silence. Okay?'

Two days later, *Tasman* sailed past the Prince Edward Islands. Murphy waited as the weatherfax machine rolled out its plot, and looked at the deep low-pressure area trundling round the northern fringes of Antarctica. Then he switched on the radio, tuned to the fleet frequency, and listened to jaw-jaw. Astern, *Chinamite* and *Siltex* were in sight of each other, with *Flag* hull-down ahead. But even *Flag* was eighteen hours' sailing behind *Tasman*. 'Hah!' said Murphy, and called up the companion, 'Steer a hundred and sixty degrees!'

He felt the boat's nose come round, the roll easing, the bow going down and the stern lifting as the wave came from astern. Then he felt the terrific lightness as she broke away, heard the roar of the bubbles passing her hull, the gurgle of the galley sink, and the hard, thin whizz of the spray on either side. He heard the cheers from the deck, too. Then the bow came up, and the ride slowed, and *Tasman* was climbing the next wave. He went on deck. The next wave came under, and *Tasman* did it again. The LCDs of the log flicked round to twenty knots, and went off the clock. Men were shouting and hitting each other on the back. 'Okay,' said Murphy. His hood was back, despite the rawness of the wind. 'She's going to blow. Let's get all the sails aft. Everything with any weight in it, to stop her nose going in.'

Sparko said, 'You want to shorten sail?'

'No,' said Tubes. 'I want to win.'

During the next four hours, the seas rose, and the wind with them. By nightfall it was up to force eight, and the watch below were below, and so was the watch on deck, sprawled on the sailbags that jammed the cabin walkways aft, except two trimmers and two helmsmen. There was sleet mixed with the gale now, and the waves were coming from astern as high as the first spreaders, their crests coming free and spilling white down their long slopes as *Tasman* raced them at twenty-five, thirty knots.

Murphy said, 'We'll change to the number four genny.'

The men were spilling on deck, bending stiffly in the cold to clip their lifeliness to the jackstays. *Tasman's* stern lifted to a wave steeper than the rest. She streaked down into a trough like a black canyon. At the bottom of the trough, her nose ripped into the upslope of the next wave. Sparko looked over his shoulder, at the crest rolling down from behind, and he shouted something. Then the deck was waist-deep in roaring water, and somewhere there was a huge explosion. *Tasman's* deck began to rise, freer, as if a big weight had been lifted away. Sparko could feel the sweat running inside his thermal vest, his knees weak with fear. Where the spinnaker had been, rags of sailcloth fluttered.

'Saved us taking it down,' said Murphy mildly. 'Let's get to it.'

The deck was going up like a lift. Sparko was facing forward, looking at the wave that was taking them up. Suddenly he felt the wind blowing on the right-hand side of his nose, heard the helmsman shout incoherently from astern. Acting by reflex, he threw himself flat on the deck as the boom came slamming across with a crash that travelled to the root of *Tasman's* keel. He heard Tubes shout, 'Everybody there?' and the answering cries.

'So let's get some sail on!' shouted Murphy, and Sparko thought: God moves in a mysterious way. If they'd gibed all standing with the big spinnaker up, they could have lost the mast. As it was, they'd just made a lot of noise and fuss –

'Down!' yelled the helmsman again, and the boom slammed across again. This time, the crash was followed by an explosion. Sparko rolled onto his back. The mast reeled silver and naked against the grey overcast. What was left of the mainsail clattered in rags from the luff and shredded downwind.

They put up a couple of headsails, boomed out trade-wind style. Then, fingers freezing in their gloves, they fumbled the ruins of the mainsail out of its racks and sweated up a new one. It took an hour. Then they heaved out the heavy running kite, and pulled it up outside the headsails, and took the headsails off. Then they went below, except for the helmsmen, and tried to warm fingers they had forgotten they had next to the cabin heater, which had decided to stink of diesel. They drank a mug of soup, and those off watch wedged themselves into bunks and crannies in the sailbags. The condensation was running down the walls, and Sparko could see his breath in the air.

'Oh well,' said Murphy, with his savage grin. 'Only three more weeks to go.'

Cooking in the Roaring Forties was a pleasure, once you got used to it. George Hart, leaning back into the loop of webbing that kept him from falling into the stove, removed a large casserole of *boeuf bourguignon* from the microwave, roared 'CHOW DOWN!' and started to deal it out, with big dollops of mashed potato and red cabbage. He had bought the red cabbage in Cape Town. In these temperatures, it was no problem keeping it fresh.

Flag's crew came quickly, except for the five men who were the minimum deck complement. The cold made them hungry for hot meat and sweet puddings. They took the plates, grunting, and ate straight away. Afterwards, as the warmth got into their blood, they started to talk.

'Terrific, George,' said one of them. 'What was it?'

'Whale,' said George. 'With boiled wet-gear.'

'*Whale meat again, don't know where, don't know when*,' they sang.

'*But I know whale meat again each goddamn day –*'

'Too kind,' said Hart, performing a deep bow.

A hooded head appeared at the hatch. 'That's your fifteen-minute allocation,' it said.

The twelve men at the table turned, unshaven chins scraping on the necks of heavy Arctic jerseys. 'Right, Hyatt,' said one of them.

'Yessir, Mr Hyatt,' said another, and laughed a closed, ironic laugh.

'Okay,' said Pal Joey. 'Let's go.'

And the five men who would replace the deck crew while they ate pulled on their gear and went up the ladder.

As they arrived on deck, the icy wind hit them like a blast from a freezer. 'I wouldn't mind, only the son of a bitch was three minutes early,' said one of them to Joey.

'Yeah,' said Joey absently. He had the wheel now, and he was not thinking about problems with Hyatt or any other members of the crew. The wake was up to the spreaders as *Flag* went down the wave front, and *Tasman* must be close to a day's sailing ahead. 'Trim, eh?'

The trimmer trimmed. *Flag* moved on, driving into the troughs, climbing the ridges, driving down again. And Art Schacker sat alone on the windward side of the cockpit, watching the monstrous swing of the sea and the roaring white fans of the wake. These waters had seen other Schackers; lean, hard men with churchyard faces, two years out from Marblehead, wives and children. Men like Abram Schacker, who had smashed a drunken harpoonist's skull with his own iron, buried the body at sea, and brought the harpoon home for use as a poker in the white house in Marblehead. Art Schacker thought of Martin Hyatt, and felt a moment of yearning for the simple, direct methods of the old days.

Twenty minutes later, it was time for jaw-jaw. *Flag* was the duty boat, and Martin Hyatt the operator. He had been trained in navy routines at Annapolis, and felt considerable scorn for the slackness of the operators on other boats. *Sirène* was having difficulty in thawing steaks in the low temperatures. *EPK Electric* gave a position from which she could save her time with ease. Hyatt didn't mind

talking to Jack Asprey; Asprey was the kind of sailor he
could respect. *Siltex* was level; *Eye* some distance to the
north, falling behind in light northwesterlies. *Tasman* was
not signing on. That was *Tasman* for you, thought Hyatt,
with a curl of the lip. He noted the fact in the log, and
added 'Suggest protest,' underlining it in red pencil. Then
he relayed a message that had come in on the SSB.
Murphy's Aunty Shar was waiting for him in Sydney.
There was no acknowledgement, but then Hyatt had not
expected one. He sat back in the padded chair, and listened to the chatter of the fleet. *Siltex*'s doctor was
treating a couple of men for diarrhoea. *EPK* were
celebrating a winchman's birthday. *Eye* was taking
measures to fix a broken bottle-screw. The ether snapped
and buzzed with the voices of operators glad to find evidence that other people were alive out there in this cold,
hostile desert of water.

Martin Hyatt did not join in. He did not see it as part of
his job to give aid and comfort or even the time of day to
his competitors. What he saw as his duty was to beat the
Australians, and everybody else, and bring honour to his
club. As a family, the Hyatts had not been close. Generation fought generation with enthusiasm. Martin had passed
a childhood first in the nursery wing of the big house in the
country outside Boston, then in military academies. His
parents had been shadowy, preoccupied figures. At first
he had been jealous of his contemporaries, whose parents
were interested in them and even affectionate. But as time
went by, the energy he put into this jealousy had been
diverted to a fierce loyalty to the group of which he was
a part.

But the group aboard *Flag* was giving him problems. He had, of course, identified their source: Schacker. Schacker, in the name of seamanship, persistently performed at less than optimum. He seemed unaware of his responsibility to his sponsors, his duty to uphold the honour of the Sound Yacht Club. Schacker the slacker, thought Hyatt, and grinned all over his sharp pink face. Well, he had promised his grandfather in Cape Town that this time he would bring Schacker up to the mark.

His eyes wandered over the readouts of the banks of instruments over the chart-table. The log repeater read twelve knots as the cabin floor lifted under his chair. Then, as the angle steepened and *Flag* began to slide, the liquid crystal figures flicked up, eighteen, twenty, and the gurgling began, and the high-frequency humming as the boat cut loose and whizzed down the face. She held it for a long time. Then the wave went under her, and the figures dropped back, twelve, ten. *Goddamn you, Schacker*, thought Hyatt. *We're not carrying enough sail, you yellow clammer*. Absentmindedly, he shifted the short-wave dial to the Cape Town met. frequency.

'. . . storm travelling east, centred on latitude fifty-one degrees, now in the vicinity of Prince Edward Islands,' said the voice. 'Winds to eighty knots.'

Hyatt leaned forward and jabbed the satnav readout. 48°S, it said. On their present course, they should get the big winds nicely astern, in a couple of hours. That would help. Except that Schacker would shorten sail, or try to steer up on to the fringes, where the winds would be smaller.

If he found out about the storm.

Hyatt climbed the companion-ladder and stuck his head out of the hatch and into the icy wind. 'Skipper,' he said. 'Trouble with the electrics. I'm stripping down the radio, right?'

'Do what you have to,' said Schacker. His square face was tired; there were exhausted shadows under his slanted eyes. 'Did you get the met. report?'

'Sure,' said Hyatt. 'More of the same.'

Schacker nodded. 'Okay,' he said.

Someone below shouted. 'Shut that goddamn hatch before we freeze.'

'Right away,' said Hyatt. Ten minutes later, he had the radio and the fax in pieces. The wind was already freshening.

It continued to freshen. The galley sole became lumpy under George Hart's feet, and he had to cling to the hand-bars as well as sitting back in his webbing. The trays in the microwaves shifted with a regular *chang*, and in the lockers the plastic plates clapped like dull castanets over the background motifs of zinging cutlery and jingling glass. Behind was the thump of heavy gear shifting an inch here, an inch there, in its stowage, and always the long, snoring bubble of the hull's openings, and the heavy roar of breaking seas from above.

The men coming below were wet, tired and white-faced. They took mugs of soup and drank them quickly, sucking warmth. Then they lay down in crevices in the sailbags, and slept.

Hart had to admit to himself that he didn't like it. The only person who did seemed to be Hyatt, sitting wedged into the corner of a bunk with a circuit tester, jabbing at the innards of the radio. Hart watched him, closely, to keep his mind off the mad writhing of the deck. He saw him apply the clips of the tester to a circuit, take them off and put them on again. As far as Hart could see, he put them on in the same place. It was difficult to tell, in the dim, yellow light of the hull; the shadows were black, and the condensation that filmed the walls gave everything a blurred, oily shine. Hart edged closer.

This time, he was sure. 'Located the problem?' he said.

Hyatt's head jerked up in surprise. 'Huh?'

'The problem,' said Hart. 'You isolated the circuit? I saw you test it, then.'

Hyatt turned a pair of furious blue eyes on him. 'I'm the radio expert here. Why don't you go cook something?' he said.

'But . . .'

'The radio works now,' said Hyatt. 'I just fixed it. Okay?'

Hart shrugged. 'Whatever you say,' he said. He swung along the catwalk to the galley, frowning. After he had peeled potatoes, he went back to the radio shack. Hyatt was seated at the desk. Static hissed over the roar of the seas outside.

'. . . winds now expected to reach ninety knots,' said a South African-accented voice on the radio. 'Earlier forecasts have revised . . . winds now expected to reach ninety –'

'What were the earlier forecasts?' said Hart.

Hyatt said, 'How should I know? The goddamn radio was out.'

The circuit tester was lying on the desk. Hart picked it up and flicked the on/off switch to on. The red pilot light glowed bloody in the gloom. Hart gazed absently at it for a moment. Then he said, 'Hey!' He was remembering Hyatt, testing connections with his crocodile clips. There had been no pilot light then . . . 'Martin,' he said. 'What was wrong with the radio?'

He never got an answer. Pal Joey's voice roared, 'ALL HANDS ON DECK!' Scrambling into wet-gear, they ran up the companionways.

Hart clipped his lifeline to the jackstay. The gale hit them like an icy sand-blaster. It was snowing hard, from dead astern. The wind howled like a chainsaw in the rigging. *Flag* was labouring, overcanvassed under triple-reefed mainsail. Out of the grey-white murk rolled something high and black, so high that for a ridiculous moment Hart thought they were under a huge basalt cliff. Then the top of the cliff curled over and crumbled, and as Joey and Schacker fought the wheel to keep her straight, white water spilled down the face until it towered above *Flag's* stern. Hart saw Hyatt, next to him, struggling with the clip of his lifeline. It seemed to have frozen open. The water roared over the transom and filled the cockpit, rising over the helmsman's shoulders and burying them. Hart saw Hyatt's head screw round at the advancing wave. The whites were showing all the way round the irises, and as the wall of water came over the deck his mouth opened to yell, but Hart could not hear it above the roar of the water. And Hart knew what was about to happen. As the water pummelled down on him, he grabbed Hyatt round the waist. His feet were swept off the deck. Hyatt became impossibly heavy. Hart's fingers were freezing, without grip. He knew he was going to have to let go. But then *Flag* rose and shook the water from her deck and the weight lessened. Hyatt lay on the deck streaming, with Hart on top of him. Someone clipped on Hyatt's lifeline. His eyes stared up at Hart in dumb fury.

'Good boy,' said Schacker to Hart. 'Now you get forward and let's get a trysail on this thing.'

Later Hart remembered breaking fingernails and not being able to feel any pain, even when they handed the mainsail and a fold of heavy Dacron slammed into his ear. At last, what seemed like hours later, they had the tiny triangle of the trysail up, and *Flag* rode easier, so she no longer took heavy water over the transom.

Finally, Hart got below. He lashed himself into the galley and made instant soup and tried not to shout about the pain in his hands. Hyatt lay in a sleeping-bag, not moving. Nobody moved, much, except when they had to.

Schacker came below, took a mug, and said, 'Thanks, George.'

Hart shrugged. He knew that he was being thanked for more than the soup.

He said, 'I think Hyatt was screwing with the radio.'

'*What?*'

Hart told him about the switched-off circuit tester. Schacker's narrow, tilted eyes rested on Hyatt in his bunk. 'He'd have to be crazy,' he said.

Hart shrugged.

'Maybe you should have let him go overboard, at that,' said Schacker grimly. 'Keep quite about it, okay. I'll fix him.'

The man on radio watch came through from aft. 'Jaw-jaw,' he said, 'We're about furthest south, except for *EPK*, and she's a day astern. None of the other guys has got this weather. Except maybe *Tasman*, last reported down this way. Nobody's heard a peep out of her for four days.'

'Maybe she went down,' said Hyatt from his bunk. 'Wouldn't that be great?'

There was a silence that dulled even the racket of the storm. Then Schacker said, 'No,' and sat down on the sailbag in the catwalk. The rest of the crew turned away, as if by common consent. Hart was closest, from his vantage point in the galley. He heard Schacker say, very quietly, 'There was something I wanted to say, and you just doubled the reason for saying it. Come Sydney, you're out. Till then, you don't touch the radio.' His voice was quiet and level, but Hart got the idea that it was something he had been wanting to say for a long, long time.

Hyatt turned his face to the wall. Schacker walked deliberately to the companionway.

Hart sat down suddenly on the galley sole and went straight to sleep.

Next morning, the wind was still howling. *Tasman's* crew had settled into a sort of numbness. Nobody had had much sleep. Hurtling down the front of the big waves under main and spinnaker, *Tasman* was barely controllable. Behind the exhilaration of sailing very fast and being two hundred miles in the lead, there was anxiety. Everybody knew that one slip would be fatal. And the anxiety became tension, and the tension had become something very like fear. Sparko for one had lain in a dank sleeping bag all night, watching the drips of water slithering down the bulkhead, every muscle tense, waiting. It was a relief to go on deck, into the insane shrieking of the wind and the tumbling wedges of water that shoved themselves under the boat. At first, anyway. But then the relief wore off, and it was just cold, and wet, and across the horizon there was more of the same, for ever and ever, amen.

Sparko sat on the weather deck and closed his eyes to the great bulge of the spinnaker and the white wing of the main waving against the sky. Whenever the boat tried to broach, he clamped his hands on the rail till they hurt. She was trying to broach a lot, now: the wind had gone round almost on to the starboard beam. The helmsmen were spelling in pairs, once an hour.

Towards the end of the third hour of the watch, Murphy came half out of the hatch and said, 'How you doing, Sparks?'

Sparko nodded, and grinned as well as he could with clenched teeth.

Tubes said, in a voice quieter than his usual bellow, 'You get used to it, mate.'

'Yeah,' said Sparko. *Tasman* heeled until her boom trailed foam.

'Tricky,' said Murphy. Then he came out of the hatch in a great bound. For the wind had suddenly gusted up, screaming in the rigging, and *Tasman* was going far, far over on her beam ends, slewing onto the wind so her spinnaker pulled her sideways instead of ahead.

'Sheet!' roared Murphy, wrenching at the wheel. The man on the spinnaker sheet let go, but there was a riding turn on the winch and it held fast. *Tasman* went on over.

The mastman ran forward with his knife, aiming for the strop at the outboard end of the jockey pole, but the deck was vertical now, and there was nothing to walk on but water.

'HATCH!' roared Murhphy from the wheel.

The water was up to the lee side winches on the gorilla pit coaming. Sparko went for the hatch and got his hand to the handles. He heard thunder behind him as his fingers closed on the brass, and the deck shuddered under his knees. He glanced round. *Tasman* was beam-on to the sea, rising on the face of a swell. Its crest arched and overhung, and began to fall. Sparks wrenched at the hatch cover. It was jammed. Roaring, he watched the water lap up to the edge of the hatch and begin to pour in. He was hanging by his harness now. Heavy objects crashed and bumped below. Water came pouring down the deck, met the water the other side. There was water everywhere, icy cold and very bitter. Sparko hung on to the hatch handles. Everything dissolved into the roar of the breaking crest.

This is it, thought Sparko, and felt strangely relieved.

Happy Birthday dear Ja-ack,
Happy Birthday to you.

Jack Asprey rose from his seat at the saloon table and blew out the four candles on the chocolate cake in front of him, bracing himself against the roll of *EPK*'s deck. His hair was brushed into a ridge-and-furrow of brilliantine, and he wore a smug smile. 'Ladies and gentlemen,' he said, 'and *especially* ladies.' He winked at Harriet. 'I'd like to say how very, *very* kind you are to have made me this cake, and to have presented me with the Birthday Bottle.' He picked up the bottle of whisky that stood on the table, and poured a slug into each of the five mugs. He stood, raising his mug. 'To me,' he said. 'And us.'

They all mumbled – all except Harriet. Harriet gulped the whisky and felt uneasy because during the last two words of his toast, Asprey had kept his dark eyes firmly on her. Now, he winked again.

She got up and said, 'I'll go and see how they're getting on upstairs.' It was one of *EPK*'s jokes that everything was 'upstairs' and 'downstairs', no 'on deck' and 'below'. It was curiously comforting. It served to shut out the cold, wet, dangerous world outside – the world which might have swallowed up *Tasman* and her whole crew.

Harriet shrugged into her wet-gear and went on deck. Emily was at the wheel, silent, hoodless, the edges of her facial bones tight against the skin. Harriet had cut her hair the previous week, a Joan of Arc crop that fluttered in the breeze from astern. 'Good party?' she said.

'A riot,' said Harriet. She handed Emily the whisky-laced tea she had brought up, and stood waiting for her body to adjust to the cold wind. Swans like *EPK* were almost too well heated below; she imagined that on a less comfortable boat, going on watch would be less of a wrench. 'He's finishing his bottle.'

'Wouldn't like to be inside his head tomorrow,' said Emily. Traditionally, birthday people got a bottle of whisky, which they could give out to their comrades as they pleased. In practice, this usually meant large tots all round, and the birthday boy polishing off the bottle solo.

'Is that ice?' said Emily, twitching the wheel to starboard.

Harriet squinted at the sea. 'No,' she said. 'White horse.'

'Hope you're right,' said Emily. It was another comfortable old gallows joke. The sea here was as full of ice as a cocktail shaker. Most were tiny; but the bigger ones, bergs or bergy-bits, were big enough to cut a boat open like a soft-boiled egg. 'They split a genoa last night. Could you cobble it up?'

'Now?' said Harriet.

'No time like the present.'

'If you're sure,' said Harriet. She was delighted at the chance of going below, into the warm cabin, and working with the sewing machine. Harriet had nothing against fresh air, but the Southern Ocean had a definite surplus of the stuff. She went back below, leaving her wet-gear in the heated hanging locker at the companionway's foot. The

303

tape machine was coming to the end of a Neil Diamond track. Jack Asprey loved Neil Diamond. Harriet hated Neil Diamond.

'Can I have the table?' she said. 'I've got a genoa to mend.'

'Sure,' said Asprey. His bottle was three-quarters empty. 'Want a hand aft with it?'

'Stay put,' said one of the hands at the table. 'I'll go.'

'No, no. I'm very happy.' His voice was slightly slurred. 'C'mon, Harriet.'

He opened the door in the bulkhead forward of the mast. Inside, the sails lay piled in their white Dacron bags. 'After you,' he said, bowing. He looked so much the courtier that Harriet could not help laughing.

'Thank you, kind sir,' she said, and walked in. He came after her, and shut the door. 'Leave it open,' she said, turning the light on. Then she saw his face, and said, 'Oh, no –'

'Why not?' he said. His flat cheeks were flushed and his eyes had a glassy look. She could smell the whisky on his breath.

'Don't be bloody stupid,' she said.

He put his right arm round her waist and his left hand sought her breast. She twisted away. 'Come *on*, Harriet,' he said. 'It's my birthday.' He was whining, like a child after sweets.

'Let me out of here or I'll shout for help.' Her back was pressed against the sails.

His face grinned at her. 'Oh, no,' he said. 'No, you won't.'

'Don't be ridiculous,' she said.

'You're forgetting who I am. If you don't have me, you don't have sponsorship, and if you don't have sponsorship, you don't go on.' He reached out and grabbed her by the shoulders. His fingers were hard and bruising. 'So why not have me? It's no problem. You'd like it. I mean you did with the little Frog in Cape Town, didn't you?'

Until that moment, Harriet had felt frightened. But now she thought of de Rochambaud, his kindness and his wit, next to Jack Asprey, false and conceited, and anger made her pulse bang in her head. His hands were round her waist now, pulling her hips away from the sailbags to grind against him. She shoved him away. As he came back at her she brought her knee up sharply. He caught it where she meant him to catch it, in the groin. As he went down on to the deck, she reached up and yanked one of the big sailbags out of the rack. It landed on his upper back, a hundredweight and a half of it. His head hit the deck with a crash. Oh my God, thought Harriet: I've killed him.

Asprey groaned. Harriet immediately felt better. Six months ago, she would not have dreamed of giving anyone a knee in the groin. Not even Jack Asprey. Now she felt she had acted responsibly in her own interests and those of the boat.

The whisky made her giggle. Placing a foot on his chest, she posed a moment for an imaginary camera. *EPK* lurched off the top of a wave. She opened the door.

'Can someone give me a hand with Jack?' she said. 'He seems to have had an acident.'

It seemed to Nicholas Eason that he could not remember a time when there had been no storms. But now, as he lay in a damp sleeping bag listening to the sound *Chinamite* made as she ploughed down her easting, he wondered. The sounds of the wind in the rigging had lessened.

He sat up, and wished he hadn't, because it was cold. The only warm place on the boat was a sleeping bag, and once the sleeping bags had got wet the only way to get warm was to climb into one that someone else had just vacated. After three weeks at sea *Chinamite* was no place for the squeamish, but then none of her crew had time for squeamishness between being on watch, eating, and sleeping.

Eason pulled on three jerseys over his thermal vest. They were all damp, but wool next to the skin kept you warm even when you were wet. He wriggled into thermal long johns, corduroy trousers, two pairs of socks, and yellow rubber seaboots with non-slip soles. Down the cabin, a couple of other figures were stirring, roused by the last watch's waker. Eason stood up, ignoring the faint twinge in his ribs what was all that remained of his encounter with Crystal.

Nobody spoke till they were aft at the saloon table, drinking coffee. Even then the talk was largely ritual. It started with the important things.

'Where are we?' said Eason.

'Fourth,' said Slicer, who had checked the last positions in the log. 'Or third. No *Tasman*.'

'Huh,' said Eason. Nobody wanted to think about *Tasman*. 'How far ahead are the rest?'

'*Flag*, a day,' said Slicer. '*Siltex*, nine hours.'

'Catching up,' said Eason.

'Slow and steady,' said Slicer. He finished his coffee, shoved a handful of biscuits into his pockets, and went on deck. Eason took course, sails, special conditions from the log and followed, into the cold dark, grunting to the dim shapes of the watch on deck.

'You steer,' said Slicer.

'Me?'

'Wind's dropped,' said Slicer. 'Now's your moment.'

'Okay,' said Eason, and took the wheel.

He had done little steering on this leg, and none at night. The leather of the wheel trembled under his glove, and he shifted it a little to starboard, aiming the long spearhead of the hull straight down in the trough. It shuddered as the speed built up, and *Chinamite* was suddenly as responsive as a dinghy as she skied down to the bottom of the hill. Then she felt heavy, wallowing in the spray of her landing, nosing indecisively towards the wind. But Eason heaved the wheel to starboard again, watching the swing of the compass card, and would not let her, and soon the next wave was buildng under her.

In a gale, she was hard to handle. But tonight the wind was force five to six, a gentle zephyr by Southern Ocean standards. And the exercise of fighting the wheel was just enough to keep Eason warm – which made a change from hot, sweaty sail-changes followed by long periods of inactivity in which the sweat congealed on your body and chilled you to the bone. It was no surprise, Eason reflected, that four men were down with some kind of flu, Henry Harper among them.

After an hour the clouds shredded back and the moon was a half-disc of silver that glittered on the jet waves and made strange monochrome rainbows which reflected in the water droplets fizzing from *Chinamite*'s flanks. The heavy 3.5 oz spinnaker and single-reefed mainsail swayed gracefully against the stars. Eason grinned and sang and wondered why he had ever bothered to stick dope up his nose. There were, it appeared, substitutes. Then he stopped grinning.

Chinamite had topped a crest, and was racing down into a trough. The water in the bottom of the trough was smooth and black. In the middle of it, visible in the space between *Chinamite*'s spinnaker and her forestay, floated something black and square-edged.

'Gibing!' roared Eason, and spun the wheel to starboard. The boom walloped over as she carved a long curve of spray down the face of a wave. The deck shuddered, and he squinted up at the mast, dreading the quick crumple to the deck.

'What is it?' said Slicer.

'Something in the water,' said Eason. The mast was holding. 'Look to port.' Slicer looked, his face invisible in the hood of his wet-gear. The object lifted on the dark wave twenty yards to port. 'There.' Eason's heart was thumping painfully.

'Can't see anything,' said Slicer.

'Could be a container,' said Eason. He was desperate

for Slicer to see it. Competent helmsmen did not risk masts with Chinese jibes.

'Oh,' said Slicer, still looking. 'Right. Got it.'

He trained his night glasses. 'Twenty-foot container, hull down. If we'd hit it, it would have had the keel off us.'

Eason felt a warm glow of achievement. Then he thought of *Chinamite* upside down and keel-less, two thousand miles from land, and the flow turned to a chill.

Harper came on deck, woken by the jibe. He looked tired, his shoulders bent and weary against the moon's glitter on the rollers. Eason concentrated on keeping the compass card steady in its pool of yellow light. The wind surged and moaned.

They were planing down a wave twenty minutes later when Eason thought he saw something else. He blinked, dazzled by the moon in the bow-wave. Then the wheel spun out of his hand, and one of the spokes smashed into his fingers and he reeled away, shouting. Harper grabbed the wheel. Eason found himself staring aft, his eyes blurred with tears of pain. Through the blur he saw something huge and black rear up from the white water of the wake, and this time his heart stopped in his chest. For the thing was *alive*; a sea serpent, he thought; I've just seen a sea serpent.

The thing turned into a letter Y that gleamed on the first streaks of dawn.

'Rudder's gone!' shouted Harper. 'Let go sheets!'

The night dissolved into the thunder of unsheeted sails. 'Whale,' thought Eason. 'It was a whale.'

Harper was not listening. He was a white mask in the glow of the compass light. 'Masthead working light!' he called. The white light at the masthead came on, spreading a pool of reflections on to the waves around. 'And let's get the main down and two genoas up.'

'Genoas?' said someone. 'What about the rudder?'

'Never mind the rudder, we're bloody racing. We'll steer with the sails,' said Harper. 'We'll take a look in the morning.'

'What's going on?' said a new voice. It was Ed Cole, still struggling into his clothes, his thin, sandy hair streaming in the icy wind.

'Hit a whale,' said Harper. 'Feels like we've got about an eighth of a rudder. Uh.' His voice trailed off in a grunt. He put his hands to his chest and sat down suddenly on the edge of the cockpit. The skin of his face was the colour of lead in the harsh white light. His shoulders slumped, and his mouth opened and hung. For a moment he remained poised. Then he toppled sideways, gaining momentum, and hit the deck with a thud.

Eason stood as if the bang of Harper's head on the fibre-glass had nailed him to the spot. Cole was already shouting. 'BONES!' he roared.

The ship's doctor padded aft from the mast, where he had been sweating up the genoa. He squatted by Harper, felt his pulse, listened to his chest. 'Below,' he shouted over the roar of sails. 'Heart attack. Get my bag.'

Eason took a leg, and they lowered Harper down the companionway and laid him on a bunk, and backed away, staggering to *Chinamite*'s rudderless bucking. Bones pulled open Harper's wet-gear, tested the vital signs and filled a hypodermic. There was shouting on deck, and a brief roar of sails. Then *Chinamite* was sailing again.

'Get on the radio,' said Bones. 'Find out where's the nearest cardiac unit.'

'Balls,' said Harper. 'This is a race.' His voice was tiny, and his face was grey. He breathed with an effort that was painful to watch. 'Sail to Sydney.'

'Perth's closer,' said Bones.

'Sod that,' said Harper. 'I . . . order you to go to Sydney.' His breath was coming in gasps. 'I didn't start this race not to finish –'

'Calm down,' said Bones. 'I'm going to give you an injection.'

'No Perth,' said Harper between blue lips.

'We'll see,' said Bones, and slid in the needle.

Eason went aft to the radio. The cabin was full of the thud of the damaged rudder. He sat himself down in the padded chair and reported in to the duty boat. As he told the story he had a sudden sense of how it all *fitted*. In cities, death was something that cleared a space in the crowd, and flashing blue lights came and swept the body under the rug. But here, in this little cramped boat, death was a member of the crew who was always on watch and never got tired.

He twisted the tuning dial, got Portishead, and booked an R/T call to *This Week*. It came through surprisingly fast. The copy-taker's voice was tiny, lapped by surges of static. He said, 'Blimey. You again? Where are you?'

'Southern Ocean,' said Eason.

'Dusky birds in grass shirts,' said the copy-taker. 'I know.' He chuckled wheezily. For a second Eason could smell the Silk Cut smoke, see the fish-belly skin of his face.

'Wotcher got, then?'

'*Chinamite*, the Great Circle entry carring *Week* man Nick Eason, today lost her rudder when she rammed a whale,' said Eason. 'Henry Harper, the oldest skipper in the race, suffered a heart attack. Harper refused to permit the ship to pull in to the nearest cardiac unit, in Perth, Australia. "This is a race," he said. "Sail on to Sydney." His condition is described as critical.'

'Got it,' said the copy-taker. 'It's on its way upstairs to His Highness and the spike.'

'What do you mean, the spike?' said Eason.

'Listen.' The copy-taker's cough merged with the fizzing of the Heaviside Layer. 'You find out about that bloke Cole, how he feels about them kids that drowned. Forget this Harper and his thrombie. Thrombies? I've had two myself, and –'

'Give up smoking,' said Eason, and cut the connection.

He went on deck. The moon was still up, and the sky ahead was grey and pink with the dawn. Most of the crew was aft, in an untidy knot round the wheel and the lazarette hatch. Cole was standing between the two genoa winches watching the twin headsails that were dragging *Chinamite* along in front of the freezing wind. 'Stock's bust above the gland!' shouted a voice from aft.

Cole said to Eason, 'Fetch up the welding gear, there's a good man.'

He dived down the hatch and ran to the forepeak. The wealding gear locker was already open. The acetylene bottle was there, but the oxygen was gone. He went back into the body of the yacht.

Bones was still kneeling beside Harper. He had the oxygen bottle wedged against the bunk, and a tube to

Harper's face. Harper's face looked pinker, as far as it was possible to tell in the dim yellow light. Eason scrambled on deck.

'Where is it?' yelled Cole, from beside the lazarette hatch.

Eason said, 'Skipper needs it.' He had never felt so powerless, or so glad that someone else had to make the decision. Save the boat and kill the skipper; save the skipper, kill the crew . . .

Cole looked at him for a moment with level blue eyes. 'Quite right,' he said at last. 'Get me the spares kit, and a genoa sheet. I'm going over the back.'

'*Over?*'

Cole repressed a surge of impatience. 'Unless you feel like swimming to Sydney,' he said. 'Move it, boy. This is a race.' Then he went to work.

Chinamite had been built with trouble in mind, and trouble had included steering-gear failure. The builders had drilled a hole into the trailing edge of her rudder. In the event of a gear failure, all the crew had to do was screw a special eyebolt through the hole, snap a shackle to each eye of the bolt, and attach the other ends of the steering lines to the tiller she carried in the lazarette, as specified by race rules. It was a well-designed, if primitive, bit of work. In the Solent, it would have been child's play. But in twenty-foot waves and with a water temperature hovering around zero, getting the bolt through the hole in the rudder was going to be like threading an embroidery needle on a roller-coaster. Eason said, 'Let me do it.'

Cole said, 'No.'

Eason said, 'Look, I'm a journalist and a spare radio

operator. This is a job requiring no, er, special skills.'

Cole looked at him. He saw the dark eyes over the hollow cheeks full of the self-deprecating humour that clouded everything Eason did. Underneath was the hint of a plea – give me a break and let's see how I make out. Cole was not particularly interested in pleas, but he knew a strong motive when he saw one. 'All right,' he said. 'Get a dry-suit on.'

Eason went below and climbed into a dry-suit, snapping the bands tight at neck, wrists and ankles. Then he put on wool gloves and thick socks and went on deck.

Cole said, 'What you have to do is look for the red spot on the rudder. It's only putty. Gouge it out with a chisel. Then you put in the ring bolt and crank it up tight. Then we'll pull you back aboard.'

'Fine,' said Eason. He kept stealing glances at the sea. The sun was up. The water was green as a cat's eyes, and it looked very cold.

'But remember,' said Cole, 'eighteen minutes in there, even in that suit, you're dead. So if you want to come out, you give us a wave. And mind your head.'

'Mind my head?'

'If you get this boat on your bonce, you've had it.'

'Ah,' said Eason. 'Well, if that happens, *This Week* might just print my obituary.'

Then he went down the slope of the transom, and into the sea.

It was incredibly cold; colder than he had imagined possible. Even through the layers of plastic and wool, he could feel the water sucking the heat from his body.

They were holding the rudder still in a bight of rope. He

crawled down the rope until he was under the overhang of the stern, clinging on tight so he rose and fell with the boat. Now the hull was a great turquoise ceiling above his head, with a six-inch gap between it and the water, a gap that came and went as the waves surged under, cut vertically by the blade of the rudder.

The red spot was six inches under water, swimming and wobbling with the refraction. He gouged awkwardly with the chisel, and for the first time lost his grip on the guide rope. The hull banged down on him, drove his face into the water as he was inhaling. For a split second he breathed in salt and panicked, choking. He dropped the chisel. It fell to the end of its lanyard as he thrashed the water. Then he pulled himself away, into the air. Faces were leaning over the stern. 'You all right?' said someone's voice.

Eason grinned from a cold-numb face. ''Course,' he said. He gathered up the chisel and went back in.

The cold was growing round his body. It steadied him. He managed to time his breathing, cleared the hole. Then he went back for the ring bolt.

The ring bolt was harder. It had its lines already attached, which was awkward, and he dropped it twice. His fingers were seizing up. Also, his head was aching. As he fumbled the bolt into the hole and worked to engage the thread of the female end, he thought: last time I had this headache was when I was a little child and I ate three ice creams too fast. The thread engaged, and he took a couple of turns, and then rested a minute, because he was thinking about his father, and then, in a slow, dreamy way, about his mother. He was sleepy, icy cold but warm at the same time. He knew he had to tighten the bolt with a pair of spikes, but he put off going to get them, remembering chill air on his face, the rest of him warm; in his pram, he suddenly realized. In Kensington Gardens.

The hull slammed down on him again, and the bitter water drove him aft. His arms moved slowly as he accepted the two spikes. He got them into the loops of the eyebolt, and applied all his strength to each, in opposite directions. But he had very little strength left, and the effort used it all up. His hands fell open and the spikes dropped out, and he laid his head sideways on the pillow of his pram and went to sleep –

Except that suddenly he was being yanked out of the water and carried somewhere, and hands were tearing at his dry-suit, and someone was saying, 'Look, silly bastard put the chisel through it,' and he was being rubbed with rough towels. And then he was cold, terribly cold, shuddering with a spastic twitching of the limbs that threatened to catapult him out of the bunk.

He dozed. From time to time, people brought him hot drinks. After an indeterminate interval, Cole was there.

'Thank you,' said Cole.

Eason's eyes were not focusing. 'What happened?' he said.

'You fixed the rudder,' said Cole. 'But you holed the suit with the chisel, so you nearly pegged out. You were in the water ten minutes.'

Eason lay there, felt the plunge of a *Chinamite* under control. 'Ah,' he said.

Cole was grinning. His face came into focus. There was an openness about his face that Eason had never seen before, not even after he had fixed the forestay off Cape Town. He looked, thought Eason with a moment of surprising clarity, like a man who had got his soul back. Now was the time for hard questions. 'That *Arpeggio* Inquiry,' he croaked. 'I don't believe a word of it.'

Cole's face flinched. 'Some people aren't what they'd like you to think,' he said finally.

'Meaning?'

'You'd better ask Clement Jones.' Cole was looking at the deck. The words sounded deformed, as if they were the wrong shape for his throat.

'I did,' said Eason. 'And one of his men threw me off the balcony.'

'That doesn't surprise me,' said Cole, flatly. 'I couldn't get near him, either. He's got powerful friends and he uses them bloody efficiently. People started to call in loans and I got the idea I'd end up broke, cut off at the knees. So I didn't have the guts to go on.' He paused. 'It took guts to go overboard today,' he said. 'I didn't think you'd do it.'

'What do *you* think happened on *Arpeggio*?' said Eason doggedly. He was beginning to feel very ill again.

'Nothing I can prove,' said Cole. His face had closed up, and he drifted out of sight.

Eason lay listening to the hum and roar of the surfing boat and trying to think. But his head was full of cold cottonwool. Soon, he went to sleep.

Three weeks out from Cape Town, *Kelly's Eye* was still afloat. Indeed, she was not only afloat, but trudging hard under a white main and a red spinnaker that shone against a deep-blue sky. Around her stern, two albatrosses rode the little air currents thrown up by the waves.

Bud Withers was at the wheel. His beard had grown, and there was a hollowness about his eyes, and a glow in the pupils, that gave him the look of an Old Testament prophet.

For the last twenty days, Withers had concentrated on sailing across the top of the weather. And he had got it right. The storms that had smashed *Tasman* and reduced *Flag* to spitfire jib and trysail had passed well to the south of *Eye*. She had winds force six and seven, from abaft the beam, and had made good, economical progress. At the last jaw-jaw, Withers had been glad to hear that *Eye* was lying equal second with *Chinamite*, sixty miles astern of *Flag*, and in a good position to catch up.

No boat under Withers' captaincy would ever be a happy ship. But without Kelly, the sand was gone from the machine, and the gears were working smoothly. The *Kelly's Eye* moving across the far southeastern corner of the Indian Ocean a little above the Great Circle course for Cape Grim at the western gate of the Bass Strait, was a slick racing unit moving fast and well.

*

318

In Fremantle, Australia, about a thousand sea miles to the north-northeast, Dave Kelly was completing his convalescence. Actually, the convalescence had not been strictly necessary, because his injuries in Mauritius had amounted to little more than severe bruising to ribs and legs. But he clung to the fiction, at first because he had to. Later, under the influence of brandy and self-justification, he had come to believe it.

Part of the fiction was his apartment, perched on the top of one of the mighty tower blocks overlooking Fremantle harbour. He had been there three weeks. He had found a local blonde, and a local brand of cognac. He had also installed a powerful ham radio, with which he monitored jaw-jaw among the race competitors, when he could pick it up.

On the twenty-second day after his arrival, he was on the balcony as usual. As usual, he had drunk a couple of big glasses of Château Tanunda, and tuned in to the race frequency. The voice of the duty boat hissed thinly across the ether; his mind went out to the cold and the wet, the lurching movement and the fetid smell of too many people in too small a space.

'Kelly here,' he said. 'Everything okay, there?'

'Sure,' said the operator – an American voice; *Flag*, Kelly guessed. 'All reporting, except *Tasman*.'

'Right,' said Kelly. 'Too bad. *Eye* okay?'

'Okay,' said the American voice.

'Right. Out,' said Kelly.

'Out.'

He poured himself another glass, and leaned back in his chair, allowing his eyes to rest on the smooth brown back of the blonde. As always, he felt pleased that *Kelly's Eye* was still afloat. Film or no film, she was a lot of good publicity. Maybe that guy in Cape Town, Lawson, maybe he didn't know his job. Maybe *Eye* was a good boat, at that.

The notion gave Kelly a surge of energy. He sat up and put his feet to the floor.

'Do my back, would you?' said the woman.

Kelly stood up. Sea and sky wobbled and swam. 'Get dressed,' said Kelly. 'Take me driving. I've just got better.'

The woman turned to look at him. She saw a thin man with hair that needed cutting. Black stubble grew on his greyish skin, and the whites of his eyes were clouded greenish-yellow. 'You don't look so great,' she said.

'Let's go,' said Kelly, and limped for the door.

The woman shrugged. She was thirty-five, and she had led the kind of life in which thirty-five means well past the first bloom of youth. Meal tickets were getting harder to come by, particularly gold-plated meal tickets like Dave Kelly.

'Show me the town,' said Kelly, once they were in the car.

She drove him round the towers and corrugated iron of Perth. Kelly sipped Château Tanunda from the bottle, looking bored. 'Christ,' he said at last. 'What a dump. Doesn't anything *happen*?'

'Yacht-racing,' said the woman. 'And rock-sitting.'

'Yacht-racing, yech,' said Kelly, and giggled. 'So what's this rock stuff?'

'I'll show you,' said the woman.

They drove out of town for about fifteen miles, to a

white beach. The foreshore was crowded with beaten-up estate cars and a scattering of pick-up trucks. On the beach, men and women were staring out to sea, drinking beer from eskies and talking. The sand was littered with empty beer cans.

Fifty yards off the beach was a rock. On the rock a man was sitting, leaning with his back against a pile of beer crates.

'There you go,' said the woman. 'There's the sitter. He's going for gold. He has to sit on that rock for, I dunno, a month or something, drinking only beer, no fridge.'

'No shit?' said Kelly. 'How long's he been there?'

'Three days,' said the woman.

Kelly sat down. 'Fascinating,' he said absentmindedly. Foggily, he knew how the rock-sitter must feel. Then he subsided into a glazed trance. Again, he chewed clumsily at the Lawson question. But the euphoria had withered, and now his cogitations had a dreary cast. He was stranded on a rock in Perth, like that asshole with his back against the beer crates. His brandy-sodden mind plodded back. What if that Lawson guy had been on the make? Maybe he'd seen Kelly coming, seen his chance of a little pot of gold. Yeah, thought Kelly. Maybe there's nothing wrong with the boat, at that.

His fingers clenched in the sand. Out in the bay, the rock-sitter climbed unsteadily to his feet and turned to scrabble in a beer crate. Arms flailing, he took a couple of steps, tripped over his feet and fell into the sea.

'End of attempt,' said the woman. 'Nice try, though.'

'Sure,' said Kelly. 'Let's get back to the apartment. I have to make some calls.'

There was only one call, to Lawson Boats, Boat Builders and Repairers, Simonstown, South Africa. A girl answered the telephone, and Kelly asked for Mr Lawson. The receptionist hesitated a moment, then said, 'I'll put you through.'

The voice on the extension was not Lawson's. It was younger and harder. It said, 'Hello. Who am I talking to?'

Alarm bells began ringing in Kelly's mind. 'You're not Lawson,' he said. 'Who are you?'

'Luitnant de Boet, Fraud Squad.'

'Where's Lawson?'

'Thet's what we'd like to know,' said the Luitnant.

'What happened?'

'I can't tell you until I know who you are.'

'Okay,' said Kelly, and rang off.

Next he got in touch with his researcher in Cape Town. It didn't take long for the researcher to get back to him.

'Lawson left two weeks ago. Wife and kid went too; destination unknown. He cleaned out the company's bank account before he left. Borrowed right up to the limits, bought Krugerrands, took a walk. It's not rare, nowadays. You want I should check further?'

'Don't bother,' said Kelly. He hung up and sat staring at the sand-coloured wall, his eyes yellow pits of rage.

'That little bastard saw me coming,' said Kelly. 'He saw a way to get a hundred grand pin money, and he got it. That boat's totally one hundred percent fine. That double-crossing shit –'

The woman frowned. Normally she found it impolitic to inquire into the private affairs of her meal tickets. But Kelly looked like he was about to have a stroke.

'I was robbed,' said Kelly. 'And I stayed off the boat because – ah, shit.'

The woman moved next to him and began to massage his neck with her long, brown fingers. 'Relax, baby,' she said. 'Have a drink, eh?'

Kelly slapped her hand away. 'Don't touch me,' he said. But he went to the sideboard and poured himself a large glass of brandy anyway. 'Baby,' she said. 'Relax. You want a back rub?'

'Ah, go to hell,' said Kelly. He fell face-down on the bed, and was dimly aware that she was taking his clothes off, felt her hands moving over his back. He was filled with a rush of self-pity. At some point, he must have gone to sleep.

He was woken by a violent crashing. At first he did not know what it was, or for that matter who he was or where he was, or anything, but he had an aching head and a sore sickness in his belly. The crashing stopped, and he heard voices. He pulled the pillow over his head and waited for them to go away, so he could get into the living-room and pour himself a drink.

The bedroom door banged open. A voice said, 'Good God!' The voice was male, with an English accent. Kelly recognized it and pulled the dirty satin sheets around his ears. It was the voice of George Carey, his agent.

The sheets were whipped back. The voice said 'My god-fathers!' in tones of deep disgust.

'He's still convalescing, really,' said the woman. 'But he usually likes a drink when he wakes up.'

'Madam,' said Carey. 'I strongly suggest that you pack your bags and hop it. I know Mr Kelly of old, and he has no further need of your . . . services.'

'Pack?' said the woman, with a note of panic.

'Precisely. This may help.' Kelly heard the crackle of banknotes.

'Oh,' said the woman, mollified.

'Five minutes,' said Carey.

'Hey!' said Kelly. At least that was what he meant to say. But his tongue seemed covered with glue, and all that came out was a croak.

'Stay there,' said Carey.

Two minutes later, Kelly heard the click of high heels as the woman walked quickly across the pink and white geometric tile floor and slammed the door.

'Right,' said Carey. 'Get up, Dave.'

Kelly groaned.

'Counting three,' said Carey. 'One.' Kelly heard a door being opened. Water hissed. 'Two.'

'Three,' said Carey, and pulled the sheets right off the thin, pot-bellied body in the bed. It moaned faintly as he grabbed its ankles and pulled. The head hit the tiles with a crack, and mewed as he dragged it into the littered bathroom.

The shower was icy cold. Carey heaved his client into a standing position and shoved him under the stinging jets of water. Kelly screamed.

'Come out when you're ready,' said Carey. 'I'll be waiting.' He left the bathroom, slamming the door behind him, and began pacing the floor of the apartment, kicking the dirty white suits and silk underwear and Hawaii shirts into a single pile in the corner, nose wrinkled against the smell of stale perfume and brandy. He was gazing at the ants marching into the garbage in the filthy kitchen when the bathroom door opened.

'Carey,' said Kelly. 'Nice to see you.' He smiled, the smile that used once to light up his face, but now seemed a perfunctory stretching of the mouth over unbrushed teeth. Carey's face must have given away his thoughts, because Kelly's eyes suddenly travelled to the dirty clothes, and his nose wrinkled at the smell. 'I've been ill,' he said.

Carey nodded slowly, his face immobile beneath his high, shining forehead. He walked into the living-room, dusted off a chair with his red bandana, and said, as if to himself, 'Mentally ill. It's the only possible explanation.'

'What?' said Kelly, who had followed him with a fuddled, anxious expression on his face.

Carey sat down, folded his hands and crossed his legs in their immaculate fawn linen trousers. 'The only explanation for one of my clients, admired by sixty million viewers for his strength of mind, courage and crispness of intellect, abandoning his career at crisis point.' He stood up. 'What the hell do you think you've been *doing*, Kelly?'

'Working,' said Kelly, with the trace of a whine in his voice. 'I was thinking I'd do a film about rock-sitting –'

'Rock-sitting?' said Carey, passing a hand over what had once been his hair. 'Listen, Dave. In your time you have interviewed Gadaffi, Abu Nidal, Ho Chi Minh. I have not flown to Australia to talk about . . . *rock-sitting*.'

'Hey,' said Kelly, stung. 'What are you trying to say?'

'I need to know why you went to Mauritius and had a little car accident and bumped your knee, and instead of straining every nerve to get out of there and back into the race, you lie in hospital –'

'Wait a minute,' said Kelly. 'I missed the plane.'

325

'So why didn't you get on the plane a day earlier?' hissed Carey. 'That's what I'd like to know. And that's what Omar Wohl would like to know, too. His lawyers are working right now to hold you in breach of contract. And I don't see any reason why they shouldn't succeed.'

'I had an accident,' said Kelly.

'Sigmund Freud was of the opinion that there is no such thing. In this case, so am I,' said Carey. 'So if you wish to continue your career, stop all this drinking and get yourself to Sydney to rejoin the boat. The rough cut of the first part was good enough so if there's any material for the second part, I'll able to take you through this one.'

'It was a nice rough cut,' said Kelly.

'I think you ought to ask yourself how much of that was due to Chuck, Herb and the editor,' said Carey. 'Now let's get you out of here and over to Sydney, and you can spend a week in a clinic and then start on the background stuff with the second unit.'

'Sure,' said Kelly. 'Let's go.' His face looked pinker, and his voice had lost its whine. Got away with it one more time, Kelly, he was thinking. Clinics? Rest cures? Kelly had been on health farms before. There was always some chick you could get around.

'And another thing,' said Carey. 'If you screw up this time, you won't have a contract and you won't have an agent. And believe me, Dave, you don't have many friends left.'

Kelly said, 'Sure, sure,' and nodded earnestly. But as soon as Carey turned away, he felt a sick panic crawl inside his stomach. Carey was right, and he knew it. Kelly had one foot over the edge of the abyss; a sour wind was close to choking him, and this time he knew that if he was not very, very careful he was going to fall.

It was clear blue day in the Great Australian Bight, and *Kelly's Eye* was lying fourth, behind *Siltex*, *Flag* and *Chinamite*. She was marching east in twenty-five knots of breeze, a couple of albatrosses skimming her wake. Compared with the freezing damp of the past weeks, the day was almost warm. The crew of *Kelly's Eye* were a dour bunch, but today they were almost blossoming. The hands in the gorilla pit were arguing about tennis. Bennett was sitting to leeward with a selection of glass bottles and the .38 that Bud Withers, for his own inscrutable reasons, carried on all his boats. She was throwing bottles into the sea and shooting them up. It made for difficult shooting, and she missed often.

At the wheel, Bud Withers was feeling less frustrated than usual. To be lying fourth was nothing to shout about. But *Eye* was not a bad fourth. Furthermore, Withers was a veteran of the SORC, and had sailed two Sydney-Hobarts, so he knew the water. In the Bass Strait and off the east coast of Victoria and New South Wales, this would count for a lot – particularly in the absence of *Tasman*. Bud Withers, braced at the wheel with his eyes flicking from sail to sea to compass, was not at all sorry about *Tasman*'s disappearance.

The radio operator's head appeared at the after companion-hatch. 'Radio, skip,' he said.

Withers gave the wheel to Bennett, and went below. Bennett pushed the .38 into the pocket of her jeans and leaned against the shove of the rudder, happy at the helm and thinking about Sydney; a few beers and a laugh, playing with Nicky Eason, maybe. He was good company, that guy. After five minutes, Withers' head appeared in the hatchway. He said, 'Your friend Kelly's coming back.'

Bennett's half-smile vanished. 'He is?' she said.

'He's waiting in Sydney. Counting the minutes, he says.'

'Oh,' said Bennett. 'Shit.' She handed the wheel back to Withers. The contentment had gone. In its place was a deep gloom.

She went to the pushpit, tossed a pop bottle overboard, brought up the pistol and blazed away at the retreating gleam of glass.

The explosions sounded flat and dull in the big wind. The bottle did not sink. 'Kelly, you sonofabitch,' she hissed, blaming him for her crooked shooting as well as everything else. One of the albatrosses soared in, ignoring the shots. Idly, Bennett pointed the gun at it. As the yellow axe-beak between the six-foot wings swayed across the barrel, she pulled the trigger. The gun went off. The albatross crumpled into the sea in a cartwheel of long white wings.

Bennett was pale. 'I thought . . . I thought I'd fired all the chambers.'

'Oh, yeah,' said Withers. His eyes were mean above the patches of brown beard that grew on his cheekbones, and his voice was harsh. 'But you hadn't.' He snatched the gun out of her hand and pushed his face in front of hers. 'And now you've killed an albatross. You know what that means?'

Bennett shrugged her shoulders and tried to laugh.

'Come on, Bud. You're not superstitious, are you?'

'I sure as hell am superstitious,' said Withers. 'If anything goes wrong with this boat, I'll throw you into the sea.'

'Okay,' said Bennett. 'I'll remember that.'

EPK Electric was a good two days behind the leaders. Harriet was on deck in the darkness, gazing into the black. Somewhere ahead was the western entrance to the Bass Strait. The wind had dropped until it was a mere whisper across the water.

Harriet was filled with a sudden expectancy. She breathed deeply, and the beat of her pulse ran hard and strong. Something was about to happen.

'Bit more mainsheet, please,' said Emily, from the wheel.

Harriet let the sheet off the drum, steadying it with her free hand – a hand now hardened by heaving wet ropes on dark nights in cold seas. She listened to the gurgle of the bow wave die away into a clop of little ripples. No wind at all.

An edge of cloud swept across the sky as if someone had drawn a great curtain. Behind it, the sky was deep blue and full of millions of stars. And under the curtain came the breeze.

It came from the north, shoving taut into *EPK*'s sails, heeling her to starboard and accelerating the wavelets from a clop to a gurgle to a hiss. It was a warm breeze. But the most remarkable thing about it was the smell. It smelt like a summer garden, honey and hayfields and warm dust. The smell transported Harriet; suddenly she was far away, walking among aromatic clumps of pinks and carnations. Walking beside Henri de Rochambaud.

The smell was confirmation that soon she would see de Rochambaud, walk with him and talk with him. After the long, empty weeks of salt water, it was the smell of the land.

Flag had come through the Bass Strait on a broad reach and turned up for Sydney on the run. The wind had backed easterly in the night – the first easterly for three weeks. At sunset, it faded away altogether. The crew worked hard changing sails as the sun sank towards the horizon and the Cape Howe light began flashing far over the smooth water.

It was good to be warm again. The temperature had been rising steadily for a week now, as *Flag* clawed northwards out of the Westerlies, rode the current past Cape Grim, marched along the southern shores of Victoria and turned north. Jaw-jaws had become terse and monosyllabic. Nobody wanted to give away positions; and radar was confusing, because after the emptiness of the Southern Ocean, the Bass Strait in midsummer was a clutter of echoes, and it was hard to tell who was who. *Flag*'s watch on deck had sweated as she had slopped around in a tiny, indecisive breeze, and the last red of the sunset faded over the mountains inland.

Then the breeze filled in from the west; the land breeze. And *Flag* began to tramp.

After supper Schacker got to his feet and said, 'Gentlemen, the end is nigh. I guess I better make a speech.' He looked down the long row of faces, lank-haired, wind-red. Beyond the crew, *Flag*'s inside stretched away, cluttered with sails and ropes and sleeping-bags wedged into cracks in the debris. 'That was part one of the Southern Ocean,' he said. 'We did well. We got through in a seamanlike manner, and we didn't break anything except a boom.'

'Is that all?' said George Hart, ironically. There was a laugh. The boom had meant two days under headsails only while the riggers lashed up heavy splints. Hyatt did not share in the laugh.

'But I want to tell you that we are still racing,' said Art. He thumbed the Brookes and Gatehouse repeater on the bulkhead. 'We have eighty-two miles to make. Maybe nine hours' sailing, if the wind holds. Not far. But far enough to lose the race in, if the concentration goes. So let's keep at it, right? And when we get to Sydney, take it easy with the booze, stay clear of journalists. If they want to talk, they can talk to me –'

'Art.' The radio operator's head appeared round the door of the navigatorium. 'Come and get a look at this.'

'That's all,' said Art, and went in.

It was a tight fit in the tiny, blacked-out space. The radar glowed with a green, submarine radiance on the console.

'This one,' said the radio operator, pointing at a blip

five miles off the coast, and fifteen miles ahead.

'Well?' said Schacker.

'She's moving eleven knots, maybe. Keeping station with us. She just came out of the coast echoes.'

'Power boat,' said Schacker.

'Not at that range,' said the radio operator. 'Too small for a ship. Too big for most pleasure yachts. She's a big sailing boat.'

'Fast, too.'

'On course for Sydney,' said the radio operator. 'What do you think?'

Schacker shrugged. But his square brown hand came up and fingered his chin. Someone in the main cabin had turned the radio to 2BL Sydney Great Circle Report.

'Well, the first boat's due in just after dawn,' said the announcer. 'And it looks like it'll be *Flag*, the Sound Yacht Club entry. There'll be some long faces about that. And longest of all will be the face of Harry Redd, chief sponsor of *Tasman*, which tragically disappeared a week out of Cape Town. Harry Redd's with me now. What do you say, Mr Redd?'

'There isn't much,' said Redd. 'Except that while there's life there's hope, and I'm still alive.'

Schacker stood in the doorway, staring at the radio.

'Tubes Murphy, *Tasman*'s skipper, was a personal friend, right?' said the announcer.

'Too right,' said Redd. 'Old Murphy's a tough bloke. I won't believe he's copped it until I see the stiff.'

'Yeah,' said the announcer. 'Well, there'll be a lot of Australians hoping you're right. But the odds aren't that great, eh?'

'Murphy's favourite kind,' said Redd. 'I wouldn't be surprised if –'

Schacker turned the set off. 'Okay,' he said. 'I want all stores overboard. And any other heavy gear we can shift.'

Blank faces turned towards him.

'Go for it,' he said. 'There's a big boat up ahead and it's the right size for *Tasman*.'

They stared at him for a moment. Then it sank in, and they began to work.

That night, *Flag* sailed stripped to the bone. The wind was fading, but she slipped through the water like a sylph. When the crew had finished work they went on deck and sat up to weather, straining their eyes into the darkness. And the blip on the radar fell back, until by five a.m. it was a mere five miles ahead.

Schacker, standing at the wheel, said, 'Dawn.'

A pale flood spread from the smooth eastern horizon, lightening the navy blue sky and rimming the world with gold. Schacker said to Joey, 'Up the mast and get a look.'

They hauled him up to the third spreaders, and he trained his glasses.

The sea was still dark grey with night. In the sky, the silver aeroplanes caught the first light. To the north, where the land was studded with the little white sugar-cubes of buildings, the sea was jagged with pleasure yachts. In between *Flag* and that first phalanx, glowing in the early rays, was a bulbous tower of sail. Joey did not have to see the logo on the sail to know the boat's name. He slid down the shroud and padded aft to Schacker.

'That's *Tasman* all right,' he said.

Schacker's eyes were flat and metallic. 'Catch her,' he said, and went down to get the weather.

Feet thundered on the deck as he tuned the radio, and *Flag*'s heel steepened. The weather forecast said easterlies, five to ten knots, falling light later. Good, thought Schacker; ideal conditions for a stripped-out boat. But further back in his mind, he was angry with himself. *Perhaps I should have been pushing harder. Maybe I was too careful.*

Then the anger transferred itself outside the boat, across the water to *Tasman*. She had neglected her radio sign-ons for three weeks. Murphy had said his Automatic Position Indicator was bust, but he had probably unscrewed it. And that was wilful disobedience of·race rules, damn it.

Schacker slammed his fist on the chart-table, stood up, and stumped on deck. 'Give me a protest flag on that backstay,' he roared. 'And catch that cheating sonofabitch!'

Flag heeled under the sudden downdraught from a helicopter's blades, and the racket made speech impossible. The sky was full of aircraft now, and the front runners of the seaborne fleet were all around, outboards howling.

'Bullhorn,' said Schacker between clenched teeth.

'Deep sixed it,' said George Hart.

Schacker swore. Then he said. 'Get down there and call that goddamn radio station and tell them to tell these guys to clear our water. Then tune in, and stay tuned.'

Hart scuttled below. Soon, the commentator's voice floated up the hatch. '*Tasman*'s changed to a light spinnaker,' it said. 'The wind's gone fluky right in sight of

the finishing line in the Heads. And way back there, *Flag*'s
moving well in five to ten knots of wind . . . flying a
protest flag, looks like.'

'Seven to twelve,' said Schacker. 'Just you keep talking,
boy.' The spinnaker ahead was getting bigger. As he
watched, it billowed and sagged. 'Losing his wind,' said
Schacker. The palms of his hands were wet with sweat.
'Come on,' he said, to the boat. The wind speed stayed
steady on nine knots. We can catch her, he thought. And
looking around, he saw the men on deck had come to the
same conclusion, but nobody was saying anything, in case
they lost the wind.

'Oh dear, oh dear,' said the commentator. '*Tasman*'s
got no wind at all. She's just slopping around out there,
within sight of the finish. And two miles away – yes,
that's all now – the American boat *Flag*'s coming in like
gangbusters. Well, those fat cats in America are certainly
going to be rubbing their hands! Oh, this looks like a
tragedy for Australia.'

'Get the ultralite,' said Schacker. It was the first time
anyone had spoken for ten minutes. 'And when I say the
word, give me a clean change of sails.' He had been getting
clean changes for fifteen thousand miles, but nobody
seemed surprised.

The foredeck men moved stealthily into position. The
figures on *Tasman*'s deck were easily visible now. One of
them waved. Nobody on *Flag* waved back.

The wind-speed indicator dropped to five knots. 'Pull it
up,' said Schacker. The huge featherweight spinnaker
bloomed, its stars and stripes glowing in the bright morning sun.

The wind speed dropped another three knots, rose, dropped again. *Tasman* got a gust two minutes later. Her spinnaker filled, and she moved perhaps four hundred yards before it collapsed. *Flag*, out in the tide, had more wind but more adverse current. 'Take her in,' said Schacker. Joey eased the wheel, and *Flag* bore down on *Tasman*'s stern.

Tasman was half a mile off the line now, with *Flag* four hundred yards away on her tail. Flat calm. Schacker was praying. Just one puff of wind, he said to himself; so I can dirty his air and keep him where I want him; mine's the lighter boat, I've got the acceleration, that'll do it –

He became aware that the commentator was babbling on. 'Well, it looks like whoever gets the sea breeze first gets the leg,' he was saying. 'And that should – well, let's say could – be *Tasman*.'

But it was *Flag* who got the wind. It was a mere zephyr, but it filled the gossamer sail, and a little vee of ripples spread from her transom as she began to move. By the time *Tasman* got it, the gap was two hundred yards. The trimmers lay flat, playing the sheets for the last breath. The gap narrowed. The commentator was incoherent with suspense, but nobody paid any attention any more. All eyes on *Flag* were fixed on *Tasman*'s transom. The transom was growing as *Flag* hauled her down. Even the spectators sensed that something was happening, and left a clear lane between the two. A lane which shortened to a hundred yards, then seventy-five. Tubes Murphy's bright-red mane shone in the sun as he stood at the wheel, never looking back. Schacker said, 'We've got his wind. Any second.' The line was three hundred yards away.

Then it happened.

A speedboat roared out of the fleet to port, a photographer lying flat on the bow, telephoto trained. The boat came straight for *Flag*'s mid-section. Schacker started to yell. The whole crew was yelling. Only Hyatt was silent, looking pink and scornful. The yells were drowned by the engine's scream. At the moment it seemed inevitable the the speedboat would ram her amidships, it turned away, heeling steeply. The wave of its turning rolled *Flag* to starboard, then back on herself, a sudden, jerky roll that knocked the wind out of her spinnaker. For perhaps fifteen seconds, it flopped and billowed. Then it filled again.

But it was too late. *Tasman* was a hundred yards clear. The gap was closing, but too slowly. A minute and a half later, the gun thudded, and every siren in the harbour howled a welcome to *Tasman*, winner of the second leg.

'*She's won!*' shrieked the commentator. '*We've won!*'

Schacker's eyes travelled to the protest flag fluttering at the backstay. 'We'll see about that,' he said as *Flag* crossed the line. Hyatt was looking at him, lip curled. Schacker ignored him. 'Now start the goddamn engine. George, let's get some breakfast, eh?'

As *Tasman* passed the layer-cake cliffs of the Heads, a helicopter clattered out of the blue sky to landward. On its nose was painted in red letters the word REDD. It lowered a box to *Tasman*'s deck. On the box was painted in large letters, CHAMPAGNE TASMAN. The press cameras of the world duly recorded the delivery. And in the open doorway of the helicopter the proprietor himself stood like a small, grinning monkey, waving.

The two boats motored in. Sydney Harbour was a pandemonium of sirens, the bridge and harbourside roads jammed end to end with cars, every driver leaning on his horn, the beaches crowded with yelling people. *Tasman* was engulfed in the press of spectator boats, her crew standing at the rail with fenders to protect her hull from over-enthusiastic supporters.

It took half an hour to get to the dock. *Flag* tied up in grim silence. Two jetties away, an ambulance backed up to *Tasman*. After it had left, Tubes Murphy soared above his crew's heads and arched into the water with an enormous splash. Schacker jumped down to the jetty and pushed his way through the crowd towards *Tasman*. His face was set hard as granite.

Tasman's deck was jammed with press photographers and journalists and people drinking champagne. He said, 'Where's Murphy?'

'Getting the water off,' said one of the crew, grinning all over his face. 'Come aboard, sport. Have a drink and congratulate us.'

'I'll have a word with Murphy, first,' said Schacker grimly.

'Feel free,' said the Australian.

Schacker pulled himself up on the lifelines and pushed his way aft. The hatches were open, and a bad, stale smell wafted up from below. Tubes Murphy's red head and barndoor shoulders were half-way out of the after hatch. He was surrounded by people. 'Art,' he said. 'Good race.'

'Yeah,' said Schacker. 'But don't get too excited. I'm protesting you for radio silence and deep-sixing your position indicator. Any objections?'

Murphy grinned, showing a wide fence of white teeth under his hooked pirate's nose. 'Only that I'd hate to see you get lynched if you get it through.' He waved a huge hand at the people on deck, the boats crowded in the harbour and the throngs of cheering, chanting well-wishers surging down to the quays.

'I'll risk it,' said Schacker.

'Tell you what,' said Murphy. 'Come and take a look below, eh?'

'What for?' said Schacker.

'You'll see,' said Murphy. Suddenly, he looked serious, and Schacker noticed that he had lost a lot of weight, and there were gaunt hollows under his cheekbones.

'If you insist,' he said.

It was the smell that hit him first. All boats smell bad after four weeks at sea in conditions where cooking is difficult and food slides and finds it way into the bilges. But *Tasman*'s smell was worse than that. It was a compound of mould and sea water and rot that caught the throat and brought bile to the stomach.

The smell was so strong that for a moment it dominated Schacker's senses. Then his eyes adjusted to the gloom.

Tasman's cabin was a shambles. Doors had come off lockers, two of her pipe cots were twisted and bent, and her galley stove had gone.

'Take a look at the flight deck,' said Murphy.

Schacker looked. The trunking was off the skeins of multicoloured wire that connected the instruments, radio, satnav. Where there should have been the bright metal of connections, there was a mass of green and white corrosion, like the terminals of a very old car battery.

'Maybe you'd like to go on deck, now,' said Murphy.

Schacker went. *Tasman* was a floating coffin, and he needed no encouragement to get into the light and air.

'Nice, eh?' said Murphy. 'Beer?'

'Beer,' said Schacker. He was not angry anymore. He took the can and drank deep, breathing the clean breeze, his ears rejoicing to the sound of the gulls wheeling over the crowds on the dock.

'Beer survived all right,' said Murphy. 'About the only thing that did.' He grinned at a photographer, then turned back to Schacker.

'What happened?' said Schacker.

'Got knocked down,' said Murphy. 'Flat on her side, with the waves breaking on to the sail so she wouldn't come up. And the bloody hatch was jammed on its runners, so she was taking water. Took a bit of a pounding, actually. Washed away the aerials and that.' Schacker would have objected, but he was too busy thinking about a vertical deck and water pouring into the hull in those fifty-foot hills of black sea.

'But we kept the mast,' said Murphy. 'And after a bit of bother we got the sails off, and up she came. Then there was a certain amount of pumping.'

'How much?' said Schacker.

'The water was up to the second bunks below,' said Murphy casually. 'Bit of a bastard getting her empty. There was about a hundredweight of rice loose and the bloody pumps kept clogging.'

'Jesus,' said Schacker.

'Yeah, well,' said Murphy. 'Prayers were said. It was bloody cold, too. But luckily we all had our dry-suits on, even the watch below. We'd been pushing reasonably hard, so when we had her dry we kept racing.'

'Electrics?'

'Right up the creek,' said Murphy. 'Thank Christ we had a diesel cabin heater and an emergency gas ring. But take my tip: unless you've got complete faith in your hatches, don't put an all-electric galley in.'

'I'll remember that,' said Schacker. He gulped beer. Then he held out his hand. 'I'm glad you made it, Murphy,' he said.

Murphy enveloped his small, hard hand in his own mighty paw. 'Nice of you to say so,' he said. He narrowed his eyes and looked into the sun, to the red protest flag fluttering at *Flag*'s backstay. 'What about the protest?' he said.

Schacker's eyebrows made two arches on his brown forehead. 'Protest?' he said. 'The protest stands, of course.'

'I thought it might,' said Murphy.

'But I guess it might not get too far once they see this mess.'

'I guess it might not,' said Murphy. He grinned, his beak of a nose nearly meeting his chin. 'Pleasure doing business with you, Schacker.'

'The feeling's mutual,' said Schacker. 'See you later.'

Tubes lay on the deck with a bottle of champagne in his hand, and watched the small, square man elbow his way through the mass of pressmen and rubberneckers.

'He'll withdraw,' said Sparko.

'No he won't,' said Murphy. 'Now, then. Where's old Reddy?'

*

After Harry Redd had lowered the case of champagne on to *Tasman*'s deck, he had gone back to sit beside the pilot. His face was grinning furiously under his cropped dome. 'Back,' he said. 'Quick.'

The pilot put the nose down, and the Bell Jet Ranger shot across the checkerboard of red-tiled bungalows and blue pools towards the heliport. Redd got on the telephone, and dialled the Stapleton residence. Mo Stapleton was in the office. But Redd had even less desire than usual to speak to Mo.

'Shar,' he said, when she answered. 'You want to see Murphy? I'll take you down, and it'll look okay, no worries from the other half, eh?'

'Oh,' breathed Shar. 'You *sweet* man. What'll I *wear*?'

Redd looked at his watch. 'I'll pick you up at the Wagga Wagga Inn in twenty minutes, okay?'

The Wagga Wagga Inn is off the Pacific Highway north of Sydney. Shar Stapleton parked in the car park and walked to the entrance. The feeder road was busy, and the exhaust fumes mingled with the heat made it hard to breathe. So did the way her heart was beating at the thought of seeing Murphy. Shar could feel sweat moistening her breasts, making the yellow silk of her dress cling to her skin. A couple of passing cars tooted and swerved. She paid no attention.

The doorman knew her well. 'Harry Redd here yet?' she said. The doorman shook his head, then looked up and over her shoulder.

'This'll be him now,' he said.

A silver Porsche was braking under the flickering shadows of the bluegums that lined the road, shifting into the centre lane to turn across the traffic. It reached the centre reservation. Harry Redd was at the wheel. Shar waved. He lifted a hand. The Porsche started forward.

She did not see where the big Holden came from. It must have been doing a hundred in the fast lane across which the Porsche was turning. There was a scream of rubber and a hideous bang. The Holden rode half-way over the Porsche and took it fifty yards up the road, and stopped. In the sudden hush, Shar could hear metal ticking. No, she thought; this hasn't happened. I shall wake up.

Suddenly the pile of steel was licked by orange flames, pale in the bright sunlight. Black smoke began to roll.

Shar started to run towards the fire. The doorman caught her arm. 'No,' he said. 'They haven't a hope.'

'Let go!' she screamed. He fell back. She started again, awkward in her high-heeled shoes. When she was thirty yards away, the wreckage went *whoomph*, and she felt the heat on her face as a ball of flame rolled into the sky.

'Not a hope,' said someone nearby. 'They've had it, all right.'

Shar watched as the flames died, leaving the blackened twisted things that five minutes ago had been two cars and their drivers, on their way somewhere. Police sirens wailed. Firemen arrived, and started squirting foam.

Shar's eyes dulled with tears. 'Too late!' she screamed. 'You're too late, you stupid bastards.'

Then she walked back to her car and drove down to the harbour, where the exulting crowds surged round the victorious *Tasman*.

SYDNEY

Sydney is not a city to be knocked on its ear by the death of a financier, even when the financier is as popular and ebullient as Harry Redd. The papers and radio and TV had a field day with it. The people of the city felt a moment's sadness, then returned to the main point. An Australian boat had come home ahead of the fleet this leg, and beaten the Sound Yacht Club. The bars were jammed. Beer, wine and whisky ran like water, and all the first day and all the first night they danced in the streets. Compared to Sydney, Cape Town had been a Salvation Army social.

But at the centre of the hurricane of celebration, Tubes Murphy found himself in a small, calm eye of grief. So far, he was numb. But he knew the numbness was an expanded version of the interval of no-pain that comes after a deep cut. There was a lot to organize, and now was the time to do it.

First of all he called Mike Trevose, who ran the yard, and told him to take *Tasman* out of the water for repairs forthwith. Then he called Wharf Sails, in which he was a partner, and told them to expect a visit. After that he went to the window of his rented office which overlooked an arm of the harbour. A motorboat was idling below.

Murphy heaved his bulk out of the window and got in. The man at the wheel winked, and said, 'Ready?'

'You bet,' said Murphy.

The boat droned across the bay, flicking past beaches and through crowded anchorages under the smooth green lawns of prosperous suburbs. At first, the newshounds tried to follow. But the driver knew his harbour, and lost them. Half an hour later, the boat sank from its wake into the still blue waters of a gum-fringed cove just big enough to hold a motor yacht, white as a wedding cake, with a gangway slanting down its side to the glassy blue water. Murphy's eyes were suddenly heavy with exhaustion. He said, 'Thanks, mate,' to the driver, and clambered up the gangway.

At the top, Shar Stapleton was waiting, dressed in white sailor trousers and a white T-shirt whose coarse cotton sang against the bloom of her brown skin. She was smiling, her teeth a gleam of white that starred in the sun, hurting Murphy's exhausted eyes. 'Like it?' she said. 'I rented it specially. Hot and cold running asses' milk in all staterooms –'

Murphy grabbed her. They clung to each other, laughing because they were at a level of emptiness where there was nothing to do but laugh. Murphy smelt the musk of her hair, felt her fingers in the big muscles under his shoulder blades. He felt the rhythm of her gasping change as her laughter turned to weeping. Then he wept, too.

He woke next day in a stream of sunlight from the picture window at the foot of the bed. It took him a minute to remember where he was. The deck was covered in oyster-coloured carpet, and a chandelier hung from the deckhead.

He reached over for Shar. She was gone. In the imprint of her head on the pillow was a note.

Hubby calls, it said. *Funeral tomorrow. Look after yourself.*

He rolled out of bed and into the clean clothes that she had brought him, a white duck suit with a red shirt. The deck swayed as his inner ear tried to compensate for *Tasman*'s heave. Breakfast was laid in the dining cabin. He picked up a slab of bread, folded it over a slice of ham, and shoved a peach into his pocket. Then he trotted down the gangway to the waiting speedboat.

As they rounded the last headland and the masts of the competitors came in view, Murphy's heavy eyebrows drew together. *Tasman* was still in the water. His big, blunt fingers tapped impatiently on his knee. At the yard dock he jumped ashore and walked quickly up to the yard office.

Mike Trevose had sun-bleached grey hair. His grey beard and horn-rimmed glasses made him look more like an academic than a boatbuilder. 'G'day,' he said, and rose from the leather chair in front of the wall of half-hull ship models. But he did not come round the big oak desk.

'*Tasman*'s still in the water,' said Murphy.

'Oh,' said Trevose. 'Yeah.'

'Lot of work to do,' said Murphy. 'Let's get cracking.'

'Siddown, Murphy,' said Trevose.

Murphy said, 'Is there something I should know about?'

Trevose gave him a smile that was all teeth and no eyes.

'Well,' he said, and drew a deep breath. 'I have to tell you that *Tasman* needs a lot of money spending on her.' He paused.

Murphy's eyes were narrow on either side of his beak of a nose. 'Go on,' he said.

'And the . . . well, the source of funds isn't evident to me,' he said finally.

'You mean Reddy's croaked and you're copping out until you know who'll pay you? Listen, mate, *Tasman*'s sponsored by Tasman Wine, not Harry Redd.'

Trevose shrugged. 'Still,' he said. 'Until things get sorted . . .'

'Okay,' said Murphy. 'I get it.' He rose, knocking his chair over. 'Thank you for your support, Mike. Next time I want someone to knife their gran for a couple of notes, I'll give you a call.'

'You don't understand,' said Trevose.

'Oh, yes, I do,' said Murphy. He stormed out into the fresh morning sunlight. The day had not yet acquired its oppressive noon heat, but he was sweating anyway.

He shouldered his way through the crowds of sightseers thronging the approaches to the yard. There was cheering: another Great Circle boat coming in. He paused and looked round. Battle flags flapped above the sea of heads. *Kelly's Eye* was in. And another, moving, coming alongside the dock under power. *EPK Electric*. He looked at the Rolex on his big, hairy wrist. *Tasman* had to beat *EPK* by forty-two hours, to save her time. *EPK* was eight hours inside that time. He felt a sinking of the heart.

'Hey!' somebody shouted. 'Tubes!'

The crowd around him suddenly focused inwards.

Anonymous bodies developed curious faces and auto-graph books. He scrawled and grinned, reversing towards the road. The crowd around him thickened. People in the front rank were cursing as those behind pushed them forward. Tubes glanced over his shoulder, saw the roofs of cars. He kept walking backwards, treading on toes. It was a month since he had seen this many people. He did not like it; it confused him, at exactly the moment when he had to think most clearly.

Tubes turned and ran. Behind him, the crowd's clamour changed to an ugly, disappointed roar. He forced his way between shoulders and bottoms. The roof sign of a taxi loomed ahead. He opened the door and jumped into the front seat. The driver said, 'Not for hire, mate.'

'Hey!' said one of the two old ladies in the back seat, the one with blue hair and swallow-tail glasses. 'Are you Tubes Murphy?'

'None other,' said Murphy. The cab windows were full of distorted faces, noses pressed against the glass. Someone was banging on the roof. 'Ladies,' said Murphy, 'Get me out of here, would you?'

'But we've just *arrived*,' protested the second old lady.

'Fair crack of the whip, young man,' said the first one. 'Cabbie, drive on.' She turned to the faces at the window. 'Piss off, you bastards!'

Old papers blew in the breeze and fluttered from the five strands of barbed wire that topped the chain-link fence surrounding the Wharf Sails building.

Murphy kissed the old ladies a gallant goodbye, slipped the driver twenty dollars and strode past the security guard on the metal gates. The reception area was light-green wood, elegant California style. But the two offices beyond were strictly practical.

In the inner office, two men in shorts were drinking coffee and peering at an IBM PC/AT. They looked round sharply as Murphy came in, then got up. 'Murphy!' they cried. 'Where you been?'

'Around,' said Murphy. 'Tolley, Creek. Good to see you.'

'Nice work,' said Tolley, the larger of the two men.

'Thanks,' said Murphy. 'EPK won on corrected time.'

'Too bad,' said Creek, pushing his horn-rimmed glasses up his nose.

'There's still the next leg,' said Murphy. 'How you doing with my sails, boys?'

'Sit down,' said Tolley, indicating the big table in the centre of the office. Tolley was the money man in the partnership. Creek was the designer, a small, introverted ex-engineer. Murphy was the public face.

'Have we got my sails?' said Murphy.

Creek looked nervously across at Tolley. Tolley said. 'Yes.'

'Great,' said Murphy. 'We'll need some more, too. Blew out a load of them this leg.'

'Yeah,' said Tolley. His face was smooth and square under a roof of straight black hair that hung down over his eyebrows. 'Murph, I might as well tell you. We've got problems.'

'Problems?' said Murphy. It was quiet in the office. Too quiet, he suddenly realized. Normally there were background noises: sewing-machines, the rumble of the sailmakers pushing themselves round on their little trollies on the polished floor of the sail-loft upstairs.

'You remember Harry Redd made us a payment for *Tasman*'s sails?' said Tolley. 'Well, it was technically a loan, for tax reasons. And some bastard from Tasman Wine called yesterday morning and served papers calling in the loan.'

'Instantly?'

'Thirty days. Unless –'

Murphy was leaning back in his chair. His eyelids were drooping; he might have been drowsing, but for the glint of anger under his thick brows. 'Unless what?'

'Unless we hang on to the sails we've got here,' said Tolley. 'Refuse to release them.'

'They can't do that.'

'They've appointed a receiver,' said Tolley. 'We're bankrupt, unless they let us off the hook.'

'Off the hook,' said Murphy. 'That little bastard.'

'Who?' said Tolley.

Murphy reached for the telephone. 'Still connected?'

'Yeah.'

Murphy dialled the number of the *Sydney Herald* and asked for the newsdesk. 'Jacko,' he said, when he got through. 'I've got a nice little exclusive for you. Meet you at the main entrance of the Tasman Tower in half an hour, okay. Oh, and bring a photographer.'

The Tasman Tower's atrium was blood-red marble and jungle-green plants. The receptionist wore eye shadow to match the plants, and lipstick to match the marble. She put down the telephone and said, 'I'm afraid no member of the board can see you right now.'

'I'll go up,' said Murphy.

The receptionist's mouth fell open. Then her hand strayed to a button, and a large man in blue uniform detached himself from the wall. 'Can I help you, sir?' he said.

He must have been six foot three. Murphy was most of a head taller. 'Nope,' said Murphy. 'I'm going upstairs.'

'Now wait –'

'And this is Jacko Starr from the *Herald* and Wally Dixon with the camera. Personally, I sail the company's boat.'

The security man's eyes flickered. His hands clasped each other as the sweat broke in his palms. 'I'm sorry, Mr Murphy. But –'

'Listen,' said Murphy quietly and reasonably. 'You want a fuss, you can have one. But before you start anything in front of the world's press, I'd have a chatette with Public Relations, eh?'

'Yeah,' said the security man, rubbing his dry lips with a dry tongue. 'Yeah.' He turned away to the telephone. Five yards away, in a bank of lifts, a door opened. 'Let's go,' said Murphy, and stepped in.

'What's happening?' said the reporter.

'Wait and see,' said Murphy. 'I think we got a change of dynasty up here.'

'Redd was a friend of yours,' said the reporter.

'Too right.'

'Who's the top dog now?' said the reporter.

'Search me.'

The lift stopped at the forty-seventh floor.

'C'mon,' said Murphy, and stumped into the grey corridor. The peach he had shoved into his pocket at breakfast had squashed, leaving an ugly stain on the white material of his jacket. He pushed open a door. The three secretaries at the desks looked up, shock in their eyes. 'G'day, ladies,' said Murphy. He marched up to the heavy oak double doors at the far end, and kicked them open. One of the secretaries screamed. Beyond Murphy, ranged in the Chippendale chairs on either side of the table, the board of Tasman Wine turned disbelieving faces towards him. 'Beaut!' breathed the photographer, and squeezed the shutter.

'G'day,' said Murphy. 'Now which one of you drongoes is trying to bugger about with my boat?'

Behind him the doors burst open, and the room was suddenly full of security men.

'Am I to understand the board's authorized a total withdrawal of funds?' said Murphy. The reporter was scribbling furiously.

Many of the faces looked away. One did not. It was the face sitting at the far end of the table, dark in silhouette against the sun glaring on the city skyline behind.

A security man grabbed Murphy by the arm. He shook him off. Two more came. They pulled him backwards. A flashbulb popped.

'Stop,' said the face at the end of the table. The voice was cold and dry. 'Now he's here, he might as well hear this. Yes, Murphy, Tasman Wine is under new management. At an extraordinary meeting of the board today, as provided for by the appropriate articles in the company's charter, I was elected chairman and managing director. It is one of the first aims of the new board to enhance stewardship of the company's assets, while redirecting its public relations into low-cost, directly beneficial channels.'

'What the bloody hell does that mean?' said Murphy.

'It means we're not paying for you to gallivant round the world like some kind of drunken schoolkid. You're fired. You and that boat,' said Mo Stapleton.

Murphy looked at him for a long, slow moment before he spoke. Stapleton's face was dull and pouchy, the eyes empty. 'I loved Harry like a brother. We all did,' he said. 'Harry's heart was in that boat and you know it.'

'Don't be childish,' said Stapleton curtly. 'Doubtless, you will be wanting to find a new sponsor. Don't let us stop you.' He paused, and a thin smile appeared on his face. 'By the way, I'm sure the board will want to join me in congratulating you on your win.'

Murphy shook the security men's hands off his arms and walked out of the room. 'Did you get all that?' he said to the reporter.

'Whew,' said the reporter, dazed. 'Something's really got up that bastard's nose. What d'you think it is?'

'Wife trouble,' said Murphy, and strode quickly away.

He broke the news to the crew that afternoon. Then he began the search for a new main sponsor.

There was a problem. Potential main sponsors knew that any boat of Murphy's would be forever Harry Redd, and Harry Redd would be forever Tasman Wine. Murphy needed a million dollars minimum to get the rest of the way round the world, and nobody was anxious to toss away that kind of money. Meanwhile, the ship's funds stood at three thousand two hundred odd dollars, which would get her out of the water and surveyed, but would not even begin to pay for any repairs. The Lord was going to have to do some rapid providing.

Harry Redd had been a man with no wife, no children, and very few close friends, so there were only a handful of people under the hot sun in Waverley Cemetery. There were his business colleagues, those of them who could spare the time. There were Tubes Murphy and *Tasman*'s crew, and various other sportsmen and artists who had been at the receiving end of his quixotic acts of generosity. They all stood round the open grave, as directed by a letter in his lawyer's possession, and waited for the coffin, which was to arrive in a manner specified by Redd but unknown to his guests. Some hundred and fifty journalists waited in a roped-off enclosure thirty yards away, marshalled by policemen.

Among the only tears were those running down the face of Shar Stapleton, as she stood beside her husband. Murphy, on the other side of the grave, caught her eye. She smiled. Stapleton swivelled his cold eyes at her. He looks at her as a man looks at his watch, thought Murphy. Checking a possession. He felt a slow surge of anger. Then his head jerked up, eyes narrowed against the sun's glare. High in the hazy blue sky, a gleaming dot sped from the direction of the city. A helicopter.

Other heads rose. Mo Stapleton shaded his eyes with a long, pale hand. The corners of his mouth drew down. The helicopter came overhead, the red letters on its silver side gaped, and something emerged into the racketing air. Stapleton drew in his breath with a hiss. It was a coffin.

The loadmaster pushed the coffin clear, and lowered it slowly groundward on a winch. It was white, and either side, in fluorescent red letters nine inches high, was written the word REDD.

The cameras of the world's press whirred like a legion of cicadas. Murphy was laughing aloud, now. So was Shar Stapleton. Her husband made a gesture of exasperation, grabbed her arm and squeezed painfully. She yanked it away.

The coffin came to rest on a patch of sprinkler-green grass. The chopper tocked away. Silence fell. Nobody spoke, because nobody knew what should happen next.

'Really,' hissed Stapleton to his aide. 'This is *ridiculous*.'

Murphy walked over to the coffin. 'Well,' he said. 'I reckon we might as well get old Reddy into the ground, eh?' Five of *Tasman*'s crew picked up the coffin. Slowly, they carried it towards the hole in the sward. Shar saw that Murphy's freckled face was convulsed with laughter, but the lines the laughter made were rivers for the tears streaming out of his eyes.

They lowered the box into the hole. Murphy threw earth on to the lid. He turned to the little group of figures at the graveside. 'Reddy didn't like priests,' he said. 'And he didn't like fuss, unless he made it –'

Mo Stapleton stepped forward. 'As Chairman of Tasman Wine, I feel I should say a few words,' he said. 'Mr Harold Redd –'

'Shut it,' said Murphy. The laughter had gone now. The tears were still running, and his face was white.

'Mr Harold Redd –'

Murphy's fist came up from the ground and smacked Stapleton hard on the hinge of the jaw. Stapleton took a step backwards, caught the heel of his Church's Oxford on a pile of earth, and crashed into the grave.

He lay still for a moment. The daylight was a man-length slot. Then faces came into the daylight, bending. He scrambled to his feet, rubbing the dirt from his suit jacket. His face hurt, and he was dazed. Hands came down to pull him up; soft hands, better at shaking than lifting.

As he scrambled out of the hole, Mo Stapleton heard the clatter of camera shutters. He remained for a moment on his knees, panting, his head ringing with the blow. As he knelt, he saw Shar pull the ring from her finger, the engagement diamond he got her in a deal with a Manila Dutch importer, a flawless blue-white, thirteen carat, and hand it to Tubes Murphy. And he heard her say, 'This is for Reddy. Use it to fix the boat.' Then she was walking away, towards the cars.

Mo Stapleton swallowed the bile of his humiliation and staggered after her.

One of the directors of Tasman Wine leaned discreetly towards Murphy. 'I didn't say this, but I reckon this is just what Reddy would have wanted.'

Murphy laughed, a sharp bark. Then he grabbed a long-handled shovel from the gravedigger, and began filling in the hole.

It was warm and still and dry in the hospital. Sunlight lay cheerfully over the white counterpane. Beyond the window, a brisk little breeze rustled the grey-green foliage of the eucalyptus in the grounds. Henry Harper pulled his eyes away from the window. It had a view of the harbour, blue and glittering in the morning sun. He had been able to watch the boats come in; two days ago *Associated Meat* and, by the sound of it, *Sirène* tomorrow. Already, his interest in the race had become that of a spectator rather than a participant. Ed Cole and Nicholas Eason looked large and untidy and too brown-skinned for the crisp, pale room, he thought. And, catching himself at the thought, he knew that the doctors were right.

Cole was still talking. 'We're third, level and on corrected time,' he said. 'Fourth over the two legs. *EPK*'s in the lead. Then *Flag*, then *Tasman*. We can make it, if we do okay in the next one.'

'The next one,' said Harper. His voice sounded remote to him, without the driving energy behind Cole's, floaty and thin. 'Yes. I don't think I'll be there.'

'Of course you will,' said Cole, frowning.

'No.' Harper grinned, and the old light came for a minute into the face which had lost its hard angles and now looked white and old. 'I'm cooked. The specialist says I'll croak if I go. So it's up to you, Ed.'

'To me?'

'You'd better take over,' said Harper. 'You know the boat. You know the crew.'

'But there are . . . other factors.'

'I talked to the marketing director of Chinamite,' said Harper. 'He's in charge. He said he'd ratify any appointment I made.'

Ed Cole reached across and shook his hand. 'If you put it like that,' he said. He got up. 'Well, we'd better be off, or you'll be tired.'

Harper pointed to a black briefcase on the bedside chair. 'All the stuff's in there,' he said. 'Good luck.'

As they went down the front steps of the hospital, Eason said, 'Felicitations, Skip. I'll buy you a drink.'

Cole shook his head. 'I don't believe it yet,' he said, and turned to Eason and grinned. It was a clear, open grin.

'Oh, come on,' said Eason. He had seen Cole use that grin on the first leg, after he had gone up the mast off Cape Town, and on the second after they had fixed the rudder. Yes, you do believe it, thought Eason. This time, you do.

Eason stopped off at a telephone on the way out of the hospital, and called Bennett's hotel. They had a date that night. But Bennett sounded depressed. 'I have to fly to the States,' she said. 'My brother's sick.'

'Right now?' said Eason.

'He's very sick,' said Bennett. 'Nicky, see you when I get back.'

'Sure,' said Eason. He hung up and gazed at the telephone. The evening had gone flat. But the sight of Cole, waiting in the marble lobby, cheered him. Cole was leaning against the reception counter, chatting up a pretty nurse. Two weeks ago, that would have been unimaginable.

Wonderful stuff, self-confidence, thought Eason.

They took a taxi to the Cruising Club of Australia, which had given guest membership to Great Circle crews. It was a low wooden building on Rushcutter's Bay. They found a table on the terrace overlooking the waters of the bay, where a fleet of Sydney Harbour 18s was roaring down on the first mark of an evening race.

'Champagne,' said Eason.

'Sod that,' said Cole. 'Let's get some rum.'

'Bundi,' said the waiter. 'Two, with coke.'

'Neat,' said Cole. 'Beer chasers.'

Eason watched him, and thought: this is a new Cole. A colt who has got on his bike and started to pedal. A couple of blonde girls at a nearby table had spotted the *Chinamite* crew shirts. One of them smiled. Eason averted his eyes, with a stern effort of will. Cole had finished his first rum. Eason raised his glass. 'Vindication,' he said.

Cole raised his. 'Vindication,' he said. 'Whatever that means.'

'It means that events have proved you right.'

Cole's eye rolled to cover him, sharp and blue.

'Whatever that means,' he said again. 'You want to ask questions, right?'

'Right.'

Cole leaned back in his rattan chair. 'Ask, then,' he said.

'Just tell me what happened on *Arpeggio*,' said Eason. 'The last moments.'

'Oh, Christ,' said Cole. 'That.' He drank from his rum, avoiding Eason's eye. Eason thought: it's no good, I'm losing him again. But Cole turned towards him and put his elbows on the table. 'All right,' he said. 'This once, and for your eyes only. We were moving along nicely, when we took a squall. I had set topsails on my own initiative and against skipper's advice, because I knew the ship better than the skipper. The squall blew her straight over, and the hatches were open, so down she went.' He paused. 'And that was that. Skipper had authorized open hatches, for ventilation. That was reasonable enough. The ship was sound. She'd been surveyed and passed the previous year. So the only explanation for her going over was that she was carrying too much sail, and that was meant to be my fault.'

'But I heard she was solid as a rock,' said Eason.

'She was, under normal circumstances,' said Cole. 'But squalls are not normal circumstances. Even so, she shouldn't have gone like that. But then it was my word against Jones, and he's a public bloody figure. So that made either me or Jones a liar. And they chose me. Negligence. Not too nice, Nick. Not nice at all.'

He gazed at his glass, then took a swig of rum.

'Still,' he said. 'Poor old Henry, but it's an ill wind. And not everybody gets a second chance.' They drained their glasses, and ordered another round.

Eason thought: so that's all. Cole disobeys the order about the topsails. If Cole disobeyed the order, he must have thought it was stupid. And if Cole thought it was stupid, then Eason, who now had first-hand knowledge of Cole's seamanship, was prepared to accept it was stupid. Or stupid in terms of what Cole knew about *Arpeggio*'s capabilities. Which implied that Jones, the politico, knew more about the boat's capabilities than Cole, the sailing master. It simply did not make sense.

That was his last coherent thought that evening. The hospitality of the Australian Cruising Club was a legend, and the members had chosen this evening to live up to their reputation. Without Bennett, Eason felt no sense of responsibility. He had vague recollections of buying a drink for the blonde girls, and talking to them long and earnestly. But he could not remember what about.

He woke the next morning fully dressed in the cabin of a strange yacht. He was wearing an unfamiliar T-shirt; he had vague memories of swapping clothes the previous night. His head felt long overdue for the dry cleaners. His watch said eight forty-five. He climbed on to the deck, squinting against the glare of the sun on the water. The yacht was anchored in a bay which was strange to him. He felt hot and sticky and three-quarters asleep, so he dived off the side. The cool water cleared his head. He swam once round, and headed for the shore, a hundred yards or so away. He landed on a stony beach at the foot of a smooth green lawn, and made his way across the lawn to the house.

A family was breakfasting beyond some French windows. He tapped, tentatively. The man of the house, large and bald and brownish in bermudas and a beach shirt, came across and opened up. He didn't look surprised. 'G'day,' he said. 'You swim out there, you'll get eaten by sharks. What are you doing on my grass?'

'I'm afraid I don't know,' said Eason.

'Strewth, it's a Pom,' said the man. He got a whiff of Eason's breath, and made a face. 'By the look of you, I'd say you came off old Porky's boat.'

'By the look of me?' said Eason.

The man grinned. 'When I see old Porky's yacht flying

that burgee, I identify the work of stinko folk.'

'Burgee?'

The man pointed. At the masthead of the yacht, something red and black fluttered in the breeze. 'A set of scanties, mate. Now step in and get a coffee, and we'll call you a cab.'

'You're very kind.'

'Kind nothing,' said the man. 'The word is habituated.'

The coffee was excellent. Eason began to take notice. The radio was playing. '*Associated Meat* came in last night,' the announcer was saying. 'She's lying ninth on corrected time – no worries for *Tasman* there. Meanwhile, controversy has flared round the British boat, *Chinamite*, currently fourth in the maxi class and on corrected time. Henry Harper, *Chinamite*'s skipper, has retired due to ill health. His chosen successor, Ed Cole, has met with disfavour from the sponsors, who have overruled Harper's decision. This is believed to be because Cole was found largely responsible for the *Arpeggio* disaster –'

'Bloody hell,' said Eason.

In the taxi, he struggled to focus his mind. The sponsors had reacted with amazing speed. And how had the press got hold of it in time to make the morning news? Henry Harper must have made an announcement immediately after he told Cole. Which meant that Eason would be in big trouble with his editor.

He ran from the taxi to the dock, his head throbbing in time to the pounding of his feet. Several of the boats were out of the water. *Tasman*'s mast was out, and the yard men were adjusting the slings under her belly. *Chinamite* was still there, down at the end of the line. Eason jumped on to her deck. The white non-slip plastic was dirty with the muck tramped aboard by hundreds of shoes. He went to the after hatch, and slid down the companionway, as he had done a thousand times.

It was dark below, after the glare on deck. It smelt of tobacco smoke. 'Ah,' said a voice. 'There you are.'

The voice was Cole's, but changed. It was flat and dry, and chilly. As his eyes grew used to the dimness, Eason saw him sitting on a quarter berth, smoking. There was a pile of butts in the saucer at his side. His face was seamed and grey under the tan, as if he had not slept.

'Ed,' said Eason. 'I heard the news.'

'Ah,' said Cole. 'He heard the news.'

'I wanted to say that –'

'Don't say anything,' said Cole. 'Not a word. That way I won't have to say anything back, and I won't end up all over the bloody newspapers.'

Eason's mouth was dry. He clutched at the galley hand-rail for support. 'What are you talking about?'

'Well, Henry Harper didn't tell anyone he was making me captain. And I didn't. Which leaves you.'

'But I thought he must have made an announcement.'

Cole made a disgusted sound. 'Do me a favour,' he said. 'And could you get out of my sight, eh?'

Eason said, 'I promise you –'

But Cole had swung his legs off the bunk, and run up the companionway steps. His feet thudded on the deck; then he was ashore. By the time Eason was on deck, he had vanished into the crowd.

Eason went below and ate a few aspirin and put the kettle

on. As he waited for it to boil he thought: if it wasn't Cole and it wasn't Harper and it wasn't me, who could it have been?

There was only one possibility. Someone last night must have overheard something he or Cole had said.

What a mess, he thought. He finished his coffee, trudged ashore to the race Press Office and dialled *This Week*.

'Hell, cock,' said the copy-taker. 'You again, is it? Funny, the editor was asking after your health last night.'

'He was?'

'Yeah. Just after the *Daily Mail* come out with a headline about your boat.'

'You want to take some copy?'

'Tell you what,' said the copy-taker, 'I'll put you through. Well, it's been nice talking to you. I'm going to miss our little chats.'

'What do you mean?' said Eason. There was no reason for his heart to sink, because he knew what was coming. But it sank anyway. A minute later the editor's voice came on.

'Nicky,' it said. 'Yeah, look, not too happy about the *Mail* getting that story before we did. I mean I know it can't be too clever down there, whales and all that, but I think we'll take what we need from the stringers and the wires.'

'So I'm fired?' said Eason.

'Nasty word,' said the editor.

'What about my money?' said Eason.

'Money? Oh yeah. Two hundred quid a thousand. We've used a hundred and twelve words. Call it a round twenty-five nicker. Can't stop, Nicky, the other line's going. See you around.'

Eason put the telephone down and stared at it. He thought: it would be an exaggeration to say that things were going Nicholas Eason's way. He was in a tight corner, from which there was only one way out: forward. First he had to find out who was splattering Cole all over the headlines. For a moment, he thought of calling the *Daily Mail*. But nobody was going to reveal their sources on a story like this. He returned to the boat and drank a beer and showed over a couple of curious girls, and tried to think strategically. At two o'clock a courier arrived with a wad of envelopes, one each for the entire crew. Eason opened his.

> *The Friends of Harry Redd*
> *at home to the*
> *Great Circle Crews*
> *Saw Ridge*
> *New Year's Eve*
> Boats sail Halley Marina 6.30

He went over to the ACC, sat down at the table he and Cole had occupied the previous night, and ordered a beer. It was the same waiter who had served them. 'I was here last night, remember?' he said when the beer arrived.

'I remember, sir.'

'Well, look, this is a rather odd question. Was there anyone sitting close enough to overhear what I was saying?' The waiter had brown eyes and an Ancient Gaul's moustache to match. 'Just about the whole terrace,' he said. 'When you started to lead the singing of "Hearts of Oak" that is.'

'Oh,' said Eason, passing a hand over his brow and taking a sedative gulp of beer. 'But earlier, when things were still . . . quiet.'

'There were a lot of members here last night,' said the waiter. He paused. 'There were those two blonde girls, of course. I'm afraid I don't actually *know* them. They were at the next table, right?'

'Sure,' said Eason. 'Hell. I need to get in touch with them, urgently.'

'Oh,' said the waiter, arching his eyebrows. 'Well, they work at the Lazy B. Anyway, that's what they had on their T-shirts. You should know. I saw you swapping shirts with one of them.'

Eason blinked, hard. Australian rum played strange tricks with the memory. 'Yes,' he said. 'Correct. Thank you.'

'Don't mention it,' said the waiter.

Eason went back to the boat and pulled out the T-shirt. There was a telephone number under the black and orange bee on the chest. He dialled. A voice he recognized answered. Behind it, voices roared and crockery clashed.

'How *are* you?' said Cheryl.

Eason outlined his symptoms. Then he said, 'Cheryl, are you a journalist?'

'*Me?*' said Cheryl. 'I can hardly spell my own name. Why?'

Eason racked his brains for subterfuge, and found none. 'You remember the bloke who was wih me?' he said eventually. 'We were all celebrating him becoming captain of the boat, right?'

'Right,' said Cheryl.

'Well, some bleeder telephoned the newspapers and made an announcement before we were ready. Any idea who it would have been?'

'No,' said Cheryl. 'Wait. Yeah. You gave me that *Chinamite* crew shirt, right? And I was wearing it when I went to the ladies', and on the way back I ran into this Pom, and he asked me what I was doing wearing it.'

'Really?' said Eason, not particularly interested.

'Yeah,' said Cheryl. 'So I told him about your mate, right, and he sort of laughed and went back to this table in the dining-room, full of big shots. They didn't look like reporters, though,' said Cheryl. 'More like they owned newspapers, if you know what I mean. The one I bumped into had a little pointy beard and a dinner suit, and he behaved like he was a duke or something –'

'And you told him about Ed Cole?' said Eason sharply.

'Sure,' said Cheryl. 'Nicky, what are you doing tonight?'

'I'll call you,' said Eason. 'Must dash.'

He rang the ACC. The telephonist put him through to the head waiter. Yes, said the head waiter. There had been a party of industrialists, at a fund-raising dinner for Youth Venture. The speaker had been Sir Clement Jones.

'Thank you,' said Eason, and hung up. There were many questions he needed to ask Sir Clement Jones.

He called the Press Office, seeking the whereabouts of *Associated Meat*'s crew. The boat was in the yard, said the Press Officer. The crew had left for the Northern Territory, where Sir Clement Jones was lecturing and his men were on exercise. They were due back on New Year's Eve.

*

Jack Asprey, sitting at the centre of one side of the long table draped with the EPK logo, ran his eye over the journalists assembled on the stacking chairs in the body of the room and permitted himself a sigh of satisfaction. Emily de Havilland was gone, on a walking tour of New Zealand's South Island. *EPK* was out of the water, under survey and repair. And Jack Asprey had been left in charge of running the campaign – running it as it should be run, with the best interests of the sponsors at heart.

The Alliance is one of Sydney's oldest and most exclusive clubs. Asprey had got it for his press conference thanks to the influence of his godfather, Lord Kimbolton. The other boats' press conferences had lacked *cachet*, Asprey felt; they had been conducted in hotels and rented halls, or in the tents provided by Lancaster, the race sponsors. The Alliance was the right place for the winner to sit and sum up the leg.

Which was precisely what he was doing, in response to a deferential question from the *Yachtsman*'s man on the spot. Next to him, EPK Electric's Marketing Manager looked pudgy, bright and eager. Flanking the two of them, the rest of *EPK*'s crew tried to look polite and interested and succeeded in looking brown and restless.

Harriet Agnew was particularly restless. She wished that Asprey would stop talking and let everybody out of this revolting Victorian gothic room. He was building up in the *Yachtsman* correspondent's mind a picture of himself as *éminence grise* behind Emily. Emily was a bloody fool to have gone to New Zealand –

Harriet stoped herself. No. Not a fool. Emily was under terrific pressure, and New Zealand was her safety-valve.

Besides, Emily had never been interested in the limelight, and knew that Asprey handled these things much better than she could. It wasn't Emily's fault that Harriet loathed Asprey. And it was up to Harriet to get along with him. She grinned, without amusement. They had the other half of the world to get round, yet.

If only *Siltex* would come in, she thought. *Siltex* had lost half her mast, and was continuing under jury rig. Nobody was hurt; she had spoken to Henri on the radio, and everything was fine. For a moment, she must concentrate on the job at hand. She remembered her father saying that. He had been wearing tropical whites at the time; the job had, as usual, been mixing one of his pharmaceutically correct Martinis, but that (as he had pointed out) made no difference to the general principle. Concentrate –

'Sorry,' said Harriet. A pimply-faced man in the third row was asking her a question. 'Could you repeat that?'

'Dan Dark. *Star*. Tell me, what's it like being a beautiful woman in a boatful of blokes?' He grinned ingratiatingly, displaying nicotine-yellow teeth.

She forced herself to smile. 'I don't think that's a very interesting question,' she said. 'So I won't bother to answer it.'

'We enjoy having her,' said Jack Asprey, and winked.

Dark said, 'I bet,' and scribbled in his notepad.

Harriet made an effort to control her exasperation. Even some of the journalists had the good grace to look embarrassed. At the back of the room, the double doors opened.

Harriet stood up. She said, 'Excuse me,' in a small, dazed voice. Then she walked quickly down the aisle

towards the light streaming in through the doors. Silhouetted against the light was the slim figure of a man. As she
drew closer she saw that he was deeply windburned. His
hair and moustache were stiff with salt. The angles of his
face were sharp and fleshless, and there were dark hollows
under his eyes. He was wearing a salt-stained *Siltex*
T-shirt, jeans and moccasins.

'Henri,' she said.

'Am I interrupting something?' he said.

The words did not seem to mean anything. 'No,' she
said. Then his arms were round her, and she could taste
the salt on his skin as he kissed her. Something dazzled
her eyes. It was only later that she realized it was
flashbulbs.

At last, Henri pulled away. 'Now,' he said, apparently
unaware of the photographers and Dan Dark, who was
shrieking questions. 'Let us go somewhere I can have a
shower. And then we will go where we do not have to think
about this bloody sea.' He looked at her with humorous
brown eyes.

'Would that suit Mademoiselle?'

Harriet smiled at him, a smile that lit up her eyes and
peeled the weeks of tension away. 'It would.'

They walked into the blazing sun beyond the double
doors. The doors closed. The press droned on like flies on
a cold window, but neither Harriet nor de Rochambaud
gave them a second's thought.

She did not remember how they got to her hotel room.
First, he showered off four weeks' salt and the *Siltex* smell
of Gauloises and sweat and bilge. Then she dried him very
carefully, every inch of his body, as if he were a delicate

object d'art she had just regained after a long separation. Then they made love.

Afterwards, as she lay with her head on his chest and listened to the even thump of his heart, he began to talk.

'I have a plan,' he said. 'I wish to go to the Hunter Valley, to see how they make their wine here. I have a friend there, a man from my part of France who makes wine. He has a nice wife. We can stay in his house, with his family, for Christmas. What do you think?'

'Lovely,' said Harriet. She paused. 'But it's my turn.'

'Your turn?'

'The first time you took me sailing. The second time you took me to the Kalahari. Now I'm going to take you somewhere.' She peered up at him.

He was smiling down at her. 'Very well,' he said. 'No Hunter Valley. But also, no sea.'

'Perish the thought,' she said, and crept up his body to find his mouth with hers.

The place was a clapboard bungalow – little more than a shack, really – at the head of a valley in the Blue Mountains. It belonged to Joe Thomas, whom Harriet's father had met when he had been stationed in Malaya. Thomas was now ancient and bedridden, living in Sydney. When Harriet had been to visit him, he had given her the key to the bungalow and told her to use it as she would.

So Harriet and de Rochambaud filled a hire car with food and wine and hit the road. Tarmac gave way to dirt some fifty miles from the city. Then the dirt steepened, and they passed the town of Yandee – two stores and a church. After Yandee the track narrowed and the gums thickened on either side. When they finally arrived at the shack, the peaks were inky cutouts against a peach-coloured afterglow. The first night, they ate dinner in bed. On the second day, they swept three years of mouse shit over the balcony and collected gumwood for the stove in woods whose aromatic leaf-litter rustled to the scuttle of mice and lizards. At nightfall, the crickets shrilled beyond the golden pools of light from the oil lamps. They played Chinese Whist, and laughed idiotically. They went to bed at nine, and got up at dawn, and walked twenty miles through air like wine without seeing anybody.

Two weeks passed in this way. On Christmas Day, they drove down to Mass in Yandee. Later, Harriet cooked a guinea fowl and de Rochambaud opened a bottle of Cabernet Shiraz. They ate on the balcony as usual. And afterwards de Rochambaud sat looking at the ridges that rolled away, blue on blue, down the flanks of the valley and into the haze of the dusk. Owls gossiped in the woods on the slopes below, their voices echoing in the ravines. Harriet sipped her wine, watching the little de Rochambaud trapped in the lens of her glass, the mountains dark against the red, vinous sky. And she thought: he is like his image in the glass; perfect, at the centre of the world. But what do I know about him? She felt a sudden chill, and looked up at the real de Rochambaud. 'Who are you?' she said.

He smiled, 'What do you mean?'

'You know all about me. I've told you. But all I know about you is the things you do at home. Not why you do them.'

He shrugged his shoulders, set his forearms on the

table, and laughed at himself. 'I am a Gascon,' he said. 'So I like to drink, and I am a keen lover – particularly of you. And I am a bit pleased with myself. You know that Gascons think that Gascon pigsties are better than non-Gascon palaces? Well, I am a de Rochambaud, from the same family that has lived in the Château St-Roch since the time of Charlemagne, and that is my home today. My family ran out of money in the Middle Ages, but they stayed at St-Roch for love. Me, I have my vineyard and I am rich as a doctor. So I was able to repair St-Roch. It has been my great enthusiasm, but now I have finished, and there are again times when I am a bit fed up and times when I am lonely.' He had lowered his eyes, and was laying crumbs of bread on the gingham tablecloth. Now he raised them again, and they were filled with an intensity that sealed Harriet off from everything else. 'That was why I came on this race. And the race has changed it, because now I have met you. I have pedalled up hills with flat tyres to be a de Rochambaud. There will be no more hills, and no more flat tyres. So I would like you to become a de Rochambaud too. If you would consider it. Soon. Tomorrow.'

The silence stretched on and on. Harriet heard her heart beat like a huge drum. Finally she reached across and took his hand. It was trembling slightly. The tremor filled her with an almost unbearable tenderness. She had a sudden glimpse of herself: head of the legal department at EPK Electric, clipped Edinburgh vowels, being proposed to by a French count at sunset on Christmas Day in a shack on the other side of the world from her two-Americanoes-at lunch –

'Oh, Henri,' she said. 'I'd *love* to.'

Sergeant Ernie Crystal met the Animal at a pub in Darwin. It was a fighting pub, which was why Crystal had gone there. At closing time, the white-tiled walls were gay with bright splashes of blood. Crystal fought three men, but they all caved in like wet paper bags, and he had started to move off when he heard a voice.

'Hey,' it said. 'Pom.'

He turned round, slow as a big cat, ready to kill. The man who had spoken was leaning against the fender of a Chevrolet pickup whose crackle-finish paintwork glittered frostily under the street-lamp. He was very tall – nearly as tall as Crystal – with a huge belly and a beard that seemed to start on his lower eyelids. He was holding out a can of Foster's.

Crystal was thirsty. The pubs were shut. He said, 'Don't mind if I do.'

The Animal hated Aborigines and women. When he started to tell him what he had done with sharpened bamboos in Vietnam, Crystal recognized a kindred spirit. During the fourth Foster's, the Animal had spoken of mud crabs.

'Mud crabs?' said Crystal. 'I don't reckon much on fucking crabs.'

'Ah,' said the Animal. 'But these fucking crabs live out in the swamps, and you catch 'em by going out at night and chasing them through water up to your waist.'

'Oh, yeah?' said Crystal. 'So fucking what?'

'So they're pretty fair tucker,' said the Animal.

'I'm a meat man,' said Crystal, and finished his beer.

' 'Course, if you're yellow,' said the Animal.

'Yellow?' said Crystal.

'I'm going down the Wildman River after crabs now,' said the Animal, heaving himself into the pickup.

Crystal jumped into the passenger seat. 'What's so special about these fucking crabs?'

The Animal drove in silence for a couple of minutes.

'Not much,' he said. ''Cept they live in the same swamps as the crocs.'

'As the *what*?'

'Estuarine crocodiles. Up to twenty feet long.'

They drove out of town until the road became a track and the track ran out. Then they were on boggy ground thick with vegetation, where the pickup's four-wheel drive whined and the headlights cut white, insect-filled cones in the velvet-black night. Finally, the Animal stopped by the side of an inlet. The air smelt of sea and thick, stinking mud. There was a glimmer of starlight on black water.

'Out you get,' said the Animal. 'What you do is, you get in and you watch around for swirls. You see swirls, net that crab. You feel teeth, kiss your ass goodbye.' He pulled a big net from the pickup's bed and threw it to Crystal.

Crystal caught it and walked down the slope of mud and into the ink-black river. He splashed angrily along the edge, aiming the beam of his flashlight at the mangrove roots, as the Animal had instructed him. He was pissed off with the Animal; nobody called Crystal yellow.

They waded around in the water for an hour. Crystal

yanked out a couple of crabs, greenish-brown monsters with bodies ten inches across, dangerous-looking claws and two-inch spines on their eyebrows. The Animal had five when they stopped for beer. 'You got to grab 'em,' said the Animal. He laughed, broken teeth showing through his froth-flecked beard. 'Not give 'em a delicate little Pom poke.'

Crystal sat in sulky silence. Biting insects whined around him. The trees of the jungle on the far bank of the inlet were a black paper cutout. Over where the black of the mangroves met the black of water, something splashed, a heavy plunging sound.

'There y'are,' said the Animal. 'Croc. Or maybe a water buffalo.' He shook his head. 'Well, we've got enough crabs, I reckon.'

Ernie Crystal grinned, a ferocious, jaw-cracking grin. Then he said, 'I'd like a couple more.'

'I'll wait,' said the Animal.

Ernie turned to face him. His eyes were pale, so far open that the whites caught the starlight all the way round. 'I think you're yellow,' he said.

The Animal's eyes narrowed in their nests of hair.

'Yellow?' he said. He picked up his pole. 'Let's go, Pom. How about fifty notes a crab?'

'Okay,' said Crystal. The two men finished their beers, slithered down the mud bank and into the water.

The tide had turned, deepening the estuary. It made the crabs harder to see, but Crystal was getting his eye in. He went after them with the sharp personal hatred he brought to bear on all his tasks. In half an hour, he had two. The Animal was level.

Half an hour later, the quick dawn of the tropics was flooding the sky when the Animal gave a yell. Crystal looked up. He was a hundred yards away, ploughing the brown water like a Dreadnought. 'She's a bleeding granny!' he was roaring. 'Size of a bin lid!'

Rage bubbled in Crystal. He refused to lose. He stared at the fat man, hating him. Then his eyes shifted, to the middle of the river.

A wide vee of ripples was spreading from an object directly behind the Animal. The object was underwater, just close enough to the surface to create a wake. The apex of the vee was heading straight for the Animal's back.

Crystal raised his hand to hide a grin, and began to sidle towards the shore, holding his breath. The Animal heaved up his net, in which an enormous mud crab waved its claws like a boxer. 'Hey, Pom!' he shouted. 'You owe me –'

It was as if he had leaped out of the water. One moment he was up to his waist. The next, his feet were out, his mouth open in his beard, too shocked to yell. The water underneath him turned to a white foam. Crystal's eyes did not flicker. The Animal screamed as the teeth in the long, warty snout clamped across his legs. Crystal watched, unblinking, as the snout slammed the Animal into the water, as the long, scaly tail – twelve feet if it was an inch – thrashed once; and the wake, bigger now, more ponderous, and studded with bubbles, moved into the middle of the inlet, then stilled as the crocodile sank to the bottom with its catch.

Ernie Crystal's eyes filled with tears. He began to laugh silently among the zinging flies. It was a laugh that racked his belly until he had to sit down. Finally, he could stand.

He got into the pickup and drove back towards Darwin, swerving from time to time as the gusts of mirth blew him away.

The no-smoking light above Art Schacker's head flicked on. He ground out the sixty-first Lucky Strike since Sydney in the ashtray, and peered out of the window. Below, the suburbs of Boston sprawled in the snow, a black and white photograph except for the occasional splash of neon at an intersection.

Schacker shuddered. It would be cold down there, and it was not just a matter of climate. In the briefcase under his seat was the letter, on SYC notepaper, inviting him to appear at an extraordinary meeting of the SYC on 28 December, to explain his conduct of the race to date with particular reference to his dismissal of Martin Hyatt in Sydney. The wording above Jasper Hyatt's crabbed signature was polite enough, but Schacker was not deceived. He was flying to Boston to fight for his life against the Sound Yacht Club.

The port wing dipped, and the engines whined and slowed as the American Airlines 747 staggered low over backyards and freeways. Ten minutes later, he was swinging his briefcase through customs and immigration. In the arrival hall, a black man in a chauffeur's cap held up a sign saying SCHACKER. Outside, the air cut through Schacker's jacket like a knife. The limousine whined smoothly among the plaited freeways, heading north for Marblehead.

Schacker had not slept for thirty-six hours. He wanted to doze in the limousine, but the idea of the meeting ahead kept him awake. His mind was getting proportions wrong. He knew he was on the same continent as Anne-Marie and the children, but the Sound Yacht Club was like a mountain range between him and them. The meeting was the pass through. Schacker set his jaw grimly, and his narrow eyes almost disappeared. It wouldn't be easy to get across. The Sound Yacht Club were a bunch of lawyers. Schackers were sailors. But Schackers were fighters, too. That was the only hope.

It was five to eleven when the limousine drew up in front of the Sound Yacht Club's bow window. Schacker went up the steps past Ernest the black butler, and into the hall. The first person he saw was Anne-Marie. She looked tiny in the cold light from the glass cupola. He kissed her. Her lips were warm, but her shoulders felt thin under the coat of her tailored navy-blue suit. She smiled at him; her face was tired. 'We'll talk after,' she said. 'The meeting starts in five minutes.'

'I know,' he said. 'I have to change.'

'Good luck,' she said, giving him a smile that only just contrived to be brave. 'I'll be there.'

He went into the washroom, rinsed his face, and changed his shirt for the clean one in his briefcase. Then as the giant clock in the hall struck eleven, he went into the chamber.

It had been built along the lines of the Pathology Theatre at the University of Gothenburg, nobody was quite sure why. Club members sat in circles of pews that rose steeply from the round table in the centre, where the committee were sitting.

Schacker swallowed. His heart was beating uncomfortably fast. Martin Hyatt's pale-blue eyes followed him from the third tier opposite.

He found an empty seat in the front row. He could feel many eyes on him; none of them felt friendly.

Jasper Hyatt was on his feet. He did not look at Schacker. He said, 'Thank you for attending this meeting, gentlemen. I'm sure we're all curious about the performance of *Flag* in the Great Circle race. After all, she carries the hopes of her club and her country. In addition to which, many of us have spent a hell of a lot of money on her.' His lipless mouth stretched in what might have been a smile. 'And now we're wondering if we're getting a bang for our buck.' He paused. 'There have also been objections to strategy and tactics, and the conduct of the race in general.' For the first time, the cold old eyes flicked to Schacker, rested a second, and flicked away to his grandson. 'I think we can most profitably start by outlining these objections. Then Mr Schacker can answer them.' Again the cold brush of the old watery eyes. 'Jasper Hyatt III will present the case.'

The Commodore's son rose from his seat at the table. He was wearing the club's blue blazer and white flannels. Schacker recalled that this guy was a partner in one of Boston's biggest law firms. 'Gentlemen,' began Hyatt. 'There are matters of concern. Matters of concern not only in that we are competing in a race we wish, as my father says, to win for club and country, but in that our captain and crew are our ambassadors abroad, and by their conduct we are judged ourselves.' His voice was round and fruity as the club's plum cake. Schacker ran his eyes round the pews opposite. These were the faces of America's aristocracy, still as marble, relaxed in the confidence of power.

There was no flicker of surprise as Hyatt's measured sentences rolled on. Schacker ticked off the accusations, his weariness turning to despondency. One, on the approaches to Cape Town, hard pressed by the opposition, Schacker did fail to set enough sail to put himself clearly in the lead, although requested to do so by members of the club. Meaning Hyatt and Lowell, thought Schacker. It would have been laughable, had it not been so serious. Two, that by transgressing the laws of a host nation, Schacker's crew did with Schacker's connivance bring the club into disrepute. Three, that by failing to set sufficient sail in the Southern Ocean, Schacker did allow the Australian boat to get away with the race. Four, that when it was shown that there were grounds for protest on the basis of Australian non-compliance with race regulations, Schacker did fail to appeal the dismissal of his protest. Five, that Schacker did maliciously dismiss Martin Hyatt from the boat. Finally, that Schacker did fraternize with Henry Harper and, worse, the Australian, Murphy, his opponents.

Mention of Murphy's name brought a hiss to the lips of the SYC's members. The pre-race taunts were an open sore.

Jasper Hyatt III wound up with a passionate plea for truth and justice. The benches opposite were studded with accusing eyes, focused on Schacker. The Commodore said in his creaky voice, 'Mr Schacker, do you agree with this account?'

Schacker said, 'No.'

'Perhaps you would have the courtesy to stand,' said the Commodore, with palpable scorn.

Schacker rose. 'Gentlemen,' he said, turning, so the crater of faces revolved under the oak-panelled ceiling. 'I will be brief. I am an experienced seaman, and when I run a boat I take the decisions about strategy and seaworthiness. That deals with numbers one and three, I reckon. As for our unpardonable behaviour in Cape Town, the only thing our crew member did that was not pardonable was to have the wrong colour skin. Finally, I reserve the right at all times and in any circumstances to choose my own friends.' He caught sight of Martin Hyatt, with the trace of a smile on his smooth pink face. Suddenly Schacker was deeply tired, and very angry. Why don't I tell the whole bunch of them to go to hell, he thought. He looked around the room, and his head had the heavy swing of a cornered bull. There was a rustle of surprised whispers. He drew breath to blast them. Then he caught sight of Anne-Marie. Her hands were joined under her chin, as if she was praying. She *was* praying. For the company, and the race, and their children's future. The breath caught in his throat. He put a hand on the smooth mahogany of the table to steady himself. 'If you will permit,' he heard himself saying, 'I would like a ten-minute adjournment. It's been a long thirty-six hours.'

It sounded like flight. The Commodore's old face took on an expression of sombre triumph. 'Of course,' he said.

Schacker walked out of the room. Anne-Marie met him in the hall. 'Tell them the truth,' she said. 'All you have to do is tell them the truth.'

'Not to lynch mobs,' said Art. 'I need a drink of water before I hang, is all.'

'Is this it? The finish?' she said.

He shrugged, tucked her into the fold of his arm. 'We can start again, somewhere.'

'There have been Schackers in Marblehead for four hundred years.'

'Looks like that was long enough,' he said.

'Hate to interrupt,' said a voice behind him. 'But did you ever consider hiring a lawyer?' Art swung round. Iron-grey hair impeccably brushed, tan radiant, Wallace DuCane grinned at him with his sharp white teeth.

'No,' said Schacker shortly.

'Well, you should,' said DuCane, not at all put out. 'Soon. Within the next seven minutes by my watch.'

'Get out of here,' said Schacker, wearily.

'Negative,' said DuCane. 'I have to tell you that I was not informed of your recall. Had I been, I should have opposed it. I'd like to speak on your behalf.'

'You said I needed a lawyer,' said Schacker.

'I am a lawyer,' said DuCane. 'By training, if not practice.'

'Let him,' said Anne-Marie.

Schacker sat down on the bottom step. He spread his hands. 'Do your worst, DuCane,' he said.

'Yeah,' said DuCane. 'Shall we go back now?'

Anne-Marie squeezed Schacker's hand and gave him a pinched, white-faced smile. He smiled back, as well as he could, and followed DuCane back into the chamber.

'Gentlemen,' said DuCane. 'Art Schacker has asked me to speak on his behalf, since I am more familiar with club procedures.' Schacker did not like DuCane, but he had to admire the man's authority as he moved urbanely through an account of events from Schacker's point of view. How could he know? thought Schacker. He must have his spies on board. But why would his spies be any different from the Hyatt's? His interests and those of the Hyatts' were identical.

Or were they?

Art sat up straight in his seat. Something was happening here. As he listened to DuCane's smooth demolition of Hyatt's points, he began to get a sense that the Great Circle was only a battle in a larger war, being fought out behind the suave exterior of the Sound Yacht Club.

'To sum up,' said DuCane. 'Art Schacker has been the victim of a campaign of vituperation, bad sportsmanship and disloyalty, prosecuted by certain elements in this august club. Elements reluctant to let go of outmoded traditions, but at the same time regarding the noble foundations of those traditions as beneath contempt. Members of *Flag*'s crew have engaged in tale-bearing and intimidation on the grand scale.' He placed his fists on the table, and leaned forward. 'Furthermore, by recklessly sabotaging radio equipment and falsifying weather reports, they have endangered the lives of all those on board.'

The faces of Jasper Hyatt II and III were hard as stone. Martin Hyatt was gazing at the ceiling.

Schacker watched them in fascination. Preliminary moves were over. The shooting was about to start.

'We are in the last quarter of the twentieth century,' said DuCane. 'Art Schacker is a man who lives in the present. We cannot expect him to win this great race if he is to be constantly harassed by . . . dinosaurs.' He spat the word out as if it were a mouthful of mud, and sat down.

A small, white-haired man half-way up the tier of benches opposite said, 'Do we have any testimony?'

Art watched the Hyatts closely. If they called witnesses, DuCane would cross-examine them, and he doubted that Martin Hyatt could stand up to much of that without giving his relations cause for severe embarrassment.

The Commodore heaved himself to his feet and turned to face DuCane, propped like a tripod on his feet and walking stick. His slot of a mouth was twitching with fury. 'I don't need testimony to show me the plain truth,' he rasped. 'We'll have a vote.'

'Very well,' said DuCane smoothly. 'I move that the motion be put: that the club approves Mr Schacker's conduct of the Great Circle campaign to date.'

'Second,' said a voice from the back of the room.

'Those in favour raise their hands.'

The tellers rose and counted, one for each hemisphere of the room. The owners of the raised hands were mostly young or middle-aged.

'Those against.'

This time, the hands were veined and brown-spotted, coming from the lower benches or rising from the committee table itself.

The tellers counted, scribbled, and passed their slips to

the Commodore. Schacker held his breath as Hyatt rose.

'Votes for the motion, seventy-eight.' There was a murmur of voices. 'Against, seventy-eight.' The murmur deepened. Hyatt raised his hand. 'In a tied vote, as Commodore, I exercise the casting vote. I vote No. Motion denied.'

He sat down heavily. Schacker watched him, numb. So this is where it ends, he thought. Not on the sea, boat for boat, but in a roomful of rich old men. He became aware that DuCane was whispering in his ear. 'You're a member,' he said. 'So's your wife. It was in our contract. Neither of you voted.'

'You're sure?' said Schacker.

'Vote first, argue later,' hissed DuCane.

Schacker stood up. The roar of voices stilled. 'Wait a minute,' he said. 'I have just been told I have a vote.'

Anne-Marie watched the small, blunt figure down in the arena through a mist of tears. Then the red-brown face turned up towards her. 'And so does my wife. Vote, Anne-Marie.'

Anne-Marie's voice came from somewhere far beyond the chamber; from a cool room in a white house, with her paintings on the walls. 'I vote aye,' she said.

'And I vote aye,' said Schacker.

DuCane stood up. 'I guess the ayes have it,' he said.

Then the hush went, and the noise spilled across the benches. Next to Anne-Marie, a little old man was shouting, 'Bully, oh *bully*!' The Hyatts rose from the committee table and marched stiffly out. Down there in the crater, Art was shaking hands mechanically, as if dazed. Someone behind Anne-Marie leaned forward and said, 'Come on. Let's get a drink.' She looked round. It was a woman, thin-lipped, deeply tanned, with expensive blonde hair and a full-length blonde mink coat. 'I'm Ellie DuCane,' she said. 'Stop crying, and let's go celebrate.'

'Celebrate?'

Ellie DuCane smiled and held out a ringed hand. Her eyes were narrow and feline. 'The end of an era,' she said. 'The King is dead. Long live the King.'

Anne-Marie didn't understand, but she let herself be led into the bar, where DuCane had already established himself in the corner, and was laughing with Art. Art was laughing too, but Anne-Marie could see he was ill at ease. He broke away and came across to her. 'What's happening?' she said.

Close up, she could see that Art's eyes were angry, and his smile did not extend past his mouth. 'DuCane's forced a vote of no confidence in the Hyatts,' he said. 'They'll have to resign. It was all fixed months ago.' The smile had gone now. 'We've been pawns, all along.'

'Pawns?'

'Us. The company. The boat. All so DuCane could be Commodore of the Sound Yacht Club.'

'Oh,' said Anne-Marie. She was thinking: it seems a lot of trouble to go to, for a yacht club. Somebody gave her a glass of champagne.

Art put his arm round her. 'Stay of execution, right?'

DuCane raised his glass. 'To the Great Circle!' he said. The crowd that had gathered in the corner joined in the toast. He came round and stood beside Art. Oh, God, thought Art, he's going to make a speech.

But what actually happened was that DuCane said out

390

of the corner of his mouth, 'Sorry about all that, Art. You'll find it easier now, I guess. By the way, we've ordered a couple of modifications to the boat, in Sydney. They'll be ready when you get back.'

'Modifications?'

DuCane gave him a grin and slapped him on the back. 'Surprise for you,' he said. Art watched him move away through the crowd, easy as a fish in water, until he became aware that he was being watched himself, by a pair of narrow, cat-like eyes under finely plucked brows. The eyes of Ellie DuCane.

Art grinned, a grin that hurt his face, and applied his Zippo to a Lucky. He was dead tired, and his throat felt like an old chimney stack, and he hated champagne, and the Sound Yacht Club. But most of all, he hated surprises.

Saw Ridge, Harry Redd's rural retreat, was a post-Modern stately home designed by Sven Lubin, architect of the Tasman Tower. The Tower reflected Lubin's brash side. Saw Ridge reflected his love affair with the Old South, and London's Spitalfields. It was a sprawling edifice of white clapboard, built on a green bite taken out of the gum forest beside an inlet on Pitt Water. Its lawns, terraced and dotted with fountains commissioned from Redd's favourite sculptors, ran down to the waters of the bay, where a dock and helicopter pad gave access to the outside world.

Actually, Redd had spent little time at Saw Ridge, preferring the penthouse of the Tasman Tower. But, as he had pointed out in the clause of his will which specified the conditions of this wake, it was a great place for a barbie.

So the cooks set out their steaks, and the barmen their bars, and the Cyril Bigsby Big Band was rowed out to the raft where it was to play. And at seven o'clock, the first of the nine hundred and ninety-nine guests arrived by paddle-steamer from Palm Beach.

Nicholas Eason was the four hundred and seventh, and as he walked across the smooth grass, towards the fires and the torches that had been lit with the coming of dusk, he felt almost light hearted. He allowed himself to bounce through the crowd like a snooker ball on a tableful of colours. There were the Fischers at a table, blown up like balloons with three weeks of high living, arguing passionately about the respective merits of *cru bourgeois* clarets and the 1979 Tasman Cabernet Sauvignon splashing from the Anthony Caro fountain at the head of the baroque stone steps. Down by the inlet, in a white glare of lights, Kelly was talking to camera. Behind him Cyril Bigsby's Big Band, lit by flambeaux, was playing 'The Heart of the Matter', his theme tune. Over to one side, in an arbour, he caught a glimpse of a table of *Siltex* people, talking and making gestures that coiled the smoke of their Gauloises round the candles lodged in the climbing-rose stems. Harriet Agnew was sitting with them. Her eyes were glowing, a glow matched by that of the big diamond on her left hand as she rested it on Henri de Rochambaud's shoulder. Emily de Havilland was there, too. But the candlelight did not touch her eyes, lost in deep, hollow sockets in her thin face.

Eason passed on, towards the bar, possessed by the smell of gum leaves and woodsmoke, wine and perfume. He paused to look down over the throng and the lights, and the spume of the fountains. Down on the floodlit quay, another load of passengers was disembarking from the paddle-steamer. One of them moved away from the crowd on his own. He was wearing blue blazer and white trousers. A Francis Drake beard jutted from his chin. Even at a range of two hundred yards Eason recognized him instantly. Clement Jones. The euphoria passed like blown cobwebs, and he began to shoulder his way purposefully through the crowd.

Half-way down to the quay, he found himself eye to eye with Ed Cole. Cole turned away. Seized by an inspiration, Eason caught him by the arm. 'Listen,' he said. 'Come with me.'

Cole said, 'Let go my arm.'

'I am going to prove it wasn't me who gave that story to the press.'

Cole turned a clammy eye on him. 'You couldn't.'

'Oh, for Christ's sake!' Eason's fuse had been shortened by wine. 'Get that bloody chip off your shoulder and listen when someone tells you something for your own good!'

Cole opened his mouth to say something. Then he shut it again. 'What do I have to do?' he said.

'Follow me. Listen to what I say. Keep out of sight, and if anyone gets violent blow the whistle.'

Cole looked down. Then he shrugged. 'Why not?' he said.

Eason led the way down to the quay. He saw Clement Jones hesitate and then move into the shadow of a grove of bamboo. As far as Eason could tell, he was alone. 'Keep well behind,' he said to Cole.

It was dark in the bamboo thicket. Clumps of stems muffled the sound of the party. There was a sound of liquid falling on leaves, and a grunt. Eason thought: caught you with your pants down, Jones. He said, 'Sir Clement.'

'Who's that?' A zipper zipped.

'I wanted to ask you some questions,' said Eason.

'I don't believe it,' said Jones, with an artificial laugh. 'You again. Really, this is too much.'

'Do you think so?' said Eason, mildly. His eyes were getting used to the dark. Jones was an obscure form, facing him. 'I think it's time we had a nice, frank chat.'

'Do you?' Jones' voice was heavy with sarcasm. '*Do* you indeed?' His dark bulk moved forward.

'I'm a journalist on a story,' said Eason, crossing his fingers. 'If you won't answer questions, I'll have to tell my readers. If you will, just a couple, you'll get a hearing.'

'Are you threatening me?' said Jones. But he had stopped moving.

'Of course not,' said Eason. 'There are some loose ends I wanted to clear up, is all.' He drew a breath for the big lie. 'A friend of mine on the *Daily Mail* said that you called him with an exclusive the night Ed Cole was appointed skipper on *Chinamite*. How come you'll talk to the *Mail*, but you won't talk to me?'

'I talk to people I can trust,' said Jones. 'That's why.'

Eason sighed happily into the dark. 'Oh,' he said. 'Is *that* it? So when that bird at the ACC told you what we were celebrating, you thought you'd give the *Mail* a tinkle, eh?'

'I find your tone offensive,' Jones' voice was thick with anger. 'By God, you wouldn't be talking to me like this if Ernie Crystal were here.'

'He's one of the ones you trust, is he?'

'Yes,' said Jones. 'Now, there are people I have to see.'

'Not immediately,' said Eason. 'What I really want to know is why you're doing everything you can to make sure Ed Cole's name's mud.'

'Look,' said Jones. 'Would you –'

'No,' said Eason. 'You look. It strikes me that you are very anxious not to discuss Cole. Maybe so anxious that you don't mind your pal Crystal putting the frighteners on me. And what I ask myself is: why? The Inquiry is over. Cole's got to make the best of its findings. So why this strange lack of magnanimity from the public-spirited Sir Clement Jones? Why should Sir Clement Jones go to the trouble of calling the *Daily Mail* with bits of tittle-tattle? Can it be that he's hoping to embarrass Ed Cole by reminding everyone of the *Arpeggio* angle just when he's on the point of making a comeback?'

'I do what I think is right,' snarled Jones. 'If you have allegations, back 'em up. If not, shut up.' His shadow advanced until he was nose to nose with Eason. 'A hundred and fifty years ago, I would have killed you for this impertinence, and nobody would have blamed me.' He paused. Eason could hear the hiss of his breath. 'We live in a dishonourable age,' he said.

Eason was opening his mouth to answer when something slammed into his stomach. He doubled over, gasping, Jones pushed by him, and was gone.

He lay in the leaf-litter, whooping for breath. When he could think again, Cole's voice was calling through the grove. 'Here,' he said, and struggled to his feet.

'I heard,' said Cole. 'I think I owe you an apology.'

Eason said, 'Trouble with a public-school education, you don't expect violence off the football pitch.'

They walked back to the party. The music was louder, the fires brighter. There was no sign of anyone from *Associated Meat*.

'Look,' said Cole, when they had got a drink. 'What does all this mean?'

'I'm not sure yet,' said Eason. 'But I think he deliberately rushed out with that story before *Chinamite*'s PR boys could get to work on it.'

There was a silence. Finally Cole said, 'Whatever it means, it looks like I'm out. They've hired Paddy Kinnersley to replace Harper. You can't expect him to want me aboard.'

'Why not?'

'The sponsors don't want me,' said Cole patiently. 'He's a good bloke. I don't want to embarrass him.'

'Can't make omelettes without breaking eggs,' said Eason. 'Kinnersley won't be damaged.'

Cole looked at him searchingly. 'Nope,' he said. 'Can't be done. Not fair on Kinnersley.'

'And if we could think of a way of it not affecting Kinnersley?'

'What the hell are you talking about?' said Cole.

Murphy had not shown up, and there was consternation among the gossip-writers. If Murphy did not arrive, the gossip-writers muttered, he must have the most pressing kind of business elsewhere. And they turned their bird heads and their hard, shiny eyes, and hoped that Shar Stapleton would not be there, either.

But she was, beside her husband, in a low-cut dress of black silk tulle. The gossip-writers muttered peevishly, and went off to look for other poison for their pens.

At six p.m., Smithy, the night watchman at Wharf Sails, was roused by the sound of a truck's engine outside his hut.

He opened the door. The face in the cab was hook-nosed, and under a wild mop of red hair blue eyes glowed fiercely. 'G'day, Smithy.'

'Mr Murphy.' The watchman liked Murphy, and was proud of him.

'Smithy, I'd like you to turn your back for a moment.'

'What?'

'Look the other way.'

'You've come to get your sails, right? Well.' He went into the hut, and came out with a typed sheet of paper. 'It says here that as Wharf Sails is in receive – uh, receivership, no assets are to be removed from the building.'

'Yeah,' said Murphy. 'But I've come for sails, not assets.' His big hands came out, and Smithy heard the crackle of money.

'Oh, well,' said Smithy, tucking the notes into his pocket. 'In that case, be my guest.' He turned his back.

He heard shoes slap on the road, and a sharp *click*. At the *click,* he turned round. A man with a pair of bolt-cutters was turning away from the mesh gates, whose chain hung severed. Up in the cab, Murphy held a massive forefinger to his lips, and winked.

The truck ground into the loading bay. The *Tasman* hands jumped down. One of them carried a chainsaw.

'Try the keys first,' said Murphy.

The locks had not been changed. The sliding door went up. Murphy hit the button on the electric hoist. 'All aboard,' he said. 'First floor, tarpaulins, covers, upholstery, sail manufacture and storage.'

The door of the store room had a new lock to it. The room filled with the snarl of the chainsaw as the blade bit into the heavy pine of the door.

'Right,' said Murphy, and kicked. Inside, sailbags lay like enormous sausages on racks. 'Look for the labels, and let's get them out of here.'

Ten minutes later, Smithy the watchman gazed out of his window as the laden truck ground towards the distant towers of the city. A big hand waved from the cab. He would have waved back, except that he was tied to his chair, and he had strict instructions not to escape for two hours. Upon escaping, he was to report that he had been attacked half an hour previously. Why, he neither knew nor cared. He would be redundant soon anyway, and what Murphy had given him would be a big help.

An hour later, Murphy and his crew arrived at the barbecue. Naturally, the first person Murphy greeted was Mo Stapleton.

'Found a sponsor?' said Stapleton.

'Not exactly,' said Murphy with a terrible grin, and turned away into the crowds.

Later, he found himself in the same circle as Shar. They kissed hello, cheek to cheek. As her mouth came close to his ear she said, 'I've had it. Can't take any more of that bastard.'

'Just till the start,' said Murphy. 'After that, we're laughing.'

She held his hand. 'Ha, ha,' she said. 'He's having me watched.' Giving his hand a final squeeze, she vanished into the crowd.

The day after Art Schacker got back to Sydney, he went early to the dock where *Flag* was moored. Pal Joey was sprawled across her cockpit, whipping sheets.

'Any problems?' said Art.

Joey looked at him blankly, his eyes glassy above his low cheekbones. 'Nope,' he said. 'Leastways, nothing you don't already know about. Survey one hunnert percent, as you know.'

'Sure,' said Art.

'So who we got in the new cabin?' said Joey, kicking a couple of cut-off sheet ends into the water.

'Cabin?'

'Aft,' said Joey.

'What the hell are you talking about?' said Art.

'We thought maybe we was goin' cruising,' said Joey, and spat.

'What the hell are you talking about?' said Schacker again.

Joey pointed down the companion ladder.

It was immediately apparent that when DuCane had spoken of surprises, he had not been joking.

Somebody had bolted a good solid bulkhead aft of the companionway, shutting off four quarter berths. Art opened the door and gaped at the double bed with twin sleeping-bags, washbasin, clothes lockers, his-and-hers reading lamps and Brookes and Gatehouse repeaters. Then he strode off the boat and up to the yard office.

Jack Millsom, the owner, looked up when Schacker barged the door open. He looked annoyed, but replaced his expression with something more welcoming when he saw who it was.

'Who authorized that goddamn stateroom on my boat?' said Art.

'I got a fax,' said Millsom. 'From –'

'I don't care where it came from,' said Schacker. His square face was purple. 'I want it out.'

'Sorry, mate, no can do,' said Millsom. 'The fax was from the bloke who pays your bills.'

'Wallace DuCane?'

Millsom smiled. 'That's him. Nice job, too.'

'There's nothing nice about a spare half-ton in the wrong place.'

'Four hundredweight,' said Millsom. 'Not too disastrous.' Schacker sat down and whacked a Lucky out of the pack. Millsom said, 'Spring it on you, did they?'

The next day, Wallace and Ellie DuCane arrived in Sydney, and sent matching sea-bags aboard.

It was a big field, burnt brownish green by the summer. The shadows of the gums on its eastern edge were long stripes flung across the grass by the red sun that was floating up out of the Tasman Sea. Four elegant horses stood head down, cropping the day's first mouthfuls. One of them raised its head as the panel truck followed the Mercedes coupé down the track at the edge of the field and back up to the door of the wooden barn in its north-eastern corner. The truck's doors opened, and the sound of a radio floated tinny in the dawn calm. A woman got out of the coupé. The horses recognized her, and strolled over, hoping for sugar.

Tubes Murphy pulled aside four of the hay bales piled against the far wall, revealing the bulge of a sailbag. The three *Tasman* hands heaved the holdalls into the back of the van. It settled deep on its suspension. Murphy refastened the padlock on the doors and went over to Shar Stapleton, who had a horse's nose in each hand. She was wearing jeans and riding boots. 'Thanks,' said Murphy, and gave her back the key. 'Mo's boys have been looking for those sails.'

Shar turned and looked up at him through thick black lashes. 'I'm moving out tonight,' she said.

Murphy's eyebrows rose. 'In whose favour?' he said.

She did not answer. Instead she took his hand in both of

hers and leaned against him, looking down.

'How about mine?' said Murphy.

Shar smiled, and her wide, high-cheekboned face lit up as she looked up at him. But she said, 'I'm too expensive for you, Murph.'

He said, 'Not yet you're not.'

'Ask again after the race,' said Shar, and stood on tip-toe and kissed him on the lips.

He hugged her once, briefly, and walked back to the van. She watched them go away. Then she saddled one of the horses, and started to put it over the jumps at the end of the field.

Nobody spoke in the truck. But the radio commentator made up for that. 'Well, it's a nice day again,' he was saying. 'The Sydney-Hobart is over for another year, and now it's the turn of the Great Circle Fleet. On this show last night, skipper Tubes Murphy revealed that he does not intend to change his boat's name, despite the withdrawal of sponsorship by Tasman Wine. I hear that Tubes is desperately short of money. But what he lacks in money he makes up for in spirit, as he amply demonstrated in a colourful graveside barney with Mo Stapleton that produced a further crop of assault charges –'

'Ah, turn it off,' said Murphy.

They drove through the northern suburbs of Sydney and on to a grimy quay where a JCB was scraping garbage out of a lighter. A gloomy-faced man wearing a greasy blue cap with a shiny peak strolled out of a corrugated-iron office, batting at the flies with a dark-brown hand.

'I got your garbage,' said Murphy.

'Beaut,' said the man in the cap, gloomily.

'See you later, then,' said Murphy.

'Beaut,' said the man in the cap. 'Bloke here to see you.'

A red Jaguar was parked across the dusty yard. Murphy went to the van, pulled out a heavy briefcase, and walked across to the Jag. A chauffeur with a dark-grey uniform and a broken nose opened the door, and Murphy slid into the back seat beside the fat man in the pale-blue suit. The fat man was sweating, dabbing with a wet handkerchief at the roll of blubber overhanging his collar.

'Maxie,' said Murphy.

Maxie Green smiled a smile that broke his face into suety crevasses. 'Murphy,' he said. 'A bet, eh?'

Murphy said, 'I'm in a bit of a hurry. You're giving me three to one against *Tasman* coming into Rio ahead of the fleet.'

'Two,' said Green, still smiling.

'You said three,' said Murphy.

'So I changed my mind,' said Green. 'So you triple your money if you win. So if that's not enough, get a price somewhere else.'

Murphy looked at him for a long moment, swallowing the anger that rose in him. 'Five to two,' he said.

Maxie shrugged. 'You twisted my arm,' he said.

Murphy opened the suitcase. It was full of banknotes; two hundred thousand dollars, the change from the three hundred thousand he had got for Shar's ring.

'Nice,' said Maxie, and his hard little eyes watched as the chauffeur counted the notes. 'So give the man a slip,' he said.

The chauffeur wrote out a receipt. Murphy tucked it

403

into his pocket, and climbed out into the dazzling sun.

Maxie waved a fat hand and the Jaguar pulled away. You bastard, thought Murphy, watching it shrink between the derelict warehouses. Then he started to walk back to the van, swinging the empty briefcase. He had done the only thing he could to finance *Tasman*'s continued progress round the world. Now, all he had to do was win the next leg.

They unloaded the van into a twenty-foot container. Then they returned it to the rental agency, and headed down for the race dock. As Murphy pushed through the crowd pressed up against the rope barriers, there was a low, throaty growl of excitment. A brass band was playing. A drift of red, white and blue balloons sailed against the sky. Bright bunting fluttered from forestays and backstays, and overhead the air was thick with the sound of aircraft engines.

'Looks like this is it,' said Murphy.

'I hate goddamn spectators,' said Bud Withers. 'I *hate* the bastards. And why don't the goddamn Race Committee arrange some goddamn stewards?'

Withers was in a mean rage. The wind, hard on *Eye*'s bow, spread his chestnut hair flat on his forehead and plastered his beard against his chin, emphasizing his prominent front teeth so he looked like a muskrat. *Eye* wove through a spectator fleet that bobbed on waters churned to froth by thousands of propellers. A big Sunseeker hovered on her bow, filming. Kelly was behind the viewfinder, checking the shot of the red and black sweaters perched up to weather like a line of cormorants, and behind it the coifs of the Opera House and the spectator-crammed bridge, and the tower blocks of downtown Sydney.

The crew of *Kelly's Eye* were a sour, edgy lot at the best of times. But today it was Kelly that had turned Withers' mood. Remembering the first leg, they had half-expected he would pull out again. But his memory seemed less sharp than theirs.

'Wind, southerly, twelve knots,' said Bennett at the repeaters. ' 'Course, you know as well as I do. Thirty-five minutes to start time. When d'you want to head into the zone?'

'Leave it as long as possible,' said Withers. 'We have to have Kelly aboard before we go in, right?'

'Right,' said Bennett. Her body prickled with the feel of Kelly's lens on her, and she turned and gave him the finger. She saw the wide white smile freeze.

Prick, thought Bennett.

Wallace and Ellie DuCane had come aboard *Flag* at ten o'clock that morning, and even Art Schacker had to admit that during the past four hours they had behaved themselves pretty well. As they headed down towards the mass of small craft obscuring the start area, the DuCanes perched out of the way in the pushpit. But Art could feel them there as he wove through the canoes and surfboards, steam yachts and ferry boats. And he did not like the feeling. It felt as if he was starting a marathon race with a pack full of rocks on his back.

'Windsurfer!' yelled the lookout.

Art passed the wheel through his hands and glanced at

the repeaters. The windsurfer swept by to port. Joey, at his side, said, 'Twenty-three minutes.'

'Let's get down to the start area,' said Art. 'Ready to tack. Helm's a-lee.'

Flag's crew had been ashore a month, but they moved with the economical precision of long practice. The winches jingled, the sails roared, and they were on port.

'Beautiful,' said Ellie DuCane.

For God's sake, thought Schacker, irritably, this is a racing crew taking a simple tack. What did you expect? Next to him, Joey turned a huge, toothless grin on Ellie DuCane, and said, 'Why *thank* you, ma'am.' The insincerity in his voice was so obvious that she blushed up to her eyebrows and looked away. Schacker kept his eyes dead ahead, repressing a grin. He had to avoid taking sides, here. This was the toughest leg, and there was no percentage in splitting the boat into camps. That was what they were supposed to have got rid of with the Hyatts.

'Ready to tack. Helm's a-lee,' he said.

The winches went again, and the boom smacked over. This time, Ellie DuCane kept her mouth shut.

Paddy Kinnersley was an Irishman with a short, blunt nose, curly brown hair, and quick green eyes. He was a delivery skipper by profession, well known in blue-water circles, and well liked. Normally, he was talkative, even ebullient. But this morning, as he sat on the uphill side of *Chinamite*'s cockpit, and watched the tall, canted sails of the other boats converge on the start area, he was not saying anything, except to read out the times to the helmsman. There was a gap in the crew, and he could feel it. A gap named Ed Cole.

Nicholas Eason crouched on the coaming of the gorilla pit and watched Kinnersley. He seemed a nice enough guy. But in the circumstances, it was not at all surprising that *Chinamite*'s crew were silent, even hostile. It was unpleasant, when you had sailed fourteen thousand odd miles as a team, to have new members foisted on you. But that was not the whole reason for the silence. The other part of it was that Nicholas Eason and three brawny grinders had arrived at Ed Cole's quarters that morning, carrying a large, empty sailbag. Since their return aboard with that sailbag, *Chinamite* was – as the sponsers would shortly discover – as full of mutineers as Captain Bligh's *Bounty*.

'Ten minutes,' said Sparko to Tubes Murphy. 'Cutting it a bit fine, aren't we?'

Tasman was still outside the start area, ploughing through the small craft between her and the launch at the left-hand end of the line.

'And we got no sails,' said Sparko. Despite the crowds of cheering spectators he was finding it cold and lonely out here, without Harry Redd on a chartered ferry, and the loudhailers and the champagne corks.

A tug towing a long line of scows was inching out from the tangle of wharves and cranes to the northwest. Murphy moved the wheel through his hands, and *Tasman*'s nose shifted and settled on the tug.

'Eight minutes to the start,' said Sparko nervously.

'Sure,' said Murphy. The scows were a hundred yards away now. He glanced to the side. A Mercruiser was closing in. The men in it were wearing dark suits. 'Off spinnaker,' he said.

The sail flapped back behind the main, and came under and down the hatch.

'Fenders,' said Murphy. 'Watch that Mercruiser.'

Four men with fenders stood along the port side as she came head to wind. The rusty plates of the garbage scows were six feet above *Tasman*'s deck as she came alongside.

'Lines,' said Murphy, glancing at the Mercruiser, which was standing off. One of the men aboard was watching through binoculars.

Fore and aft, mooring lines snaked down from the scow and were made fast.

'Hatches open. Stand by.'

A bulging white sailbag appeared on the scow's deck. Three men shoved it over. It landed on *Tasman* with a thump, and the crew bundled it down the forehatch. The first bag was followed by eight others.

The man on the bow of the Mercruiser started to shout. Murphy bent and picked up a boathook, and held it threateningly in his two hands. 'Cast off,' he said.

The mooring lines went. The fenders came inboard, and were stowed. The spinnaker went up. Four men went below to stack the new sails in the racks.

'Right,' said Murphy, twitching the wheel to dodge a catamaran streaking across the nose. 'Going down for the line.' The Mercruiser came to within twenty feet of *Tasman*'s port side. 'I have here a writ for the recovery of sails,' shouted the man with the glasses, 'property of Tasman Holdings.'

Murphy shifted his grip on his boathook. 'What sails?' he yelled. 'We've got a race to start.' He waved an arm at the thousands of boats in the harbour. 'And if you get in

408

the way, there'll be a lot of people happy to drown you.'

The man waved a white envelope.

'Piss off!' roared Murphy. A steward's boat bore down, and headed off the Mercruiser. An argument started. *Tasman* drew away, heading into the bight of clear blue water on the shore side of the start boat.

'Six minutes,' said Sparko.

On *EPK*, Harriet was sitting in the gorilla pit, snapping elastic bands on to the spinnaker and trying to persuade herself to get up and wave to *Siltex-France*. But every time she gave the matter serious thought, the lump in her throat nearly choked her.

A shadow fell across her. When she looked up, Jack Asprey was grinning down at her. 'How's tricks, Countess?' he said.

Harriet shrugged. His tone was light and easy, but she knew he resented her.

'Rum old honeymoon,' said Asprey. 'Separate boats, ha, ha. Well, at least you're on the same ocean.' He padded forward to organize the foredeck. For a moment, Harriet was mastered by grief and confusion. To be married and separated, Harriet Agnew and a countess, to have a partner and yet be lonely; it was too much. Then she recovered her toughness. *Damn you, Agnew*, she thought. *Where's your bottle?*

She finished the spinnaker and went aft to where Emily was at the wheel. Emily smiled at her. Her time in New Zealand had done nothing to take the tautness out of her smile. She was very thin, Harriet thought. She said, 'Half-way round.'

Emily's eyes snapped across at her. 'Oh,' she said. 'Yes,' as if the idea surprised her. 'I bet you can't wait to get back to your husband.'

Harriet said, 'We've started this, so we'll finish.'

Emily nodded crisply. 'Yes,' she said. 'Eric and I have the same arrangement.' Again she smiled. But the smile faded, and for a second she looked sad and wounded. 'Had,' she said.

Harriet wanted to put her arm round Emily. But Emily loathed being touched, and recently her reserve had deepened so it surrounded her like a carapace. Harriet was suddenly conscious of her hands, and found herself smiling mechanically, as if her very presence was an upsetting reminder of Emily's widowhood. Well, it was up to her to make things as easy as possible for Emily.

But Jack Asprey was going to do his damnedest to get in the way. The more withdrawn Emily became, the more assertive Jack Asprey would be. Emily needed support if *EPK* was going to win the leg. And Harriet had to face up to the task of providing that support.

Just at the moment, she did not know if she had the strength. *Siltex* was a hundred yards to leeward. She waved. The small figure of Henri de Rochambaud stood up, his arms in the air. Gallic cheers floated up the wind. The brooding silence of *EPK* lifted, and Harriet's cheeks pinkened with pleasure.

Rockinghorsing in the wash of the spectator fleet, *EPK Electric* set her nose for the line.

On *Sirène*, the Fischers were readying themselves for the start in their usual way. Georg had unwired a bottle of

Bollinger and was preparing to remove the cork. His brother was holding the tray of glasses, ready to receive the libations to Neptune. The rest of the crew stood to windward, awaiting the nectar.

More by luck than judgement, *Sirène* was in an excellent starting position, on port tack at the pin end of the line. The Fischers were feeling pleased with themselves, smiling and waving at other boats in the fleet, and getting a lot of waves back. Overall, *Sirène* was lying firmly in last place, even behind *Siltex*, who had been knocked far down the fleet by the loss of her mast on the previous leg. Even the hard chargers kept clear of her as she worked her way to the line; *Sirène* had become a sort of mascot.

But nobody had told Ellie DuCane.

Schacker had got on to the final starboard tack, and courteously handed the wheel to Mrs DuCane. It was simply a matter of her keeping the present course over the line and into the Heads. Close-hauled on starboard, she had right of way. *Flag* heeled steeply as she caught a puff, and the spray whizzed in a white fan from her red, white and blue bow.

'*Sirène* on port ahead,' called the lookout.

'Forty seconds,' said Pal Joey, on the readout.

The fleet was moving down in line abreast, a long row of white sails curtseying in the confused wakes of the spectator boats.

'Collision course with *Sirène*,' shouted the lookout.

'Hail,' said Ellie DuCane, a tight little smile on her red lips.

Schacker said, 'He's not a problem. Let him through.'

'Balls,' said Ellie DuCane.

'Starboard!' roared the lookout.

On *Sirène*, Georg Fischer was raising his glass to his lips for the first delicious sip, when he saw *Flag*'s bow, bearing down to cut him in half. *'Mein Gott!'* he cried. 'Tack!'

The glass flew out of his hand as the boom banged over. As the boat heeled on the starboard tack, the bottle rolled on its side, two crewmen diving after it as its precious contents bubbled through the toe-rail.

'Scheiss!' cried Fischer.

Ellie DuCane luffed gently as she went under *Sirène's* stern, on course for the start boat.

'You didn't have to do that,' said Joey.

Ellie DuCane laughed like a sleek blonde mink, eyes glittering and triumphant over a kill.

Murphy looked over his shoulder. The Mercruiser and the steward's boat were bobbing side by side. As he watched, the small figure of the steward shrugged his shoulders in resignation, and the Mercruiser's nose lifted over her wake as she came into the clear water of the start area.

Murphy left the wheel, and picked up the boathook again. 'Keep her straight,' he said. 'Don't stop, whatever.'

'One minute,' said Sparko.

The Mercruiser was close astern. This time, one of the men in dark suits was up on the decking of the bow, hanging on to the little chromium rail with the hand that did not contain the envelope. The power boat's nose glided up alongside, half-planing, a mere three feet away. The man in the suit reached out a hand with the envelope. 'I call upon you to –'

'No, ta,' said Murphy, and cracked the fingers that held the rail with the boathook.

The man yelped and let go. Murphy let him have the butt of the boathook in the chest. His heels caught the rail. He fell backwards into the sea, Murphy's giant laughter ringing in his ears.

'Ten seconds,' said Sparko. 'Nine. Eight. Seven.'

'Here we go,' said Murphy. 'Now let's get out of territorial waters. Roll on Cape Horn!'

In the wake, the Mercruiser was picking up the process-server. Some distance away, a white envelope flopped on the surface of a wave, leaking ink.

Whump went the starting gun. The harbour filled with the wail of sirens. In the blue water inside the horseshoe of spectator boats, the white mainsails passed between the two grey destroyers at either end of the line.

The third leg of the Lancaster Great Circle had begun.

LEG 3 · SYDNEY ~ RIO

Nicholas Eason had crossed the starting line with a bad conscience. Once *Chinamite* was leaning away from the wind and her deck was clear of the debris of the start, he knew he had passed the point of no return. He scuttled under the boom aft, where Paddy Kinnersley was leaning on the pushpit rail. Ashore, what he was about to do had seemed perfectly logical. But now, he saw Kinnersley against the blue water and the horde of spectators, and he could not imagine how he had the nerve in the first place.

'Paddy,' he said. 'Confession time.'

Kinnersley was squinting under the boom at *Siltex*. 'Wonder if he'll try a luff,' he said. 'What is it, then?'

'We've got an extra man aboard.'

Kinnersley's green eyes did not deviate from the French boat. 'Really?' he said.

Eason paused for the racket of a dive-bombing press plane. 'We brought him aboard in a sailbag,' he said. 'We thought it was bloody unfair –'

Kinnersley's green eyes turned on him, hardening. 'That was nice of you,' he said, with sarcasm. 'Lucky someone warned me, or it could have got bloody embarrassing.'

'Warned you?'

'What else did you expect?' said Kinnersley. 'As soon as you'd put the proposition Ed came over and told me what was going on. He told me, and he was right, that it put him in an impossible position. He offered to go home. But he wasn't the only one who was in an impossible position. How do you think I felt, taking over a crew from a bloke like Ed when as far as I was concerned he's a bloody good skipper? I'm not Captain Bligh.' He paused as *Chinamite* dived through the trough of a motor boat's wake. 'So we've come to an arrangement – part of which is that you carry the can. Satisfied?'

'Fletcher Christian, at your service,' said Eason.

Cole had come up the hatch. He said, 'You're lucky he didn't send the whole lot of you home.'

Eason's eyes flicked between the two of them. 'Yes,' he said.

Kinnersley said, 'We've got a deal. Ed sails the boat, I'm the skipper. Career moves for all. If the sponsors ever let us sail again.'

Eason thought and said, 'Don't worry about the sponsors. The sponsors are going to love this.'

Kinnersley's mouth was cynical. 'I wouldn't bet on that.'

'Headlines all over the world,' said Eason. 'Intrigue, high adventure. Ed Cole, the man the crew would not leave behind.'

'Oh,' said Kinnersley. 'Well, as your skipper I find you guilty of mutiny. So you can bloody well go and make coffee and fairy cakes. And then you can get on the radio, and tell the press what you've done.'

'Journalists,' said Cole. 'I hate 'em.' But Eason had the

distinct impression that just this once, what Cole said and what Cole thought were two different things.

As the day wore on, the fleet headed out into the south-setting current, riding it down towards Tasmania. The wind kicked in easterly, raising a short, dirty chop. The roast lamb with broccoli and roast potatoes that came from the galley that evening was not well received; a lot of people had lost their sea legs ashore. Nicholas Eason was no exception. But when the radio watch buzzer squawked for the sixth time that evening at the beginning of the fourth watch of the leg, he took the call cheerfully. It was the editor of *This Week*.

'Nicky,' he said. 'Long time no hear.'

'You fired me,' said Eason.

'Administrative error,' said the editor. 'I heard that piece you did on the *Today* programme this morning, about your mutiny. Nice piece. I want you to keep sending stuff like that, to us, that is. Quid a word, okay?'

'Sorry,' said Eason. 'No can do.'

'You crazy?' said the editor. 'Who else would make you an offer like that?'

'The *News*.'

'The *News*?' said the editor. Even at a range of twelve thousand miles, Eason could hear the steel come into his voice. 'Nicky, I get the impression you have changed.'

'Possibly. How's that copy-taker I used?'

'Harry? Dead. Clock stopped. Silly bugger wouldn't stop smoking. The paper tried. No loyalty. Like you.'

'Yes,' said Eason. All of a sudden, the radio shack was making him sad. 'Excuse me, I must pop and be seasick.'

He cut the connection, and went on deck to throw up. It is by no means easy to vomit and laugh at the same time. But that night, as the spray whipped his face, and the black seas grew under the big wind, and *Chinamite's* main and spinnaker gleamed like wings under the Southern Cross, Nicholas Eason managed it.

During the next week, the fleet dropped away into the Southern Ocean. The winds were fresh northerly at first, and the last stirrings of the East Australian Current under their keels drew them southeastward and into the Westerlies. Little by little the smaller boats fell behind. The large boats stayed well together. As on the last leg, the Great Circle course, the shortest distance from Sydney to Cape Horn on the globe, passes over the Antarctic mainland. As on the last leg, the big Westerlies blow to the north of the low-pressure systems that girdle the continent, roughly along the limit of the Polar drift ice. So they were taking the Great Circle course to a point around 55°, where they would twitch the wheel a little to port, and sail down the rhumb line to the Horn, following the line of latitude round the globe.

As the latitude rose, the temperature fell. The cold bred a

gloom aboard the boats, driving home the perversity of leaving the warmth of Sydney for another month in the icy waters above the Pole. But four hours on, four hours off, is a routine that brings its own anaesthesia. And soon most of the crews had lapsed into a coma of work, alternately running with sweat and shivering with cold, looking forward only to eating big hot meals washed down with vast mugs of sweet, milky coffee as an antidote to the bitter whips of icy spray that lashed uncovered skin.

For the first two weeks the winds blew steady, west and southwest. Dave Kelly was surprised to find that he was better equipped for this leg than for the first one. For one thing, he found it easier to live aboard. There was a niche among the sailbags forward that he made his own, padding it with bits of cloth and foam that he dug out of lockers and appropriated to his own use. In this rat's nest he spent much of his time. Crouched in his corner, the new, cleareyed, pale-skinned Kelly even looked something like a rat. His delicate bone structure seemed to have come forward into a point, his nose lengthening and his chin receding, as his eyes flicked cautiously about his surroundings.

Eye was sailing extraordinarily well. She was firmly in the lead, better than a hundred miles in front of *Flag*, closing fast on the Horn. But Kelly was not really interested in the race.

He went on deck very little. He loathed the cold, and it had been getting steadily colder. The only inducement was filming. Then, he went on deck to do his duty, and after he had done it, he burrowed straight back into his nest.

On the eighteenth day, he went on deck to find *Eye* running across a smooth, green-black swell. Chuck was filming a flat-topped iceberg half a mile away. The berg might have been a mile long, and it moved with a heavy, uncomfortable plunging. Fog wisped its surface, and the sound of the waves breaking on its glacis was like the mutter of big guns.

Kelly huddled into his parka, shivering. They had not been so close to a berg before. Then he said, 'Let's do a little live to camera, Chuck.' He looked round for Bud Withers. Withers was at the wheel, his hood pulled down and a rime of frost on his beard. 'You got any iceberg facts, Bud?'

Withers did not smile. 'Yeah,' he said. 'The fact is I hope we don't hit one in the dark.'

'You'd see it,' said Kelly.

'Uh-uh,' said Withers. 'Not in the weather we got coming.'

'What weather?' said Kelly nervously. Suddenly his belly felt sore and shrunken, and ached for brandy.

'Little blow,' said Withers. 'Maybe force nine, ten.'

'Shit,' said Kelly.

'You said it,' said Withers. 'This is where we hope that surveyor in Cape Town knew what he was doing.' He laughed.

Kelly tried to laugh back, but the sound that came out was a grating croak. What if Lawson hadn't been on the make? What if the boat was unsound? A bucketful of water caught him in the face. It was freezing cold. Panic rose in Kelly at the thought of all that cold water, waiting to suck him down into its black deeps. He went below, and snuggled into his nest, and tried not to think about it.

The sun set early, into the thick mat of cloud that had

come up to cover the sky astern. *Eye* had been running under a small kite, with three slabs out of the main. As the wind rose, Withers took out another slab, and changed down to the number six genoa. The wind was bang astern now, and the waves were growing. Chuck was out filming. Kelly found the motion uncomfortable below, so he went on deck and crouched next to Chuck. Astern, the swells built up until their black crests, netted with foam, merged with the low black sky. Chuck kept swearing gently to himself at the splendour of the shots he was getting. Kelly sat beside him and clenched his jaws until the muscles ached, to stop his teeth from chattering. Every time a shining black wave hung over the stern and it started to go up, up, up, sweat squirted from Kelly's pores, and his gloved hands clamped onto the pushpit rail, and his bowels loosened within him.

It was hard to tell when the darkness of the clouds became the long Antarctic twilight. But as the eight-to-midnight watch wore on, the waves became gradually invisible, and the night gathered in on the red and green jewels of the running lights and the churchyard glimmer of the compass and windspeed repeater. The three deckmen of the watch stayed on deck. The rest of them wedged themselves into crevices in the chaos below, and tried not to let the seas smash them into the sweating white walls of the boat.

Kelly stayed on deck, too. Below had suddenly lost its cosiness, and become a trap. The wind shrieked appallingly in the rigging as *Eye* flung herself down the wave fronts.

At about eleven a new noise came above the sound of the

wind and the waves; a hard rumbling to the north. Bud Withers' lips, greenish in the compass light, framed the word 'thunder'. *Eye* rose to a wave-crest as a blue-white glare lit the slaty roof of cloud.

The light spread across a black sea streaked with the spume of breaking waves. And dead ahead, something long and low and white.

'Berg!' said Withers, in a conversational tone. He moved the wheel hard-a-port. The rigging groaned at the sudden load, and the grinders slacked off the lee runner and winched in the genoa.

Kelly looked at Withers, motionless still in the flicker of the lightning. His heart was thumping. What if the lightning had not chosen that moment to flash? They would have piled into that berg –

He swallowed. *Eye* was heeled over steeply to starboard as she reached across the swell. There was a nasty cross-chop. Her big flat bow went up and came down with a *boom* that shivered her to her keel. And again. A column of blue fire slashed into the sea two hundred yards away, and the sky bellowed thunder. The bow came up again, and slammed down.

This time, it did not come up.

Withers heaved at the wheel. *Eye*'s movements were suddenly sluggish. There was shouting below. Bennett's bare head came up the companion-hatch, hair lashing in the gale. 'Making water forward!' she shouted. 'Hull's split forward!'

'Check,' said Withers. 'Damage report. Stand by to transmit mayday.'

Bennett dived away again.

Kelly thought his heart would come through the wall of his chest.

Two minutes later, Bennett's head came up the hatch. 'There's an eight-foot split forward of the bulkhead.'

'Shut the door,' shouted Withers. *Eye's* sails, head to wind, roared above his head. 'Brace it. Send out the mayday.'

'What's happening?' whimpered Kelly. 'What's *happening*?'

'We're sinking, that's what,' screamed Withers.

Kelly thought he could hear the accusation in his voice. *The survey*, he wanted to shriek. *The guy who did the survey was a crook. It was a mistake. I thought –*

Kelly clung to the rail, with the voices roaring in his mind. Then it happened.

Thunder banged like a mighty cannon in the sky. The night turned a violent blue-white. Kelly was suddenly flying through the air. As he went, he saw the backstay and the aerials outlined red against the darkness, glowing. His face smashed into fibreglass, and he felt himself sliding through the lifelines. It was his safety harness that brought him up short. There was a strong smell of ozone. Lightning, he thought. We've been struck by lightning. But I'm all right. Thank God, I'm all right.

Lightning flashed again, and he flinched. By its glow, he saw that *Eye's* wheel was bent and twisted, and that the aerials on her transom were gone. And there was something else missing.

He crawled aft. Bud Withers' safety-harness clip was still attached to the jackstay. But half-way up, the nylon strap was severed, charred and melted.

Dave Kelly put his head down the hatch, into the noise of the cabin. A wave rolled slowly over *Eye*'s nose, and sluiced a foot deep down the deck.

'Man overboard!' croaked Kelly. 'Man overboard!'

People spilled on to the deck, and the beams of flashlights swept futilely at the empty sea. *Kelly's Eye* started, very slowly, the long process of sinking.

Flag was flying. On the eighteenth day, she was dead level with *Tasman* and *Chinamite*, but some fifty miles further north – on virtualy the same track as *Kelly's Eye*, better placed for the Horn than the boats to the south of her.

On the morning of the nineteenth day, she was surfing down the enormous swells flung up by the storm astern. The sky was overcast, the wind WSW force seven. It was the weather she had been built for, and she was eating it up.

The crew had settled, too. Even with the opposition out of sight, they kept racing. Pal Joey drove his watch remorselessly, and the men drove themselves. George Hart seemed to have gone into a kind of culinary trance, propped up in his webbing in the galley while the sink outlets howled with the rush of water passing them. And the

DuCanes – the DuCanes were behaving surprisingly well. Even Schacker had to admit that.

Not that Wallace DuCane was much in evidence. He was putting in a lot of time in the back cabin. He had been very sick for the first week. Now, he did not seem at all interested in the sailing of the boat, though he displayed an intelligent curiosity about Schacker's strategy and his handling of the weather systems.

Ellie DuCane was different. She had done some racing, and it showed. She did not have the physical strength to work a winch, but she was a useful helmswoman, and did not hold back from her share of chores. Yet she was not part of the crew. It was not only the fact that she slept in the absurd stern cabin: but rather that there was always calculation in her narrow, black-fringed eyes. A good crew-member takes you for what you are and is happy to be taken for what he or she is. Ellie DuCane was visibly possessed by a sense of her difference. As Joey observed to Schacker, when she looked at you, you could never tell whether she wanted to buy you or eat you.

This morning, she was up in the gorilla pit with George Hart. Hart was taking a break from the galley; he liked to get a couple of hours' air every day, and this morning there was plenty available, moving over the deck at between thirty and forty knots. He was trimming the spinnaker. Ellie DuCane was watching the gull-wing curve of the sail suspended high above the bow. George was not talking; somehow she made him feel plump and adolescent. He bent his head to his task, conscious of her perfume, sharp and exciting.

'You must get lonely in that galley,' she said.

'Oh, I dunno,' said George, grinning. 'You meet all kinds of people, on a boat.'

'But none of them doing the same things as you.'

George shrugged. 'It's fine,' he said.

She got her shoulders under the coaming and lay back, staring at the sky. It was a curiously abandoned pose, and it left George uncomfortably aware that it was nigh on three weeks since he had seen a woman. 'What made a guy like you sign on as cook?' she said, looking at him out of the sides of her eyes.

He shrugged again. 'I wanted to come on the race. I'm not so great at sailing, but I can cook.'

'You sure can,' said Ellie DuCane, and she narrowed her eyes and smiled a smile loaded with complicity. Oh, wow, thought George; she wants a piece of Hart. The sweat of embarrassment prickled under his wet-gear, and he knelt up and cranked the winch half an unnecessary turn. 'Maybe you could give me some lessons?'

'Sure,' said George. 'Any time. But I bet you can cook too, right?'

'Oh no,' she said. 'I open cans. I can sew, though.'

'Is that right?' said George. He had had some weird conversations in his life, but this was one of the weirdest.

'I was going to be a sailmaker,' she said. 'Come down forward, and I'll show you.'

'I'm trimming right now,' said Hart.

Ellie DuCane smiled, a sharp flash of teeth between thin carmine lips. Then she called down the deck to the mainsheet man, 'Take over here a second, would you?'

The mainsheet man came forward and took the ice-stiffened sheet. 'Sure,' he said.

'Come give me a hand,' said Ellie DuCane. The helms-man watched without curiosity as the two figures walked to the fore-hatch, opened it and dived in.

It was dark down there. The door into the crew quarters was closed. The sail-locker was almost empty of sails; they were piled in the gangways aft, to keep the trim bow-high.

'So where's the sewing?' said Hart.

Ellie DuCane turned towards him. He could see nothing. 'Here,' she said. She took his hand and removed the glove and tossed it away. Then she pulled his hand inside her parka.

'Oh,' said Hart, as he felt the swell of her breast under her thermal underwear.

'Shh,' said Ellie DuCane, and grabbed him round the neck with one arm. Her mouth was on his like a hot limpet, and he could feel her tongue moving and searching. Her other hand was on his waterproof trousers, pulling at the zip.

'It's too cold,' he said feebly.

She ignored him. 'Why, *George*,' she said, her fingers burrowing. 'That's what I call a *very* nice compliment.' And she pulled him on to the sailbags, and undressed him with strong, definite fingers.

'Oh,' moaned Hart. 'What about your husband?'

She moved so he could feel the heat of her upper thighs against his groin. 'He's on radio watch,' she said. 'Don't worry about a *thing*.' Then she lowered herself on to him with a deep, gastronomic sigh.

Morning jaw-jaw was over. *Eye* had not called in; but Bud Withers was like that. Nor did Wallace DuCane care much about illusions of warmth and safety. What he wanted from jaw-jaw was the positions of the other boats.

So far this morning, there was a woman on *EPK Electric* talking to her husband on *Siltex*. DuCane could hear the need in her voice even through the crackle of the lightning from the storms astern. DuCane was not interested in need unless he could make money out of it, and he found it a little disgusting. Far away, an Austrian was complaining on short wave that the seas were making it difficult to cook. DuCane, who was still a little queasy, changed back to the fleet distress frequency. And his long, coppery face stiffened, his lips tightening over his teeth.

Buried under the layers of stressed and crepitating ether, a voice was gabbling. The voice was tiny, and obliterated by frequent roars of lightning. But it was repeating its message. '*Mayday*,' it was saying, '*Mayday, Mayday. Kelly's Eye sinking, position 57°, 01' S 70°.13' W.*'

DuCane checked the given positions of the other yachts on his chart. *Eye* was dead astern of *Flag*. They must have sailed virtually over the top of her in the night. His fingers drummed on the table. *Flag* was only sixty miles ahead of her position. But if *Flag* went to her rescue, she would be delayed. *Flag* was radio watch boat till noon, and it was her duty to promulgate the distress call, and turn back to the rescue. He looked at his watch. It said eleven forty-five. DuCane stroked his chin with his fingers. If he turned a deaf ear for fifteen short minutes, she would be the responsibility of the next watch boat, and *Flag* would be under no obligation to tune her radio until the evening jaw-jaw – if then. DuCane hesitated. On the edge of his mind, there flickered a picture of a boat, awash in huge, freezing seas.

But closer to the centre of his consciousness was the immensely detailed vision of the Sound Yacht Club, in its place near the top of the pyramid of Wallace DuCane's achievements and ambitions. He could go to the rescue, and maybe share in a hero's accolade. Or he could close his ears, and go on to win. DuCane's conscience nagged him. But he had not come this far by listening to his conscience. Anyway, it was probably too late anyway . . . Whistling between his teeth, he put out his hand and twisted the dial. The desperate gibbering in the headset ceased abruptly.

Nicholas Eason was tired and bored. As he sat down at the navigator's table under the bank of radio sets, there were two ideas dominant in his mind. In the foreground was the notion that he was very angry with Noddy. Because Noddy had, without provocation, pinched the last of the chocolate digestive biscuits from the galley, when he knew damn well that they were Nicholas Eason's favourite kind of biscuit. The foreground of Eason's mind was full of hatred for Noddy. Noddy was his very good friend, of course. He knew that, and could maintain the hatred and the friendship simultaneously in his mind. The foreground thought was intimately connected with the background thought, which was that he had been stuck in this cold, wet, rackety roomful of large people called *Chinamite* for too long. He was bored silly by it, and tired nearly to death. He wanted it to be all over, and soon.

Eason reached up practised fingers and flicked on the radar. The screen was empty, except for one hazy blip ten miles to the north. *Tasman*, judging by the positions of the opposition marked on the chart since the morning's jaw-jaw. What bloody silly names boats had, he reflected as he twisted the radio dials. *Siltex*. Or *Chinamite*, come to that. Why couldn't companies give themselves decent names any more? The *Téméraire* Trading Corp, maybe. *Flying Cloud* –

His fingers had reached the VHF dial and spun to the open channel, checking, ready to leave it open. The room filled with static from the speaker. He frowned. Behind the static was an insect muttering. Eason switched to the headset and put in some filters.

'. . . *sinking position 57°.01'S 70°.13'W Mayday Mayday Mayday Kelly's Eye sinking . . .*'

The muttering faded away in a roar of atmospherics. Eason's pencil scratched as he noted down the position. Sixty miles away, northwest. Judging by last reported positions, *Flag* was closest. He called her up. There was no reply; nobody on radio watch. He tried *Tasman*. Nothing. There were no merchant ships within a thousand miles, and no Chilean navy within twelve hours' steaming. That left *Chinamite*, eighty miles away, bang on the wind. He ran for the companion-ladder.

Ed Cole, at the wheel, looked amazed at the coatless figure, black hair flying in the icy gale. Eason shouted out his message. Cole said, 'Go below before you get frostbite, you silly bastard. And send out a general call.'

Before Eason was down the ladder, the wind was cutting over the deck as Cole brought her round and the main-sheetman hardened up. The mastman let go the spinnaker halyard, and the kite came in under the main. Three minutes later the number five genoa was up and sheeted hard in, and *Chinamite*'s axe bow was chopping into the black monsters trundling out of the west.

'Main engine!' roared Cole, and hit the button. The vibrations of the donkey shivered through the hull. But when he threw the gear lever, smoke poured from the box. 'Bloody thing's seized!' yelled Slicer, the mechanic. 'Stripping her down.'

'Oh, Lord,' said Cole. 'We'll have to sail.'

And he hunched down beside the wheel, and concentrated on keeping the compass card on the dot.

It took eight hours to sail back to *Kelly's Eye*'s last reported position. The wind was up to force eight and nine, and the tops of the waves blew off solid and came down the deck feet deep. The watch below came up and crouched on the weather deck for trim, and the water came into their hoods and trickled down over their bodies until they were clammy and shuddering with cold. And the change in movement, from the long swoop of the downhill run to the tight, hard slam and pitch of clawing to windward, took away the sea legs, so a lot of them were sick again. But perhaps that was just as well, because the rockinghorse pitch made it impossible to keep anything on the galley stove. After two hours of it, Slicer staggered on deck. His face was pale green. He said, 'Can't be done, Ed. Parts everywhere. Maybe if you turned her stern to sea –'

'Can't spare the time,' said Cole. His eyes returned to the luff of the mainsail. For the next six hours he stayed at the wheel, one foot on the cockpit sole, the other leg on the cockpit coaming, his safety harness connecting him like an umbilicus to the boat.

At 1953 hours by Nicholas Eason's salt-crusted Swatch, Ed Cole shouted, 'We're at rendezvous!' Eason jumped to the pushpit rail, steadying himself on the backstay.

A thin, biting sleet was pouring out of the west, pocking the dirty grey surface of the sea. A wave passed under and swept away. From the next crest it looked the size of a fair range of hills with a valley between. There was something infinitely evil in the roll and shift of it. Beyond the ugly waves there were more waves, and beyond them, more: grey giants, trudging on for ever. There was no *Kelly's Eye*. Radio transmissions had stopped.

For the first time, Eason felt horror at the desolation of the sea.

'Right,' said Cole, sounding as brisk as if he were on the Solent. 'Box search, downwind.'

The next two hours were worse even than the preceding eight. Cole sailed due north twenty minutes, turned ninety degrees starboard, sailed two minutes, then turned another ninety degrees starboard and sailed a reciprocal south, forty minutes. Then at the end of the southerly leg, he did two ninety-degree port turns.

Eason's gloved hands were numb. The genoa sheets were frozen and inflexible. Across the winch from him, he could see Noddy's teeth chattering. Soon it would be dark.

'Go! Go! Go!' someone yelled.

Eason put his head down and ground the winch. It generated a sort of heat, but he knew that the sweat would turn clammy, and –

'THERE!' shouted Slicer from the foredeck, the triumph in his voice cutting through the gale. 'STARBOARD BOW!'

Down there in the trough, something lifted. It was a slow, soggy movement, with a heave of black under it, a flash of gold. The hull of *Kelly's Eye*, nose down, stern out of the water. Aft on her deck, little red figures huddled, clutching to their ship like barnacles on a piece of driftwood. Eason watched, mesmerized, as a wave surged over them, swirling among the red parkas.

Chinamite inched down the wind and under *Eye*'s stern. The eyes of the survivors followed her. One of them lifted an arm: Bennett. Cold forgotten, Eason shouted and waved, and she managed the ghost of a smile. *Chinamite* came alongside, shrouded in spray, rubbing on fenders. They held the two hulls together with springs on the genoa winches, Cole nursing the wheel, ready to break away at the first sign of trouble. One of the men had a camera on his shoulder. The first thing he passed over was a big duffle bag, full of film cans.

Eye's crew could scarcely move. Their legs were rubbery, and they crawled over the side like old men.

Eason helped a man he recognized as a grinder. He was muttering, the words lost above the scream of the wind in the rigging. Eason put his head down. 'Exercise,' the man was saying. 'Keep moving, she says. Exercise.'

'Who says?'

'Bennett,' said the grinder.

Dave Kelly was next. Eason could feel his thin arm

shaking under the wet-gear. They tried to take him below, but he would not go. He crouched at the foot of the mast and clung to the halyards. *Chinamite*'s people were busy, so they clipped him on and left him there for later.

Bennett was the last to come. Her face was grey in the hood, and her lips were bluish, but she was smiling, her old damn-your-eyes smile. Her movements were slow, as if she were underwater. Eason clipped his harness to the footrail and went over to *Eye*, to give her a hand. As she stopped to unclip herself from the jackstay, the air suddenly stilled. Eason looked up.

The wave was over *Eye*'s first spreaders. It was a grey-black precipice topped with a cornice of foam that hissed like an express train. Then the slope of it banged *Eye* like a wall and Bennett looked over her shoulder. The sudden movement put her off balance. She fell through a wrecked section of *Eye*'s pushpit and into the sea. For a hundredth of second, Eason saw her head reappear in the four-foot gap between the two boats. It passed very clearly before his mind's eye what would happen next. The crest would grab her. She had no lifeline. She would be gone.

He did not consider that the two boats would be ground together by the crest, crushing anything that came between them. Instead, he jumped.

The water was so cold it knocked the breath out of him. His arms grabbed Bennett and locked about her stomach. Then the crest came down in a chaos of noise and water. There was a colossal impact as the two hulls slammed together above his head, and something yanked at his safety harness so hard he was sure it must come out of his parka. But it held, and he held Bennett. And suddenly his head was above water, and he and Bennett were being towed downwind by *Chinamite*. And hands were tugging the lifeline, and pulling first Bennett, then him, over the side. And a second later, he was crouching on the deck, spitting out water; while upwind a gold and black hull rolled on the upslope of a wave, made bubbles and slid under the surface of the icy black sea. Then there was a new sound. The sound of Dave Kelly, screaming and screaming and screaming.

Eason shook his head. 'Cup of tea,' he said, and went below.

Half an hour later, he was still shivering in a wet sleeping-bag when Paddy Kinnersley came and sat beside him. 'Stupid bastard,' said Kinnersley.

'Me?'

'If you ever go overboard on a boat of mine again, I'll kill you,' said Kinnersley. He sighed. It was not an angry sigh, and his short Irish face was humorous and resigned.

'How's Bennett?' said Eason.

'Asleep. Bones says hypothermia and shock, but no problems.'

'How many did we get?' said Eason.

'The lot. Except Bud Withers. He went over the side, poor devil.'

Eason said nothing. There was nothing left to say.

'Look,' said Kinnersley, 'I don't know if you realize, but what Cole just did is not only brilliant, but just about impossible. I think you ought to tell that rag you work for.'

'I was about to,' said Eason.

Eason rolled out of his bunk, dressed, and collected a

cup of sweet tea from the galley. Then he shuffled aft to the radio shack and switched on the SSB. Half an hour later, he was in contact with the *News*.

'Nicholas Eason here,' he said, and checked the satnav and the chart. 'Two hundred and nine miles west of Cape Horn. I have something you're going to want to hear.'

For the first time in eighteen thousand miles, Art Schacker sat at *Flag*'s chart-table and banged a Lucky Strike out of the packet, and in defiance of his own rules, lit it. He stared woodenly ahead at the banks of radios. The radios which had just dropped a bombshell in his lap.

Forward, George Hart was banging a pan with a ladle and yelling 'Chow down!' The door behind Schacker opened – the door of the DuCanes' new after cabin. Wallace DuCane looked blithe and chipper in a shiny-peaked yachting cap and the inners of a three-layer suit of wet-gear.

'Eat time, huh?' said DuCane. 'I sure am hungry!'

Schacker blew smoke from nostrils flared like an angry bull's. 'Siddown,' he said.

'Can't it wait,' said DuCane. 'I'm starv –'

'Siddown,' said Schacker again. His eyes were chips of

438

blue ice, and the muscles at the corners of his jaw were hard as stone.

DuCane sat, in the padded navigator's chair next to Schacker's. There was no alternative.

Schacker said, 'You were on radio watch this morning.'

'Sure,' said DuCane.

'You logged all the calls?'

DuCane's eyes became wary. 'Something on your mind?' he said.

'*Kelly's Eye* sank an hour ago,' he said. 'She was sending out signals on VHF frequencies from an antenna pulled up her main halyard, constantly from 1100 hours until 1300 hours. The job of the watch boat is to pick up that kind of stuff. We're within range. How come we didn't pick it up?'

DuCane said nothing for a moment. Then he said, 'Jesus, Art, that's terrible. Were they rescued?'

'*Chinamite* got to them. She was south of here, maybe fifteen miles further away from *Eye* than we were. *Chinamite*'s engine was out. She had to sail back. Do you understand what that means?'

DuCane said, 'I guess not. Listen, right now I'm hungry. What about supper?'

Schacker moved his head so his nose was inches from DuCane's. DuCane could smell the stale smoke on his breath, see the lines of strain round his eyes. 'At best, you are an incompetent radio operator,' he said quietly. 'At worst, you heard those poor bastards and you ignored them. Since the log doesn't show that you received their call, I'll give you the benefit of the doubt. Only you know what happened. But for your information, we have been protested by every boat in the goddamn fleet for gross negligence. And my reputation stinks, and so does the boat's. And if I was on the committee that hears the protest, I'd uphold it and make goddamn sure everybody knows why.'

DuCane was pale, and his mouth was clamped in a hard line. 'We'll get our lawyers down from Boston,' he said. 'They can't do this to us.'

'Oh, yes, they can,' said Art. 'This is an international race, not a college regatta. Never mind that, though. People could have died back there. One of them did. DuCane, are you human?'

DuCane stood up, staggering to the roll of the boat. 'Have Hart bring supper to my cabin,' he said, and opened the door.

'Get your own,' said Schacker. 'And while you're at it, you can explain to the crew how you lost them the race.'

The door slammed in his face.

In the saloon, Ellie DuCane sat at the table and smiled her steely smile as the watches shovelled in canned stew and freeze-dried potatoes and George Hart's special apple pie à la mode.

Wallace DuCane ate no dinner that night.

The following morning at 0800, *Tasman* was butting her way across a sea like a cold, wet switchback. The watch on deck were all up to weather, because the wind had gone north-northwest, and *Tasman* was on a reach. The men were cold, and wet, and fed up almost past endurance.

When Sparko came down the ladder for jaw-jaw that morning, he found Murphy at the set. The big man was leaning back in his chair. His arms dangled by his sides, and his eyes were closed. The lids were red with lack of sleep; stone the crows, thought Sparko, even his *eyelids* are bloodshot.

'Skipper,' said Sparko nervously. 'Jaw-jaw.'

'We'll listen,' said Murphy. 'But no talking. No need to tell 'em where we are.' His big, hairy hand went up and turned on the radios, set by set. Then, as an afterthought, he punched the buttons by the satnav readout, and compared them with ones on the chart on the table in front of him. Sparko peered over his shoulder. The position was three minutes different from the previous one, close to the group of ragged-edged islands at the foot of Patagonia. Tubes must have taken a fix less than half an hour previously.

'Breakfast,' said Sparko. 'I got an ovenful of bacon in there.'

Murphy grinned. It was his old grin, but the flesh had fallen away from his cheeks, and there was something wolfish about it now. 'Nah,' he said. 'I'll get something later.'

Sparko shrugged. 'Great bacon,' he said. Murphy had been off his food for two weeks now. And he wasn't sleeping, either. Sparko was beginning to get seriously worried about him. But there was nothing he could do. So he stood and felt lonely as the voices of the jaw-jaw squawked from the speakers.

After a while, Murphy levered himself out of the chair, pulled up his hood and went on deck. *Tasman* was moving hard. The wind had gone round full north, pulling a nasty cross-chop off the precipitous swells from the west. It was a very cold wind: much too cold for a wind that has spent its career at sea. Murphy walked forward and climbed on to the spinnaker pole, watching as the bow went for ever up a wave, and screwing his eyes up as it hung on the summit. But the sea ahead was obscured by a silvery fog. He jumped down again and went aft. 'See anything?' he said.

'Nope,' said the man at the helm. 'But we'll want the kite off if we get the wind any further on the nose.'

They turned and looked at the sail. It was a 1.5 oz Mylar spinnaker, not designed for heavy running. None of the sails Murphy had appropriated in Sydney were. But there was no chance of getting any more made. They had been going through them at a frightening rate, down there in the South Pacific.

'Bastard,' said the man on the wheel, struggling with the spokes. *Tasman*'s bow nosed up towards the wind, which struck hard in her oversized kite and dragged her over until her main boom tore a furrow of white spray from the sea to starboard. Murphy went to help him. But the wind was freshening and heading. The luff of the spinnaker billowed back, then filled again with a crack. Murphy shouted 'Get it off!' Too late. There was a dull, heavy *bang*, and a streak of grey sky appeared across one of the sail's horizontal seams. The wind got its fingers in the streak and tore. Ten seconds later, there was no sail left.

'Fifteen thousand dollars,' said Murphy. He spat, and watched the saliva fly over the rail and into the sea to starboard. Then he heard Sparko's voice. He recognized it as Sparko's, though there were no words. And the helmsman was howling too. And he raised his head.

The foredeck men were putting on the next sail. Ahead of them, the freshening wind had torn the mist off the sea. Off the port bow there hung a huge black brow of rock that scaled the sky, hundred feet on hundred feet, until it faded into a vague swirl of vapour.

'Well, wouldn't it rot your socks,' said Sparko. 'Cape Horn.'

As Harriet switched off the sets after jaw-jaw, she felt desperately cold and desperately lonely. *EPK* had sailed very far south. They had seen a lot of ice: too much ice, some of the crew said. But the winds were blowing hard and steady from abaft the beam, and that, as Jack Asprey pointed out, was the main thing. Harriet was somewhat surprised to hear him endorsing Emily's judgement; it seemed unlike him. There was even a hint of conspiracy between them. But for Emily's sake, she was glad.

She was worried about Emily.

Every day she looked thinner and more fragile. Now she seemed animated only by whatever slow fire it was that glowed in the big, dark eyes shadowed by the hood of her parka. Before, Harriet and she had always been able to talk. But since Sydney – since before Sydney – Emily seemed to inhabit mental country in which Harriet was a stranger.

Harriet sighed. She felt suspended: between Sydney and Buenos Aires, between wedding and honeymoon, between Emily and the crew. The little voices on the radio were her only company. Every time she spoke to Henri de Rochambaud it was as if he were in the room with her, and she could feel his firm hand on her shoulder. It was the only moment of warmth in the day, and now it was cooling with the radio sets. She was back to the cold and the feeling, lurking at the edge of her consciousness, that something, somehow, was very badly wrong.

She got up stiffly, her joints aching with cold, and went to the saloon. Jack Asprey was sitting at the table, writing in a notebook. He looked up and laid his forearm across what he had written, like a schoolboy hiding his exam paper. 'How's hubby?' he said. 'Garlic holding out?'

Harriet said, 'Fine,' and forced a smile. She pulled down the flap of the table, clamped on the twelve-volt sewing-machine and started to repair a splitting seam in the number five genoa. When she had finished she went on deck.

'What's the met.?' said Emily.

'Storm coming up astern.'

'Oh,' said Emily. *EPK* was moving fast and well across a long ten-foot swell, reaching to the northerly wind sweeping across her deck at force five to six. White horses played on the green water. The horizon was close and hazy. The sun was shining, but it failed to lift the spirits. Harriet looked at the haze, and shivered with the knowledge of ice.

'We'll save our time yet,' said Emily. Her eyes swivelled under the peak of her hood. Harriet thought there was a slyness in them, as if she was only making polite conversation, and smiled back uneasily.

After a while, Asprey came on deck. He grinned at Emily, and said, 'How are we doing?'

'Fine,' said Emily.

'Looks like you were right,' said Asprey.

Emily smiled mechanically, as if she scarcely knew what he was talking about. But Harriet knew. Emily had announced at the beginning of the leg that *EPK* would be sticking as closely as possible to the Great Circle route, plunging far to the south. There was a bigger risk of ice down there; but it was shorter.

They had been lucky with the ice. Now, *EPK* was on the northeastern fringes of the Bellingshausen Sea, running parallel to the ice-hidden shore of Antarctica, leaving the South Shetlands four hundred miles to starboard and lifting her nose gently to run northeastwards.

When Emily had set out her strategy, the most experienced grinder had said, 'This is bleeding loopy.' But Asprey had rapped him down. 'She's the skipper,' he had said. 'She knows what she's at.'

445

And so far it had worked very well. The big boats could make time with an orgy of surfing, but the shorter distance was a big advantage to a smaller boat like *EPK*.

During the last couple of hours, the wind had begun to rise and the sky clouded over from the southwest. At midnight, Harriet rolled into her damp bunk above the saloon table and fell instantly asleep. As she slept she was aware that *EPK*'s motion was increasing, and that the sound of wind in the rigging had risen from a moan to a scream. But while she was aware of these things, they did not make her sleep uneasy. It was her dreams that did that; one dream in particular, of Jack Asprey, listening to Emily, head cocked; smiling and nodding, and writing in his notebook. But the letters his pen made were written not in ink, but blood.

It seemed a very short time before she was awakened by someone shaking her arm. She sat up, rolled out of her sleeping bag and into the second layer of her wet-gear in one movement. *EPK* was moving in a series of sideways slews, a heel to port lasting perhaps ten seconds, then an indecisive yawing, and off again, this time heeled to starboard. The cabin sole seemed wet. It was bitingly cold.

She got the dregs of the coffee from the galley thermoses. It was all there was left. A few of the crew were milling around in the half-dark. She tried to say something; but the noise of the sea and the wind were too loud. It was not the wind but the absence of coffee that made her realize for the first time that this was not an ordinary storm.

Emily was not in her cabin. She must be on deck. Harriet punched the repeaters beside the photograph of Eric which hung above the bunk. Wind speed, sixty-six knots. She felt a hollowness in her stomach. Force twelve. Hurricane. She had never sailed in a wind like that before. Few people had. Or few people who had lived to tell the tale. Her eyes were drawn again to the photograph. It shivered slightly, as the vibration of *EPK*'s passage through the water gave it life.

Life. Harriet slammed the cabin door and ran up the companion-ladder, clawing at the hatch with frantic hands.

Water hit her in the face – heavy, icy water. She wriggled through the opening, clipped on her safety harness and slammed the hatch again. The water trickled over her breasts inside her suit. It made her gasp. But the air was so cold it burned her throat, and she cut the gasp midway.

The world was white. The sea was a confused white mass where the wind had caught the waves and ripped them to shreds. The surface was invisible under the whizzing spindrift. And mixing with the spindrift, whipping horizontally out of the low black sky, came the snow.

All this Harriet took in in one quick glance aft. The wind slammed stinging snow into her face. She jerked her head away, clinging to the rail with gloves which accumualted little drifts.

EPK's boom and forestay were naked of sail. She was driving through the water under bare poles. Harriet tried to shout to the helmsman, 'Are you okay?' But the words were wrenched away by the gale. So she banged the figure at the wheel on the shoulder.

The hood turned towards her. Inside it, Emily's eyes caught the white reflections of the snow. Her face was pale too, with the alabaster translucency of a saint in a cathedral. She smiled. It was a strange, soft smile; the smile of a woman going to meet her lover.

And suddenly Harriet understood. 'No!' she shouted. But the wind tore the word away. She put her arm round Emily's shoulders. They felt thin and unresisting under the bulky parka. Harriet knew that as far as Emily was concerned, she might as well not have been there.

Asprey was crouching in the gorilla pit. She struggled forward, her feet slithering in the frozen snow on the deck, and jerked her thumb towards the hatch. They went below.

'What is it?' said Asprey. His face was cold and hard under his hood.

'Emily's . . . not well,' said Harriet. 'You must relieve her.'

Asprey grinned at her. 'What?' he said. 'Come *on*, Harriet. This sounds like disloyalty.'

'For God's sake,' said Harriet.

'You forget,' said Asprey, and his grin had gone now. 'Emily's the skipper. You've made it pretty plain that you trust her, not me.'

'Be reasonable,' said Harriet. 'She needs help –'

'We all need help,' said Jack Asprey harshly. 'Taking the southern route's one thing. But at this rate, we're going to land up in the bloody ice.' He went back on deck.

And *EPK Electric* reeled on through the howling milky sea, due east, towards the jagged coast of the Antarctic peninsula and her rendezvous with the dead.

They stood watch in pairs. Those not on watch stayed below, as there was nothing to be done on deck. The helmsman was relieved at half-hourly intervals by his or her companion. At the end of the first day, the wind went round northwest. Jack Asprey went into the navigatorium, and did some calculations with a chart and a pencil and a ruler.

When he had finished, he made a note in his notebook.

Harriet watched his face. It was haggard, the brown skin sallow and pale. And she found that for the first time, she was properly frightened.

She turned and stared at the wall in front of her eyes. What would it look like when the ice came through, she thought. The blue-green shard that would go through the boat like a gutting knife through the belly of a fish; and after it the cold, green water. You would freeze before you drowned –

'Harriet,' Emily was saying. 'On deck.'

And so it went on. On deck, freezing in the icy twilight. Then below, looking at the side and wondering what dying felt like.

At jaw-jaw time, she felt a sudden desperate urge to talk to de Rochambaud. She went to the radio, and called the duty boat. But the duty boat was too far away, or the aerials were blown flat, or her icy fingers were too numb to tune. She began to cry, and climbed into her bunk. The last thing she saw before she went to sleep was Jack Asprey, a small, terrible smile spreading across his face as he snapped shut his notebook.

Harriet thought: of course, we are none of us strictly normal, just now. She smiled. Henri would be vastly amused when she told him. And she fell into a deep, peaceful sleep.

It was the quiet that woke her. It was an uncanny quiet; an absence of all sound, the only movement a long, regular heave of the sea, as if she were lying on the chest of some huge animal, rising and falling with its breathing. Then she opened her eyes.

The porthole above her head glared dazzling white. Her footsteps were loud on the cabin sole as she went for the companion-ladder.

On deck, the light was blinding. For a moment, she could see nothing at all. Gradually her eyes adjusted.

EPK was lying in the middle of a white sheet of ice. At first, the glare made Harriet think the sheet was unbroken. Then she saw that it was criss-crossed with lines of black water, ranging in width from a few inches to thirty feet. There was no wind: *EPK*'s sails flopped listlessly.

The ice stretched away to the eastern horizon, where it was broken by a series of long humps. At first, Harriet thought that these were icebergs. Then she saw patches of black basalt; cliffs.

'What are they?' she said to the man sitting by the wheel.

'South Shetlands,' he said. His eyes were bloodshot, and his voice was unsteady. 'Missed 'em by a whisker. A bloody whisker.'

There was a knot of people round the bottom of the mast. Emily was there, and Jack Asprey, and a couple of grinders. Emily was in the bosun's chair, attached to the spare main halyard. Harriet felt a chill that had nothing to do with the icy air. 'What are you doing?' she said.

Emily turned. There was a pair of binoculars round her neck. Her eyes were big and soft, and her smile radiant with joy. 'We have arrived,' she said. 'He's out there, beyond the ice. I'm just going up to see exactly where. Then we'll go and get him.'

'Get him?' said Harriet.

'Pick him up,' said Emily. 'Poor Eric. He's been so cold. Okay, boys.'

The grinders ground the winches, and Emily rose from the deck as if being transported to another world. Jack Asprey watched her from the deck, shaking his head. The corners of his mouth twitched with the beginnings of a self-satisfied smirk.

'Oh, my God,' said Harriet.

'I'm afraid she's had a nervous breakdown,' said Asprey, shaking his head. 'I blame myself. I should have spotted it earlier.' He looked solemn. But Harriet could see the skin around his eyes twitching with triumph. 'I think we should . . . well, humour her.'

Harriet stared at him in horror. 'You *bastard*,' she said. She turned to the grinders. 'Bring her down,' she said.

'Keep her up,' said Asprey. His smile was gone now, and his face looked hard and dangerous. 'It'll cool her off. Silly bitch could have drowned the lot of us.'

'And now you'll be skipper,' said Harriet quietly.

Asprey shrugged.

High at the maintruck, Emily de Havilland screamed. She screamed again and again. Asprey said, 'Lower away. She's cooked.'

Harriet caught her as she came down. She had stopped screaming now. Her eyes were tight shut, as if to exclude something she didn't want to see. The grinders avoided Harriet's eyes uneasily. 'Don't just stand there,' she snapped. 'Help me carry her below.'

Emily lay rigid as a plank as they carried her below and laid her on her bunk. Harriet sat beside her and took her hand. It was clawed like a bird's.

'It's all right,' said Harriet mechanically. 'It's all right.'

Emily de Havilland did not stir, or give any sign that she

was alive except for the hiss of her breath between her clenched teeth. Harriet went to the first-aid kit, and got out four Valium. When she came back into the cabin, Emily's knees had come up to her chest, and she was clasping them with her hands, moaning. Harriet forced the pills down her throat. Then she sat crouched in the tiny floor space of the cabin, and waited.

After an hour, Emily began to mumble. 'He said he'd be there,' she was saying. 'He said he'd be there.'

An hour later, the wind came up, and the swell jostled aside the drift ice. *EPK's* sails filled, and her nose came round northeastward, and the water gurgled at her transom as she began to move down a wide blue lead. Within two hours, she was in open water, tramping hard, with her nose fixed on Staten Island, five hundred miles away at the tip of Cape Horn. Astern, the horizon was lit with a white glare like the glow of a cold fire. It was the ice-blink, the reflection from the thousands of miles of ice that stretched, deadly and sparkling, south to the Pole.

'Turn left,' said Cole.

'After you,' said Nicholas Eason, and handed him the

wheel. Cape Horn, tall and black under an untypically clear blue sky with untypically brilliant sunshine, slid by seven and a half miles to port. A pair of albatrosses rode the air astern of *Chinamite*'s forest of aerials. As the day wore on and they came under the lee of the land, the huge swells that had followed them for the best part of a month died down to a solid roll. *Chinamite* heeled to the cold north-westerlies from the mountains, and began to trudge heavily up the western arm of the Falkland Current, heading for the tropics.

But the tropics were still a long way away, and *Chinamite* was intolerably cramped below. The *Kelly's Eye* crew were not good company. Once they were over their shock, disappointment set in. It made them ill-tempered and edgy. The only one who was in a good mood was Dave Kelly. He had saved his film, and Chuck the cameraman had got his camera working again. Kelly seemed almost indecently cheerful.

Somewhere northeast of Rio Gallegos, the call he had booked came through.

Bennett was convalescing in one of the quarter berths. She was taking a long time to recover from her freezing; as it transpired, she had kept *Eye*'s crew busy, which was how they had stayed alive. But the effort had taken a lot out of her, and she was ill with what Bones said was exhaustion. Kelly's voice came loud and clear through the wall of the radio shack.

'Sure,' it said. 'So you'll have us taken off, right. And I'll film the fleet on the final approach, and do some background for the Mardi Gras piece, right?'

'He's going,' said Bennett. 'Thank the Lord.' Her voice

was weak and dry. Eason was sitting on the bottom of her bunk. 'Do me a favour,' said Bennett. 'Keep me aboard. I don't want to go anywhere with that prick.'

'Not my decision,' said Eason. She was squeezing his hand. The strength of her grip was surprising.

'I was watching him when I was sitting there on that goddamn boat,' said Bennett. 'He didn't go more than two feet from the liferaft the whole goddamn time. He had all his film in his coat, and he borrowed the cameraman's gloves, and now Chuck's got frostbite in two fingers. And ne helped Bud to specify that goddamn boat.' She paused. 'I was crazy to go near it. First time I saw the thing, I thought, this is like sending a Formula One car on the Baja race. But I went.' She shut her eyes. 'I was crazy. I spent a long time being crazy. You know, I shot a goddamn albatross.' She laughed, a high grating sound.

Eason said, 'Relax. You're not crazy.'

'Not any more,' said Bennett. 'You can get to know yourself real well when your boat's sinking and you're responsible for fifteen guys sitting up to their asses in ocean.' She opened her eyes again. 'But I guess you know that. You're real nice, Nicky.'

'Oh, for heaven's *sake*,' said Eason, acutely embarrassed.

'I owe you one,' said Bennett.

Next door, Kelly was saying, 'Yeah. Great. Great. *Great*.'

'Rubbish,' said Eason. 'You owe me nothing.'

'No,' said Bennett. 'Listen. When I was in the States I found out some stuff you might be interested in. About *Arpeggio*, right?' She was up on her elbows. Her face was a dreadful brownish grey, her eyes sunk far back in her head.

'*Arpeggio?*'

'I know a . . . a guy who was on the dock gang in Toronto, before she sailed.'

There was a great stillness in Eason's mind. 'Tell me,' he said.

Bennett opened her mouth to speak. But at that moment, Cole's voice roared from the deck. 'ALL HANDS!' And *Chinamite* heeled far to starboard under the whizzing spray of a *pampero*, a storm of cold wind rolled down from the Andes to the west. After the new sails were set, all hands were ordered up to windward. Cole was not the man to get an extra ton and a half of movable ballast on board without taking the opportunity to carry some extra sail. By the time Eason was back with Bennett, she was asleep.

That night they ate supper in shifts. Afterwards they crammed into the weather bunks, and sat in silence, except for the Rolling Stones playing 'Brown Sugar' on the stereo and the mumbled chatter of Noddy and Slicer, who were discussing exactly how they planned to surprise and delight the womanhood of Rio. Bennett was still asleep. The atmosphere was damp, jolted, and unmistakably sullen.

In the middle of the sprawled bodies, Kelly stood up. Chuck the cameraman switched on a set of lights he had rescued from *Eye* and charged from *Chinamite*'s generator. Kelly said, 'I have to make an announcement,' and looked across to Herb, who was holding a big mike and trying for a level. 'Can we have quiet?' said Herb.

Kelly switched off the stereo, said, 'Thanks, guys,' to Noddy and Slicer, and gave them the famous Kelly smile.

Kelly started speaking to camera. He knew that the bodies in the background would give the shot a dramatic, Death of Nelson, Raft of the Medusa quality.

He said, 'I want to thank you for the work you did.' He paused, and looked sincere. 'A lot of people in the past have maybe felt grateful to Dave Kelly for, well, doing a little to straighten out lives that have been twisted by injustice or abuse of power. Well, it's Kelly's turn to be grateful. And when we leave this boat, *Chinamite*, and Ed Cole who tracked us down in the middle of some of the worst seas in the world, we will leave a little piece of our hearts here. Thank you, guys. Okay, we can cut the end part later.' He cleared his throat and patted his nicely brushed hair. 'There's a ship on its way out of Comodoro Rivadavia to pick us up,' he said.

Eason went on deck, to where Cole was conning *Chinamite* through the tough, steep sea the wind was raising off the current. He said, 'Ed, do me a favour.'

Cole's raised a sandy eyebrow.

'Keep Bennett aboard when the rest go.'

Cole's other eyebrow went up. 'Why?'

'Robbie's broken his arm. He has to go ashore. That leaves us a man short. Bennett'll be fine in a day or so. And I have to talk to her about things. They concern you.'

'How?'

'You'll have to trust me.'

Cole looked at him sourly. 'Trust a journalist?' He brushed a slap of spray out of his eyes. 'Okay,' he said. 'This once.'

Two hours later, the crew of *Kelly's Eye* went up the rusty side of a ship, crusted with dung and loud with the

456

mooing of live cattle bound for Buenos Aires. Kelly went last, as if he had been the captain, and Chuck got a shot of him shaking hands with Ed Cole and Paddy Kinnersley before he clambered up the Jacob's ladder.

'Can't say I'm sorry to see the last of *him*,' said Cole, as the ship went hull-down on the western horizon.

When Eason went below Bennett was awake, propped up in the bunk with a cup of coffee in her hand. 'Listen,' she said. '*Arpeggio*. The guy on the dock gang. He was the foreman. He's my brother.'

'Your brother?' said Eason.

'My twin brother. Identical. Scott Bennett. Everybody knew old Scott. Real character, Scott.' There was bitterness in her voice. 'There was something funny about *Arpeggio*.'

'There was?'

She said. 'I was with him when they said on the radio she'd gone down. Scott kind of ran out of the room and got sick.'

'Got *sick*?'

'It was like somebody punched him in the gut. He just seemed to . . . crumple up.'

'Did you ever find out why?'

She shrugged. 'He was on the dock gang. *Arpeggio* went down. Maybe there was something weird going on. Who knows?'

Eason picked at the quilting of the sleeping-bag. In his mind the faint outlines of a picture were forming, like a ship seen at dawn in the mist. 'So,' he said. 'Your brother would have given evidence at the Inquiry. And that's why Cole said in Cape Town that he knew your face. That's why you didn't want to talk about it, and you seduced me instead.'

Bennett looked straight at him. 'Right,' she said. 'It was kind of nice, at that.'

'Yes,' said Eason. 'Where's your brother now?'

'In Toronto,' Bennett said, 'I went up to see him. Nick, you saved my life back there. Scott's a weird guy. He'll talk to me, but he wouldn't talk to anyone else. Do you want I should go see him again when we get ashore in Rio?'

'Yes,' said Eason. 'I think that's a very, very good idea. But I still don't understand why you didn't tell me all this the first time we met.'

Bennett looked at him coolly. 'I thought you were supposed to be smart,' she said. 'If your brother was a junkie who told a bunch of lies at a formal inquiry into the death of thirty kids, would you tell the whole story to a Limey you met twice?'

'I see,' said Eason. 'What's changed?'

'I owe you one,' said Bennett. 'And Scott's not going to be around for long. That's why I went up to see him, last stopover.' She stopped. Eason saw to his amazement that her eyes were glazed with tears. Somehow it had never entered his head that Bennett, the titanic Bennett, would be capable of tears. 'Maybe he'll want to tell me about it, before he goes,' she said.

Twelve days up from the Horn, the green mountains of Brazil were silhouetted on the rim of the world as *Tasman* marched northwestward, canted steeply under light main and number two genoa in eighteen knots of wind. The sunset was a particularly good one, and Sparko was explaining it to the other men in the gorilla pit. 'The mountains of Spain,' he said. 'And there's El Cid, leaping across the plains to rescue his sheila from the terrorists –'

'Shaddup,' said Murphy, at the wheel. Sparko looked up, grinning. But there was no answering grin on Murphy's face.

'What's up?' said Sparko.

'I can't stand your bloody drivel any more,' said Murphy. 'It's time we did some racing on this boat.'

Sparko felt the blood rising into his cheeks. Then he thought, hang on. There's something not right here. Totally unlike Murphy. So he said, quietly, 'Hair across, Skip?'

Murphy said nothing. His face, high forehead, eagle nose and vast chin in silhouette against the sky, looked as if it was carved out of stone. Finally, he said, 'Sorry. Where's the opposition?'

'*Flag,* fifty miles astern. *Siltex*, a hundred, *Chinamite* most of a day.' Sparko kept his voice patient, wandered aft to the cockpit, and started to fiddle with the bearing compass he was resetting.

He took a deep breath. 'You got a problem?' he said.

This time, Murphy looked down at him with a wretched parody of his carnivorous grin. 'Nah,' said Murphy. 'Only we got to win this leg.'

' 'Course we have,' said Sparko.

Murphy sat down heavily and squinted up at the luff of the mainsail. 'We need money,' he said. 'If we don't win this one, we won't have any money to sail the next one.'

'What?' said Sparko.

'I got some change out of that ring Shar gave me,' said Murphy. 'Quite a lot of change. So I whipped down to old Maxie Green the bookie. I put it all on the old girl's nose.'

'Nose?' said Sparko.

'Half a million dollars to two hundred thousand.'

'*How much?*' said Sparko.

Murphy did not answer directly. Instead, he said: 'We need some more sails. We didn't get enough heavy-air kit out of the loft, and we've been going through it this leg. If we get a bad blow on the last leg, we could be scuppered.'

'Ah well,' said Sparko.

'Yeah,' said Murphy.

After that, there seemed very little to say.

It was blowing force five over the deck from the east, a sparkling breeze that blew the tops of the low swell to white horses and pushed *Tasman* along at a clear eleven knots under a big Mylar genoa and her fairweather mainsail. The watch drank coffee, and woke up slightly. At 0515, the wind veered southerly, force five, and the watch captain ordered the 1.5 ounce running kite. At 0525, the wind went southwest for a time, and stiffened. The log entry read:

Downhill for Rio! (for 5 minutes anyway).

At 0530, Tubes Murphy woke from an hour's fitful sleep in his bunk. As usual, he had a sore head and a sore stomach. His eyes went straight to the Brookes and Gatehouse repeaters over his bunk. He crawled out of his sleeping-bag, shoved his feet into his boots, and punched the satnav. His heart, which had been thudding hard, slowed. Progress was being made. He crawled out of the stuffy cabin and up the ladder into the cockpit.

· It happened as he stuck his head out into the cool dawn air. The helmsman glanced down and said, 'Morning, Skip.' That was why he did not see the puff of wind that came from the wrong direction, out of the east, and knocked the mainsail aback so the boom scythed across the deck and landed on the opposite tack with a crash that made the hull ring.

The helmsman swore.

'And again,' said Murphy.

The wind gusted from its old quarter. This time the helmsman and the mainsheetman were ready, and they passed the boom gently overhead, and the spinnaker filled once again. But as they took the full weight of the wind, there was a sharp *bang* from somewhere half-way up the mast. And the mast itself bent double above the first spreader, folded gently forward and went into the sea.

There was a moment of complete silence. Then Tubes Murphy sat down on the deck, and held his throbbing head in his hands.

It took four hours to get the mess cut away, and another six to fix a jury rig and cut the sails crudely to fit. And by four o'clock, *Tasman*'s aching, sweat-stained crew were once again sailing for Rio. But by four o'clock, she had been overhauled first by *Flag*, and then by *Siltex* and *Flag*. And *Chinamite*'s high wedge of sail was cutting the horizon ten miles to the southward.

As *EPK* worked her way past the Falklands, Harriet Agnew made a careful study of Jack Asprey's routine. Now that he was acting skipper, he was not standing regular watch. The only fixed point in his day was breakfast, just after the 0800 change of watches. After breakfast, he shaved, slowly and meticulously. It took him, Harriet had observed, precisely eight and a half minutes from the time he closed the head door to the time he replaced his washbag with the rest of his effects in the locker outside. Among the effects was his private diary.

So all Harriet had to do was wait for a day when the sun would be high enough to suit her purpose.

As *EPK* moved up the tropics, Asprey's routine did not deviate. Harriet kept daily observations of the patch of bright sun the skylight threw on the wall of Emily's cabin. Off Buenos Aires, the light-meter of her camera told her that the light was bright enough for her purpose. And on the next day but one, there was no cloud.

On that day, Harriet watched Asprey go into the head and lock the door behind him. Then she tiptoed aft, opened his locker, and peered inside. The hard-covered diary was at the back, behind his spare shirts. She twitched it out, closed the locker door silently, and went into Emily's cabin. Emily was torpid on the bunk.

Harriet rifled the diary's pages until she came to the entries dealing with the third leg. Then she raised her compact Olympus 35mm camera, held the book open in the patch of sunlight with her free hand, and aimed. The autofocus whined. She shot, double page spread, turned the page, shot again. Asprey's writing was small and crabbed, and she did not even have to finish the roll.

When she had done, she checked her watch. One minute to go. She ran out, pushed the book in the back of the locker, jammed the shirts up against it, and shut the door as she heard Asprey's fingers rattle the lock of the head.

When he came out, she was replacing her camera in her own locker. 'Morning,' said Asprey, leering. 'What are you up to, eh?'

'Oh, not much,' said Harriet, giving him the sort of smile that she knew he expected from women. 'Just getting organized.'

'Let's talk strategy,' said DuCane.

Art Schacker was sitting beside him at the tilting chart-table. DuCane looked puffy and pale. Schacker did not want to talk to him about strategy or anything else. He pulled a Lucky out of the pack and stuck it in his mouth, but did not light it. 'Yeah?' he said.

DuCane switched on the radar. He was great on the electronics, thought Schacker, on the stuff you switched on and off. Probably he thought people worked in the same way. 'Okay,' said DuCane, pointing at the blips. 'No chance of catching *Siltex*, right?'

'I guess not,' said Schacker. *Siltex* had come through when *Flag* had stuck in a private calm two nights before. 'But we're giving her a good run for her money.'

'Sure we are,' said DuCane soothingly. 'And I'm protesting her. Well, you're protesting her. It is my – our – view that she needs remeasuring, and that rudder they put on her in Cape Town will put her rating through the roof.'

'She was checked in Sydney,' said Schacker. 'Anyway, she was so far down on the last leg that she's no chance for the race.'

'She has a chance for this leg,' said DuCane. 'I want us to win this leg. And I have lawyers coming down from Boston to present our case to the committee.'

'Your case,' said Schacker. 'Not ours.'

DuCane looked at him from over the hammock-like

464

pouches slung under his hard blue eyes. 'Your case is our case,' he said. 'That was why I yanked you out of the shit when you were drowning up there in Marblehead. Remember?'

'I remember,' said Schacker dully. 'But this is a British Race Committee. They might not take too kindly to your lawyers. Particularly when there's more than *Siltex* to argue about.'

DuCane grinned. 'Touché,' he said, and waved a well-manicured brown hand. 'But these are very, very good lawyers.'

'They'll need to be,' said Schacker. 'To explain exactly how you managed to overlook a continuous distress signal.'

DuCane ignored him. '*Tasman*, now.' He stabbed with his finger at the green blip far astern, and laughed. '*Tasman*'s no threat, right? I guess I have never seen a sweeter sight than ol' *Tasman* with her mast over the side.'

'He sailed a good race,' said Schacker, simply. 'It could have happened to anyone. Sure, it was useful. But I like to win clean.'

'I like to win, period. I shall personally propose a toast to that bust shroud at the club's next annual general meeting,' said DuCane.

'I won't drink to it,' said Schacker.

A hand descended on his shoulder. He looked around. Ellie DuCane was smiling down at him. 'Having fun, boys?' she said.

'Discussing tactics,' said DuCane.

'Ah,' said Ellie. Then, to Schacker. 'I find the best tactic is just to let Wallace win, otherwise he goes all nasty.' She smiled with her black-fringed eyes, and walked round into the accommodation. The weather was hot, and she was wearing a T-shirt and shorts that showed off her long brown legs. The shorts were just tight enough to show that she was not wearing anything underneath them.

Schacker was not unduly sensitive to such matters, but he had noticed that Ellie DuCane had become rather partial to George Hart. He hoped that that was not going to cause trouble with her husband. Running a boat and dealing with DuCane was as much as he could handle already, and if the DuCanes started having love troubles, he could not even bear to think of the fallout on a small, cramped boat.

'Bloody hell,' said Slicer. 'Listen to that. Just *listen* to it.'

Chinamite was ghosting towards the green hills of Rio de Janeiro. Ahead, the Christ on Corcovado Mountain stretched out his arms in welcome above the clustered white buildings of the city. Already, the headlands of the vast natural harbour had folded them in. The finish line was two hundred feet ahead. Beyond and to port was a long, white beach, packed with brown bodies and dark glasses. The roar of the traffic and the blare of automobile horns drifted from the high-rise buildings. And woven into the roar of the traffic, drums emulating the thunder of exhausts and brass contrapuntal to the car horns, were drifts of music.

Slicer's docksiders were executing involuntary dance steps on the deck. The whole of *Chinamite*'s crew was there, watching the land come up. The bow moved very slowly between the buoy and the grey gunboat at the far end. The finishing gun sounded.

And the town went wild.

All the people on that white sand began to cheer. The sirens of the spectator fleet began screaming. Even the crew of the gunboat waved and cheered. The captain of the gunboat switched on his loudhailer and began to make a speech in rapid Portuguese. The spectator boats came alongside, full of slender brown women in tiny bikinis. Slicer groaned, and went into a trance of lust. Then the champagne bottles started spinning through the air. And after a couple of gulps, Slicer got possession of himself, and started collecting telephone numbers.

A bay opened to port, under the vertical cliffs of the Sugar Loaf. *Chinamite*'s bow turned in. It was full of yachts. At a dock were two masts taller than the rest, flying battle flags: *Flag* and *Siltex*.

Noddy had stripped down *Chinamite*'s gearbox soon after the rescue. She motored up to the race dock, stopped alongside *Siltex*'s wide grey spearhead of deck. A couple of Frenchmen took the mooring lines, grinning. A small man with a camera jumped on to the deck.

'Where Cole? Where Cole?' he shouted.

'Here,' said Cole.

The man raised his camera, and shot. 'Congratulations,' he said. 'Nice thing to meet hero. Where Eason?'

Eason found himself staring down a lens, and having his hand pumped wildly. 'What is this?' he said, dazed.

One of the Frenchmen grinned, revealing missing front teeth. 'You're world-wide headlines,' he said. 'You better get used to being a hero.'

Chinamite Inc's PR Office then took control, stationing security men on the gangplanks to keep the decks clear while the crew prepared themselves for the joys of Ashore.

Below, Bennett was pushing the last of her washing gear into a seabag. 'Well,' she said to Eason, 'I have to go.'

'So soon? Wait for the party.'

She shook her head. 'I have a flight. I have to see Scott.'

'Yes,' said Eason. 'True. And then what are your plans?'

'Maybe you'd like to sail the last leg?' said Kinnersley's voice from behind them. 'Robbie's arm isn't going to be up to it.'

Bennett's eyes flicked from Kinnersley to Eason. A smile started at the corners of her wide, red mouth. 'What the hell?' she said. 'I started. I'll finish. Sure.' She looked at her watch. 'Now I have to go. See you in a month, right? Have a nice carnival, Nicky.'

'Good luck,' said Eason. She did not look back, and he watched her go down the gangplank square-shouldered, long-legged, tracked by the eyes of the dockside gawpers with their unbuttoned white shirts and brown chests jingling with gold chains.

Half an hour later, an envelope arrived from the Race Committee, announcing an Extraordinary Meeting.

'You go,' said Kinnersley to Cole. 'I'll stay here, talk to the press.'

'I don't know about that,' said Cole, his eyes shifting.

'It's supposed to be the skipper who goes to the committee.'

Kinnersley said, 'It's a toss-up between that and meeting the journalists.'

Cole swallowed. Whenever he thought of committees, he could hear the heavy buzz of the flies round that still, hot room in Plymouth. He took a deep breath. 'If you insist,' he said.

'Take Eason,' said Kinnersley.

Cole ran his fingers through his thin, sandy hair. 'Yes,' he said. 'Good idea.'

Kinnersley watched him go down the deck, and thought: I wonder how long it's going to take him to realize he's turning from a pariah into a hero. Perhaps he never would. A man like Cole did not pay any attention to what they said on TV and in the newspapers. He formed his own opinion of himself, and he would not be merciful.

Kinnersley sighed. Then he announced a crew party on deck at 1830 hours, drink provided by sponsors. Cole and Eason jumped down to the quay and fought their way through the crowd, dizzied with the smell of people, the noises, the brilliant colours of flesh and clothing. The ground waved under them as they flagged down a taxi.

In the taxi, Cole said, 'It looks like you did a good job with your reporting.'

'And I suspect old Cole's flavour of the month with the sponsors,' said Eason.

'Oh,' said Cole, wincing as the taxi skidded broadside across a pedestrian crossing. 'I hadn't thought of it like that.'

For the rest of the ride, they gaped as Rio streaked past the windows. 'Strewth,' said Eason, after they had got out, and were leaning against a lamp-post to recover their composure. 'Give me the Horn any day.'

The meeting was in an aggressive silver and white shoe-box of a building. Its entrance hall was a sheet of echoing marble, and the air-conditioning chilled the sweat of the taxi ride on their bodies as they ascended to the thir-tieth floor. They were steered into a room panelled in mahogany with a large round table in the middle. There were ten men at the table: four of the committee, their faces pale after a British winter; Dave Kelly, barbered and smiling in a cream tropical suit with a Panama hat on the table in front of him; Jean-Luc Jarré of *Siltex*, his jaw covered with a two-day beard, scowling over his perpetual Gauloise; and Art Schacker and Wallace DuCane of *Flag*, backed by two smooth, well-fed men with dark suits and golf-course tans. DuCane was talking to the smaller of them. Schacker sat apart. Eason thought he looked uncomfortable. He was sucking deeply on a Lucky Strike, knocking its ash off into an ashtray that already held half a dozen butts.

A large, red-faced man rose. He said, 'I think we're all present and correct. Good afternoon.' The chairman of the committee perched a pair of half-moon glasses on his nose. 'We're here to hear two protests. One, that *Siltex-France*'s rudder form was changed in Sydney.' He turned to Jean-Luc Jarré. 'Any objection to measurement?'

Jarré shrugged his shoulders. 'And if I object, what?'

'Then you will be disqualified, I fear.'

'Then of course I do not object. Is this why you ask me here?'

The chairman frowned, but his downward-slanting eyes

were amused. 'We must do these things by the book,' he said.

'Okay, we remeasure,' said Jarré.

'Thank you,' said the chairman. He turned to the secretary. 'John, please notify the scrutineers.' He frowned. This time his eyes were not at all amused. 'A protest against *Flag* for dereliction of radio duty. Protest lodged by' – he pushed his half-moon spectacles up his nose – '*Chinamite* and *Siltex*, *Sirène*, and of course *Kelly's Eye*. There are others, but I'll accept *Chinamite* as spokesman. As for *Flag* . . . I recognize Mr Schacker and Mr DuCane. But who are these other gentlemen?'

The smaller of the dark-suited Americans rose. 'We are the legal representatives of the Sound Yacht Club, sponsors and owners of *Flag*, sir.'

The chairman looked at him with distaste. 'So am I to understand that you are here to argue your . . . clients' case? Looks pretty cut and dried to me, I must say.'

'The truth will no doubt emerge,' said the lawyer with a small, perfunctory smile. 'I believe that one of the protestors, Mr Cole of *Chinamite*, is no stranger to Inquiries.'

Eason saw Cole's head jerk back as if he had been hit. The colour drained from his face, then returned, dark beetroot red. His mouth opened to speak.

But it was not him who spoke. It was Art Schacker. 'Withdraw that remark.'

The lawyer looked up. 'Are you addressing me?'

Schacker turned, slowly, his slanted eyes burning in his oaken face. 'You're damn right I am,' he said. 'This protest is being defended in my name, but not at my request, and I no longer require your services.' He stood up, keeping his hands flat on the table. 'Ed, I would like to apologize for that offensive remark.'

'Oh,' said Ed Cole. 'Yes. Thanks.'

Schacker turned to face the chairman. 'Chairman, I admit dereliction of radio-watch duty.'

DuCane jumped to his feet, knocking over his chair. 'Schacker!' he yelled. 'You're out of order. Sit down!'

The chairman cleared his throat. 'I think that is up to Mr Schacker. He is the captain of *Flag*, Mr DuCane. You are the, er, financier. Protests are against the captain.' He waited as DuCane retrieved his chair and took his place. 'Now, I think we all want to get on.'

DuCane looked around him and found no sympathetic eye to catch. The small lawyer leaned forward to whisper in his ear, but DuCane shook his head.

'The committee will now confer,' said the admiral. The four members rose and left the room.

For five minutes there was no sound except the faraway snarl of the traffic and the low hum of the air-conditioning. Then the four members returned to their places.

The chairman put his finger-ends together, and looked owlishly over his half-moon glasses. 'The committee has unanimously agreed that in the event of a protest standing unopposed, it shall be best dealt with by time penalties. The decision of the committee is therefore that *Flag* shall incur a sixteen-hour time penalty. And that *Chinamite* shall have the sixteen hours occupied by the rescue deducted from her time. Furthermore, the committee would like to offer its congratulations to the crew of *Chinamite* and in particular to Mr Cole, on an outstanding piece of seamanship.' He paused. 'And of course this makes *Chinamite* the winner of this leg.'

Art Schacker stood up and shook Cole's hand across the table. Jarré said, '*Merde,*' and grinned. Eason looked at the two captains and Cole, all small men, all hard, all grinning. Then he looked at the soft-skinned, tight-mouthed lawyers. And he thought: there's us and there's them. We started out racing crew against crew. But now perhaps it's changed. It's the people on the boats against the people on the land.

'Er . . .,' said Cole, with a slow, tentative grin on his narrow face. 'I hear they sell rum in Rio. I think I'd better take you out and buy you some.'

RIO DE JANEIRO

FROM THE NOTICE OF RACE

The final leg of the Lancaster Great Circle will be sailed as a pursuit. Class 2, 3 and 4 Yachts will start from Rio de Janeiro at intervals determined by their ratings or handicaps, slowest first. Class I boats or Maxis will start level.

A week after the maxis had come ashore, Dave Kelly called a press conference at the Iate Club do Pão do Açucar, which had given all the Great Circle boats use of its dock and honorary membership for the duration of the stopover. The aim of the conference was for the world's press to meet Ed Cole, in his capacity as hero, and Dave Kelly, on whom some of the heroism was intended to rub off. It was a well-attended event. Newspapers from all over the world had correspondents in Rio for Carnival, and the correspondents were looking for stories.

The press conference featured a stage with a row of chairs, facing more rows of chairs for the journalists, and a large quantity of Taittinger champagne paid for by Dave Kelly. Attendance was not confined to journalists. From his seat on the platform, Nicholas Eason could see twenty or thirty crewmen from other maxis at the bar, wearing shorts and T-shirts, taking the opportunity for a free carouse handily placed near the race dock, in the intervals of patching up their boats for the final leg.

Kelly was ten minutes late. Eason could feel Ed Cole's uneasiness. 'Okay?' he said.

Cole scowled, lowering his small, sandy head. 'If he's

not here in five minutes, I'm off. Got work to do.'

'Probably putting his face on,' said Eason.

Cole grinned, the sudden grin that lit up his face. There was a commotion at the entrance. 'Look out,' he said. 'Here he comes.'

Dave Kelly was wearing a white tropical suit with a gold and orange Hawaiian shirt. He trotted down the aisle between the chairs, gained the dais with an agile leap and said, 'Ladies. Gentlemen. Thanks for being here, people.' He smiled, and the TV lights were dazzling in the snowy enamel of his incisors. 'Now,' he said. 'The reason I asked you to be here with me today is to join me in greeting the man who saved my life.' The cameras purred at the side of the dais. Some American reporters began to look interested. A couple of obvious Englishmen sidled towards the bar, looking pink and hot. 'Ladies and gentlemen, I give you Edward Cale!'

'Cole,' said Cole.

'Cole,' said Kelly, darting a look of veiled fury at his researcher. 'Shake hands, Ed!'

Cole got up, looking acutely embarrassed, and offered his hand. Kelly took it. Flashbulbs popped. Cole tried to withdraw his hand, but Kelly held it tight. And the bulbs continued to pop as Kelly began to talk, his white-suited shoulders shaking slightly at Cole's attempts to tug free.

'This man,' said Kelly. 'What can I tell you? This man sailed a hundred miles through mountainous seas to locate the stricken *Kelly's Eye*. His finding was an astonishing feat of seamanship –'

Cole yanked his hand free. 'Rubbish,' he snapped, his voice made curt by embarrassment. 'Pure bloody fluke.

You were lucky, that's all. Anyway, it was only eighty miles. And if you want to thank everyone you'd better thank Nick Eason here, because he was the one that picked up your distress call. Nick, tell 'em.'

Eason grinned. 'Nah,' he said. 'Mr Kelly can explain.'

Kelly's smile was fraying at the edges. 'Thank you,' he said. 'Thank you . . . er, both for saving my life and that of my crew. And thank you for being here today.'

'Fine,' muttered Cole. Then he leaned across to Eason and whispered, 'Let's get the bloody hell out of here and get a beer.' He had not noticed the microphone a foot away from his head. The aside boomed through the room. A titter ran through the representatives of the world's press. Some of the crewmen cheered hoarsely.

'No hope,' said Eason. 'They're waiting for you out there.'

Cole winced, and Eason thought of the Inquiry. The questions began. Eason slipped off the dais, and got himself a glass of champagne from the bar. Kelly had interrupted a question and was plugging his film for all he was worth. Eason made a face, and pushed his glass across for a refill.

'Mr Eason,' said a voice at his side. He turned, to find himself face to face with a grey-jowled man wearing horn-rimmed glasses and a drip-dry suit. 'I'm Armstrong, *This Week*. I read your pieces. I thought they were very nice.'

'You fired me,' said Eason.

'I'm the Features Editor,' said Armstrong. 'This race will be over in a couple of months. What are your plans?'

Eason shrugged. 'I haven't made any.'

Armstrong said, 'I want your story.'

Eason stared at the small brown eyes swimming behind the thick glasses. 'Not a hope,' he said.

'You can have a cheque,' Armstrong went on as if he hadn't heard. 'Or you can have a job. Forty K a year, invent your own expenses –'

'Excuse me,' said Nicholas Eason. 'I've seen someone I want to talk to.'

Armstrong followed his eyes across the room to Harriet Agnew, who had come in with de Rochambaud. 'Ah, yes,' he said. 'How about Loneliness of Round the World Wife?'

'Do me a favour,' said Eason and walked away.

Armstrong sighed. He had told his editor that when blokes like Eason got a sniff of money, they got big-headed. But the editor had told him to come out and have a go anyway. Well, there were worse places to be. These Dago birds were crying out for it. He poured himself two more glasses of champagne, lit a Senior Serice and considered his next move.

His editor had given him the telephone scratchpad he had used during his conversations with Eason. One of the notes said: *Eason digging dirt on Clem Jones Kt. Making progress – crew member Crystal CHECK??* Right, thought Armstrong, draining the glass in his left hand and then swigging at the one in his right. If Eason won't play, we'll use our own initiative. Let's follow up this Crystal lad.

The champagne was now getting the better of the press conference; the noise was increasing, and Kelly was looking harassed. Cole was sitting in the corner of the dais, surrounded by an eager crowd of reporters. Eason thought that Harriet was looking tired; there were hollows under her high, wide cheekbones, and a suspicion of fine lines at the corners of her eyes. Tired or not, she was happy. As he came close, she was laughing at de Rochambaud, and he was looking down at her with a clown's straight face. Eason felt he was butting in. But he greeted them anyway.

'Nick!' said Harriet.

'Glad you could get here,' said Eason. 'Bit late on this leg, weren't you?'

Harriet made a face. For a moment, she looked sad. 'A bit,' she said. *EPK* had come in the previous afternoon, twelfth on handicap for the leg. Emily de Havilland had gone off in an ambulance. She had been strong enough to make a fuss about that. Finally, Harriet had accompanied her. The diagnosis was mental exhaustion; which, in the circumstances, was the best that could have been hoped for.

'But you're well placed for the race.'

Harriet shrugged. 'Fourth on total corrected time,' she said. 'Your side did well.'

'We all did well,' said de Rochambaud, smiling. 'And I have to say I am very happy that we are on the shore again.'

'How's Emily de Havilland?'

Harriet's blue eyes shifted away. 'Not very well. She's in for a check-up, and when she gets out we're taking her off to Bahia, to lie on the beach.' She paused. 'Oh, Nick, yes. Are you busy tomorrow night? The Ambassador is giving a party for Henri and his lot, at Henri's cousin's house in Ipanema. Then we're all off to some ball or other.'

'I'd love to,' said Eason. Bennett had gone North, to see her brother. Rio was noisy and full of beautiful women but Eason was pining for peace and quiet, on ground that did not behave like a ride in an amusement park.

Someone had opened the double doors into the bar, and the press conference had dissolved like a sugar lump in hot tea. The Comte and Comtesse de Rochambaud faded away, and Eason found himself drinking hard and talking to two exquisite *mulattas* and one of *Tasman*'s grinders. He was getting on very well with one of the *mulattas*, who had a grave classical face that turned into a beautiful child's when she smiled, which she did every time he made a joke. Somewhere in the crowd, a band had struck up a samba. The girls began moving, hips and arms, small movements like seaweed in the turning tide.

People were dancing now, and his heart was beating a nice, solid back-rhythm to the congas. 'Do you think you could see your way clear to teaching me to samba?'

The *mulatta*'s smile lit up the room. 'But of *course*,' she said. And they moved on to the floor.

Ed Cole was sweating as he came down off the dais. He had had enough of being asked questions in public at the *Arpeggio* Inquiry. These were a different kind of question, but questions nevertheless, and he hated them.

Paddy Kinnersley was waiting in the crowd. 'Ed,' he said. 'Well done.'

'Stupid bloody fuss,' said Cole. 'Let's get a drink.'

'There's someone I want you to meet,' said Kinnersley. 'Maurice Quain, Chinamite's Marketing Manager.'

'Oh,' said Cole, gazing at the plump, smiling man in a light tan suit. 'We've met.'

'Nice to see you,' said Quain, who had watchful eyes in a clean-shaven face. 'We've been following your adventures, Mr Cole. We weren't very pleased with you in Sydney.'

'Oh,' said Cole.

'But we now accept that that was a . . . communication problem. In view of your remarkable achievements so far in the race, I'd like to express our appreciation of your contribution, and our . . . regret at any misunderstanding that may have affected our relationship in the past. Meanwhile, the board has asked me to congratulate you. A sentiment which, I may say, I echo. Heartily echo.' He raised his glass, and looked at his watch. 'I'll let Paddy fill you in. Then you can give me a call, and we'll go over the details.'

When he had gone, Cole said to Kinnersley, 'What the bloody hell was that all about?'

'He's sorry he sodded you about. He thinks you're a great guy, because of all the publicity you got them. I'm standing down so you can sail *Chinamite* back to England.'

'*What?*' said Cole.

Kinnersley was grinning at him. 'You'd better do it,' he said. 'I resigned this morning. Delivering a boat to Athens. Sailing next week. If you don't accept, someone else will.'

Cole stared at him in disbelief. 'You resigned?'

'Just make sure you win, that's all.'

Armstrong finally tracked down Sergeant Ernie Crystal at the Bar Fatima. It was small and dirty and the Commandoes from *Associated Meat* had adopted it as their own.

He moved to the bar, pulled up a stool alongside Crystal, and ordered beer. Then he said. 'You're Crystal. Let's talk.'

Crystal turned pale-blue eyes on him, but did not answer. Armstrong's antennae began to vibrate to the signals he gave off. This man was news. Lots and lots of news.

'Tell you what,' said Armstrong, after a couple of beers. 'Let's get out of here.' He waved a hand at the dirty electric fan, the flies buzzing under the fluorescent tubes, the footballers' portraits cut from old magazines. 'It's Carnival. I'll take you to a really nice place.' Armstrong winked, a wink dreadfully magnified by the lens of his glasses. 'And we can talk.'

Crystal looked at him, then looked at the bar. 'Okay,' he said. But he was thinking: I'll take this bloke for a few beers. He must be a queer or a reporter or something. And if he takes a liberty, I'll kill him. Crystal smiled. He half hoped that Armstrong would take a liberty.

But as bottle after bottle emptied, Crystal began to develop a certain respect for Armstrong. He knew a lot, Armstrong. And he was a laugh. Besides, they had a lot in

485

common, like the fact that they were each interested in people only for what they could get out of them.

They landed up at one o'clock in the morning in a samba bar, drinking rum. On the stage, a thin brown man in leather shorts was writhing between the thighs of a dark, voluptuous woman. The lights were low and blue, and they shone in the sweat on the faces of the drummers. The bar was packed, the sounds of its customers animal grunts and parrot-like screeches.

Ernie Crystal had been pouring his rum into flowerpots for an hour now. Armstrong's rum had gone down Armstrong's throat, and Armstrong was drunk. He rested his head on an unsteady hand, and said, 'Whass your boss like?'

'Sir Clement Jones?'

'Thass him.'

'What's it to you?' said Crystal. His blue eyes were full of innocent curiosity.

'I got an idea you don't like him. I got an idea you were going to tell that twerp Eason something about ol' Jones,' said Armstrong. 'I think Eason is working on Jones. Creckshun. I *know* Eason's working on Jones. And I think you're his source.' He leaned towards Crystal. His head slipped off his hand, and banged on the bar. ' 'Scuse me,' he said. 'Big cheque if you tell all to me, not Eason. Besides, Eason doesn't need you.'

'That right?' said Crystal, mystified. He had no idea what Armstrong was talking about. Source of what? he thought. All he knew was that Jones didn't like Eason sniffing around. It was no business of his to ask why.

'Naaah,' said Armstrong. 'Eason's got the facts.'

Drunkenly, he saw that his only hope of getting the story was to get this thug to cough the lot up, and run it as a total quote before Eason laboriously tied up his loose ends. 'He knows Jones is a wrong 'un.'

Crystal looked up suddenly. 'He does?' he said. On the stage, the man in leather shorts was spinning like a Catherine wheel on the woman's pubic bone.

'Yeah,' said Armstrong. 'Got proof.' He started to slide, made a grab at the bar, and landed in a dark forest of legs on the floor. 'Proof,' he said once again. Then he passed out.

Crystal left him where he lay. As he strode through the glittering night, Rio raged around him: gleaming flesh, laughter, and the thrash and clatter of drums. He paid it no heed. He did not know what Armstrong had been on about. But he did believe that Eason knew things about the Skipper he ought not to know. Before, he had got after Eason to stop him nosing around. But it sounded like warnings would be no good any more. Complete silence was what was needed. *Complete* silence.

Nicholas Eason was woken by the noise of loud music and the hammer of feet immediately above his head. He rolled out of his bunk automatically, using reflexes conditioned by weeks of standing watches. Then his headache reminded him what he had been doing the previous night. He groped his way aft to the medicine locker, and swallowed a couple of aspirins. The clamour on deck continued. The voices were Noddy's and Slicer's. They were singing *La Cucaracha*, and they probably thought they were dancing.

Eason grabbed a towel and his shaving gear, and went on deck. The day was already hot and bright.

'*La Cucaracha's* Mexican,' said Eason. 'And it's not a samba.'

They did not hear. Each of them had a rum bottle in his pocket, and they were wearing the same clothes as the previous evening, somewhat crumpled. Eason went ashore and washed his headache away with cold water from the Iate Club's showers. Then he returned to *Chinamite*, ate breakfast, and went on deck to touch up the paint of the aircraft identification number on the foredeck.

The Great Circle fleet lay at a series of jetties at the western end of the yacht club's basin. This time, most of the crew-members who had not left Rio were staying aboard. Accommodation ashore in Carnival week was expensive and virtually impossible to find. As Eason worked, he exchanged greetings with people working on the boats moored around him. As he flaked away loose paint with a chisel, he reflected. The fleet had begun fiercely competitive, reluctant to give opposing crews so much as a sight of their deck layouts. Six months later, the fury of the race had not abated. But ashore, they were like a floating village.

He worked for a couple of hours, by which time Noddy and Slicer had finished their Latin American repertoire and passed out on the deck. He dragged them out of the sun, then went to meet the *mulattas* at the beach at Ipanema. He returned at two, sore from the sun and the pounding surf. *Chinamite* and the rest of the fleet were wrapped in sleep on the glassy waters of the bay. He clattered below, into the hot, dim cabin, and took a siesta.

When he awoke he walked up to the hot green squares

of the University, and caught a bus over to Copacabana. There, at a table on the black and white mosaic sidewalk of the Avenida Atlantica, he gave himself up to the sinful luxury of drinking *cafezhino,* the infamous and coal-black Brazilian coffee, reading the English newspapers, and being alone.

The Avenida Atlantica was a maelstrom of humanity; brown girls swayed by in *tangas,* the minute bikini invented in Rio, pursued by men in crisp shirts and gold chains, strutting like cock sparrows in the glory of their *macho.* Underfoot, ragged children from the shanty-towns scuttled for loose change and swiped the sugar from the café tables, chased by white-coated waiters who might well have been their fathers. And weaving through them all, the ordinary people, shopping, making assignations, yelling, laughing, in a state of what anywhere else in the world would have been frenzy, but in Rio was merely the lull before the storm of Carnival.

In the middle of all this, the claustrophobia of being one of twenty-two in a boat the size of a suburban living-room fell away. And Eason began to feel human again.

As it got dark, he ordered a couple of *batidas,* cocktails of rum and fruit juice squeezed from fruits whose ancestors grew wild in the forests that creep right up to Rio's outer margins. He began to hear the drums, penetrating the ground under his feet. *Carnival*, they throbbed. *Car-ni-val, nival.* He got up and paid his bill, and was immediately caught up in a crowd of people, bobbing down the street behind a band, singing a song whose words he did not know. But he sang anyway.

Somehow he lost the band. He bought a big cigar from a

vendor, stuck it between his teeth and lit it. Someone jostled him from behind.

'Hello,' said a flat English voice. 'Nicholas Eason, innit?'

Eason look around, and found himself staring into the pale-blue eyes of Ernie Crystal. The music and the laughter seemed to still. They stood with the river of people flowing round them.

'I'm going to kill you, Nicky,' said Crystal, still smiling. 'Look.'

Eason looked down. From Crystal's right hand protruded a short blade of blued steel.

'Short, innit?' said Crystal. 'Long enough to cut your kidneys out, though.' His grin widened. 'Frightening, innit?' Eason looked into his pale eyes and knew how a rabbit feels face to face with a stoat. Crystal meant to kill him. There was no doubt of that.

'Why?' he said.

'Because you're upsetting my guv'nor,' said Crystal. 'You been nosing round looking for dirt, and I know you newspaper bastards, you'll make it up even if you don't bleeding find any. Right?'

'What makes you think he's clean?' said Eason.

'He's my skipper,' said Crystal. 'And I believe in team spirit. Something you wouldn't understand.'

Eason would have laughed, if he hadn't been so frightened. 'Very sporting,' he said, looking down at the stubby blade.

'Now then' said Crystal, and came round to Eason's side. 'You and me is going for a little walk down a side street. And only one of us is coming back.' He tittered.

Eason's eyes flicked right and left. The crowd moved past, unstoppable. Why had Crystal not stabbed him in the crowd, without introducing himself? thought Eason. But suddenly, he understood. Crystal needed to gloat, to spin it out, to feed on his fear.

Irrationally, the knowledge that Crystal possessed human frailties made him feel less frightened. Immediately to his left, a queue of people was climbing on to a bus. Crystal was raising his arm to drape around Eason's shoulders. Eason took the cigar out of his mouth, and exhaled smoke. Instead of putting it back again, he jammed it into Crystal's shirt front, and lurched away into the crowd boarding the bus. Hoarse voices yelled at him, and he felt a sudden sickening pain in his side. He fought his way grimly through, gave money to the driver, and struggled down the aisle to a place near the exit. He stood gasping for breath as the bus ground away from the crowds on the sidewalk.

A running figure pulled away from the crowd. It was Ernie Crystal. His face was white, and his grin was gone. Eason saw his mouth twist as he shouted something, but the words were lost in the roar of the bus's old diesel engine. Eason took his hand away from the pain in his side and waved through the window. The hand was the wrong colour, black and gleaming. Blood. Crystal shrank in the darkness. People around him were looking and muttering to each other. Eason grinned and said, 'It's perfectly all right.' But it was becoming clear that it wasn't. He could feel blood running all the way down his leg, and he felt dizzy and sick at the same time. He had to get out.

He got off at the first stop, and leaned against a

lamp-post, looking around him. Far down the road, he caught a glimpse of a figure running doggedly. Crystal. The fear came back. He had done the wrong thing, getting off the bus. He looked desperately for a taxi.

There were no taxis. The traffic had suddenly gone. Instead, a huge crowd of dancers was approaching. The women's hips moved as if on universal joints, while around them half-naked young men leaped and writhed. Somewhere in the midst of the throng, a *bateria* was crashing out the inevitable samba.

He looked round. He could not see Crystal any more, but far down the enigmatic darkness, he seemed to detect a rippling in the crowd. He tried to think, but his brain was fogged. He had to get out of here. But there was no way – Yes, there was.

As the dancers came level, Eason plunged into the midst of them. The dancers grinned and yelled. Their faces whirled past him as he danced his way through, to the tailgate of the truck that carried the band. There was a step there, and he jumped for it, gasping for breath. The music seemed fantastically loud. Gleaming faces surged around him. Above the bobbing heads, the neon signs moved slowly by.

And Crystal did not come.

Eason fought to keep his eyes open as he clung to the side of the truck, waiting for the neon signs to change. When he thought they had changed enough, he jumped down and stumbled through the dancers. Diving into a street running away from the sea, he lurched on rubber legs towards the lights at the far end.

Traffic was flowing on the Avenida Nuestra Senhora de

la Copacabana, and he found a taxi almost immediately. He showed the driver the address on the paper Harriet had given him, and fell into the back seat.

Henri de Rochambaud's cousin lived in a white house inside a high wall, in a street of other white houses inside high walls. A sea breeze rustled in the acai palms, and there was a smell of barbecue smoke and frangipani. Eason's side throbbed as he gave his name to the armed guard in the sentry box at the iron gate. The man's sharp black eyes flicked over his blood-soaked shirt, the greenish-white face with the dark shadows under the eyes, then checked him off against the list. He showed no surprise.

Eason had a sudden vision of a dinner-party invitation: *Dress: blood-stained.* He laughed, then stopped because his side hurt. He made it on to the verandah, where the other guests were drinking cocktails, before he fell down.

It was Henri de Rochambaud who put fourteen stitches into the long wound in the muscle that ran from his spine to his right flank, just under the bottom rib. 'You were lucky,' said de Rochambaud, after he had washed the blood off his hands. 'Another couple of inches and this person would have dug out your kidney.'

Eason smiled feebly. Inside, he felt even feebler. 'That was the idea.'

'Excuse me?'

'It doesn't matter.' He sat up, and groaned at the pull of the stitches.

'Relax,' said de Rochambaud. 'They will bring you some dinner. Then you can see the police.'

'Not the police,' said Eason.

Harriet Agnew put her hand round the door. 'How's he doing?' she said.

'Extremely well,' said de Rochambaud. 'He had the sense to choose a mugger with a very sharp knife. Now he does not want the police.' He twirled a corner of his enormous moustache between a neat finger and thumb. 'Perhaps he wishes to take his revenge.'

'Not exactly,' said Eason. 'It's part of a story.'

'A *story*?' said de Rochambaud.

Eason lay back and closed his eyes. It was quiet and calm and cool, except for his side, which throbbed fiercely, despite the painkillers de Rochambaud had given him. Soon he would have to return to *Chinamite*. And that would be a problem, because he was pretty sure that Crystal would try again, and next time he would undoubtedly do a good job.

When he opened his eyes, Harriet and de Rochambaud were watching him. Harriet looked worried. She said, 'Nick, why don't you tell us what's going on?'

Eason was about to clam up when de Rochambaud turned to Harriet and said, 'You cannot ask him that. The man is a journalist.' And once again there was that half-humorous, half-worldly glint in his eye. It was suddenly borne in on Eason that if there were two entirely trustworthy people in the race, these were they.

So he told them as much as he knew.

When he had finished, there was a silence. Eason could hear the tree frogs piping in the big garden, the quiet voices of the diners below. Then de Rochambaud said, 'You have proof of all this?'

'There's more to come.'

'Ah,' said de Rochambaud, looking down at him thoughtfully.

'Oh, for God's sake, Henri,' said Harriet. 'We must take him with us.'

'Of course, my love,' said de Rochambaud. 'I am sorry. I was thinking that this Cole is lucky to have so honourable a friend.'

Eason suddenly felt embarrassed. 'Oh, no,' he said. 'Listen, I've cocked up your dinner party. And as for your taking me with you –'.

'I am sorry,' said de Rochambaud. 'We have been treating you as if you are not here, which of course you are.'

'Look, Nick,' said Harriet. 'A friend has lent us a house near Bahia. There is a beach and a village with a few bars. A good place to convalesce, if you can stand the sight of us.'

Eason thought for a moment and then whispered, 'I should love to.' He was floating off. He was back in the playground at his prep school. Out there the Thugs were running with ash sticks, whacking at the Squirts who had not made it across the line. Eason was across, though, in the shadow of the lime tree. In Tom Tiddler's Ground.

Georg and Anton Fischer were early at the Iate Club Carnival Ball, which is to say they arrived from dinner at eleven thirty. The Iate Club's gardens were a blaze of lanterns and coloured lights, and on daises cunningly tucked away in the trees, six separate samba orchestras were thrashing away. The swimming-pool was a great blue jewel, and round it surged the dancers. Some of the Australians were singing, 'Teach Yourself to Samba'. The Fischers were not in need of tutorials. Anton and his dental nurse had in the past been the toast of *thés dansants* in Zermatt, and he was something of an expert.

His brother Georg was also reminded of the nurse. 'Think,' he cried. 'One more leg, and you will be back in the arms of Trixi!'

Georg smiled across the table. Anton had lost weight in the big seas down south. However, *Sirène's* freezers had been restocked with excellent beef and lobster, and her galley was draped with strings of *chouriço* sausage. The cellars had held out very well, considering. He raised his hand, and ordered another round of rum and cashew juice. The rum was doing wonders for his sense of rhythm. He eyed the long legs of the woman at the next table. She was wearing two shreds of scarlet satin and drinking something bright green that looked as if it ought to contain an anaconda. When she licked her straw, her tongue was shocking pink, and her big, friendly brown eyes were fixed on Anton. The vision of white-skinned, statuesque Trixi melted like whipped cream in the sun. Two minutes later, their pelvises were undulating with a synchronization that reminded Georg of a Tissot watch.

'Bum bum, bum di bum,' crooned Georg, conducting the band with a cocktail umbrella. 'Bum bum, bum di bum.'

'Starve the lizards,' said Sparko, who was sitting at a table. '*What* a barbie!'

'Yeah,' said Murphy, taking a swig of beer.

The noise of the shouting and laughter, and the swaying throb of the six bands, had blended into an ecstatic roar. The Murphy table was on the fringes of the action, but even so, the racket was stunning.

'I'm not a dancing man myself,' said Sparko.

'No,' said Murphy.

Sparko eyed him nervously. Murphy had been speaking in monosyllables for two days, now. His hair was matted, and there was a rash of flaking skin on his cheekbone. Shar had arrived a week previously, and Sparko reckoned she was worried, too. He got up. 'I think I'll, er, have a look round for a game of cards,' he said.

'Yeah,' said Murphy.

He sat with his chin in his hands, watching the flesh whizzing past. Nearby was a long table covered in food. A woman in a bikini was standing in a large bowl of fruit salad. Chunks of paw-paw and banana and strawberry were slithering down her shoulders and breasts, belly and thighs. A clown was attempting to eat the fruit as it slid. Naturally, they were both dancing the samba.

Shar Stapleton emerged from the throng. Like most of the other women at the ball, she was wearing an exiguous bikini. Behind her, a masked red demon prodded the air with his trident, in samba rhythm. She sat down, drained a glass of rum, and said, 'See you later, Meffy,' to the devil, who vanished. 'Poor lamb doesn't speak English,' she said.

'Oh,' said Murphy.

She stared at him, her eyes screwed up. 'Now,' she said. 'Tell Aunty Shar what's wrong?'

'Nothing,' said Murphy. 'You want a drink?'

'Not till you tell me why the Great Stone Face,' said Shar. 'Are you going off me?'

Murphy's vast hand covered hers. 'Not a hope,' he said. 'If you want to know, it's the bloody boat.'

'What's the problem?'

'I need a new mast,' said Murphy. 'And some current expenses. Last week I mortgaged a half share in a sheep station Reddy gave me to raise some loot.'

'So?' said Shar.

'Ah, I dunno,' said Murphy.

'You paid your bills, right?'

'Some of them.'

'So what's your difficulty?' said Shar.

'There's two charges of assault outstanding back home. There's no way I can pay off the mortgage, so the bastards will foreclose. I've got a load of light-air sails for the final leg, but nothing worth having for heavy weather. Me good mate Reddy's pushing up the daisies. I'm letting the blokes down left, right and sodding centre. And I reckon those bloody Yanks are going to walk off with the race.'

Shar's eyes were solemn. 'You know what I think?' she said. 'I think you need looking after, mate.'

Murphy shifted his head until he was looking her full in the face. 'You want the job?' he said.

'I'm still considering, long term,' said Shar, with a grin. 'Short term, fine. And the first thing you can do is come on back to the flat.'

'Ah, give over,' said Murphy. 'There's a party going on.'

'We'll have a private one,' said Shar. 'Now do what Aunty says.'

She dragged him away. Couples were sambaing underwater in the pool; on the surface, sections of guava and paw-paw bobbed.

Murphy fell immediately asleep in the back of the taxi with his head on Shar's shoulder. She looked at his leonine profile, the wild mane of hair, and clicked her tongue. Then she looked out of the window and said, '*Well!*'

They were in a queue of cars at the gates of the club grounds, alongside a row of lighted windows in what looked like a private room. Through the knots of revellers she caught a glimpse of men in shirtsleeves, one of them looking over the top of a fan of playing cards. In the middle of the table was a big pile of banknotes. And on the left-hand side, scratching his armpit under his red *Tasman* crew-shirt and frowning at his cards, was the unmistakable figure of Sparko.

The following morning, Anton Fischer's woman in the scarlet tanga drank a glass of champagne and ate a paw-paw at *Sirène*'s mahogany saloon table, then walked down the gangplank and sat on a chair in the early sun, watching the Fischers and their crew working on deck. She saw the last-minute cartons of vegetables go aboard, the mooring-lines flipped off the bollards, the blue exhaust of the engine float away from the dock. *Sirène* moved out of Botafogo Inlet, through the anchored boats and into the tiny ripple of the morning zephyr on Guanabara Bay. There her sails went up, white like the wings of a gull. There was a tiny *pop*, and the woman waved as Georg raised his glass of champagne to her. *Sirène* heeled, and the figures on her deck shrank as she moved alone on the water towards the distant start line. The distant thud of the gun travelled to the woman's ears. She turned, and walked with the easy *carioca* sway, long brown legs and sinuous waist, towards her Fiat. She was going back to real life, on the beach.

Sirène leaned into the long Atlantic swells, and turned her nose for England.

'Look,' said Jack Asprey. 'You and I have got to have a conference.' He was working on one of *EPK*'s deck winches. Harriet was in the cockpit, ramming a sail needle through the heavy Dacron of the mainsail, patching a batten pocket.

'What about?' said Harriet.

Asprey plied a socket wrench, hard. 'Emily,' he said. 'We're off in two days. She hasn't shown up.'

'She's on her way now,' said Harriet, turning innocent blue eyes on him.

'But what's she going to be like when she gets here?' said Asprey. 'I mean, last leg she puts us slap into the bloody ice. And I had to drive the boat up here.'

'She's better,' said Harriet.

Asprey wiped his greasy hands on a rag. 'How do we know? It's all very well acting sane when you're lying on a beach. But this leg, well, it's a month bang on the wind. And we're in a good position. We can win. How do we know Emily is up to it?'

Harriet watched him without blinking. There was a little smile at the corners of her mouth. 'So what do you propose? Asprey takes over?'

He shrugged. 'It looks logical. I mean I know you're Emily's friend and we haven't always seen eye to eye, but . . . well, even you have to see the logic of it. Don't you?' He grinned his charming, overgrown schoolboy's grin.

Harriet banged the needle with a maul, and tugged it through the tough cloth with a pair of pliers. 'No,' she said. 'Not actually.'

'Oh, come *on*,' he said. 'Why –'

'*Talked to the Old Boot this morning*,' said Harriet, quoting. '*Told her I had very strong feeling wreckage further south. Claimed seen E in dream, and that he was looking forward to meeting her.*'

Asprey's face was grey. His mouth was hanging open, the lower lip pendulous and self-indulgent.

'*Doing nicely. Told me she thinks E dead. Told her had same dream, heard E sounding foghorn near tabular berg 50 miles SE.* Interesting diary, Jack,' said Harriet.

'I-don't-know-what-you're talking-about,' said Asprey in a churchyard voice.

'Of course you do,' said Harriet. 'I photographed your diary for the last leg. It wasn't a bad idea. I suppose. You knew Emily was in bad shape, so you thought you'd capitalize on it, and drive her round the bend.' She put her hands on her knees, and leaned forward. 'And you damn nearly succeeded.'

'Prove it,' said Asprey. 'Just prove it.'

'I don't think you'd like me to try,' said Harriet. 'But if you would, all you've got to do is offer to skipper the boat home. As it is, I don't see any point in raking all this up, because it will only distress Emily, and you've put her through enough already. So from now on, you do as you're told, and don't play any more of your little games.'

'But . . .'

'She doesn't remember,' said Harriet. 'Not a thing. And she's fine. And as you said, we can win.'

'Who's fine?' said a quiet voice behind them. Asprey's head jerked round. 'I agree that we can win. I intend to do just that,' said Emily de Havilland.

She was thin, burned almost black by the sun. There was more grey in her hair, and her cheeks were high and gaunt. But her eyes were clear; they had lost their inward glare. Now they were ordinary, capable eyes that saw things as they were.

Jack Asprey was dark red, like a schoolboy caught cribbing in a maths test.

'I owe you an apology,' said Emily. 'On the last leg, I lost my self-control; it was inexcusable. I was . . . overcome. Now I understand that Eric is gone and I will never see him again.' She sighed, but her eyes did not falter. 'But I think the least we can do is sail hard, and win the race. For Eric and for ourselves.'

There was a silence. Jack Asprey opened his mouth, lips stretching back from his teeth, ready to snarl. But he sat down and took a deep breath, and said, 'Yes.' When he put out his hand to pick up the socket wrench, his fingers were shaking so much that he knocked it into the harbour.

'Oh, *shit*,' said Jack Asprey.

The following day, *EPK* sailed down to the start and slipped over the blue horizon.

The Nicholas Eason who had returned with Emily de Havilland from Bahia to the Iate Club do Pão de Açucar was a lean, brown, fit Eason. The reason he had returned on this specific day was because at noon, *Associated Meat* was to cross the start line, and he wanted to be quite sure that Ernie Crystal and Clement Jones were aboard.

So at five minutes to noon, Eason was out in the press boat, engines idling, some hundred feet off *Associated Meat*'s quarter. The harsh grunts of the mastmen as they sweated up her mainsail came clearly across the water. Sir Clement Jones stood at the wheel, legs apart, head jutting as he squinted at the set of the sail. Crystal was in the bow, braced in the pulpit. His close-cropped head shifted as the press boat revved its engine. His eyes caught Eason, and levelled like gun-barrels. The boat driver throttled down.

'See you in England!' shouted Eason.

Crystal slowly passed the edge of his hand across his throat. 'Blimey,' said the reporter next to Eason. 'Nasty bit of work, that one.'

'Pussycat, really,' said Eason.

Associated Meat lumbered down on the line. The starting gun puffed smoke. And Eason returned to the harbour, to begin the final act of the Great Circle.

Four days before the maxis' start date, Wallace DuCane called the fourth of the weekly meetings he had instituted to review progress and (as he put it) facilitate crew-sponsor communication with special reference to race objectives. That meant him and Art Schacker, head to head across a desk in an office of a banking subsidiary of DuCane's in Avenida Rio Branco. Outside, the traffic roared like wild animals, and dense clouds of exhaust fumes licked the office towers. In DuCane's office, despite the Danish modern desk and the two Dufys discreetly lit on the wall, the atmosphere was scarcely less poisonous. DuCane was looking trim and bronzed once again, and he was smiling. He made no further mention of the Race Committee meeting. Schacker, on the other hand, looked tired and haggard. The skin under his eyes had a greyish pallor, and there was a suspicion of sag to the flesh under his square jaw. But his slanting blue eyes were uncompromising. 'The boat's in good shape,' he said. 'We've stripped her out and taken her on trials. You lost the panelling in the back cabin, but you kept your bulkhead. She's beautiful.'

'That's terrific,' said DuCane, showing his sharp teeth. 'I'm glad to hear that. Uh, Art, we'll have three extra crew this time, hope you don't mind?'

Schacker eyed him coldly.

'Dave Kelly wants to film,' said DuCane. 'Now his own

boat's gone, he wants to be aboard the winner.' The manicured hands played with an ebony ruler. 'He'll be bringing a cameraman and a sound man. It'd be great publicity, Art.'

Schacker slumped back in his chair and banged out a Lucky. 'And you and your wife will be in the back cabin, right?'

'Wouldn't miss it for the world,' said DuCane.

Schacker said, 'You sure you wouldn't like to take along the Washington Redskins, just in case somebody feels he needs a game of football?'

'Art,' said DuCane. 'Wait –'

Schacker raised a hand. 'You're asking me to take on three passengers, over and above you and Mrs DuCane. Me and the guys have sweated blood to take out a ton weight, to get us across the doldrums before any other sucker. And now you want me to put most of that back. Do you want to win the race, or not?'

DuCane looked calm, but slightly pained. 'Art,' he said. 'Let's talk this through. How come you can't lay off a couple of other hands? That college boy cook. He's no great shakes as a cook, and he sure weighs plenty.'

Schacker said, 'Hungry men don't work.'

'Okay,' said DuCane. He was not smiling any more. 'Bottom line time. I saved your company. If I hadn't put money into Marblehead –'

'You had your reasons,' said Schacker.

'Everybody has his reasons.'

A secretary put her head round the door. 'Mr Schacker,' she said. 'Telephone.'

'Excuse me,' said Art, and went into the next room. It was Anne-Marie.

'I knew I'd catch you there,' she said. 'How's it going?'

'Tell you later,' said Schacker. Her voice sounded high, slightly breathless. 'How 'bout you?'

'Fine,' she said. 'I mean terrific. Listen, Art. Someone made an offer for the company.'

'They did?' Schacker's voice was dull.

'East Coast Boats,' she said. 'The lawyers say we could pay off the bankers, and the SYC. They want the cannery site for a marina.'

'A marina?' said Schacker.

'And a boatyard, holiday apartments, all that stuff. Art, we've got to do it.'

'So what's left the far end? Nothing?'

'Wait,' said Anne-Marie. 'They know Dave Kelly's aboard. They're tying in with this movie he's making.'

'Oh,' said Schacker.

'There's a million-dollar bonus if you beat the maxi fleet into England.'

Schacker thought: it means caving in to DuCane. But then he thought: it's the only chance of freedom. The only chance of getting out of the clutches of DuCane and all those white-trousered sons of bitches at the SYC.

'I'll go for it,' said Schacker.

'I love you,' said Anne-Marie. 'So do the boys.'

'Me too,' said Schacker. 'Sign that contract, right?'

But as he walked back through to DuCane, his face was grim and savage.

He sat down in the chair and lit his Lucky, drawing the harsh smoke deep into his lungs. 'Okay,' he said. 'I'll take your guys. But I'm sailing to win, so don't expect a goddamn cruise.'

'We won't. Now.' DuCane rubbed his hands briskly. 'Time to get the Race Committee decision on *Siltex*.'

Schacker said, 'If you want. Tell me later, though. I'm busy right now.'

When he had gone, DuCane called the Race Committee.

'The *Siltex* measurement protest?' said the voice on the other end. 'Measurers rate her exactly seventy feet. She starts, as planned.'

'Send me a copy of the ruling,' growled DuCane. 'And lodge an appeal against it, right now.'

'Who am I talking to,' said the voice.

'DuCane, SYC.'

'I'm sorry, sir. Appeals must come from the individual captains.'

DuCane slammed the phone down. His fist crashed on the table and his face twisted into a vicious snarl. He was pretty sure he couldn't get Schacker to appeal against *Siltex*. And worse, he was no longer sure he had the power to make him.

Matters were moving beyond his control.

The woman was blonde, of medium height, dressed in a black linen two-piece suit and a white blouse. Once she must have been very pretty. But now there were bags under her eyes, and the eyes themselves were red. She stood on the jetty at the Iate Club, with the hibiscus bushes of the garden banked behind her, red and gold and green, and looked sad and faded. She held two small red-haired boys by the hand. They looked pale and tired, and confused. 'Could I talk to Dave Kelly?' she said, in a voice that held the remnants of long Texan vowels.

George Hart jumped down from *Flag*'s deck and on to the dock beside her. 'He's not here right now,' he said. 'But he'll be over for lunch, I guess. You want to see over the boat while you wait?'

'Sure. I guess,' said the woman. 'Scott? Bud?'

'Is this boat like Daddy's?' said the larger of the two boys.

'Kind of,' said the woman, and turned her face away so she was looking at the horizon. Hart saw a tear glitter in the sun. 'Hey,' he said, quickly. 'Come on, guys. Let's give you the tour.'

The boys began to look a little happier. Hart took them on deck and sent them below. 'Grab a Coke in the ice box,' he called after them.

The woman smiled at him. The best you could say for the smile was that it was brave. 'Thanks,' she said. 'I appreciate that.'

George Hart introduced himself.

'I'm Cindy Withers,' she said. 'We flew in this morning. I wanted to see Dave Kelly.' From the way she said it, Hart got the impression that it was the only fixed point in her existence.

'He'll be along soon,' he said. 'You're Bud's wife?'

She nodded, dumbly. Hart said, 'Come on up. I'll make coffee.'

They sat in the cockpit and drank the coffee. The boys played below. Cindy Withers smoked Kools, tossing them overboard after three or four drags. There was a raft of butts floating in the water at *Flag*'s transom by the time Dave Kelly trotted down the jetty.

Cindy Withers looked up. Her hand shook slightly. 'Mr Kelly,' she said.

Kelly turned his white professional smile on her. It narrowed fractionally as he registered that she was not as pretty as he had at first thought. 'Yeah,' he said.

'This is Cindy, Bud's widow,' said George Hart.

'Bud?' Kelly's face was blank for a moment. 'Oh, *Bud*!' He assumed an air of concern. 'Mrs Withers, I'm terribly sorry. More sorry than I can say –'

'That's what the letter from your researcher said,' said Mrs Withers. 'I've just brought the kids down. Since you were the last person to see their Daddy alive, they wanted to meet you.'

'Sure,' said Kelly, beaming. 'Is that them I can hear?'

They came on deck and shook his hand and stood shifting from foot to foot in the cockpit, tongue-tied. Hart watched as Kelly threw loops of his charm over them and drew them close. He is human, after all, he thought, and so strong was the Kelly spell that he felt ashamed of himself for having doubted the man's sincerity.

The children were soon laughing and talking, and even the mother brightened. 'Now, you listen here,' Kelly said, after twenty minutes or so. 'I can see the crew coming back. We'll be taking the boat out in a while. I want you to stay right here and wave, and I'll take pictures of you from the boat as you stand on the dock. Then we'll come and pick you up, and we'll take you out with us. We have some real important filming to do today.'

'Gee!' said the elder of the boys, who must have been about eight. 'You mean it?'

'Sure I mean it,' said Kelly.

The crew were aboard by now. The shore lines were cast off, and *Flag* moved out into Guanabara Bay. Under

Kelly's direction, Chuck filmed the woman and two children on the jetty. They stood, waving, as instructed. *Flag* moved away from the shore in the light breeze. Soon, they were four hundred yards off.

Hart said, 'Let's go back and pick them up.'

Kelly turned his head. His face was completely blank, as if he had not understood. 'Back?' he said. 'Why?'

'We're taking those little guys for a ride, right?'

'A *ride*? Long lens,' said Kelly to Chuck. 'Listen, get out of my way, will you?'

'You're going to leave them ashore?' said Hart.

'Sure,' said Kelly. 'Noisy little bastards. Excuse me, okay?' He turned away again. Through his binoculars, Hart could see the expressions on the three faces on the jetty were changing. The waving became slower. The bright smiles became fixed, then slipped altogether.

'*Fantastic*,' said Kelly. 'The last farewell, right? Daddy sailing to death or glory . . . still in shot?'

'Sure,' said Chuck.

'Keep rolling.'

Hart listened to the whirr of the camera, the chuckle of the wake as *Flag* picked up speed. Schacker was standing at the big wheel, squinting up at the sail. He moved closer to Schacker. 'Kelly promised those kids a ride,' he said, pointing back at the dock.

'He didn't say anything to me,' said Schacker.

'Maybe he didn't mean to keep his promise,' said Hart loudly.

Schacker passed the wheel through his hands. *Flag's* nose turned away from the horizon, and the boom went out as Christ the Redeemer emerged from behind the sail, arms raised in blessing.

'Hey!' said Kelly. 'What about my shot?'

'What about your promise?' said Hart.

Kelly's face was mean and closed. 'Promise?' he said. 'This is television, not a Girl Scout cruise.' The two small red-headed figures on the dock began to grin and caper.

'I don't know anything about television,' said Schacker.

At ten o'clock on the morning of start day, Bennett tossed her sea-bag on to *Chinamite*'s deck and pulled herself aboard by the lifelines. Eason was passing boxes of long-life milk down the main hatch. 'What happened?' he said.

'I got cold,' said Bennett. 'It's winter up there.'

'Get up here on the bow line!' yelled Cole. 'We're going to the gas dock.'

'Tell you later,' said Bennett, running forward. 'You'll love it.'

Eason passed the last case of milk into thin air. 'What the hell's going on?' screeched Horace the cook.

'Sorry,' said Eason, and went below to mop up.

The land breeze began to blow at two o'clock, frosting the waters of Guanabara Bay as the maxis moved slowly away from the cheering crowds and towards the line. The wind filled in from the east. The big Mylar genoas came

down, and number twos went up. The boats heeled, showing bottoms scrubbed clean of weed and barnacle. The
crews sat up on the weather decks, looking overboard at
the Sugar Loaf and the Christ, arms outspread over the
fleet. Bennett was in charge of the foredeck crew, making
ready for a lot of sail changes in the notoriously fluky
winds after the start, so Eason did not get a chance to talk
to her. He sat on the weather deck, legs through the lifelines, and fretted.

'Comfy?' said Cole.

Eason hung his chin on the lifeline and said, 'Not
particularly.'

'Pity,' said Cole, grinning. 'Because you're going to be
sitting here for the next month.'

'Here?' said Eason, blankly.

'One month, bang on the wind. Up through the southeast trades, across the doldrums if we're lucky. Then ho
for the jolly old northeast trades, and more starboard
tack, and salt-water ulcers on your arse. READY TO TACK!'
Cole swung the wheel. The grinders ground. The people
on the weather deck changed sides.

'Ten minutes to the gun,' said Cole. 'Sharpen up, now.'

LEG 4 · RIO ~ PORTSMOUTH

East of Rio, the coast runs due east for nearly a hundred miles to Cabo Frio. The starting line lay north-south, and the wind blew over it at a steady fifteen knots.

A hundred feet away, on *Chinamite's* starboard bow, *Flag* was going for the committee boat on port. 'Watch him,' said Eason. 'Is he feeling nasty today?'

The American boat's big buff mainsail bulged back, and her red, white and blue hull showed itself full length to *Chinamite* as she tacked.

'Nasty,' said Cole. 'TACKING!'

And then they were both on starboard, heading for the line. 'He's trying to push us over the end,' said Cole. Across sixty feet of water, Dave Kelly's thin figure, dressed in all-white deck gear, bent his head towards Art Schacker.

On *Flag's* deck, the only sound was Dave Kelly's voice, talking loudly and confidently into a tape recorder, wrapping up an interview with Schacker.

Schacker, at the wheel, sighted grimly down at the buoy end of the line. The buoy trembled on his forestay. He felt a tight satisfaction as *Chinamite* tacked off his quarter.

'Three minutes,' said Joey, at his side.

'Where are the rest?' said Schacker to himself, glaring round. *Siltex* was moving up on the blue and white launch flying the Brazilian flag at the right-hand end of the line. And *Tasman* –

Tasman was a couple of hundred yards down to port, heeled steeply to port, tearing a white plume of foam from her bow. She can't get across my bow, thought Schacker. We're on a collision course. I've got right of way. She can go under my stern, and tack. But that wouldn't be like her. And if she tacks downwind of me, I'll knock her off the line. 'What's he playing at?' he said to Joey.

Joey peered under the boom. 'Couldn't say,' he said. Murphy was braced solidly at *Tasman*'s wheel, his mane of red hair blowing back from his hook nose. 'Unless he's planning to ram.'

Schacker did not reply. He was watching the imaginary point off the port bow where *Tasman* would have to tack. The muscles in his shoulders tensed as the fan of spray at her bow hissed close to the spot.

'She ain't going,' said Joey, jerking the mainsheet out of the self-tailer.

'STARBOARD!' roared Schacker.

Tasman came on. Chuck the cameraman ran down to the lee side, aiming his camera as the plastic wall of her hull, lined with the polite blank faces of her crew, moved across *Flag*'s bow. The hindmost of the crew lifted his feet up on to the toe-rail to prevent their getting crushed.

'PROTEST!' shouted Schacker, spinning the wheel to port. *Flag*'s nose came ten degrees off the wind, and flashed three feet under *Tasman*'s stern.

'BALLS!' roared Murphy. 'YOU CHICKENED OUT!' He

was thirty yards up to windward, now. 'TACKING!' he yelled. *Tasman* came round on a dime, slightly ahead of *Flag* and upwind. Schacker looked up, saw ripples in the main and genoa, the telltales in the slot writhing like leeches in *Tasman*'s dirty wind. Up on the foredeck, the lookout was indicating frantically with his right hand.

'You're going to go the wrong side of the buoy,' said DuCane, stating the glaringly obvious from the weather rail. 'And you can't tack because he's in the way.'

Schacker shot him a look of pure hatred.

'Ten seconds,' said Joey.

'Stand by to jibe!' roared Schacker. *Flag* twisted viciously to port. The start gun went as she was running away from the line, the mountains and the sea turning 360°, boom banging over as she came across the front of the wind. 'Come on,' said Schacker. 'Someone fly me a protest flag, for chrissake.'

Flag crossed the line on the port tack, half a minute behind *Tasman*. George Hart was up on the rail, watching the rest of the fleet to windward and ahead: *Siltex* lean and black, *Chinamite* moving well. 'Here we go,' he said, largely to himself. But Ellie DuCane was sitting next to him, legs dangling. And she smiled, and ran her tongue round her thin red lips, and he felt the pressure of her foot. And his heart began to beat faster, and there was nothing he could do to stop it.

The Rio spectator fleet was thinner than at the other stops, and the boats that did give chase decided at about nightfall that they had better things to do, and turned for the distant loom of the mountains. At dusk, the wind dropped as the land cooled. It went fluky; *Chinamite's* crew changed headsails five times in an hour. When Nicholas Eason went down at eight o'clock to begin his watch below, he was tired and wet. Normally, after supper he would have rolled into a bunk and caught three hours' sleep before the midnight watch. But a month ashore had broken the rhythms of watchkeeping. Besides, it was time he spoke to Bennett.

When he went on deck, the lights of the fleet were all round. Far to port, over the glittering black roll of the sea, the lights of the holiday towns of the Costa do Sol winked as they rose on the crest of the swells. The wind had filled in. It was blowing from the southeast, crisp and steady; the trade.

The watch on deck were up by the starboard rail, dressed in jerseys and waterproof trousers. Bennett was at the wheel, her hair reflecting the lights of the instruments, the close-hauled indicator making a tiny green reflection in each of her pupils.

'Well?' said Eason to Bennett.

'I spoke with him,' said Bennett.

'And?'

Bennett eased the wheel to ride a swell. 'He was dying.'

'Dying?'

'Smack,' said Bennett. 'He was all worn out by it. He'd had hepatitis so many times his liver was like a bath sponge.'

'Oh,' said Eason. He was trying to imagine Bennett up there in the freezing Canadian winter, with a dying brother, asking questions. But they were in the trades, and the wind was pleasantly cool, and that was Brazil on the horizon. He gave up. 'What did you find out?' he said.

'You'll be very pleased,' said Bennett, dull-voiced.

'I will?'

'It lets your friend Cole off the hook. Right off. And that Jones guy . . . it's not too useful for him.'

'Did you –' Eason was about to ask if Bennett had witnesses to her meeting. But she cut him off.

'I made a tape,' she said. 'So what I suggest is that you get below, into the nav shack maybe, and you and Ed play it through. But leave me out, from now on. I've had enough.'

Eason was shivering with excitement. 'Come *on*,' he said. 'Don't you want to see Ed's face when he hears it?'

'No,' said Bennett. 'I want to sit up here and steer. And I never want to hear that tape again. Poor Scott.'

Eason put his hand on her shoulder. 'Take it easy,' he said.

She shook his hand away. 'Keep your hands off me,' she said. 'I want to think about sailing this boat.' Her voice cracked. 'The poor bastard died this morning.'

'Oh,' said Eason. A chill had fallen.

'The tape's in my wash-bag,' said Bennett. 'In my locker.'

Eason went below and collected it. Then he found Cole in the captain's cabin.

The voice on the tape was flat and very, very tired. Towards the end, it nearly faded out altogether. Eason could understand Bennett's agony.

When it was over, Cole leaned back, his eyes moving over the instrument repeaters, checking. 'Well,' he said. 'That sort of changes things, doesn't it?'

'Yes,' said Eason.

Cole's eyes were distant and withdrawn. Eason tried to

imagine the years of disgrace they were seeing; the polite smiles, the whispers behind copies of *Lloyd's List*; *don't look now, but that's the chap who sank* Arpeggio, they would have muttered. *Wonder what he's up to now.* Finally, Cole laughed. He said, 'I think we'd better catch Sir Clement bloody Jones, and see what he's got to say. Eh, Nick?

'By all means,' said Eason.

'Er, by the way,' said Cole. 'Thank you for everything.'

'Same to you,' said Eason.

'Roll on the bloody doldrums,' said Sparko.

'What do you mean?' said Murphy, looking up from the saloon table on which he was resting a cup of coffee and studying a weatherfax map. 'We don't want no bloody doldrums.'

'Yes we do,' said Sparko. He pointed to a frayed patch on the left-hand hip of his jeans. 'You see that? That's the hole the deck wears in my strides on starboard tack, which is bloody mortifying for a fashion-conscious person such as myself. Maybe we'll get on an even keel in the doldrums.'

'Well, you'll have to roll over, or patch your jeans.' Murphy shoved the weather map across the Formica top. 'I reckon you're hardly going to notice the doldrums. The northeast trades have nipped down to meet the southeast trades, and there's a couple of thunderstorms in the middle, and that's the lot.' He took a gulp of his coffee. 'But I'm not sure that we'll tell all those other guys. If they haven't worked it out for themselves, they hardly need to know, right?'

'Right,' said Sparko.

'Good,' said Murphy. 'I'll have a little natter, come jaw-jaw, and see what I can find out.'

He finished his coffee, picked his way over a couple of sleeping bodies and went on deck.

They were a degree south of the Equator, but *Tasman* was hard on the wind, moving through a glittering blue chop, in force four-to-five easterlies. There were three more sleepers face-down on the weather deck, jammed into the angle of the coachroof. Automatically, he looked around the horizon. No sails in sight. Which did not entirely surprise him; he reckoned he was a hundred miles to the east of the rest of the fleet, well off radar. It was not an accident. He had a powerful feeling about the doldrums. He wanted to get across at the narrowest spot, and he reckoned that the narrowest spot would be out this way. There was no rational basis for the idea – the Intertropical Convergence Zone was too fickle for rational analysis. But Murphy trusted to his gambler's intuition. It had stood him in good stead before.

He had the sudden unpleasant thought that it had not done him so well on this race. But he brushed it aside. Confidence, he said to himself. Confidence. And he had a sudden vision of Shar Stapleton, the last night of the Rio layover, in the fleabag hotel where they had been staying. The neon had been reflecting on the ceiling, and Shar had been lying outside the covers, her body like brown marble. And she had got up on her elbows, and said, 'Murphy, what are we going to do about us?'

Murphy had been hypnotized by the black cavern between her breasts. 'Dunno,' he said.

As her skin slid over his, she had said, 'What I want to know is, will I be waiting for you in England?'

'Up to you,' said Murphy, holding his breath.

'I love you all right, Murph.' Her fingers drew slow circles on his chest. 'But I also like my little comforts.' She paused, and he felt her breath hot in his ear. 'Sometimes I wonder if you'll be able to *provide* them?'

Murphy grabbed her round her narrow waist, 'No worries,' he said. The neon light lit her face framed in black hair on the pillow, and she smiled. But both of them knew the question had not been answered.

Now, as he screwed his eyes up at the empty blue rim of the world, the answers came. They were not all encouraging. Shar was beautiful and she was a laugh, and they understood each other. Furthermore, she had been amazingly generous. Without her jewellery, *Tasman* would have stuck in Sydney. She had already exerted herself far beyond the call of duty; she could be forgiven for thinking she had done enough. But there was more to it than that. Murphy grinned, a not altogether humorous grin. She had what he supposed a poet might call a rival. The rival was the sea, and in particular racing bloody great boats on the sea until either he won, or the boats broke. As a racer in boats, Murphy thought dispassionately, he was good, if on the rash side. As a provider, particularly for one of Shar's refined tastes, he was a non-starter.

Ah, forget it, thought Murphy. What you need is a night's kip.

That evening, after the huge red sun had plunged over the western horizon, lightning danced on the rim of the sea to the north. At jaw-jaw, Murphy checked round. *Chinamite* was sailing in line abreast. *Siltex* and *Flag* did not report. No doubt they wished to keep their positions to themselves. But they would be listening in. Murphy thumbed the mike. 'Lucky bastards,' he said to the others. 'We're in a bloody great hole. Sitting still. And no sign of a breeze.' The deck heeled sharply under the navigator's chair, and the rush of the wake swelled to a roar. 'Slop, bloody slop,' said Murphy.

'Too bad,' said the thin voice from *Chinamite*.

'Yeah,' said Murphy. He could hardly hear himself speak above the wake. 'Well, me for a swim.' He signed off. As he went for the companion-ladder, the sound of the wind in the rigging rose to a scream. There was the creak of the genoa sheet being eased off the drum, then a sudden tearing, like a giant sheet of paper.

And the best number two genoa shredded out of its ropes, and its twenty thousand dollars' worth of invisible fragments fluttered away towards the coast of Brazil.

The fleet made it through the doldrums with an exhausting succession of sail changes, but no real difficulty. The boats moved northward, hard on the wind, starboard tack, heading for the Azores, and the next set of fluky winds in the Azores High. Until then, it was a matter of tramping the trades, with the weight to weather, and keeping the best windward helmsmen on.

Two weeks out, Dave Kelly shut himself in the head, shaved carefully, and cleaned his teeth with Pearl Drops until they shone brilliant white. The tan was no problem. All in all (thought Kelly) you look in terrific shape, boy. He pulled his wide, thin-faced grin in the tiny mirror. There was a touch of grey at the temples. Yeah, he thought. Maturity. The face of a man who had been shipwrecked off Cape Horn, fought the good fight with the booze, and won. A face that belonged way up the ratings.

Patting aside a stray tendril of hair, he went to summon up Chuck the cameraman. It was time to interview Wallace DuCane.

Flag was corkscrewing over a long, low swell, and the motion was almost pleasant. There had been no doubt about where to set up the interview; in the radio shack, with the scuttle open to admit the warm breeze. DuCane was alert but relaxed in the padded chair at the navigation table, with the lights and bar indicators glowing, and the computer screen showing a map of the Atlantic, with the cursor winking at *Flag*'s position. Kelly had rightly judged that Wallace DuCane was a happy man when he had a desk under his wrists.

The first questions were designed to keep him happy. Smooth as glycerine, Kelly led DuCane through his early life, stacking shelves on Long Island, his first corporate ventures, and on to the Stock Exchange. He could see DuCane's coppery face relaxing as he expertly massaged his ego. Kelly knew that after ten minutes DuCane would be thinking he was the smartest, most important man in the world. It was a state akin to anaesthesia. When Kelly had his patients like this, he could operate without their feeling pain.

'So,' said Kelly. 'You worked your way up until now you're the biggest management consultant in the US. And you joined the Sound Yacht Club, huh? Why the Sound Yacht Club, in particular?

'It was convenient,' said DuCane. 'And my wife was an associate member, a keen sailor. It seemed like a nice thing to do.'

'Your wife's family is from Boston, right?'

'Sure,' said DuCane. 'Since way back.' The tinge of pride in his voice did not escape Kelly.

'And the Sound Yacht Club is one of the more . . . blue blooded, right?'

DuCane shrugged. 'I guess so.'

'So what did they think of having a new member who'd started out stacking shelves on Long Island?' Kelly laughed, to show it was a joke.

DuCane was so far under the Kelly spell that he forgot to parry the question. 'They didn't like it,' he said. 'Some of them, anyway.'

'But now you're the Commodore,' said Kelly. 'Why did you become Commodore?'

'I was voted in,' said DuCane.

'That's quite an achievement,' said Kelly. 'But I said *why*, not how. You're a busy man. You have commitments. Why take on a whole lot more?'

'Why does anyone do anything?' said DuCane.

Kelly smiled, sweetly. 'I think you're not levelling with me,' he said. 'I think Wallace DuCane wanted to prove that he was better than any Hyatt or Lowell or Cabot, right?' Out of the corner of his eye, he could see Chuck's hand operating the zoom. He could see a sheen of sweat on DuCane's forehead, as he came out of the pleasant, soothing dream and realized that whatever he answered, he stood convicted of naked social ambition. Kelly paused a beat. Then he said, 'And I guess it worked. Whatever the human cost. How many resignations from the SYC since you became Commodore, Mr DuCane?'

DuCane said, 'Seventy-nine.'

'Would these members have been the ones who opposed your recruiting of Art Schacker as skipper?'

'Sure,' said DuCane. Kelly saw the frustration smooth out of his face as he saw a way out. 'And I have to say that appointing Art was a carefully calculated move.'

'Please explain.'

'He's a great seaman,' said DuCane. 'A dedicated, single-minded professional sportsman.'

'Like you.'

DuCane smiled, and shrugged. 'If you like. The object of the SYC's challenge in the Great Circle is to show that Americans can beat the world in the toughest race there is.

And when we've brought the Great Circle Cup to America, we'll bring the race there, too. We'll be lobbying for a stopover in Boston on the next Great Circle.'

'Ah,' said Kelly. 'So there's money in it, right?'

'It's nice to have fun, and it's fun to make money,' said DuCane.

'Is Schacker here for the money?' said Kelly.

'You'd better ask him that,' said DuCane.

He's coming round, Kelly thought. 'I heard you imported lawyers to argue technical points with your competitors,' he said. 'I also hear that Schacker wasn't exactly happy about that.'

DuCane said, 'Schacker has a sailing background. I have a management background. There are differences in approach.'

'Sure,' said Kelly. That was what he wanted: an unequivocal statement of difference, into which he could cut Schacker, dour and monosyllabic and obviously at odds with DuCane. 'Well, I guess we have enough here,' he said. 'Thank you.'

'Fine,' said DuCane, relaxing visibly. 'Hey, wait right here for a moment.' He went aft. Chuck muttered, 'You got enough there to hang him?'

'I guess,' said Kelly.

DuCane was returning. 'Here,' he said, and thrust something into Kelly's hand. Kelly looked down. It was a tumbler, half-full of bourbon. 'Always buy the press a drink,' said DuCane. 'Owner's supply, under my bunk.' He raised his glass. 'Cheers.'

Kelly raised his. 'Cheers,' he said, and before he had time to tell himself to stop, he poured it down his throat. His mind went back to the clinic in Australia, the Antabuse, the encounter groups; one day at a time, they had said. But this would not really be drinking. Just cementing a professional relationship, right? Far away he heard DuCane offering him another, and a voice he recognized as his own said, 'Sure.'

'Oh,' said Ellie DuCane, in the forepeak. She was dressed only in a T-shirt, and her head was on George Hart's shoulder, and her sharp white teeth were nibbling George Hart's neck. 'That was *beautiful*.'

'Sure,' said George Hart, his hand moving gently on the smooth skin of her naked buttock. It was pitch black in the sail-locker. But since he and Ellie DuCane had spent so much time down there he was beginning to know it by feel. 'Listen, one of these days we're going to be down here when the watch on deck decides to change a sail.'

'Trust me,' said Ellie DuCane, her hand sliding down his stomach.

'Never,' said George Hart.

The bourbon burned through Kelly's stomach like worms of fire. DuCane filled his glass again. He had another drink, then another. He was talking to DuCane, felt he'd known the guy all his life. Then DuCane was gone, leaving the bottle, and he was talking to Chuck. He felt tremendous affection for Chuck. Good old Chuck, who had sat in his survival suit on *Kelly's Eye*. Good old *Kelly's Eye*. She had kept going for much, much longer than the surveyor in Cape Town had said she would –

'What did the surveyor say?' said Chuck.

And through the hot fog of his drunkenness, there came to Kelly the notion that he had said something deadly; that he had armed a bomb that he was doomed to carry around with him for ever. So he took another drink, and by the time the glass had left his lips, he had forgotten.

But Chuck had not forgotten. Chuck looked at Kelly's sallow face and glassy eyes, and the writhing of his thin, mobile lips over the perfect teeth. He kept talking to Kelly until Kelly slid to the floor of the navigatorium. Then he switched off the tape recorder, which had been running throughout the interview, and removed the tape. Finally, he got Art Schacker's permission to make an RT hook-up with Los Angeles, California.

EPK was travelling across a bright blue sea in brilliant evening sunlight. Fifteen miles to the west, the seven-thousand foot fang of Pico, tallest island in the Azores, jabbed through a mat of white cloud. A school of porpoises rolled and plunged around the bow. The Azores High, which makes this part of the Atlantic notorious for calms, was over to the west, producing a crisp northeasterly, and *EPK* was making excellent time. But below, where most of the crew were eating dinner, the air was poisonous with hatred.

'Ketchup's run out,' said Harriet.

'What do you mean?' said Asprey, turning cold eyes on her.

'Gone. Finished. None left.'

Asprey laid his knife and fork down carefully and pushed his plate away. 'How the hell am I supposed to eat this . . . muck, without ketchup?'

Emily looked up and said, 'Control yourself, Jack.'

Harriet looked from her across to Asprey. Asprey's face had turned dark and heavy. To change the subject, she said, 'Anybody get a met. report?'

'No,' said Asprey, sullenly.

'Not far to go, Jack,' said Emily. Her thin face was entirely calm. 'We're in line to win on corrected time. So let's not squabble about ketchup now. It's only another week.'

Asprey stared at her with a face blank with hatred. 'Can't wait,' he said, and went on deck. Emily went on stolidly eating. She did not even look after him.

That night, Emily sat in on jaw-jaw. The fleet was closing up astern; but *EPK* was an easy thirty-six hours ahead of the maxis.

'I said we can do it,' she said to Harriet later. 'I mean we've got to do it.' A dark glitter was back in her eyes. Harriet thought: oh, dear, she's got Eric on her mind again. But this time the glitter died away, and the flat, tanned skin of her cheeks stretched in a grin that was closer to being mischievous than anything she had managed for months. 'And it's not because of Eric,' she said. 'Though he would have been pleased, poor chap. It's to show everyone out there. Including Mr Asprey.'

At midnight that night, the northeasterly died on them. *EPK* sat on a long swell, her sails slatting and banging. The weatherfax showed the Azores High over to the west and south. But that was no consolation.

By morning, three-knot zephyrs were chasing their shadows across the sea. The sun boomed down out of a clear sky, and a pair of whales surged black on the starboard bow. Emily's fingers beat a nervous rhythm on the deck.

'We're too heavy,' she said. 'Everything over the side. Saloon table, food, booze, the lot, except three bags of rice and twenty gallons of water.'

'Twenty gallons?' said Harriet. 'That's a week's worth.'

'If we don't get home within a week, we're better off dead,' said Emily. The mischievous grin was on her face again. 'Win or bust, Agnew.'

Harriet laughed. 'Win or bust,' she said.

EPK was floating nearly six inches higher when the last of the food went overboard at three p.m. At six, while the rice boiled in sea water and the watch on deck were sipping a sundowner of weak orange squash, the wind filled in from the west.

'Here we go,' said Emily. 'Fly us a kite, boys.'

EPK shrugged her way into the waves, and began to move steadily northward.

Two days north of the Azores, *Associated Meat* was trudging along in fifteen knots of wind coming in from the west. Along her waterline, a fringe of green weed waved in the blue water. Her sides were faded with sun and salt, and her Dacron sails had been punched baggy and shapeless by twenty-six thousand miles of wind. There were bits of Terylene rope reinforcing her lifelines, and the varnish on the handrail on her coachroof was flaking away, revealing the sun-greyed wood beneath. Five thousand miles on the starboard tack had worked her mast loose where it went through her deck, and every time a wave came aboard, a portion of it landed below, so her cabin was a slimy, reeking swamp.

Her Commando crew, never very talkative, had become more silent than ever. Nobody complained: they were too highly trained for that. But each of them had gone into a hard inner shell where stinking bilges, and wet sleeping-bags, and the knowledge that *EPK Electric* was even now slipping away from them sixty miles to the west, could not touch them. Each of them, but not Ernie Crystal.

Crystal seemed entirely unaffected by the wet and stench. There were simple tricks he practised constantly; he carried several Brazilian coins which he made disappear, and displayed great dexterity with a bandana handkerchief. Now, as the watch on deck huddled up to weather like cattle in a blow, he was eating razor blades.

'Dead easy,' he said, nudging his neighbour hard in the ribs. 'Look.' He placed a Gillette in his almost lipless mouth, chewed and swallowed.

'Ech,' said the man next to him. Like most of the rest of the crewmen, he did not bother Crystal, or allow himself to be bothered by him. Inasmuch as he thought about Crystal at all, he had the idea that he was a bit of a nutter, but reliable. 'You'll kill yourself'

'Nah,' said Crystal, and popped in another blade. 'It's a knack. You can do beer glasses too, the same way.'

'Oh,' said the neighbour.

Sir Clement Jones at the wheel, said, 'Ernie, you are a bloody lunatic.' There was pride in his voice: the kind of pride a man might feel for a guard dog only barely under control. 'Next time you crap, hose out the head after yourself.'

The deep, bellowing laughter of the soldiers rolled over the waves, down the wind towards Spain.

At dusk on the twenty-fifth day out of Rio, Pal Joey went up *Flag*'s mast on his daily check of halyards and headfoils. He was wearing full wet-gear again; the March winds struck cold up here, high as a church tower above the grey rollers of the Western Approaches.

Far below his feet, *Flag*'s hull squashed the waves to foam. The watch on deck were perched up to windward of the cockpit; the wind had gone northeasterly, moderating, bringing a tongue of cold air from Continental Europe down across the Atlantic, and frosts to the gardens and farms of England over the horizon to the northeast. Joey pulled a pair of water-proof Schmidts from the kangaroo pocket of his parka, and swept the horizon, razor sharp in the clear air.

Beyond a couple of tankers to the westward, a thin blade of dirty white cut the primose-coloured sunset sky. *Siltex-France*. Joey spat far to leeward. She must be ten miles off. Which was ridiculous, after twenty-five days' racing. They were good, these French guys. But on balance, they were too far to leeward to be much of a threat, until the wind changed. Which it undoubtedly would.

He swept the south again. Somewhere down there were *Tasman* and *Chinamite*. On jaw-jaw, they had claimed to be in sight of each other, in a fresh westerly. Joey spat again, and shifted his bony rear end in the bosun's chair. Eastern Atlantic weather was too goddamn chancy for his liking.

He turned his binoculars to the north. Somewhere up here, EPK *Electric* and *Associated Meat* were plugging into the chops of the Channel.

The lens moved on, completing the sweep. To the north-eastward, right down on the horizon beyond a container ship heading north, a tiny pinprick of light showed itself above the back of a swell. 'Shit,' said Joey. He kept the glasses trained, braced against *Flag*'s roll, which was intensifying as the failing breeze took the stiffness out of her.

On the next crest but two, the light winked again.

He waited for the interval. But next time it did not come. Instead, a long black shadow was spreading across the sea, inking in the approaching night with a deeper, thicker darkness.

Joey looked up. The sky was clear, except for a high plane with a condensation trail that the setting sun turned to a bright needle pulling a strand of gold lamé. 'Let go!' he shouted to the man on the halyard. When he hit the deck, he trotted aft to Art Schacker, at the wheel.

'Bishop Rock Light to the northeast,' he said. 'And plenty fog.'

Twenty minutes later, the wind died, and the fog bank rolled over them like a huge, formless ghost. *Flag* lay in the glow of her running lights, blind in the thick, wet vapour, the slop and crash of her sails a rhythm section for the blasts of her foghorn.

The aeroplane overhead had been an RAF Nimrod from St Mawgan, and its mission was to send back met. reports from which, with others like it, the met. men would complete the North Atlantic maps. Two hundred miles west of the fleet, the ancient aircraft began to rattle and bump in the turbulence of high mounds of cloud. 'Yuk,' said the signals officer, eyeing his instruments.

'Nasty one.'

The Nimrod banked, and ran straight and level across the centre of the great whirlpool of air ploughing across the ocean towards Ireland. 'There'll be some breeze in that,' said the Signals Officer, who sailed a Drascombe Longboat out of Fowey. 'Me for a weekend by the fire, and hope the bloody chimney pot doesn't blow off again.'

The signals flowed out to the aerials on the Met. Office Roof, and the computers in the building swallowed them, mixed them with satellite data, and digested them. At 0033, they were on a desk in a dusty grey studio in Broadcasting House, and a balding man with an expensive toupée cleared his throat and began to read.

'Get this,' said Kelly, as the introduction came over the radio in *Flag*'s main cabin. 'Jesus, that guy's *voice*!'

'Shut up,' said Schacker, without looking at him.

'. . . warnings of gales in Portland, Plymouth, Sole, Lundy, Fastnet,' said the voice.

'That's us,' said Wallace DuCane. Schacker shushed him with a hand.

'. . . variable three to four, veering westerly gale force eight, severe gale force nine in Plymouth, Sole, Fastnet, Lundy later.'

They listened to the detailed forecast in a silence punctuated by the flop of *Flag*'s sails. When it had finished, Kelly said, 'These limeys make a hell of a fuss about a little weather.'

Schacker turned his hard, wide face, and gazed upon him expressionlessly. 'You ever sailed round here?'

'Only on the way south,' said Kelly.

'Well, I suggest you button your lip till you see what she can do,' said Schacker, and went to send men into the forepeak to swing up the storm canvas.

The wind rose enough to blow the fog away, but the gales held off. At 0800, the breeze had turned southwesterly, but remained light. *Chinamite* had ghosted up on the Isles of Scilly, with the green hump of St Mary's low on the northern horizon. Through his glasses, Eason could see boats at anchor in a white-beached cove. A green motor yacht cruised along forty feet to port. There were a lot of small children in the cockpit. One, taller than the rest, yelled in a high, piercing voice, 'GO ON CHINAMITE!' The rest, who had fair hair and looked vaguely alike, took up the refrain. 'BEAT THE YANKS!' They yelled, before their father, a red-faced man with blond hair, came out and told them in a loud British voice to shut up and stop being unsporting. The boat was called *Melledgan*. As the wind rose and *Chinamite* dug in her rail, she turned away, children watching, and headed back for the islands. Lucky devils, thought Eason, waving. Breakfast time, hot tea, bacon and eggs, fresh milk, fruit.

The wind was blowing up now, force five, six in the flurries of rain bustling across the grey, foam-streaked sea. Cole was at the wheel, squinting at the set of the big, flat reaching kite. They were surfing again, riding down the fronts of the following seas on angels' wings of spray. Eason went forward, pulled himself up the mast to the first spreaders. As he stood there, balancing easily against *Chinamite*'s roll, his mind went back eight months, when he had passed far to the south, retching over the pushpit rails on the second day out from the Solent. A good many things had changed since then. Not the least of them Nicholas Eason.

Tasman's sails were down to the south. She was slow, thought Eason; it looked to him as if she was flying too much headsail, and was staggering. He grabbed a halyard, and let himself down the mast. It was a pity they were not going to win, though. That would put the lid on it for Cole. Eason grinned to himself. It would be satisfying for him, too. But there were other victories in store.

He padded aft at the rapid half-shuffle that was now second nature, and said to Cole, 'Why don't we all pop below for a minute, and have a chat with Sir Clement?' Bennett was on the weather deck. 'Come on,' he said. She shook her head.

In the radio shack, Eason plugged a small cassette machine into the VHF, switched to the open channel, and picked up the handset. '*Associated Meat, Chinamite*,' he said. '*Associated Meat, Chinamite*.'

'*Chinamite, Asscociated Meat,*' said a loud, distinct voice.

'Sir Clement Jones, please,' said Eason, after the preliminary formalities.

'Will do, over,' said the voice. There was a pause. Then another voice, hard and firm even through the distortions of the ether. 'Jones.'

'This is Nicholas Eason, *Chinamite*. Ed Cole is with me. I want to play you a tape.'

Jones said, 'Look, I've had about enough of you. I'm trying to finish off a race with my chaps. So forgive me if I don't want to chat.'

'It concerns *Arpeggio*. It is a statement made by the head of the dock gang in Toronto. You will be interested in it. So will the police.'

The speaker emitted a thin, whispering crackle. A hard gust banged *Chinamite* over on her side. 'He's disconnected,' said Cole quietly.

Eason shook his head. 'Here goes,' he said. 'Reading begins now.

' "My name is Scott Bennett I am making this tape because I want to, and because my sister has asked me to. Immediately before the start of the Route des Voyageurs Tall Ships Race, I was in charge of the gang working on the topsail schooner *Arpeggio* in Toronto Harbour. The night after she had returned from her sailing trails on the lake, in the course of which she was inspected and passed sound by Ed Cole, her sailing master, I took a call from Sir Clement Jones. He offered me five thousand dollars to take out half *Arpeggio*'s ballast pigs and pitch them in the harbour. I can prove this with statements from the gang who helped me do it. Also, the pigs are still right there on the bottom of the harbour.

' "I got to know Sir Clement Jones when *Arpeggio* first came to Toronto. He reckoned that if we took out some ballast, *Arpeggio* would be lighter, and move better downwind. She was an okay ship, but real solid and kind of slow, Jones told me, and he wanted to give himself a little of the best of it. I didn't see nothing wrong with that. After all, the guy was skipper of the boat, so I got the idea he would know her tolerances. I guess he would have been okay, except he took a squall. And then there wasn't too much I could say without giving myself big problems.

' "Well, I guess that wraps it up. I hope this statement is some good to somebody. Copies are lodged with Hamilton and McFee, my lawyers in Toronto." ' Eason paused. The whisper of static filled the cabin. Finally, he said, 'That tape was made five weeks ago. Toronto police pulled that ballast ashore today.'

'Have you finished?' said Jones' voice. Normally it was full and booming. Now, it was thin and harsh.

Ed Cole twitched the handset away from Eason. 'No,' he said. 'I want to tell you, on behalf of those kids you drowned, that I am bloody glad Nick Eason had the guts to sniff you out. Over.'

There was a silence. Then Jones' voice rasped, 'How dare you! How *dare* you!'

'I didn't, for a long time.' said Cole. 'All those days sitting and watching you at the Inquiry. Do you know, by the end of it, you had me believing it was my fault? So what was it all about? Trying for your peerage, were you?'

The speaker was growling. 'And what if I was? What's

wrong with wanting to cover your country with glory? By God, man, you are degenerate. You and your friend Eason. Rotten to the core. Cynics and scoffers. People who have sold your country down the line. No loyalty. No enterprise, no valour – damn you, Cole, you knew that ship was over-ballasted. She *was* over-ballasted. All we did was take a little out, so she would perform. *Perform*. We weren't looking to sail the Atlantic in single bloody file and let a lot of foreigners win. We were sailing for glory. Glory, Cole. Glory. We, the heirs of Drake, of Nelson, of –'

The speaker went dead.

'He's off his head,' said Cole.

'Sorry to bust this up,' said Slicer, from the doorway. 'But we've got *Associated Meat* in sight on the port bow. 'Bout three miles ahead, and we're hauling her down nicely.'

As Eason came out of the hatch, the wind slammed into him as if it were solid. When he looked aft, his eyes filled with water. The anenometer on the cockpit coaming read forty-six knots. *Chinamite* was moving through the water between white wings of spray.

Overhead, the wind had torn great rents in the cloud.

Behind the rents was a sky crusted with stars, at their centre the silver Easter moon, half-grown. Directly overhead, a shooting star trailed fire across the sky, and vanished. The blood was thumping painfully in Eason's ears, and he could feel his facial muscles stiff with a grin of pure excitement. The night was full of omens, and the omens were about to bear fruit.

For the moonlight lay over the sea on the port bow. It was an awe-inspiring sight; a mass of hills and valleys, gleaming black, with crests that the wind hacked at and shattered into white spume that tore away eastward. And out there in that patch of moonlight, a genoa and a close-reefed main rose from a trough, revealing beneath them a long hull with tiny figures huddled about its stern. *Associated Meat*.

Cole put his face close to Eason's ear. 'I WANT HIM TO SEE US GO BY,' he bellowed, and pushed *Chinamite*'s nose a couple of points towards the wind, so she went across the waves in a mad, soaking corkscrew. Eason huddled behind the dodger, and looked up. Cole was standing in a cloud of spray that diffused the moonlight into a silvery glow. His head was bare, and his thin hair blew about his head in snaky whips.

The figures on *Associated Meat*'s deck grew larger. Their faces began to turn. *Chinamite* bore down on them as if they were standing still. A hundred feet under her starboard quarter he paid off, so the two boats were running parallel, with the wind dead astern. The crews stood and watched. Nobody moved. They just stood, faces shaded by their hoods, the only still things in that roaring chaos of sky and wind and sea.

Then Cole turned his head. 'This is bloody stupid,' he

541

said. 'Let's get on and win, and sod them.'

But on the deck of *Associated Meat* a figure came down to the starboard rail. It was wrapped in its wet-gear, but everyone knew it was Clement Jones. His arms lifted: he was raving, and the sound of his voice was a thin gabble above the roar of the gale. The man at *Associated Meat*'s wheel glanced across. Eason knew suddenly who it was, and that something terrible was going to happen. He saw the mouth open black in the moonlit white of the helmsman's face, saw the man stoop to get a good purchase on the wheel with his left hand, and swing the wheel over.

'LOOK OUT!' roared Eason. He did not know exactly what he was shouting at; for *Associated Meat*'s bow yawed towards him, suddenly, like a knife-blade ready to carve into *Chinamite*'s side. Then her mainsail billowed back as the gale caught the wrong side of it. Clement Jones looked up. He was standing inboard of the boom as the full gale hit the back of the sail, snapped the vang, and whacked the boom across the deck like a great alloy flail. Eason heard the crash, watched *Associated Meat* stagger. And the place where Clement Jones had been was empty.

'He's OVERBOARD!' yelled Eason. 'MAN OVERBOARD!'

Then he saw Crystal's face. He was fighting two other crewmen off the wheel, heaving at the spokes to bring *Meat*'s bow to bear on *Chinamite*'s hull. The moon glistened on his teeth, bared like a wild animal's. But *Meat* was no longer sailing. She was heeled away from the wind, spinnaker taking it side-on. Her mast arched over *Chinamite*'s foredeck.

'LOOK OUT!' somebody roared.

Meat's maintruck cleared the spinnaker by two feet.

Cole heaved at the wheel. The alloy casting swept past the mast, missing by inches. Eason breathed a sigh of relief. Then he saw at its tip a thin wisp of something that lashed in the gale, and felt a jolt.

'IT'S OFF THE TOP SPREADER!' yelled Bennett's voice.

Associated Meat fell away astern. The top forty feet of *Chinamite*'s mast leaned downwind from the runner tangs, and collapsed. The spinnaker tore across, and vanished. There was a second of what felt like silence. Eason saw that because there were five slabs out of the mainsail, the peak was actually below the break in the mast. She was still sailing, and there were only a hundred and thirty miles to the finish line. He thought for a second about *Associated Meat* in the blackness astern, Clement Jones swept off his own deck by the boom. *Chinamite* was impossible to manoeuvre. Impossible to go back and help with the search. 'Can't do it,' he kept saying. 'Can't do it.' His mouth was dry, and he was shaking.

Bennett was organizing the work parties. 'Nick!' she bellowed. 'Halyard winch!'

He stumbled forward to the gorilla pit. He knew he should be filing a story. But newspapers and England seemed ludicrously remote and shadowy. What was real was what they had spent the last eight months trying to do: to get to the finish line.

It was 0110 hours, and *Flag* had a hundred miles left to sail. The wind was up to force nine now, and the surface of the sea was a confused mass of white in the puddles of moonlight that spilled from the shrinking cracks between the clouds. *Flag* was moving well, tight and neat with five slabs out of her mainsail, and her smallest, heaviest running kite. They had not used the small kite since the booming gales of 60° south, and even there they had not used it in winds like this. But *Siltex* was fifteen miles ahead, and Art Schacker was sailing for his life.

'Can't you go any faster?' said Wallace DuCane, at his side.

Schacker ignored him, as he would have ignored a buzzing fly. He kept his eyes flicking from the log to the white loom of the masthead light on the sail. Part of his mind was there in the boat, in the terrible stresses of her rigging. Another part was back in Marblehead, in the sheds behind the quay at the dock, in the white house with Anne-Marie. But to get back and to be a free man, he had to win his bonus. He had to be first maxi over the line stretched across the entrance to Portsmouth Harbour, a hundred miles ahead in the screaming dark. To do that, he was going to have to sail fifteen percent faster than *Siltex*. And that was impossible.

A hooded figure appeared in the after hatch, and mouthed something that the wind grabbed away.

'What?' roared Schacker.

The figure came aft, and bellowed in his ear. '*EPK's* crossed the line!' it roared. '*Chinamite* lost half her mast, but she's coming up behind under jury rig.'

Schacker nodded. *EPK* had won. She had saved her time. She was the right size; small enough to get handicap advantage from her rating, but big enough to have the speed. And *Chinamite* – well, it could happen to anybody. It could still happen to anybody. He would have liked to win outright, but there was nothing to be ashamed of in being beaten by *EPK*. It was *Siltex* that was the big problem.

At 0300 hours he went and got a cup of coffee from George Hart, who was wedged into the galley, talking to Ellie DuCane. She gave him a slow, lascivious wink. He thought fleetingly that one of the big pleasures of ending this race would be not having to see the DuCanes. If he won, he need never see them again.

At the navigator's table he marked the new position on the English Channel chart. The tide would be turning soon; time to head up for the cover of the shore and stay out of the ebb. By the time *Flag* was in sight of home, there would be the flood to sweep her up into the Solent. Meanwhile, boat speed was eleven knots –

The figures on the Brookes and Gatehouse flickered and collapsed. 00.00, said the black-on-grey readouts. *Flag* shuddered and heeled steeply to port. Schacker jumped out of the navigator's seat and ran up the companion-ladder. The wind nearly knocked him over. Joey was struggling with the wheel. *Flag*'s nose was dug into the seas, and her motion was heavy and sluggish. Schacker went to the wheel, and heaved. The rudder moved reluctantly. *Flag* did not answer. Schacker grabbed the big waterproof flashlight from its clips and shone it over the side. White polystyrene floats thrashed in the spray. His heart went cold in his chest. 'Get the kite off!' he roared. 'We've fouled a net!'

The foredeck gang ran along the rail. 'No!' roared Schacker. 'Belay that!'

'Do something, God damn you!' yelled DuCane.

Schacker ignored him. *Flag* was lurching downwind, her rigging protesting at the new, unfair load. He pulled the wheel up, inch by inch. *Flag* came round, her nose turning up for the wind. The gale tore across the deck as her angle of heel steepened. DuCane screamed, 'What the hell are you doing?' Then he sat down and laced his arms through the pushpit railings. *Flag*'s masthead went down, foot by foot, towards the sea. Schacker's teeth were clenched so hard that his jaw muscles were cramping. His breath was coming in gasps, from the effort of keeping the helm over. But he clung on, and slowly, foot by foot, *Flag* lay over on her beam ends.

As her rail came between Schacker and the wind, there was an instant of strange quiet. In the quiet, DuCane could be heard roaring, 'You're crazy! Crazy!'

'Now,' said Schacker, between clenched teeth.

What was meant to happen was that with *Flag* on her beam ends, the keel would present no impediment to the fishing net. Her rate of drift downwind would be faster than the net's; she would simply slip out of the noose. But instead, she lay over and wallowed. For a whole minute she wallowed. Then, with a sudden lurch, the sluggishness left her. Her mast began to rise. Schacker hauled the wheel round again, and the deck levelled and the main filled, and the spinnaker came round. And *Flag* was running.

But she was slow, the rudder still stiff and ponderous under Schacker's hands.

'Joey!' roared Art. 'Get a look over the stern!'

They let him down on two lifelines, slithering between the aerials on the transom. When they brought him up, blood from his nose was pouring down his thin, monkey face. 'Still a lot of stuff on there!' he shouted. He unshipped the big diver's knife from its scabbard on the backstay.

This time, he was down for twenty minutes. The rudder improved slightly. But the log readout stayed below ten knots; it should have been close to fifteen. When Joey came up again, Art snapped, 'Is that the best you can do?'

Joey's face was a pale mask, shining with black blood in the dim lights. 'Yeah,' he said. 'You're out of the net, but there's a whole lot of rope down there. I guess it's wrapped round the rudder. I'll go get it when we get some light.'

Schacker resisted the urge to say that that would be too late. 'Sure,' he said. And *Flag* ploughed on towards the dawn, three hours away.

There was another, worse problem.

As the eastern sky began to grey, the wind had dropped back to force eight. Gradually, sea and spars emerged from the darkness. None of the crew had slept. They were watching; watching the Portland Bill light coming up on the port bow at the end of the long, pale, pencil-line of the Chesil. And, to the south, a red sidelight of a sailing boat's running lights. The sidelight had started on the starboard quarter. During the last three hours it had come abeam. Now it was ahead on the starboard bow, perhaps two miles ahead. As the light grew, it became possible to make out a weirdly truncated mast carrying a much-reefed mainsail, and a small spinnaker.

It was *Chinamite*.

The light grew. A swarm of aircraft buzzed about them like flies. George Hart went below to the radio, came up ten minutes later, glanced at *Chinamite*, now well ahead, and said, '*Siltex*.'

'Yes?' said Schacker.

'She's lost her mast. She's out of the race.'

There was a moment of stunned silence. 'Yeehaa!' whooped Wallace DuCane. 'Thank you, God!'

There was another moment of stunned silence. Then Schacker yelled, 'Joey! Get over the side!'

Joey vanished under the stern with the diver's knife. This time, he came up grinning. 'I cut away some leadline,' he said. 'There's some stuff round the rudder stock, but it's hard as rock. She'll go now.'

The Brookes and Gatehouse steadied on twelve knots. The rudder was still stiff and awkward, and it would not last. So what, thought Art: it only had another four hours, at the outside.

On the starboard bow, *Chinamite* steadied. George Hart crouched in the gorilla pit, lining up a winch-top with a stanchion to give him a precise sight-line. The sight-line crossed five miles of tossing grey water and arrived at the foot of her mast. He looked away, at the chimneys on the low, dark coast. Then he looked back. The sight-line ended forward of *Chinamite*'s bow.

'We're catching her,' he said. 'We're catching her.'

Beyond *Chinamite*, a great lump of land was growing from the sea. It was dull coloured and grim, except at its base, where it was lined with a smile of white chalk.

'What's that?' said George Hart.

'The Isle of Wight,' said Schacker. 'Where we finish, boy.' And he went below.

He needed coffee. When he had poured some and lit a new Lucky from the stub of the old, he knew he did not want to go on deck again. DuCane was there, and Kelly. And he did not, just for the moment, want to know how close he was to catching *Chinamite* or whether he could catch her before the line. So he went to the VHF and said, '*Tasman, Flag.*'

The reply sounded distant, full of interference.

'We're about to finish,' said Schacker. 'Where are you?'

The voice at the far end was weary. Tubes Murphy's voice. 'Off the Lizard,' he said.

'What kept you?' said Schacker.

'I ran out of sails,' said Murphy.

'*What?*'

'True,' said Murphy. 'All I got in the locker was light-airs stuff. Also storm jib and storm trysail, as per race rules. Which I'm flying now.'

Schacker shook his head. 'Sorry to hear that,' he said. 'Buy you a drink in England.'

He disconnected and went on deck. *Chinamite*'s lead was down to a mile and a half. To starboard the white jags of the Needles churned the swell. The wide corridor of sea between the Isle of Wight and the mainland was dotted with the shapes of spectator boats.

Joey said, 'We're doing it.'

'Good,' said Schacker. His eyes travelled to Kelly, talking excitedly on the foredeck, and DuCane, crouching in the gorilla pit. 'If any of them spectators gets in your way, go straight through them.'

Joey's eyes did not deviate from the truncated triangle of *Chinamite*'s sail, jutting against the distant line of Portsmouth. 'Sure will,' he said.

The whole of *Chinamite*'s crew was on deck now. Eason's mouth was dry as he looked astern. *Flag* was wearing a huge spinnaker, red, white and blue, stars and stripes. It was swelling like a balloon inflating. She was getting closer.

Under the foot of the sail, the black eye of a camera lens pointed forward. Dave Kelly was there too, spidery in his white wet-gear, making the commentary. The wind was down to force seven. Eason swallowed and turned away.

At the wheel, Ed Cole's teeth were bared as he glanced down at the log. Twelve knots. Twelve knots under jury rig. Not bad, thought Cole. Not bloody bad. But when he looked round at *Flag*, the gap of lashing water was narrower, the spinnaker taller.

As they moved past Cowes, there was half a mile between them. The wind was dropping all the time. Cole knew the Solent well; he kept in the tide, looking over the bow at the stone drum of Horse Sand Fort. The swell was gone now, the dirty water whipped into a three-foot chop, nothing more. *Chinamite* moved through it hard and well. But *Flag* was moving better.

'She's going to catch us,' said Bennett.

'No,' said Eason.

She shoved the blonde hair out of her eyes. It had grown on the long tramp northward. 'She's faster,' she said. 'Nothing we can do. If he comes through to windward, we'll luff him. But if we go down to port to cut him out we'll have to jibe, and even if we keep the mast he'll be on starboard tack and we'll be on port, so he'll have right of way.'

Eason watched *Flag*'s bow creep up astern. He could see Kelly's teeth now, set in the famous smile. And suddenly, he was grinning himself. He thought: twenty-seven thousand miles' racing. And here we are, a couple of hundred yards apart at the finish.

A puff of air darkened the waves astern. 'Here they come!' said Cole, wearily. He looked up at the mainsail, the jury spinnaker, wrinkled and sagging. 'Nothing we can do but lie back and enjoy it.'

For *Flag* had caught the puff and gone to port. And suddenly she was only three lengths away, and Cole was no longer permitted by the rules of racing to sail below his natural course to the line, even if he wanted to. Eason felt suddenly tired. He leaned against the lifelines and watched the platform of *Flag*'s deck go past: the foredeck, with a genoa rammed down along the rail, the foredeck man standing, watching; the gorilla pit, with the trimmers lying down, sighting up at the taut balloon of red, white and blue nylon floating against the overcast; the faces of the crew on the deck, burned black by the sun. George Hart, gazing with something like sadness across the strip of water between the two boats, next to sharp-faced Ellie DuCane. And in the cockpit Dave Kelly, preoccupied, talking to camera; Pal Joey, stacked loosely against the coaming, chewing a matchstick, his baggy eyes travelling ceaselessly from horizon to readouts. Art Schacker, stocky at the wheel. Despite the March chill of the wind, Schacker's square face was glistening with sweat. And above him, sitting on the pushpit rail, Wallace DuCane. As *Flag*'s transom went past, DuCane's head turned. His eyes were alight with glory, his lips pulled back in a snarl of triumph. He raised his right arm. Eason watched in amazement as his middle finger rose in an unmistakable gesture.

'The finger,' drawled Bennett. 'A sportsman and a gentleman.'

Eason's eyes were fixed on DuCane under the sail. He saw Chuck the cameraman turn his lens on him, triumphant against the sky. Then he saw Schacker's head turn on DuCane, his mouth drop open with astonishment. And he heard him bellow with rage. *Flag* yawed as he dropped the wheel. His right fist went back and slammed into DuCane's grinning jaw. DuCane fell face down on the deck. Not a single member of *Flag*'s crew even looked at him as the red, white and blue hull drew ahead of *Chinamite* and bore down on the line.

Five minutes later, *Flag* passed south of Gilkicker Point, and every siren in the Solent roared a welcome. The blast had not ended when *Chinamite* crossed the line and plunged into the crowd of spectator boats.

Cole sat down on the coaming, and ran his small hands through his sparse, sandy forelock. 'Well,' he said, above the roar and clatter of the three helicopters circling the deck. 'Not a bad morning's work. Not brilliant, but not bad. Anyone fancy a beer?'

HOME

In the marina at Gosport, the Customs rummage crews came aboard. Very politely, they prised up floorboards, looked in lockers, and prodded mattresses. Then they went away empty handed. It would have been a depressing welcome to England, if anyone had noticed it. But the champagne was flowing, and for a few hours even a dismal April drizzle failed to dampen spirits.

The coastguard had been out since morning, looking for Sir Clement Jones. They had not found him. But the cutter had come alongside *Associated Meat* and taken off Ernie Crystal and the fellow-Commando whose finger he had bitten off as he had wrenched him away from the wheel. An ambulance had been waiting for Crystal on Weymouth quay. The attendants had been surprised to find him trussed like a turkey, his neck corded with sinews and black veins standing out on his forehead, hissing obscenities at things only he could see. It was early days to diagnose paranoid schizophrenia, but it looked very much like that to the duty doctor at the Herrison Psychiatric Hospital.

In the evening, *Tasman* came in, and the festivities changed into a higher gear.

Sometime after midnight, Chuck the cameraman laid

his camera down, and said to Dave Kelly, 'I guess that's enough.'

'Enough?' said Kelly. They were in a restaurant somewhere outside Southampton. At the other side of the room Nicholas Eason from *Chinamite* was attempting to teach George Hart from *Flag* the tune of 'Rule Britannia.'

'Let's wrap,' said Chuck. 'We have to talk.'

'Talk?' said Kelly.

'About our partnership,' said Chuck. 'I've been thinking. What we need to do is form a production company, you and me.'

'*What?*' said Kelly.

'Partnership,' said Chuck. He was smiling, a hard smile. 'I guess I've had a bellyful of being on staff. So I provide the expertise, and you provide the finance.'

'Wait a *minute*,' said Kelly. 'Are you crazy? The world is full of cameramen –'

'Yeah,' said Chuck, looking at Kelly with hard, flat eyes. 'But not all of them know what I know.'

Kelly stopped breathing.

'The survey in Cape Town,' said Chuck. 'You mentioned it on the boat. Well, I know a guy who's a private investigator in LA. And I had him check on this guy Lawson. So now I know where I can put my hands on him, if I want to.'

Kelly said. 'He's been talking to Lawson?'

Chuck raised his hands. 'Nobody's going to talk to Lawson. Not unless they feel they have to. Now, maybe we should talk contracts, and I can have my lawyer draw it up. Okay?'

Kelly looked at him from eyes that were suddenly sunk

deep in their sockets. 'You sonafabitch,' he said. 'You can't get away with this.'

'Sure I can,' said Chuck. 'Don't misunderstand me. I understand your motive. Television's television, right? I can identify with that. But television's teamwork, also. Right, Dave?'

Kelly stared bleakly at the future. 'Right, Chuck,' he said.

On the morning after *Tasman* docked, Sparko was seen to be throwing clothes into a backpack.

'Where are you going?' said Murphy.

'Me brother's in London,' said Sparko. 'Off to say hi. Back in a couple.'

'Fair enough,' said Murphy. He had a lot on his mind. First of all, there was no Shar, and no news from her. Second, some of his sub-sponsors, who had provided things like winches and ropes and food, were queuing up for rides. He didn't have a lot of time to worry about his crew's social engagements. As Sparko shouldered his backpack and started to tramp up the quay under the screaming gulls, Murphy waved absentmindedly.

Sparko returned two days later. His backpack looked significantly slimmer. He pulled himself up on *Tasman*'s deck, and said, 'Word in your ear, Skip.'

'Hold it,' said Murphy. He was staring down the jetty, between the bows of the moored boats. A woman was walking towards *Tasman* with a long, easy stride. The breeze ruffled her thick black hair, and the spring sunshine lit her vivid brown skin. Murphy jumped down and ran towards her. She disappeared in his vast embrace.

'That's two bits of good news for the skip,' said Sparko enigmatically to a seagull on a piling. Murphy and Shar returned, grinning grins that they could not extinguish. 'Bloody marvellous you arrived,' said Murphy. 'We're off for a photo session, and we need something to distract the punters from the state of the paintwork.'

They cast off, motored out into the Solent and put the sails up. When they were sailing and the photographic boat was buzzing about, Murphy turned to Shar and said, 'Are you back?'

'I'm back,' she said. 'I'd rather be poor and honest than rich and kept.'

Sparko had been hovering on the weather deck, nearby.

'Er . . . Skip,' he said.

'Yeah?' The wind blew back the red hair from Murphy's forehead.

'I got you some loot,' said Sparko.

'Loot?'

'Yeah.' Sparko looked shamefaced. 'I got to playing poker, at that barbie in Rio.'

Shar said, 'That's right, I saw you. Through the window.

'Yeah?' said Sparko. 'And I won, er, quite a lot of loot. About seven grand, US.'

'Hang *on*,' said Murphy. 'That's real nice but –'

'No,' said Sparko. 'Wait. One of the blokes at the game was a, well, dope dealer. I gave him the seven thousand, and he gave me fifty pounds of weed and a fake gas bottle to stash it in. So when I was up with me brother I flogged it to a bloke he knows, right?' He reached into the side pocket of his parka, and pulled out a bulky brown paper bag. 'And he gave me twenty-five thousand quid for it. I know it's been, well, difficult, with Reddy and all. So I thought I'd donate it to the boat fund.'

Murphy looked at Sparko's round face, and then at the parcel. 'You jammy little bastard,' he said. He took the brown paper bag, opened it and pulled out one of the hundred-pound notes it contained. 'But no dope money, ta. Except to replace the gas cylinders you must have tossed overboard in Rio.' He shoved the note into his pocket, and handed the bag back. 'All yours,' he said.

Sparko looked at him. Then he dipped into the bag, and came up with a fistful of notes. He opened his hand, and the wind caught them, and they fluttered away, tumbling in the air, over and over until the grey waves caught them.

'Take it,' he said, holding out the bag.

Murphy shook his head, grinning.

Sparko dipped in his hand and threw away another fistful; then another, and another. Finally he upended it. And down the wind, after the notes, there floated a great noise. Murphy, his arm round Shar's shoulders for support, was roaring, bellowing with laughter.

The carnations were already out on the terrace clasped between the turrets of the east wing of the Château St-Roch. The morning sun caught their petals and wafted their clove scent to Harriet, Comtesse de Rochambaud, as she poured coffee for her husband and herself. To the east, the vine-yards fell away towards the valley of the Garonne.

Harriet had had fifteen breakfasts at St-Roch, and she had loved them all. Like her, Henri de Rochambaud was a quiet breakfaster; he liked to drink his coffee and read the newspapers, and think about things for a while before embarking on the day's endeavours. It had been a worry to Harriet that perhaps they would be incompatible in such matters. She picked up her letters, and looked through them. One of them was addressed in Emily de Havilland's neat, firm handwriting.

> *I had hoped to come and stay in your new house* [she read]. *It sounds beautiful. But I'm afraid I have got mixed up in something rather exciting.* EPK *Electric has offered to sponsor me in the Single-Handed Translantic Race. So of course I can't possibly refuse, even though I shall have to start work straight away . . .*

She read till the end of the letter. Then she said, 'Emily's off again.'

'Oh?' said Henri, cocking an eyebrow. 'Are you going with her?'

Harriet looked down at her belly, standing high with the baby she was expecting in September. She laughed. 'Even if she wanted me, there wouldn't be room.'

'I am very happy,' said Henri. 'And now we have the little problems out of the way, the big ones. What shall we eat for lunch?'

The sun was pouring through the windows of the *piano nobile*, glinting from the sharp little steel instruments that Trixi had placed ready on the circular marble plinth by the chair. Anton Fischer took a grateful breath of the antiseptic air of his surgery, and smoothed his thin rubber gloves over the callouses that had not faded from his hands in the ten days since *Sirène* had tied up in Vilamoura. He caught Trixi's china-blue eyes, and smiled a secret smile. She smiled back, a smile heavy with the remnants of their reunion the previous night. Then he spoke to the patient in the chair, a stout banker draped in green plastic.

'Any problems?' he said.

'No,' said the banker. 'Just my annual checkup. It's been a hell of a year. The only good thing about it's been my teeth.'

Albrecht moved up to him and said, 'Open wide.'

Looking up into his brown, smooth face, the banker said, 'Maybe I should be a dentist. A nice even life, patient follows patient, no problem that lasts more than a couple of days . . . bliss. God, it's been a terrible year.'

Albrecht pulled down the lower jaw and peered inside, renewing his acquaintance with the familiar landscape of gum, ivory and amalgam. 'Aha,' he said remotely. 'Yes. A lot can happen in a year.'

The snakebark maples lining the path to the white house in Marblehead were lobster pink with new leaf as Schacker walked up to the door. His footsteps boomed in the high, white hall. Children's voices sounded from the back of the house.

'That's Daddy!'

The hall echoed with the racket as they all tried to tell him at once what they had been doing these last eight months.

'One at a time,' said Schacker.

Anne-Marie came in, wearing her smock with the paint stains. She looked tired, but very happy. 'Art,' she said. 'Welcome home. And don't go away again.'

'Right,' said his eldest son. 'We saw you on TV.'

561

Schacker smiled. There had been a brass band and a lot of speeches. Wallace DuCane had made a speech, and he had made one too, though it had not been as long as they had probably wanted. And after the speech, he had handed DuCane the cheque with which he had purchased back control of Marblehead Clam and Lobster. Schacker had enjoyed the look on Wallace's face. As of today, he was a free man, with a million-dollar bonus in the bank.

After supper, the boys went away to play. Schacker and Anne-Marie went into the drawing-room.

He put his arm around her shoulder. She looked up at him with her deep, dark eyes, and said, 'We missed you.' Above the telephone table, Nathaniel Schacker gazed impassively down from his portrait. Nathaniel, who had brained the harpooner with his own iron, down there in the icy South. Schacker rubbed his knuckles where the skin had grown back after he had hit Wallace DuCane.

'What are we going to do?' she said.

'Take a vacation,' said Schacker. 'Then we'll see.'

'Oh, yes,' said Anne-Marie. 'You got a cable.'

It was leaning on the mantelpiece. He opened the envelope. '*HEREBY REQUEST YOU BECOME MANAGER NEW YORK BANKS SYNDICATE AMERICAS CUP CHALLENGE*', it said. He showed it to Anne-Marie. She laughed, and so did he. He crumpled it up and pulled his hand back, to throw it in the fire. Then he changed his mind, smoothed it out and pushed in into his coat pocket. Anne-Marie looked up again. His hard, square face was pensive, the tilted blue eyes far away.

'Oh, *Art*,' she said.

*

The Royal Yacht Racing Club is a small but distinguished building in a cul-de-sac off St James's Street, Piccadilly. Its members are mostly oldish and reddish, with successful careers in the Navy and big business behind them. On a warm June evening eight weeks after the finish of the Great Circle, a lot of non-members were pushing through the mahogany swing doors with brass portholes, carrying gold-edged paste-board invitations. For tonight was the preview of Dave Kelly's film.

Among them was Nicholas Eason, wearing a blue light-weight suit with a copy of the *Independent* sticking out of the pocket. His hair was shorter, and his tan had largely faded. There was a brisk purpose to his walk as he passed through the lobby and into the smoking room.

It was meant to be full of Great Circle people. Actually, there was only a sprinkling. The bulk of the people in the room were the usual journalists and potential sponsors and notabilities and freeloaders who turn up at official yachting cocktail parties. Those Great Circle people who were there, Eason found almost unrecognizable. In the dark, solid room, they were somehow diminished; Noddy and Slicer, drinking hard in the corner, looked even a little intimidated. There were no Australians, and few Americans. It was all very polite.

'Nick,' said a small man with receding sandy hair and bright blue eyes. He was wearing a blazer and cavalry twill trousers, and a dreadful shirt. Eason had to look twice before he recognized them as Ed Cole. 'You're late, you slovenly devil,' said Cole, and grinned.

'Sorry, Cap'n,' said Eason. 'Congratulations on the job.' Cole had just been appointed to the command of

Janus, a barque owned by Operation Drake, and one of the biggest square-riggers still in service.

'Praise be,' said a female voice. 'Humans.' There was no trouble about recognizing Bennett. She was wearing a suit of green linen, with a skirt short enough to show her astounding legs to good advantage. There was still that old screw-you-Jack look in her eye. Eason grabbed her and kissed her on the mouth, partly because he was pleased to see her and partly because he was pleased she had not changed.

'So when's the main feature?' he said.

'Right now,' said Bennett.

They went into another room, with rows of seats facing a screen. Music began: Vaughan Williams' *Sea Symphony*. Waves rolled across the screen, the heavy green waves of the South Atlantic.

A title appeared:

Great Circle

A
Dave Kelly/Chuck Butz Production

for
USTS

Then there were boats. There were little cries of recognition in the darkened room. Dave Kelly began to speak. The room became silent. The first leg started. The commentary continued; there were sighs of pleasure from the audience –

those members who had not sailed the race. Jack Asprey had gathered round him a tight knot of Great Circle veterans. In the odd and unfamiliar surroundings of St James's, he had been a familiar face, a link between all this sherry and blazers and the hard graft of flogging round the world. And Jack had switched on the charm, and they had pulled their chairs together, and settled down.

But as the film started to run, something happened. Asprey kept nudging them in the ribs, pointing out familiar sights, spreading bonhomie. And the people in the chairs around him began to drift away, as if they did not believe him. And Jack Asprey found himself in the dark, with no-one to charm. Alone. For the film was . . . well, *wrong*. The men and women who had sailed the race looked at the pictures and heard the words, and knew that it had not been like that. It had not been the same for any two people. There had been one constant, and only one: the sea, the smell of it, the sound of it, the way it changed. The film might be a good film, of its kind. But a film was all it was.

Eason leaned over to Cole and Bennett. 'I'm going to catch this on video. How about some dinner?'

They got up and walked out, away from Kelly's voice and his celluloid waves. Pigeons were cooing on the ledges of the buildings, and the warm air of the evening lapped at them as if it was water. And they came out of the cul-de-sac and into the roar of St James's Street, and were swept away into the sea of people and buildings.

Headline books are available at your book-shop or newsagent, or can be ordered from the following address:

Headline Book Publishing PLC
Cash Sales Department
PO Box 11
Falmouth
Cornwall
TR10 9EN
England

UK customers please send cheque or postal order (no currency), allowing 60p for postage and packing for the first book, plus 25p for the second book and 15p for each additional book ordered up to a maximum charge of £1.90 in UK.

BFPO customers please allow 60p for postage and packing for the first book, plus 25p for the second book and 15p per copy for the next seven books, thereafter 9p per book.

Overseas and Eire customers please allow £1.25 for postage and packing for the first book, plus 75p for the second book and 28p for each subsequent book.